C0-BKK-191

PRAISE FOR THOMAS E. KENNEDY

"Thomas E. Kennedy is an astonishment, and *In the Company of Angels* is as elegant as it is beautiful, as important as it is profound. A marvel of a read."
    — Junot Dìaz, author of *The Brief Wondrous Life of Oscar Wao*

"Wonderful and of the moment...[Kennedy] is a writer to be reckoned with."   —*Washington Post*

". . . artful and empathetic . . ."   — *Time Out New York*

". . . extraordinarily powerful and illuminating . . ."
                                    — *The Guardian* (U.K.)

"With generous and elegant prose, Kennedy takes us from the darkest, most violent regions of our collective behavior to our most exalted: our enduring hope for something higher, our need to forgive and be forgiven, our human hunger to love and be loved. This is a deeply stirring novel suffused with intelligence, grace, and that rarest of qualities—written or otherwise—wisdom."
    — Andre Dubus III, author of *House of Sand and Fog*

". . . truly an original voice, the sort one discovers with enthusiasm and delight; the gifts he brings us are formidable, memorable, and lasting."   — Gladys Swan, author of *Carnival for the Gods*

"Thomas E. Kennedy's . . . stories pulse with humor, moral edge, and a deep sympathy for the human predicament . . . These stories come as a gift from across the sea of a fine writer's untamed imagination."
    — James Carroll, National Book Award-winner

"[Kennedy writes] . . . about grown-ups, people battered and dinged by life, painfully aware of their own responsibility, whose understanding of their past never stops evolving. It's the dignity of their adulthood . . . that makes them so admirable and, above all, so moving."   — *Salon*

"Kennedy . . . doesn't disappoint. His characters are pleasingly multifaceted . . . [He] knows how to whisper and to let his reader discover the patterns he makes of teeth, silence and sky."
— *Cleveland Plain Dealer*

"Tragic, wise, comic, profound, [Kennedy writes] an epic of the human heart struggling for meaning and redemption." — *RainTaxi*

". . . complex and poignant and resonant, full of literary pleasures."
— René Steinke, National Book Award Finalist

"Kennedy's force is his ear for good dialogue, those understated conversations between irony and intimacy of which Anglo-Saxon and Irish literature have always been world champion."
— *Politiken* (Copenhagen)

"Thomas Kennedy is a true discovery, an author of rare intelligence and moral vision . . . immensely compelling and beautifully written.'
— Alain de Botton, author of *How Proust Can Change Your Life*

". . . some of the most intelligent and beautifully crafted short fiction in America… fresh and contemporary and very much his own."
— W. D. Wetherell, Drue Heinz Prize-winner

"Kennedy is a writer's writer and a reader's fortunate discovery."
—*Cape Cod Voice*, "Our Favorite Fiction of 2003"

"Intense, humorous, sexually charged, emotionally powerful, the stories of Thomas E. Kennedy . . . brilliantly mine the hidden recesses of the human heart. Kennedy is a dazzling writer—literary, compelling, and profound."
— Duff Brenna, AWP Novel Award-winner

"Kennedy is at his best when catching the arbitrary leaps and descents of thought as his characters muse on their position . . . in a minor key, as nimble and intimate as a piece of chamber music . . . it touches on the contemporary moment with a deft precision . . . of the utmost timeliness." — *Financial Times*

"The narrative skill of a great fiction writer drives the writing here."
— Robert Stewart, *New Letters*

"No one writes about the loves and lives of men better than Kennedy, including their relationships with their own children."
— *Kansas City Star*, "Noteworthy Novels of 2003"

". . . Kennedy's power to relate sight and sound on the page borders on the supernatural . . ."
—*Abiko* (Tokyo)

OTHER BOOKS BY THOMAS E. KENNEDY

NOVELS
Kerrigan in Copenhagen, A Love Story (2013)
Falling Sideways (2011)
In the Company of Angels (2010)
A Passion in the Desert (2007)
Danish Fall (2005)
Greene's Summer (2004)
Bluett's Blue Hours (2003)
Kerrigan's Copenhagen, A Love Story (2002)
The Book of Angels (1997)
A Weather of the Eye (1996)
Crossing Borders (1990)

STORY AND ESSAY COLLECTIONS
Last Night My Bed a Boat of Whiskey Going Down (2010)
Riding the Dog: A Look Back at America (2008)
Cast Upon the Day (2007)
The Literary Traveler (with Walter Cummins) (2005)
Realism & Other Illusions: Essays on the Craft of Fiction (2002)
Drive Dive Dance & Fight (1997)
Unreal City (1996)

LITERARY CRITICISM
Robert Coover: A Study of the Short Fiction (1992)
Andre Dubus: A Study of the Short Fiction (1988)
The American Short Story Today (Ed.) (1991)
American Short Story Award Collections (1993)

EDITED ANTHOLOGIES & JOURNAL ISSUES
Winter Tales: Men Write About Aging (with Duff Brenna) (2011)
The Girl with Red Hair (with Walter Cummins) (2010)
The Book of Worst Meals (with Walter Cummins) (2010)
New Danish Writing (*The Literary Review*, 2008)
Writers on the Job (with Walter Cummins) (2007)
Poems & Sources (*The Literary Review*, 2000)
Stories & Sources (*The Literary Review*, 1998)
New Irish Writing (*The Literary Review*, 1996)
New Danish Fiction (with Frank Hugus) (*Review of Contemporary Fiction*, 1995)

TRANSLATIONS
Dan Turèll, *Last Walk Through the City* (2010)
Thomas Larsen, *The Meeting with Evil: Inge Genefke's Fight against Torture* (2010)

POETRY
Verses for Drunks, Lechers & Other Miscreants (2010)

GETTING LUCKY

GETTING LUCKY

New & Selected Stories

1982 - 2012

THOMAS E. KENNEDY

newamericanpress

Milwaukee, Wisconsin • Urbana, Illinois

new american press

www.NewAmericanPress.com

© 2013 by Thomas E. Kennedy

All rights reserved. No part of this publication may be reproduced, stored in a retrieval system, or transmitted, in any form or by any means, electronic, mechanical, photocopying, recording, or otherwise, without the prior written permission of the copyright holder.

Printed in the United States of America

ISBN 978-0-9849439-2-0

For ordering information, please contact:

Ingram Book Group
One Ingram Blvd.
La Vergne, TN 37086
(800) 937—8000
orders@ingrambook.com

For my father, George Ryan Kennedy, Sr. (1906-64),
who made our home sing with poetry.

For my mother, Ethel P. Kennedy (1905-86),
and my sister Joan O'Connor,
who always listened with enthusiasm to my childish tales.

For my brothers—
Jack, who taught me there was music to be found inside;
Jerry, who taught me dialogue with his quick ripostes;
George, who taught me to tell time
and to stand on my head.

Always for Daniel, Isabel, Søren, and Leo

And for the Mademoiselle.

We are left with who or what we have made of ourselves.

CONTENTS

...and to die is different
from what anyone supposed,
and luckier.

— Walt Whitman, "Song of Myself"

ACKNOWLEDGMENTS

The following stories appeared previously in the journals and anthologies indicated:

"Is Dog?" in *Fiction*; "Little Sinners" in *American Fiction* and reprinted in *REDUX: A Literary Journal*; "Bliss Street" in *Patchwork of Dreams* (The Spirit That Moves Us Press); "The Sins of Generals" in *Confrontation* and reprinted in *Into the Silence* (Green Street Press); "Here's My Story, It's Sad But True" in *Black Warrior Review*; "The Author of Things" in *The Girl with Red Hair* (Serving House Books); "Getting Lucky" in *South Carolina* Review; "The Great Master" in *Missouri Review* and reprinted in *Writers Notes Magazine* and *The Booktrader Christmas Album*; "What Does God Care About Your Dignity, Victor Travesti?" in *New Letters* and reprinted in *The Whole Story* (The Bench Press); "Gasparini's Organ" in *Crosscurrents* and reprinted in *Literary Olympians II* and *Best of Crosscurrents*; "Murphy's Angel" in *New Delta Review* and *Pushcart Prize XV*; "Bonner's Women" in *Glimmer Train* and reprinted in *Rosebud*; "Kansas City" in *New Letters*; "Drive Dive Dance & Fight" in *New Letters*; "Landing Zone X-Ray" in *New Letters* and reprinted in *O. Henry Awards 1994*; "The Pleasure of Man and Woman Together on Earth" in *New Letters*; "Years in Kaldar" in *The Literary Review*; and "A Cheerful Death" in *Gulf Coast*.

PREFACE

THE FIRST OF MY STORIES to be published, written in 1981, was accepted by Martin Tucker, editor of *Confrontation*, in January 1982, but didn't see print until 1984. Mr. Tucker paid me twenty dollars for it, and that was the sweetest, most succulent double sawbuck I had earned until then. At that time I had been writing and submitting short fiction since I was seventeen years old—twenty doubt-troubled years. But when I was a few pages into that story, "The Sins of Generals" (included here in section one), I *knew* that it would be my first published short fiction.

Into a bar in Montpelier, Vermont, I took the twenty bucks, and Andre Dubus, a master of the short story, happened to be there. I approached him, introduced myself and suggested that we drink my honorarium up. He was kind enough to offer to read the story and apparently liked it sufficiently that he included it in an anthology he was editing (*Into the Silence. American Stories*, 1988), alongside some of my heroes: Gina Berriault ("Stone Boy"), Mark Costello ("Murphy's Xmas"), Susan Dodd ("Public Appearances"), Leonard Gardner (*Fat City*), Tobias Wolff ("The Barracks Thief"), and others.

So it seems I took twenty years to learn to write a publishable story (retrospectively receiving payment of a dollar a year for the work)—a lengthy apprenticeship with no guarantee of establishing myself as an author—and in what manner does one manage to establish that? Throughout those twenty years I became increasingly desperate. I was in danger of becoming a bitter man. Writing was the only thing I wanted to do; I had a good job with a comfortable salary, a good career, a family, a nice house, but all I wanted to do was write—for a lengthy period most days I even got up at five in the morning to write. And I had seen what the thwarted desire to be a writer had done to my own father—through years of trying, he published only three poems and died in his fifties. I felt as though an important part of my spirit was   already dying, maybe was already dead. I had not yet realized that the sustenance must primarily be in the writing itself, in the process, in the trying, in the discovery—it would be further years before I came to understand that.

Meanwhile I felt like a dead tree. But as Rilke pointed out, a tree in winter might look dead when really it is gathering the forces necessary to bloom in spring. That long season was my winter of discontent, stretching out over two decades.

Over the following thirty years, however, I would publish well over a hundred stories and many novels and other books, including the four collections represented here, and a few dozen personal essays constructed of the same craft elements as short fiction.

My earliest style was what I would call "uninformed realism." Then, when I began to realize that realism was as much an illusion as other styles, all of which, at their best, were seeking to discover some small and in some way entertaining purchase on the inscrutable, reality, I began to experiment with surrealism, magical realism, absurdism, and metafiction, eventually to return to realism and, as Eliot put it, finally know the place—somewhat. One of the things that I came to understand with those experiments is that anything in a story—as anything in a dream—is magical regardless whether the story is realism or magical realism. Another of the things that had been blocking me from writing a viable story was the mistaken assumption that I had to "understand" the story I was writing, that I had to have a preconceived understanding of it, which is a fast track to writer's block. In about 1980, I read a sentence by Wright Morris—"How do I know what I want to say until I've said it?"—which fortunately derailed me from that dead-end track.

The stories in this volume represent all the types of story I have written so far, insofar as I can typify them, and all of my collections. The first section includes new and previously uncollected short fictions. The stories in this volume appeared originally in *Glimmer Train*, *The Literary Review*, *Fiction*, *Rosebud*, *South Carolina Review*, *Patchwork of Dreams*, *Black Warrior Review*, *Missouri Review*, *New Delta Review*, *Crosscurrents*, *Literary Olympians*, *The Girl with Red Hair*, *American Fiction*, *Confrontation*, *Writers Notes*, *Gulf Coast*, *The Booktrader Christmas Album*, and five of them appeared first in *New Letters* at University of Missouri Kansas City. Some of them have been reprinted various other places, and some won prizes—inter alia a Pushcart Prize, an O. Henry Award, the Charles Angoff Award, the *Gulf Coast* Short Story Competition, and several others received honorable mention in the *Pushcart Prize* and *Best American Short Stories*. Thirteen are from four previous collections—four each from *Unreal City* (Wordcraft of

Oregon, 1996) and *Drive Dive Dance & Fight* (BkMk Press, 1997), three from *Cast Upon the Day* (Hopewell Publications, 2007), and two from *Last Night My Bed a Boat of Whiskey Going Down* (New American Press, 2010), billed as "a novel in essays" mainly because it consisted of a mix of creative nonfiction and fiction, and we did not know what to call it until David Bowen came up with that neat solution.

Of the seven stories in the first part of this book, four are very new and none was previously collected; one appears here for close to the first time (the title story, a novella)—it was published in *South Carolina Review* the month before this book appeared. All represent, along with the other pieces in this volume, examples of what I consider some of my more successful short stories—insofar as a writer can make that claim about his own work. One of the stories in the first section I wrote in the mid-'80s—it is a parody of sexist male behavior—and, in celebration of free expression, I read it on a public occasion at a writing seminar to the consternation of some present; one woman in the audience expressed her distress that the story existed in the same world as her children (she had, in fact, earlier that year infected one of my friends with an STD), resulting in the expression by the seminar director of that program that I should refrain from expressing "that sort of thing" there again. Which I took as a compliment, confirmed by the editor of *Black Warrior Review* who telephoned me a month later in Copenhagen to express her view that the story was "simply hilarious" and that she would be publishing it in her magazine. (I got fifty bucks for that one.)

It is good to have an opportunity to showcase storie
I still care very much about and to give them a new life in a
new book.

I thank David Bowen and Okla Elliott as well as Liana Bowen of
New American Press; Robert Stewart of *New Letters* (an early and
consistent supporter of my writing for which I am deeply
grateful); Walter Cummins and René Steinke and Minna Proctor
of *The Literary Review*; R. A. Rycraft and particularly Duff Brenna
of *Serving House Journal*; Wayne Chapman of the *South Carolina
Review*, which has devoted many pages to work about my work;
David Memmott inter alia of Wordcraft of Oregon; Ben Furnish
of BkMk Press; Linda Swanson-Davies and Susan Burmeister of
Glimmer Train (probably the best-paying literary journal in
America); Rock and Roll Professor Greg Herriges of Harper
College who, with Tom Knoff, generously honored my work by
making two documentary DVDs about it; Christopher Klim of
Hopewell Press; Dwayne D. Hayes of *Absinthe: New European
Writing*; David Applefield of *Frank* magazine in Paris; Gladys
Swan, Rick Mulkey, Susan Tekulve, Susan M. Dodd, Gordon
Weaver, and the Roaring Boys of Vermont College (Paul Casey,
Dennis Bormann, Mike Duffy, and Jim Marengo); all of my
colleagues and friends and students at Fairleigh Dickinson
University as well as at Serving House Books, all of whom make
life so much less lonely; and all of the other editors, professors,
mentors, colleagues, and friends who have encouraged me over
the years with that ultimate compliment for a writer—publishing
or teaching or even just reading or in some manner valuing one
or more of his stories.

Many of these people have become friends, some very close and cherished friends indeed.

I especially thank Alain de Botton, Junot Dìaz, and Andre Dubus III; my editors at Bloomsbury Publishers—Anton Mueller in New York and Helen Garnons-Williams in London as well as all their colleagues—my agents Nat Sobel and Judith Weber; and my original Irish publisher, Roger Derham, for helping give me a new literary life in this new millennium.

Most of all I thank my father, for his hyperbolic praise of my fledgling teenaged efforts and for making our home a place that sang with poetry, the value of which becomes increasingly clear to me with the years, and my mother and my sister Joan who always amazed me by always being willing to listen with enthusiasm to my tales and stories and accounts. I remember coming home from some adventure or other and sitting in the kitchen with them and their tirelessly listening as I recounted the doings of some of my friends or a place I had biked to or funny people I had seen in school or on the street or even just a movie I had watched in those days when a movie was watched in an ornate, many-tiered movie house. I did not know then that I was subject to paroxysms of language and that Mom and Joan, two beautiful women, were helping me away from the abyss of silence. And I thank my brothers—Jack, Jerry, George—for their friendship.

*   *   *

Finally, and not least, I salute the literary magazines and small presses of the United States and Canada, which are an American treasure; without them, our culture would be in danger and many, perhaps most, American writers would live in a desert, lacking the encouragement necessary to go on.

— Thomas E. Kennedy
Copenhagen, 2012

ONE: THE SINS OF GENERALS

New & Previously Uncollected Stories

Is Dog?

Sklar jolts off his sweaty sofa in the ungodly dark to get the phone, thinking, *Pop's gone.* But his father's phlegmy voice, without greeting or apology for the hour, wheezes in his ear, "I'm *alone* here! I need things. I'm out of vodka!"

Sklar needs things, too. He needs his sleep. He needs to find a job. He needs to pick up a gift for Nicoline's twenty-fifth birthday and to make this crappy little place presentable for when she comes over this evening. And he needs to talk to his father. Resolve some stuff.

So he showers—pointless in this New York August heat—slurps down some instant and foots it north, plowing through the sweltering west side streets to Tenth and 38th, Sammy's Books and Music, which opens at 9:00.

As Sklar watches the blade of Sammy's Swiss Army knife slice the foil from the bottle of Cab, he talks about Nicoline, realizing that he is trying to explain her to himself.

"You got it bad," says Sammy and wrestles out the wine cork with a pop.

"She's so…sweet."

"Even the sweet ones got hair on their ass." Sammy is a dozen years Sklars' senior, has a pretty wife whose mouth seems to get harder by the year, and a boy in high school with a face full of studs. Sklar wonders how that might be for a twist of fate, kid like that, but Sammy seems cool with it:. "I told him if he absolutely had to be pierced, have it done by a pro. Don't scar up your kisser, kiddo—you'll need that for the duration. So, how's your old man, Sklar?"

"Raging."

"Why don't you just tell the girl you need to be with him? She'd understand that. And if she don't, well, fuck 'er."

Sammy pours the Cab, and they stand over the remainder table, lift their glasses. Sklar often brings a bottle when he visits Sammy. Helps him think. Sammy has a massive chest and short legs; beige dreadlocks dangle from the fringe of his shiny, tan bald pate. He occasionally shows himself to be a man of compassion, even if he does write sci fi stories about creatures that kill by devouring the genitals of earthlings and cremators who collect and trade the handsomer corpses instead of incinerating them and other assorted horrors that Sklar won't read for fear of screaming nightmares.

"I can't expose Nicoline to Pop," says Sklar. "Our relationship is too new."

"Ain't poked her yet?"

Sklar makes a face that says gimme a break. "If I tell her about my father, she's so nice she'll insist on coming to visit him, and then…." Sklar sighs, sips his wine. "This is corky."

"Let's pretend not," says Sammy, putting down his glass on a yellowing paperback of Paradiso to tend to a customer. Sklar can smell the customer all the way across the room, glances over to see the telltale greasy hair and wet red complexion of a homeless wino sweating beneath a frayed Harris Tweed. Where do they all get those gray pants? Sklar wonders. The wino is holding up a battered book as if it were a jewel box. Sklar recognizes it as a stray volume from a supermarket encyclopedia.

"Can I interest you in this art book?" the wino asks. His voice is coarse and phlegmy and reminds Sklar of his father's. His father could've been a bum, few wrong choices. Sklar still could be.

Sammy takes the book, turns pages with an expert touch. "Five bucks," he says gruffly. "Take it or leave it."

When the wino is gone, the folded sawbuck clutched happily in the horrible pocket of his filthy gray pants, Sammy chucks the book into the trash bucket behind his counter.

"Where do they all get those gray pants?" Sklar asks.

"'Ey. There but for the grace."

Sklar peers at his friend. "You believe in God?"

"Woulden it be pretty to think so."

They sip their corky wine. It's not so bad really. Sklar thinks of the homeless man with his five dollars. Will he rush out and buy a gallon of even cheaper wine than this? Sklar wonders where the man sleeps, marvels again about the fact that when his father dies he will inherit the five-room condo in which he is dying. Without that condo, Sklar himself could easily become homeless, hanging on by the teeth to that tiny Chelsea studio rented by the month for more than he can manage. He could drop the studio and stay with his father, but then there would be no respite from the old man's dying, his stink. The wasp nest of his thoughts rouses guilt. Soon he'll own a property worth a million easy. Hold your horses. What kind of a greedy fuck-head are you? Think what Nicoline would think.

"Shit," says Sklar. "What the fuck am I gonna give Nicoline for her birthday?"

Sammy holds up one blunt, tobacco-stained finger, reaches beneath the counter to produce an intriguing, long flat box. It is woven of some kind of brown grass and has a spring top. Arrayed artfully within is a string of dark beads set in smithed silver on a silver chain. Sammy tells him he picked it up in South Africa when he was on an acquisition tour for vintage township jazz. "This belonged to the mother of Abraham Ibrahim. It's more than a hundred years old. You know his wife has a two-room at the Chelsea? Costs five grand. A month. No wonder he sold this so cheap. Needed the dough."

"How much? It's beautiful."

"For you: Eighty."

In Sklar's wallet are two hundred in twenties. Which should have gone toward this month's rent. "Can I owe you?"

"No. Want a bag?"

Only when he's ready to leave, turning back from the door, his wallet thinner by four Jeffersons, does Sklar think to ask, "What kind of beads are they anyway?"

"They're said to have magical properties. If I don't tell you what they are, you won't have to decide whether to tell Nicoline."

Sklar stares at the man's Slavic face, his high cheekbones, his bleached blue eyes. "It's better to know," Sklar says. A statement he will regret. Because Sammy, for all his virtues, has a no-refunds policy.

"Caveat emptor," the little, broad-chested Slav tells him.

Rattling downtown on the 8th Avenue, Sklar sweats in a cattle car of sweaty meat-smelling bodies, his purchase tucked inside a plain white plastic bag. In his haste, he jumped on the wrong train and hasn't the patience to get off and wait for the right one. He springs off at Spring and hoofs, puffing, up the grimy stairway, considering that it is not yet eleven and he's already consumed half a bottle of corky Cab that is oozing stinkily out his pores. When will he ever learn not to drink before noon? Through the soupy heat he wades east toward Alphabet City, Avenue C, stops at a neon Wine & Liquors sign to purchase four packs of L&Ms and a double handle of Babushka, cheapest on the market. Taste is not an issue here, only the intoxicant value. Then he drags south to 2nd and lets himself into the building with the giant NO sign showing through the glass door:

NO ballplaying cardgames congregating
drinking dancing necking nuttin'

Allen Ginsberg once lived here, where Sklar's father is now dying and where Sklar has been camping sporadically on a futon in the musty living room, unwilling to choose a room for himself, certainly not the tiny closet he occupied as a child.

Why did we live here? Because it was cheap. Pop was not the big shot I was led to believe. Never made professor. Never even got tenure. So we lived here. Where he sat in his back room office and did math, always on the verge of some great discovery. A vain man. Thought he was handsome, great. You're vain, too. No I'm not. Yes you are. Your father was no worse than you are. Took you for walks sometimes too. Hated him. A little. Because of the way Mom coddled him like a big baby. Your father this, your father that. Coddled you too. Not enough. Your father is a professor. You only found out later he wasn't. Saw that she didn't even know. He's not. He's an adjunct. Hand to mouth. She thought he was a god. Gave it to her straight: You know Pop is not really a professor. Her tilted smile. Why that's crazy, son, of course he is. She didn't believe you. He was her god. But she had Jesus too. Didn't have the brain to see it was all metaphor. They tried to do your brain in too, nip it in the bud with all the memorizing, chains of words: Whomadeus? Godmadeus. Who is God? God is a supreme being who sees all knows all and is infinitely good. Why did God make us? God made us to show forth his goodness and to share with us his infinite happiness in heaven… But you broke the chains, read books they never read, mom couldn't, Pop wouldn't. Joyce. And then you didn't need them anymore. Not true. Still loved them. A little. Still had the religion-shaped hole in your heart, something Pop never had. I could give him that now. Show him something he doesn't have. That I have. Why this spite? I love you, Pop. That word conveys nothing of what I feel for him.

A little black kid peeks out from next door. "Whachoo doin' dash."

"Visiting my Pop."

"You Pop live in there dash."

"Yeah."

"Kin I meet 'im dash."

"How come you always say dash at the end of everything?"

"Cuz I don't know if I'm done so I leave it open dash."

"Where'd you ever get an idea like that?"

"Dreamed it dash. Hey, kin I come in witchoo dash?"

"Probly not a good idea right now."

"Okay dash. See you dash."

Sklar watches the kid slip in behind the door again, decides to baptize him Dash, wishes he had dreams like that, wishes he could visit with the kid instead of his father. As he keys open the apartment door, the old man's smell rushes into his nostrils. Remember Pop could smell when you were sick: Boy's got the measles. Pop's got the C.

"Where's my vodka!" the phlegmy voice grumbles from the "master" bedroom. Phrases from childhood: The master bedroom. Your father's office. Go to your room. Closet, you mean.

In the kitchen, Sklar pours a deep tumbler of the vod, then plugs his nose with tissue wads before bearing it in to his father. Even through the tissue, he can smell impending death. His father is propped up in a rented hospital bed, a drop in either arm—one of nutrient, the other morphine. There is a plunger hanging from the bed frame by which his father can regulate the morphine dose. He can take as much as he wants. He can kill himself if he chooses. Sklar considers that this could be a nice way to go, OD on morphine. He himself was given morphine once, before an operation, and he could not believe how good it made him feel. But his father prefers to "keep his mind clear" and dose himself to sleep with vodka. Twice a day a giant gentle black man comes to replenish the nutrient and morphine bags and take the old man's

L&Ms away from him. Even at their cut rate price, Sklar is going broke on cigarettes.

"Can't you hide them under your pillow, Pop?"

"He smells the fuckin' things." Sklar's father never used profanity before. Sklar wonders if all these years he had thought it, privately, inside his skull.

On the thin, wilted sheet that covers his father's lower half, pencil thin legs swathed in graying cotton, is a range of things: the remote to a flat screen TV that plays mutely at the foot of the bed, an ashtray, scattered sections of the *New York Times*.

Sklar sits in a straight back chair beside the bed and breathes normally, inhaling enough of the stench that he has to suppress a gag. The cancer is in the colon, but the smell is everywhere. Sklar tells himself it is a smell like any smell, that he needn't place a value on it, but another part of him asserts that it is the smell of death, of a sick, decaying body and that it is unnatural not to be repulsed by it. He thinks of Nicoline's fragrance, her honey-blond hair, her smile, gentle blue Italian eyes. Maybe Sammy is right, but he does not want to put her to this test. He does not want to lose her before he's even won her. Why take chances? As is, he finds it hard to believe that she spends time with him, a paunchy homely man past thirty with few prospects other than the ghoulish profit he will reap from selling his father's home after the man is dead. Unlike Sklar, Nicoline has a steady job, teaching in a Catholic grade school in Little Italy. The kids love her. She goes to Mass on Sundays but has never bugged him to join her. How come you go? he asked her. It makes me feel good. And so far she has had no questions about his sketchy

CV, his poetic aspirations that so far have yielded sparse publication in journals of questionable repute, mostly on-line. But Nicoline is enthusiastic about them. She's too good to be true, but Sklar is determined to believe. What's the alternative? Drop her for her bad taste in poetry? Anyway, so far is so far not so far. All he's ever done is kiss her under the Moorish Wall. Two little kisses and a cryptic gaze that said maybe later. Women so damn eloquent with the eyes. Their eyes tell all—if you can only decipher it.

He doesn't ask his father how he feels. No point in that. Instead he glances at the pile of books on his night table, silted with dust and L&M ash. Arcane math treatises. Ought to try some poetry, philosophy. Embarrassing to have a father who never even read Eliot not to mention Stevens.

"Been reading, Pop?"

"What's the point." Glowering eyes, knotted mouth. "You see those pictures in the Times?" he asks. "Boys returning from Iraq? One called 'Marine Wedding'? Kid whose face was blown off, getting married to his highschool sweetheart? Kid had no face. Nothing. No fuckin' face! Just like a blank dome with eye-ear-nose holes in it. Didn't even have a skull, just a plastic reconstruction." He glares at his son, then exhales with surrender. "What's the fuckin' point. It's all over."

Sklar shakes his head. He's already maxed out on war news. His father's glass is empty, and he thrusts it toward his son. "Whyn't you leave the bottle with me?"

"I don't mind serving it to you, Pop." In truth it is an excuse to retreat to the slightly fainter air of the kitchen. He takes his time pouring an even steeper one.

"You're begging the question!" the phlegmy voice wheeze-barks after him, but Sklar is humming a tune that spares him from acknowledging. Then he realizes the tune is Billy Strayhorn's "Blood Count." His father knows jazz, always talking about math and music, would recognize it if Sklar managed to hum it in key, might find it taunting. Sklar glides into "Take the A Train," wonders if that will remind the old man of his years at CCNY, letting people think he was a professor. One stop express from 59th to 125th & Lex. Sklar went to City, too, a decade before, where he found out his father was far from an honored leader of the math department. Sklar himself is still a few credits short of his BA. Ought to get that done.

The skin on back of the hand clutching the glass of Babushka is gray as ash, shot through with thin brown threads and mottled with beige spots. Sklar glances briefly at the face but cannot bear it, turns his eyes back to the hands, tries to focus on good memories, his father's gentle gruffness, years ago, mussing his son's hair, tender-tough. The accomplishment of getting Pop to laugh, walking with him down by the harbor, in Central Park, museum visits, historic tours. *See that building—shaped like a flat iron and that's what they call it. See here, Bowling Green? The Dutch used to bury Indians up to their necks and bowl at their heads. Fact. Hey, you wanna see the mummies up at the Met?*

"Pop, I've been thinking about something you said the other day," Sklar says. "You said, 'My past is your future and vice versa.' What does that mean?"

"I didn't say that."

"Oh yes you did."

"Prove it."

Sklar chuckles, grateful for the repartee. "Prove you didn't."

"The burden of proof is on the claimant." Then the vodka and the joking turn sour again. "I know what you're up to. I should never have let her send you to Catholic school. You actually believe that horseshit."

"Not literally. Not like eternal reward or punishment, not a tunnel of light even, not even the survival of the ego, but it seems evident to me that there must be something. All of this this this existence didn't come of nothing."

"Horseshit."

"Mom believed in it."

"Mom was a woman. Are you a woman?"

"We don't think that way anymore."

"We! You don't think. You feel. Like a little girl. Are you a little girl?"

Sklar doesn't take this personally. He knows what his father is thinking about when he says that. He's thinking about Bobby Kennedy in the House hearings on organized crime, telling some Mafia boss that he giggled like a little girl, asking, "Are you a little girl, Mr. Gian-something-or-other?" His father had loved to catch politicians saying stupid things. He had a whole collection of these sayings logged into spiral notebooks, but in the old days they enlivened him. Now they seem only to reinforce his despair, give him ammunition against anyone trying to take it away from him. Sklar wonders if the whole exercise hadn't been to cover up his own sense of inferiority. Prove everybody in the world is an asshole, then it's not so bad if you are, too.

"Seems to me," his father grumbles, "you'd do a hell of a lot better living this life a little better. You're fucking wasting it."

"What does that matter, if there's nothing else? What do all your years of study and math matter then?"

"Fuck you!" he wheeze-shouts, bulging-eyed, gasping, glowering. "Fuck you! You're just like your mother!"

"Easy, Pop," Sklar whispers. "I was just talking. Here, let me get you something more to drink."

Sklar's mother was Catholic, died fingering her rosary beads, and Sklar knelt by her bedside, wondering whether Joyce truly had refused to kneel and pray with his dying mother or if that was just in his fiction. What a pointless gesture, to deny comfort to a dying woman. If all you believed in was nothingness, what difference did it make to support a lie if it gave comfort. On the other hand, it was Joyce—not his father—who saved him from that death of the mind.

He and his father sat up late together the night after her funeral, and Sklar could see the man had been working up to something. Finally he flung it out. "I can't believe you knelt and prayed. And received communion. You still believe all that crap, don't you?"

"Not literally," Sklar said. "But I do believe something of us survives. Even Einstein said energy can neither be created nor destroyed..."

"You think you can teach me physics?"

Sklar shrugged. He was weak at science—had just got a C in the only physics course he ever took, but still.

*   *   *

Now, nearly a dozen years later, Sklar schemes to rekindle that conversation. "That's really terrible. About that Marine. I didn't see the picture, but…"

His father shrugs, scowling. "Whatever. What does it matter? People screaming about the fate of the human race. I think: who gives a fuck? Don't they know they're gonna die? Don't they know they're gonna forget everything? Don't you know—you phony existentialist!—that nothing is real?"

"I choose to live and be happy."

"Ha! Even I know Camus when I hear it. As an existentialist you're a big fat phoney-baloney! You're a goddamned Roman Catholic in your heart. I should never have agreed to let her send you to that Catholic school. They runed you."

"How? By giving me something to believe in?"

"So you do believe in it! I knew it!"

"No, not anymore, but I do believe that something of us survives. Not the ego. Something deeper. And I regret that you won't open your heart to that possibility…"

"Fuck off!" the old man barks and sits there, heaving for breath. Then, "Sorry, son," he begins and for one instant Sklar thinks he is truly apologizing, but then sees the apology was rhetorical. "That would mean time is real which as far as we know is not the case. It's not false that something of us survives. Rather, 'Something of us survives' is meaningless. Do you remember what I told you years ago when you asked me about infinity? I told you the universe is finite. And you asked me, then what lies on the outside of it? And I told you asking that is like asking, 'Is dog?' Because the words string together properly according to the rules in grammar books, but they do not signify anything. It's the same with time, death, survival. As far as I'm concerned, 'Something of us survives' equals 'Is dog?' It's not that past and future are illusions —more like they're tricks of perspective, not worth worrying about. My past is your future and vice versa. That's Einstein! Maybe it's easy for me to talk this way because I'm a Jew and I allowed your mother to talk me into sending you to Catholic school so it's 'natural' for you to believe something survives because you're still Catholic underneath all the existential patter. We think we're independent thinkers, meanwhile we're really the servants of some priest or rabbi, Christ or Maimonides, from a thousand years ago."

"Then you could be wrong, too."

After his long speech the old man has trouble finding wind to go on, but he finds it. "No no no, what I'm saying is right! The universe is finite, so what's around it?" he adds scornfully and shakes his head, lumping up his lips sourly, eyelids drooping from his exertions.

The third tumbler of vodka is empty, glass clutched in the ashen fist, the big-browed head slumps forward. Sklar holds his breath, then leans in through the cloud of stench to kiss his father's cheek.

"I love you, Pop," he whispers, hoping the words might seep in and become the simple, final truth. The only answer is a faint snore.

The red August light of mid-afternoon slants through the cracked window blinds, and Sklar still is sheened with chill sweat despite the air conditioner. The only sound in the apartment is the combined hum of the AC and refrigerator, and it seems the hum of eternity. In a finite universe. With nothing outside it. Because there is no outside. Only an end. And a senseless question. Is dog? And a soldier with no face, marrying his high school sweetheart. And the fragrance of Nicoline's hair.

Sklar goes out to the kitchen and drops ice cubes into a dusty glass, splashes in six fingers of Babushka and sips. The liquor is coarse, barely distilled. Hospital spirit. His father is too young to die. Sixty-seven. Sklar does not want him to die bitter. Wants to help the old man see what he himself can almost see, can sense, can…what? And who is it for? Him? Me? Both maybe. Why? So I'll be able to enjoy my inheritance? His mother went a decade ago, in her early 50s, and her death started the old man's. Despite all his understanding, when she slipped away and took with her all the illusions that had sweetened their life, it was the beginning of the end for the man of science.

Sklar sits in an old wooden chair and listens to a car whisper past two stories below on 2nd Street and tries to comprehend his own thoughts. A line of poetry floats up: If the soul is ever to know itself it must look into the soul. Impossible. Oxymoron. Maybe if the soul could look in a mirror? From an apartment above he hears a baby howling with what sounds like terror. Alarming sound. Abuse? Or simply the terror of incarnation? He wonders what a baby knows. What do you see in the depth of infant eyes? He is aware that he has already begun to move away from the questions of existence his father made him want to discuss. He is also aware that he is much too tired to take the train uptown and clean his apartment.

He sits nodding in the wooden chair, thinks briefly of the little kid next door. Dash. Call him Dash. Never finished speaking. Never noticed that kid before. Seemed to know me. So many people I never notice. Like in school, back then. Fear. I don't see them, they don't see me. Don't know who's there. Lot of blank spaces. Fill 'em in with words, people-shaped words. Always been this way. Too dangerous otherwise. Else they get you. Right back to the first day of school. Before. People on the street. Come right up to you on those Alphabet streets, mean teeth smiling to see what they can get, how they can use you. Stay still, make like nothing. Don't answer, don't hear, don't see, just keep looking away and they think you're not there. Just an illusion. Like a dog that comes barking. Just ignore 'im your father said.

His nodding head snaps up and he wonders where he was, is.

Before he leaves, he looks in on his father one more time and is startled to find him awake, his face awash in the flicker of the flatscreen, but his dark eyes are fixed on Sklar's, and in them, he sees an expression he has never before seen—not in his father's eyes, not anywhere. It is as though the man is looking back at him from the other side, as though he is about to vanish but his spirit is still glowing, like a dwarf star, dark one.

Sklar steps closer. "Pop," he whispers, but the old eyes just keep staring. Then he says, "My fucking butt hurts. Gimme some vodka."

*   *   *

Sklar is ashamed bringing Nicoline up in the filthy elevator of his Chelsea building, walking her along the grimey tile floor to his door. "You'll have to excuse the mess," Sklar says as they stand in the hall, bodies touching lightly, before he slides the key into the lock. "This is only temporary quarters. My actual place is being fixed up for me." Why'd I say that?

Nicoline smiles that smile that zapped him from the first moment he saw her, three months before, drinking a giant martini at the outside bar of the Tavern on the Green, and what were the odds that he would go into the Tavern on the Green, where he never went, at just the moment he would see her there, sitting beneath the hedge clip-sculptured to look like King Kong. She was new in town, a refugee from Upper Darby who not only let him talk to her but even turned upon him those blue Italian eyes with such intensity that they wound up dancing to Lou Reed's "Walk on the Wild Side" at CBGB where his knowledge of the city wowed her. What were the odds of all that in a finite universe?

Yet what was it really about? Genetic programming? Just one more illusion? He thinks of his father's dark, intense eyes, that silent staring. A phrase floats up: Now and at the hour of our death...

He seats Nicoline at one end of the black corduroy sofa in the sparse light of two faux Tiffany lamps where, he hopes, she cannot see the sofa lint or floor dust.. He puts on Getz while he unwraps, unwires, uncorks a bottle of Cremant. The cork pops clean to let a little foam dribble off the lip of the bottle. Their smiles are droll, observing, and their eyes meet. From where he sits he can see her twice—in person and in the wall mirror which he mounted there to increase the depth perception of this tiny crappy pad that he could lose at any moment. His worry is immediately alleviated by the memory of what his father's five-room is worth, purchased way back when a normal human being could still own a five-room in a decent building in the East Village. He remembers again those staring eyes. Perhaps part of his reason for not telling Nicoline about his father is the fear that the prospect of his inheritance might pique her interest. Already hoarding your gold? Won't make him rich, but enough for a good start. What's a good start? Will you drink it all away? Do I deserve a good start? Whether or not, you'll get it. And he remembers the eyes. The eyes have been with him ever since, every time his mind pauses.

Now he shields his own eyes, then uncovers them to look at Nicoline. She has a classic profile—Roman—and he pictures her kneeling at Mass, a little hanky on her head, the way his mother used to cover her hair in church. Probably don't do that anymore. Then he notices that Getz is playing Billy Strayhorn's "Bloodcount," written by Strayhorn in '67 when he was dying of cancer and recorded by Getz in '87, when he was dying of cancer, and now it is '07 and his father is dying of cancer—Pop!—about to leave him, a 32-year-old orphan. With a five-room condo. A million easy, maybe. Or even half that. He remembers reading that Getz said he could hear Billy talking to God everytime he played the notes of that composition. Four minutes finger-fucking eternity. In a finite universe.

His mouth opens, and the words that come out are, "Is dog?"

Nicoline smiles that smile, tilting her head in a way that says she'll go along with the fun if he will but give her a clue.

He pours a bit of the cremant into her glass and lets it foam off, then pours more, recalling that it was his father who taught him how to do that, and he repeats aloud the words of Churchill his father loved to quote about the bubbly: "Three requisites about champagne: It must be dry, it must be chill, it must be free."

Nicoline's laughter is pure as mountain water, and they clink flutes while Getz enunciates Strayhorn's speech to God, and Sklar murmurs, "If the soul is ever to know itself it must look into the soul," looking into blue eyes that seem to reveal the depth of a soul that might live forever even if, in truth, he knows nothing about it, has no idea really what he sees in her. Sweetness and light? Haven't poked her yet? This is not just about sex, no way. What's it about for her? A guy who can show her the CBGB?

The tilt of her smile now tells him that he is unsettling her, and he remembers the gift. He has failed to wrap it so he folds the white plastic bag smoothly over the box and holds it out to her.

"Happy birthday," he whispers, thinking that twenty-five years is absolutely no age, but still a long time, a lengthy illusion perhaps, her future his past and vice versa. Maybe.

She thanks him as though her eyes might tear up, though they don't. They only peer a respectful moment into his as though she adores him, which she surely doesn't. Is she playing me?

"I bet you look at all the boys like that."

"Not quite like that," she says with a cryptic movement of lips before she opens the box. "Oh, they're beautiful!" she exclaims and gives them to him, twisting in her place, so he can clasp the chain at the nape of her pretty neck. Is that what this is all about really—just a pretty neck?

She beholds herself in the mirror, glossy nail-pointed fingertips running over the beads, fingering them. "They are just so gorgeous," she says. "Wherever are they from?"

"Africa. They're said to possess magical properties."

Her nostrils crinkle. "They have a funny smell."

"They're very old," he says and refrains, at least for the moment, from telling her the settings are purest silver, but the beads are made of petrified leopard dung.

"Thank you," she whispers and allows him to kiss her, and for just that moment it seems to him that if the question "Is dog?" were to look at itself in the mirror, it would see "God is?" The fact dazzles him, seems to prove something. Then he realizes it is not quite so. The 'g' would be twisted and 'is' would be 'si' and the question mark would come first, backwards, like a lopsided question in Spanglish. "The trick doesn't work," he mutters.

"You say such unusual things," she tells him, and he realizes she is being diplomatic. By unusual she means weird. Already he's losing her. Maybe his father came between them after all. You don't have what it takes to hold onto a woman like this. Yet the expression on her face, in her eyes, seems to say, Show me what you want to do. I'm in your hands.

Miles is now doing magical fusion with "Sweet Sweet Surrender" and Sklar moves closer, wondering, for that instant before the passion seizes and overpowers him, whether he really believes in or even knows what he is doing. But then she looks into his eyes, and her teeth part, and he forgets the dog, the universe, his father's eyes as, with a cry of surrender, he goes under.

(2008)

LITTLE SINNERS

MY NINTH SUMMER, in 1952, I ran with a kid named Billy Reichert, a classmate from the Christian Brothers Boys School. We were thieves. We used foul language. We smoked Lucky Strike cigarettes purchased with stolen quarters. We pored over the dirty pictures on a pack of Tijuana playing cards Billy had secreted in his basement. It was a lovely summer.

I loved stealing. You had to be quick and brave. I loved that feeling in my stomach just before I made my move. I glanced at whatever it was—a Milky Way bar, a cap pistol, a comic book—walked past, scanned the shop in front of me, turned, scanned behind, and if the coast was clear, *zip!* I moved, shoved it in my pocket, under my shirt, down my pants. Then I hung around a while as a precaution, but also as part of the fun: that incredible sense of power it gave me to stay there, moving slowly amongst the enemy, the loot on my person, the danger, the triumph, the sheer belly-tingling risk! I asked the shop clerk, the guy with the pencil moustache and underslung jaw at Gerstie's, say, the price of some impossibly expensive item, HO gauge electric trains or a glittering package of imported hand-painted lead soldiers in red coats, looked wistful, wandered out with my head down. I understood from overhearing my father, who was a legal counselor for the State of New York, that the law said you could not be arrested for shoplifting until you were actually out the door, so I was prepared to put the booty back on the shelf again at the least suspicious glance. But none ever came. I was too quick. Me and Billy could lift just about anything—coins out of the cigar box on the brick and plank newspaper stand in front of the Roosevelt Avenue cigar shop, comic books out of Gerstenharber's, cupcakes and Mission sodas from the A&P or Frisch's Market, toys from the glass shelves of Kresge's or Woolworth's, and assorted junk, mostly mysterious small automotive gadgets, out of Sears & Roebuck's which, for some reason, we called Searsie's. If there wasn't anything in particular we desired, we would lift any old thing, just for the joy of it.

Billy was a nice-looking good-natured boy, blond and tan and blue-eyed with a big white smile and easy laugh. My feeling for him was a little like love. We were together all the time that summer, morning to night. We rose early in the mornings to go out prowling in the mild air, breathing the aroma of honey-suckle and cut grass. Usually I rose first and called for him because of his sister.

The Reicherts lived in an attached house on Ithaca Street, and he and his older sister, Fran, shared a bedroom at the rear of the second floor. When I called for him, his mother used to send me straight up to Billy's room, and because his sister just saw us as little squirts, she went about her business without paying us any mind. Lots of times she would come out of the bathroom wearing nothing but underpants and bra or wrapped in a towel with beads of water on her tan shoulders and long thighs.

Once I remember she sat on her vanity bench wearing just a

skirt and bra and slowly pulled on her nylon stockings the way women do, even when they're only fifteen as she was, so slowly and wonderfully, the leg extended out in the air and curving like heaven. Billy and I sat there pretending to play checkers. We watched her draw one all the way up to the top of her thigh. I sighed, and Billy said, in a singsong kind of way, "It's gettin' ha-ard." And she didn't get ticked off or anything. She just glanced over and smiled as she pulled on the other stocking. To this day, I don't know whether she knew what her little brother meant, whether she enjoyed us watching her as much as we enjoyed watching, or whether she was completely oblivious of us as males and was just smiling innocently, maternally at us. If I knew that, maybe I would have a better handle on women today, but all I know and knew was how happy I felt at that moment with my eyes full of her and the whole long wonderful August morning and afternoon stretched out before us.

In my memory, that was in fact the last day of that summer, the day when it all hit the fan. Probably my memory is not completely right. It seems hard to believe that so many things could have happened in one single day. But then again I was only nine then, and when you're nine, any day can be full of wonders.

It was Tuesday. Indian Head Penny day at the Jackson Movie House. Every Tuesday morning the Jackson had a special offer for kids where you could get in for a can of soup or for an Indian Head Penny. I think it was to benefit charity, or maybe the owner of the movie house was a coin collector and was hoping to acquire some rare and valuable dates. Anyway, my father had a box of old pennies, and we had standing permission to help ourselves. Otherwise, we would have had to lift a can of soup from the A&P. My parents would have given us the cans of soup, too—they were generous—but we'd just as soon have lifted them.

Most fifties movies, when I see them today, are junk. But back then, to a nine-year-old, they were magic. Wonder tales of heroes and desperadoes, love and murder, cruelty and kindness, theft and retribution, dueling and dancing and fighting with fists or guns. I can't recall the titles or even the stories, only a scene here and there: Jimmy Stewart in a lambskin jacket rolling in the dust cradling a pump action rifle against his chest. Gary Cooper's face glistening with sweat as he poled a raft through the Everglades. Dale Robertson on horseback, riding up a rocky hillside along the foaming Red River where, no doubt, some woman, an Indian squaw or a white woman abducted by the Indians, would be bathing her bosoms.

This particular Tuesday, we paid our Indian Head pennies to the gray-haired, white-faced matron in her white dress—the same one who would later prowl amongst the dark aisles, clutching in her white, blue-veined hand a steel-cased flashlight that she would shine and swat at our feet to make us take them down—and took our usual seats in the front where the great blue-gray screen loomed up above us like a billboard for the gods. The film that day, all I can remember of it, included a lovely scene in some jungle somewhere, and we watched Clark Gable watch Ava Gardner take a bath in a wooden tub underneath the vines and palm trees. She lifted one creamy leg from the water. Gable's moustache stretched across his grin, and she gave him that incredible smile of hers which hinted of things whose beauty no imagination could match.

"It's gettin' ha-ard," Billy sang.

As we stumbled out of the dark movie house into the midday sunlight, blinking, laughing, we ate the last of the Jujubes we'd hoisted from the Cigar Store, made a horn out of the empty box, ripped the flap off one end and blew into it, and it honked like a duck. I got to thinking about a girl we knew named Sally Donnell who lived in the Hampton Apartments. She was a friend of one of the other kids in our class. I played with them one day months before in the basement of her building.

"She took her underpants down," I told Billy.

"Bull."

"She did. I dared her, and she did."

"What did it look like?"

"I'm not sure. It was kind of dark. She lives just around the corner here."

We looked at each other. "Let's go!" And we took off running.

The lobby of the apartment was dim, solemn as a church with its old dark wood and smell like the bottom of an empty fountain. We rode the wooden walled elevator up to the third floor and found the door halfway down the dim corridor. The two-noted sound of the bell was lonely in the empty hallway. Then Mrs. Donnell, a smiling, gray-eyed woman, was looking down at us.

"We're in the same class as John Brandt at Christian Brothers School," I said. "He had my reader from school and said he'd give it to Sally for me."

I was pretty nervous in case she questioned me further about it, but she just called Sally, who came out into the hall

and fixed the door so it wouldn't lock before closing it behind her.
I was glad she didn't invite us in. "Johnny didn't give me no
book," she said.

I smiled. Billy smiled. She looked at us. She smiled. Down in
the basement was a meter room with a single window, high up on
the wall, through which motes of dusty sunlight slanted down
across a patch of the concrete floor. I don't remember too many
details, but until the day I die I will never forget how beautiful
Sally looked taking her clothes off and folding them, piece by
piece, into a neat pile on an old trunk in the corner, how she
looked with no clothes on in those motes of sunlight, smiling and
showing herself, slender and blond, her face flushed and shining.
We sat on seltzer crates and watched her turn for us in the light
beneath the window.

"Gee, it's gettin' hard," Billy said, but there was a reverence to
his voice, and all at once, I made the connection between getting
hard and looking at a girl with her underpants down, and I wanted to talk about it, but I didn't even know where to begin and
anyway couldn't speak for the lump in my throat. I just watched. I
just drank her in through my eyes, into my heart, to fill my
memory with enough of her to last forever.

Somehow the moment, the meeting, found its end, I don't
remember how, but next thing I knew we were out in the sunlight
again wearing cap pistols in holsters slung low on our thighs and
tied with strips of rawhide, gunfighter style, our pockets bulging
with cigarettes and pop bottles, all acquired by virtue of our
special talents. We were waiting for the bus to Forest Park, to visit
a secret little pond there that not many people knew about and

where we could be alone to exchange our thoughts about the beauties and wonders of Sally Donnell.

Our pond was up behind the golf course, through a path that wound between the hills and back behind a wall of tangled overgrowth. You never saw grown-ups there and only rarely other kids. We had a favorite rock we sat on, a big slate-gray boulder, the kind my father had once told me was the very thing New York was built on, the same kind of rock that the Mespatches Indians and the Dutch and British colonists saw hundreds of years before. "Just think," he said, "Indians might have camped right there, hunted over across the river, in that park. Wolves and wildcats and brown bears and rattlesnakes..."

I drew my pistol. "Watch it!" I shouted. "Snake!" And fired a roll of red paper caps, smoke and the smell of gunpowder rising from the little pistol as a diamondback twitched and bounced into the air, twisting, dead. I blew the smoke from the barrel of my shooter, holstered it again, sat on the warm sunny rock, and popped the cap from my Mission orange soda.

"If this was real jungle wilderness, like in the movies about Africa or something," Billy said, "we'd take off our clothes here and dry ourselves in the sun."

"We're not even wet."

"We would be if this was the real jungle. That pond would've been a river where we had to wash ourselves, like Stewart Granger and that woman did there in *King Solomon's Mines.* "

"They still had clothes on."

"That's all the movie shows. In the real life part, they were nude." He tore the cellophane off the pack of Luckies and tapped out two cigarettes for us. I dug a matchbook from my pocket and we lit up. We smoked in silence for a while. Then I said, "You want to?"

"What?"

"Take off all our clothes?"

He smiled. He was pretty. We unbuckled our cap guns and doffed our clothes, admired each other for a while—he was almost as pretty as Sally, the way his tan skin rippled over his ribs and stretched tight across his belly—but looking at him didn't make me hard, and I wanted to ask if he knew what that was all about, but I didn't have the words I needed.

So we lay back in the sun, the warm rock beneath our naked flesh, sunlight tingling in our faces and chests and bellies, as we smoked cigarettes, blew smoke rings at the sky, washed the bitter smoke from our mouths with orange soda. I twisted out my cigarette, closed my eyes, and turned my face to the sun and I guess I've never felt more content, more completely alive than I did just then.

Then we heard footsteps, voices, giggling, on the path behind the overgrowth. We hid our cigarette pack, ditched the empty soda bottles and pulled on our clothes, tied the holsters to our thighs. Someone was moving closer. We practiced drawing on each other while we waited to see whether we would have to make a run for it or stand and fight or what. Two older kids came crashing out of the overgrowth. They had funny looks on their faces, like they knew something we didn't, like maybe they had seen us. I recognized them both, but I didn't think they knew me. The one kid, William Zipler, used to be in my older brother's class at school, and the other, a Latin kid named Manuel, always hung around with him. Manuel was older, too, though small and dark-haired with big dark eyes and long black eyelashes like a girl's. Zipler was a tall skinny kid with a big nose and a mouth that made me think of an owl's beak. He drew a deck of cards from his pants pocket. "You guys want to play some poker?"

"We got no money," Billy said.

"No sweat," said Zipler. "We can just play for fun."

So we all sat on the rock, and Zipler dealt a couple of hands of stud. Billy got brave and lit up, offering the pack around. "Estunt your growth," Manuel said, but Zipler took one, and I did, too.

The Lucky wobbling between his lips, eyes squinted against the smoke, Zipler said, "Hey, I got an idea. Let's play strip poker."

Manuel giggled. "Panty ante,"

Billy said, "That's no fun unless there's girls."

"Well, look," Zipler said. "You don't have to play. You can just watch."

Pretty soon, the two of them, Zipler and Manuel, were naked. Me and Billy sat where we were and watched. It was fascinating, but a little sickening, too. Zipler had a very big dark cock with hair around it. He started rubbing it between his palms, and it got bigger. Then he said, "Manuel, tell them about your dream you had." To us, he explained, "Manuel had this crazy dream about something, something he had to do to someone."

Billy flipped his cigarette into the pond. We were backing away, gun hands poised over our holstered cap guns.

"Show these kids what you dreamt about, Manuel," Zipler

said and lay back on the rock with his cock sticking up in the air, but we had already backed up to the tree line.

"Hey, where you going!" Zipler called out as we dashed across through the scrub and out to the path, running like hell. There were snakes all around us, hanging from tree branches, coiled at our feet, wrapped hissing around the trunks of trees, and we fired our cap pistols as we ran, killing the one after the other, but they kept on coming as we ran along the sunlight-dappled path beneath the leafy trees.

"That guy's a queer," Billy said.

"He's pretty weird," I agreed.

The bus wheezed in to the curb, and we climbed on. We sat in the back seat, rode in silence for a time. Then I said, "Hey, what was he doing that with his cock for? Rubbing it like that?"

"Who knows? The two of them are probly just queers."

"Oh, right." And, "What's a queer again?"

"A queer is just a queer guy who does queer stuff like that. That's all. My old man says if a queer takes a drink in a bar, the bartender smashes the glass with a ballbat afterwards."

"How come?"

"Cause that's what they do."

The bus pulled in along the curb at 82nd Street, and we climbed down to the pavement and started walking again. The day, which had been so perfect, so wonderfully beautifully perfect, suddenly, inexplicably was blemished. Something needed to be done. Of course, we couldn't understand that or know what had to be done. We could only sense that all the beauties of that day, all the beauties of the female body and of our own, the wildness of our freedom was in threat, the day was in danger of being lost somehow.

The sun was no longer high in the sky. Our shadows were long and slender before us as we walked. "What you want to do now?" I asked.

"I don't know. Somethin'."

We were passing by the local tavern at just that moment, and a man named Mr. Sweeney stepped out, blinking into the late afternoon sunlight. He had wild hair and a swollen red nose and white gunk in the corners of his mouth. He didn't know us at all, but he pointed at me and said, "You. What the hell you think you're doin'?"

"We're walkin'," I said.

"Where to? You walkin' to the ballfield?" His nose was bumpy and full of broken veins. His eyes were bloodshot.

"You play any ball today?"

"Uh-uhn."

He leaned close to us with fierce eyes and snapped, "Why the hell not? You a shit-heel, are you? Get out and play some ball, the two of you! Little baseball. Basketball. Football! Don't be a goddamn shit-heel all your goddamn worthless life!"

This was just what we needed to lift the mood. We went right into a dialogue. I turned to Billy and said, "Get your ass out and play some baseball!"

"You shit-heel!" Billy said.

"Some bowling ball!"

"Damn shit-heel!"

"Tennis ball!"

"Shit-heel!"

"Ping pong ball!"

That one broke us up pretty good. We started giggling and staggering along the street, and old man Sweeney was yelling after us as we took off running.

"Snot noses!" he hollered, waving his fist in the air. "Idiots! You goddamned little sinners!"

We threw our stolen capguns, holsters and all, off the top of the Long Island Railroad Trestle, and decided to head over to Searsie's to hoist just one more thing, something really great, something to remember the day by, to heal its wound. As we headed on up to Roosevelt again, I watched the long weird shadows strutting out from the tips of our sneakers before us, and I couldn't help thinking about Zipler, about what Manuel's dream might have been, what they were out after, what Zipler looked like lying there with it sticking up in the air. I didn't like it. It wasn't good. It wasn't beautiful as Sally had been in the meter room, turning in the sunlight with her slender golden body. Or as Billy had looked sitting naked on the warm rock with his smiling face.

At Searsie's, we took a drink of cold water from the stainless steel water fountain and wandered around looking at the objects displayed in the glass-partitioned counterspaces: sparkplugs, fuses, batteries, headlight bulbs, flashlights—and then we saw it. A beautiful little flashlight charm on a chain. It was wondrous to behold. A yellow and white plastic oblong on a golden drainplug chain. You flipped open the top and thumbed a switch on the side, and a strong, clear, pencil beam shone forth. My heart thumped with desire to have it in my pocket, the cool plastic against my palm, to have it home with me, crawl into the depths of my closet, lighting my way into the unknown with its scalpel sharp beam, studying the secrets of floor cracks, the mysteries in the corners of upper shelves, beneath beds…

We made our move fast. Once around the counter, a glance at the guy in the white short-sleeve shirt through which you could see his strapped undershirt as he slouched up against a counter waiting for a customer, back to the end of another circuit and zip! Our pockets were thick with treasure.

The guy in the transparent white shirt glanced at us. He was chewing something very slowly with his lips closed. "What's the story with you two?" he said.

"Huh?"

"What's the story? What are you looking for?"

Billy said, "Uh, where do you have the toothbrushes and toothpaste and all?"

The man wrinkled his brow. "This look like a freakin' drug store to you, kid?"

"Sorry, mister," Billy said. "Guess we better try the drug store," he said to me. I felt the man's eyes on my back as we headed for the door. I felt fear in my knees, in the pit of my stomach. Is it this time? I thought. Is it now? Waiting for a hand to clutch my shoulder. Just for good measure, we took another drink of water from the fountain before exiting. Then we hit the street, spun: no eyes watched, no hands reached for us.

We ran like hell.

Maybe it's only something manufactured by my imagination,

by the retrospect of memory, but there seemed something sad in the way we parted that evening. Dusk lay across the town. The streetlights had just been lit. We parted at the corner of Gleane and Baxter, I to proceed to my house through the tunnel of trees that was our street, Billy to head along beneath the El to his own house. He had chained his flashlight to one of his belt loops. Mine was secreted in my hip pocket. I don't remember what we said. I only remember, or think I remember, a melancholy yellow light from a streetlamp, a sadness of dusk, Billy's downturned face and the shadows on his yellow hair, a sharp sense of loss, though of what I could not know.

That evening as I lay on the living room floor on my belly, chin propped in my palms, watching "The Big Story" on TV the telephone rang. My father answered, spoke quietly for a time into the black mouthpiece. Then he hung up, and he and my mother went into the kitchen and shut the door. A few minutes later, the door opened again and he invited me to join them.

They sat in the ladderback chairs at the beige metal kitchen table. My father motioned me to sit. Then he said, "I just spoke with Billy Reichert's mother on the phone. She said he came home with a little flashlight on his beltloop, and when she asked him where he got it, he finally admitted that he stole it. She said he told her you stole one, too. Is that true?"

"Yes," I said and lowered my eyes.

"Why?"

I shrugged, shook my head.

"Don't we give you enough? Do you feel cheated? Do the

other boys have more than you?"

"No," I whispered. Which was true. My parents were very generous.

"Then *why?*"

I shook my head, stared at the black and white checked linoleum.

"Have you stolen other things, too?" my mother asked.

"Yes," I said. "Twice. A pack of gum and a quarter from the newspaperman's box outside the cigar shop."

"You'll have to put that quarter back," my mother said.

I nodded.

"And the flashlight, too."

"I threw it away. Down the sewer."

"Well, then, I'll have to go up to Searsie's and make amends for that," my father said. "I won't make you come with me. Unless the priest says you should. The gum I suppose we can just forget. You can put a dime in the poor box to make up for that. Out of your allowance. But you'll have to tell the priest in confession about each of the things you've stolen, and then we'll see what else there is to do about this."

I nodded, raised my eyes for a moment, swallowed, whispered, "Are you mad?"

"Not mad," my mother said. "Just confused. And disappointed."

"And puzzled," my father added. "We don't understand *why* you would steal. You have a good allowance. We don't deny you anything within reason. Why would you steal? *Why?*"

I looked into my mother's sad blue-gray eyes, my father's

brown troubled ones. Their sadness pierced me as nothing could. If they had yelled, beat me, my heart could have hidden from it, but there was no escape from this. I wanted to explain to them, but the truth, the fact of it, the experience, which had never found or needed words in my consciousness, that it was beautiful to steal, already was beyond the reach of my tongue, hiding away like a shy fish beneath some deep rock of consciousness. But their eyes, their sadness, disappointment was a wound that needed comfort, an emptiness that needed filling.

I said, "William Zipler made us do it."

They leapt at my words, sat up straight and stared at me. *"Who?"*

"William Zipler."   .

"Who the hell is William Zipler?" my father said.

"He was in Ralph's class at school, wasn't he?" mother said.

"He's much older than you."

"Promise not to tell Ralph," I pleaded. "Ralph will kill him. Promise not to tell." I knew they would honor the confidence. My mother and father were reasonable, dependable people.

"How did he *make* you do it?" my father asked.

"He just, he didn't *make* us exactly, he just showed us how, and then he said we should do it, too, or he'd make us sorry."

"The little *creep,*" my mother said.

"That makes it at least a little bit more understandable," my father said. "But still it doesn't *excuse* you. I *still* want you to tell this in confession."

"I know," I said.

"You stay away from William Zipler from now on," my

mother said. "The little *creep.*"

"Do you have anything else to tell now?" my father said. I shook my head. Then I whispered, "I'm sorry."

My father placed his gentle warm hand on the back of my neck. "It's all right, son," he said. "It was an experiment. Now you've tried it once and it's *over,* and I want your promise that you won't *ever* do anything like that again."

I promised, was hugged, allowed to hug back, released, and went up to my room where, in bed, in the dark beneath the covers, I played with my plastic flashlight on a chain. I pressed it up behind my fingers, inside my fist, and saw the light glow eerie red through my flesh, limning the bones of my fingers. I realized I was going to have to ditch the flashlight, for if they saw me with it they wouldn't understand, it would bring that sadness to their eyes again, and this time they wouldn't believe me. Yet there were so many things I wanted to do with that light, so many small corners and crevices, floor cracks, to explore, the inner depths of the closet, the dim far reaches of the basement....

On Saturday, as always, I got my allowance, thirty-five cents, with instructions to return a quarter to the news stand, put a dime in the poor box at Blessed Virgin Church, and go to confession.

I *did* put the quarter in the cigar box, reversing my talents, getting it in there without being observed. The challenge distracted me from the pain of forking over the two bits. But putting my last dime for the whole week in the poor box, with no prospect of other means of procuring the goods I wanted, was something else again. I stood there for quite some time just inside the church doors, the little silver coin sweaty in my palm. I decided *not* to do it, was about to turn away, but saw my hand lift to the coin slot, felt the dime slip from my fingers. It clunked and echoed into the depths of the tall metal box. Then, in confession, my little flashlight in my pocket (how I would have liked to explore the dark shadows inside the confessional box!), I spoke to the dim outline of Father Walsh behind the screen, told him I had stolen gum, a quarter and a flashlight.

"Have you made retribution for these things, bub?"

"I returned the quarter, Father, and put the gum money in the poor box, and my father made retribution for the flashlight."

"And are you sorry for these sins?"

"Yes, Father," I lied—though it didn't really seem a lie so much as a formality, a concession to the social order.

"Okay, bub, then say ten Hail Mary's and make a good act of contrition now."

As I prayed, "Oh my God, I am heartily sorry for having offended Thee...." I couldn't help thinking how ironic it was that, in fact, I had never stolen gum in my life. That has always seemed a funny kind of administrative irony to me.

I've often wondered about the fact that it didn't bother me, lying in confession. It was no doubt also a sin to have lied about William Zipler as I had, but I never confessed that, never really regretted it either, never felt either way about it. It was just a convenient way to appease my parents.

That day was the end of my friendship with Billy Reichert. I *did* regret that. He was such a nice, good-looking kid, and we had shared so much joy that summer.

I still have the flashlight. It doesn't light anymore, been dead for years, but I keep it in a cigar box where I have a bunch of little doodads and souvenirs, a broken watch, an old tarnished silver miraculous medal, an Indian Head penny, things like that. From time to time, I take the flashlight out and hold it in my palm, dangle it by the little gilt chain from my finger. In all the years since, I never did steal again. I never felt real sorrow for what I did or remorse, but I never did steal again. In fact, I don't think I *ever* sinned again with such pure joy.

(1989)

BLISS STREET

I WAS BORN on Bliss Street in Sunnyside, Queens, just down from White Castle—ironic names for a place that crouched in the shadows and din of the great hulking El tracks. The IRT Flushing Main Street line rattled past overhead every ten minutes or so when it was on schedule, usually just as Perry Mason was about to make a crucial revelation to Della Street.

We lived in the finished basement of a two-family house owned by two cross-eyed brothers named David and Wilfred Darling. My little brother Dennis used to joke about their names and their affliction in a quavering falsetto: "Oh, David, darling! Oh, Wilfred, darling!" Unkind as it was, we also used to do a routine of the astigmatic David directing the astigmatic Wilfred as he steered his big beige 1954 Plymouth, which we called The Brown Cow, into the driveway.

The Darling brothers had finished the basement themselves and rented it out illegally. We had two bedrooms and a living/dining room beneath a seven-foot ceiling. The pipes, of which there were many, were boxed and the walls panelled in grain-masked plywood, and just outside the water closet was a metal shower stall whose walls rumbled like radio thunder if you bumped them. The windows, at the top of the walls, looked out on the tires of the Darlings' Plymouth parked in the alley.

My brother and I were only allowed to invite kids home in good weather when we could play in the yard and my mother could give us a snack at the old redwood lawn table. The Darlings did not care for us playing in the yard, though. They worried we disturbed the second-floor tenants, who had a balcony and liked to keep the glass doors open. "Maybe they're afraid the kids'll drown out the El," my father said, but my mother thought the real reason was that they were afraid people would notice that a third family was living there illegally.

"It's against the fire laws," she said.

My father, in his arm chair reading the sports pages of the Daily News, grunted.

"They don't want us to be seen at all," my mother said. "They'd like the boys to stay hidden away down here all day in this, this..."

My father looked at her. His face was mild, but she stopped speaking. She smirked, rolled her eyes.

Dennis and I were lying on our stomachs on the floor, playing cars. The purple carpet had a series of borders which served as roads, and our little metal roadsters cut right angles around the corners of the rug. The floor beneath us vibrated as the Flushing line rumbled past out above Roosevelt Avenue—whether named for Teddy or Franklin none of us knew. Dennis had a toy motorcycle cop tied to the bumper of his car and was dragging him along the purple carpet road, uttering a low murmur of agony. The MC cop, which he called Flynn, made of flesh-colored flexible plastic that smelled like a cheap shower curtain, was the hero of all Dennis's games. Dennis would put him through great adversity—he would be bound, hung, scalded with matches, buried to his neck in the dirt of the yard and painted with honey to attract the little red ants or the big black ones, but always, when the odds were worst, Flynn would break free, overpower his invisible enemies, put things right again.

Dennis was two years younger than I, but still his games always seemed more original and interesting than mine. When he wasn't around, sometimes I would co-opt his plots, but I was too proud to do it in front of him. After all, I was the big brother. He should imitate me.

My mother was twenty-six years old, a very pretty, dark-haired woman, and I feared she regretted having married my father, a short balding redhead who was seven years older than she and drove a laundry truck for a living. My father was a joker, always had a quick, dry retort, but my mother didn't smile much any more, and she never let him forget why. She didn't have to say much, just a phrase once in a while, muttered with her back to him, while she did the dishes, saying, "Hm. A basement. Live in a basement."

He would look up from his paper or the TV, say, "Got somethin in your eye, Beth?" like he did the time she had a bad hemorrhoid and was limping around all the time and could always make her laugh with that. But she didn't crack a smile now. She didn't even answer and wouldn't repeat what she'd said, although we all knew very well what it was.

I didn't mind so much living there. The only thing I really wished was that there would have been windows in the little bedroom where Dennis and I slept, but if they only looked out on somebody's dirty retreads, what would be the difference?

Dennis and I knew every inch of our home and we had no complaints. We knew the places where the plywood had separated from the white-limed walls and you could put secret messages written in candle wax on typing paper that you made look old by scorching the edges with a match flame. We knew about the empty alcove behind the curtain and the secret closet there that led into the furnace room, and we knew about the crawlspace under the front porch, a wonderful, terrifying place closed off with a woodskid on hinges that was bolted shut.

Dennis and I also knew the secret of this place; the bolts were not fast, but could be jerked out and the wood skid opened onto a dark, earth-floored cavity. We would sneak it open and peer into the darkness to try to imagine what was in there: buried treasure, jewels, arrowheads, old pirate pistols, a corpse. We tried shining the five-battery flashlight in, but you couldn't see much, just the rumpled dirt floor and dungeon-gray walls.

What I especially liked about the crawlspace was that Dennis was more scared of it than I was. One day as we were peering in, I told him I had seen something moving in there, something big, and that I was going in to take a look. He started to cry, begged me not to, and his terror was so exquisite I just had to have more. I hoisted myself up onto the sill, and one hoist got me in. I heard him crying out, running, and then suddenly I was inside in the cool dark quiet, the soft damp earth beneath me, my nose full of the musty, grave-like smell.

Stupidly, I didn't think about who Dennis would run to for help, but just about the time he was coming back with my mother, I felt something crawling inside my pants leg.

I screamed. Dennis screamed.

"Be still!" my mother screamed. "Stop that screaming! Oh, God! What's happening in there!"

She reached in and grabbed hold of my foot and dragged me out through the dirt, got me down on the floor, and started shaking me by the shoulders, screaming into my face, "I thought I told you never to..."

"There's something crawling inside my pants!" I yelled to make her stop. Dennis ran into the shower stall and pulled the curtain after him, while my mother alternately screaming, slapping, laughing, hugging me, unbuckled my belt and pulled off my pants.

Her search of my clothes produced two large black beetles which she sealed, alive, into a mailing envelope to show my father when he came home from work. Further, I was ordered to dress again in my dirt-smudged clothes and sit in a chair in the hall and was not permitted to wash myself until my father had a chance to see with his own eyes.

"I wouldn't have got so dirty if you hadn't pulled me out through the dirt like that!" I hollered.

But she didn't seem to hear me. She paced and muttered to herself, went around wiping out clean ashtrays, scrubbing the sink, the shower stall (Dennis was now out in the yard reading a Beatle Bailey comic and munching cornflakes dry from the box).

"This is it," she said. "This. Is. It. A basement. A cellar. Insects. Insects!"

I knew what she meant by the word insects. She meant the unspeakable thing which happened only to filthy undesirable humans.

"They're not cockroaches!" I said. "They were just ordinary everyday beetles."

"You shut your mouth!" she hissed, and her eyes fixed me in a way that made me frightened.

It was only about an hour before my father got home, but my mother was waiting for him up the stairs by the side door which led into our apartment when he climbed down out of his laundry van.

My father was still wearing his gray laundry driver's uniform and had the gray cap tipped back on his bald red pate. "Hah," he said when he saw my mother standing there at the door. "What do you know, the royal welcome, hey? Where's the red carpet?"

"This is no joke, buster," she snapped. Buster was a serious word with my mother. "Go down and take a look at your oldest son."

I could see my father's face before he saw me as he came down the narrow stairway, saw the look on his face saw that he expected to find me minus an eye or with a hand torn open from a cherry bomb, or wrapped in a body cast or something. When he got down to the little place at the foot of the stairs that my mother, with dripping sarcasm, called the foyer, he stopped and saw me there, all smeared with dirt, and I saw the startled relief in his eyes. "Jingo netties," he said, "You look like the wreck of the Hesperas."

I started to laugh, but my mother was already on him. "Do you know where he got that way? Do you know what was on him?" She had the sealed envelope in her hand and was tearing back the flap. My father looked from her to me to the furnace room door.

"Beetles," he said, peering into the envelope.

"Insects!" she said. And, "You filthy Irish failure!"

Then there was silence. I waited for some evil word from him, some word I had never heard him speak before, but which would be the only possible response: Bitch. Slut. Or worse. But he said nothing to her. To me, he said, "Go wash up your face, son." Then he turned and went back up the stairs. I heard the door of his laundry truck smack shut and the engine start, and then I was alone with my mother.

Dennis lingered at the foot of the stairs. He made a face at me. "Puke for brains," he whispered, "It was your fault."

"Wouldn't of happened if you didn't call Mom," I said. "Baby ass."

When my father was't back by eight, my mother served dinner without him. We ate our fishcakes in silence, and afterwards watched *Have Gun Will Travel* and *The Rifleman*, and my mother let us stay up all the way to the late news, when my father still was not back.

I woke sometime during the night to the rattle of a key in the door upstairs, listened intensely for whiskey sounds, but there were none. I reached beneath the bed for my Little Ben alarm clock. The luminous dial said it was 2:15 in the morning. The basement was quiet but for the sounds of his footsteps, slow, but not heavy like they would be if he had gone over to Ryan's like he did once in a while to drink shots of rye and talk with the men and women there.

When I woke in the morning, he was gone again, his truck was gone. My mother said, "Your father came home very late and had to leave early today."

"When's he coming back?" I asked.

"He has some things to do," she said, and I recognized the evasion, asked no more. I hated to go to school that day, hated leaving Dennis alone with my mother, the two of them with their dark hair and fine features and little feet, hated going off on my own, a round-faced little redhead whose father was off god knew where. I recall it was a spring day, the first day that year I noticed buds on the hedges and trees. It was only my eighth spring so I did not yet recognize this as the triumph of life over death, was not yet able to put together the phase that we had just been through, the dead of winter, the long bleak stretch between Christmas and Easter, did not realize that the good weather was coming again or identify my parent's behaviour as the strain of being cooped up all those weeks with kids who could not invite friends home and could not go out to play in the yard, being locked in a basement which made my mother think constantly of shame and failure.

At eight, you do not yet know that things change, that things can be changed. All I knew was that there were buds on the hedges, the sky was blue, the air mild on my face, and my mother and father were fighting and it was my fault.

When I got home from school at three, my father's truck was parked outside the house. Its panel doors were wide open, and a mattress stuck out of it. On the sidewalk were a pile of planks which I suddenly recognized as the frame of my own bed.

Dennis was sitting at the redwood table in the yard, playing with his collection of ice cream sticks. He opened his mouth to speak, but I covered my ears, pressed the heels of my hands against them. I could not bear to hear it from him. I had to have it straight from Mom and Dad. That way, maybe I could make them change their minds. I ran down the cellar stairs to find my father standing in front of our dining table which lay on its back, like a beetle, legs up in the air. He was screwing the legs off, one by one.

"Where's Mom?" I asked.

"She'll be right back."

"What are you doing?"

"Surprise. I'll tell you all at the same time when she gets back."

I joined Dennis at the redwood table. One of the Darlings watched us through the kitchen window, his eyes crossed and his little moustache knotted above sour puckered lips.

"Screw him," I muttered

"Oh yeah?" said Dennis. "You want to get us in even more trouble?"

"Wasn't my fault in the first place!"

"Was, too!"

My father appeared at the top of the basement stairs with the big round table top in his outstretched arms, hugged close to his body. That table had belonged to my mother's mother, one of the three pieces of furniture we had which we were really proud of. The way he was carrying it you could see underneath where the wood was not finished, and there was some kind of label pasted. It made you feel good the way the paper looked, yellow, kind of antique. It made you think of the past, of grandmothers and grandfathers, visits and all.

Gingerly, my father rested the table on the tops of his shoes, not to scratch it, just as my mother came into the yard carrying two brown paper A&P bags.

"What's going on here?" she demanded.

My father said, "We're moving. Bought us a house. Up on 34th Avenue. There's a tree outside."

My mother smiled the way she did only when she was very perplexed. "A *house*?" she said. "Who would sell *you* a house?"

From the sidelines, Dennis and I watched. "She shouldn't of said it like that," I whispered.

"Don't be so touchy," Dennis said. "She didn't mean it like that."

My father said, "I got a mortgage."

My mother's smile grew increasingly lopsided. "A mortgage? On what you make?"

"Hey," he said, "This guy at the bank, this Mr. Fowler, he looks at my baby blues, and he says, 'Oh, well, Mr. Duggan, so you got your down payment, do you? Well, that's fine, then.'"

My mother stared off at the Darlings' apple tree, the one that got twisted by Hurricane Alice the summer before, and without even looking at my father, she said, "Where'd you get the down payment, big shot?"

"She shouldn't of said it like that," I said.

"She didn't mean it that way," Dennis said, but he was as scared as me, I could tell, especially because she asked it without looking at him.

My father shifted the table on his shoes. He was looking down at the pavement, and he was smiling the way he did when you knew there was no discussing something. Anybody from the outside who saw him would think he was smiling merrily, but both Dennis and I could see the smile and knew it meant something drastic. Maybe my mother did, too. Maybe that's why she wasn't looking at him. Her smile disappeared. She was no longer perplexed. Now her mouth was small, her dark pretty eyes even bigger than usual, and she stood with her legs apart but the toes of her scuffed loafers pointed in toward each other. "How will you ever pay it?" she whispered. "How will we eat?"

He took out his handkerchief and wiped his forehead. He was

looking down the alley now, toward the laundry truck, and I could see he was getting ready to lift the table top again, that he was through talking. He dipped his knees and lifted the heavy round oak piece. When he had it up in his arms again, and his knees locked, he said, "I'll be working nights for a while. I got some extra hours over at Elmhurst General."

We slept in our own house that night. A red brick row house up on 84th Street between 34th Avenue and Northern Boulevard. There were trees spaced along the street, and you couldn't hear, smell, or feel the el train running along the tracks sixteen blocks southwest. Our neighbors on the one side were a lawyer named MacPhillips—the family name was written in metal script, built right into their front screen door—and on the other side a single man, a chiropodist named Dr. Digit. He had a white poodle.

It was a tall, narrow house, and Dennis and I each got our own bedroom, on the third floor, with windows that looked out to our own yard, which had trees and bushes and a rusted swing set. But Dennis came in and slept in my bed anyway, so we could discuss the meaning of these events. I didn't see that there was anything wrong. Mom was sore, but she had her own ideas about things, and I couldn't see that there was anything but good going on there. But Dennis thought Dad borrowed the money from this guy we knew about named Tony Beggs, who lived in Corona and who would break somebody's legs for you if you paid him fifty dollars. That scared me pretty good. Tony Beggs was also a collector, and I had seen a film called *The Kiss of Death* about people like that which showed what Richard Widmark did to people who failed to keep up with the interest payments on the loans made to innocent family fathers in tight situations.

"You know what they do?" Dennis said. "They push old ladies in wheelchairs down the stairs. They set fire to your house and they beat up your father in an alley."

I said, "They file the silver fillings out of your teeth, too, and snatch toys from weeping orphans" trying to make a joke out of it, but I was pretty scared there in the dark in our new house, and the presence of my little brother's body in the bed with me didn't help much. I ran through it over and over in my head as I lay there, studying the new ceiling above my face. First I ran through the idea that it was not at all what we feared, that nothing bad was going to happen, that Dad had just taken a loan and had to work a couple extra hours a week over at Elmhurst General. But after I ran through that in my head, all the other possibilities still waited, things that had to do with shadows and alleys and Tony Beggs, who had a nose that looked like it had been creased by wearing a tight heavy rubber band around it. I saw him pushing my father, hitting him, and I couldn't stand it, tried to go back to the other idea where nothing was wrong, but it wasn't easy to keep that alive.

The truth of the situation was different, maybe worse in a way. My father had taken a loan from a bona fide finance company that had a little office on 37th Avenue run by a guy with a pencil mustache who drove around in one of those insect-looking German cars. The interest on the loan sounded like it was very low, but the thing is, it was paid out by the month, so really you were paying more than twenty percent a year.

This meant my father drove the laundry truck every day from 8:30 to 4:30, came home to eat and take a nap and was at the hospital from six in the evening til one in the morning. By not taking any meal break, he did it in a seven-hour shift, and he got paid ten percent extra for working nights.

"It's a deal," I heard him tell my mother. "All they want's that and my left nougat, and we're home free."

My mother was not amused.

Apparently he ate on the move, while he worked, carried apples and bananas and leftover boiled potatoes in the tool pockets of his work pants. He had a voracious appetite, but we didn't get much meat to eat any more. We ate a lot of spaghetti and potatoes for dinner, and I can still remember the expression on my father's face when he looked at what was on the table, and the way he looked afterwards when it was all eaten up and he refilled his glass of water and took another slice of Wonder bread and looked from bowl to empty bowl. As hungry as he always was, he lost weight, and I could tell my mother was worried. She used to make baloney sandwiches for him to take to the hospital. Sometimes, when he was really tired, he got forgetful, and I would have to go over to the hospital to bring the food to him because he left the brown bag on the hall table.

Usually he was having a smoke outside the glass doors on Elmhurst Avenue when I got there, and I would hand over the bag, hang around with him there for a few minutes and shoot the bull while he ate. He always offered me a piece of the baloney sandwich. I felt a little bit like I was visiting him in jail or something. After a few minutes, he'd flip away the butt of his cigarette and go his way inside the building, and I'd go my way down Elmhurst Avenue to Roosevelt, up 84th to our brick row house, where my mother sat alone in front of the TV, knitting or darning while Dennis did his homework at the dining table.

She looked so lonely there, kind of dazed, and the house was so quiet all the time now, without my father's jokes. Sometimes I even missed the sound of their arguments. She was much easier with Dennis and me during those first months, but it wasn't much of a relief because we knew it was not because she loved us more, but just because she was too confused or hurt to get mad.

One time when I brought the food bag over to my father, he wasn't outside waiting for me, so I went in to look for him. I saw him in the hall between the elevator banks shoving a bucket. It was on wheels and had a ringer in it. He pulled the mop up through the ringer so gray water squeezed out of it, then slapped the wet mop head onto the tile floor and started mopping. I stepped behind a pillar, my heart beating, to watch him there, a short, redheaded balding man in a white uniform shoving a mop through an empty hallway. Somehow, I hadn't known that was his job there. I remembered once or twice he took me on his rounds in the laundry truck when I was eight years old. It was fun. I felt proud to sit up in the front of the truck with him, help him lift out the folded, clean laundry wrapped in neat brown-paper packages, enjoyed how he joked with all the people where he made pickups and deliveries. But in the hospital, I didn't see him with anybody. He was alone with his bucket and mop in an empty corridor slopping up dirt.

I hurried away after giving him his food and never went inside the hospital again. I feel ashamed to admit it, but it bothered me, too, that others might see him there like that. My friends, the neighbors. What would Judge MacPhillips think if he saw his next door neighbor pushing a mop along a hospital corridor, mopping up other people's shoe filth?

My mother didn't much like it either, but for other reasons. She never saw him any more, only on weekends, and half the time, he slept most of Saturday away. When he wasn't sleeping, he worked on the house. It was in bad shape, which is why he got it so cheap. The windows needed putty and sanding and paint. It needed paint everywhere. The wiring was bad, and the plumbing was set to go, piece by piece. The roof needed patching, and the yard was a mess.

It got to where Dennis and I didn't want to be home on the weekends any more. It was the same thing every week. My father on a ladder, scraping, sanding, painting, hammering, trying to get us to run after tools for him or down to the hardware store, or hold something or clean up after him, and all the while my mother would be in and out of the doorway to holler at him to let it be, forget it, sit down and relax and stop wasting his time on this broken-down wreck that nobody but he would be so stupid to buy.

Usually he wouldn't answer. Sometimes he'd say, "You wanted a house. You got a house."

"I never said I wanted a house. You could of just rented a decent apartment."

"Rent. Sure. Throw your damn money out the window."

Then there were long periods where no one spoke at all in the house, only me and Dennis. I don't honestly know which was worse, the silence or the yelling.

That was how our life got to be then. I only remember it in little takes. My mother at the kitchen table peeling something, her eyes staring off out the window at the yard. My father in his armchair in the half-furnished living room, elbows on his knees, staring at the floor, or snoring in front of the TV. He was skinny now, so his gray laundry uniform hung on him, and one time, on a Saturday evening, he went out for a walk without his shoes on. He walked in his sock feet down the middle of the road along our street. I went down to tell my mother about it, but she was sitting alone in the living room with just a single lamp lit, rubbing cold cream into her hands, and I didn't know what to say to her.

So I went back upstairs and sat by the front window and watched the street. About an hour later, I saw my father coming back. One of the men he used to go to Ryan's with, a blond round-faced man with a deep voice, was walking with him, leading him by the arm, walked him up to the door and rang the bell, then went away again.

The holidays were not much relief either, Christmas, Easter, summer vacations. There was never enough of anything except silence, which there was too much of. I actually got to dislike Christmas for a while, would get a sick feeling in my stomach hearing Gene Autry sing "Rudolph the Red-Nosed Reindeer" on the radio in the quiet house while my mother put together the old artificial Christmas tree that she kept in a cardboard box in the attic.

Then one Christmas Eve, my father put a little box under the tree with a tag that said "To Mom" on it, and when she opened it up, there was just a piece of paper inside, folded in four, with printing and some kind of rubber stamps on it.

"What's this?" she said. Her eyes had dark circles under them, and there was gray now in her dark hair.

"It's the loan I took for the down payment."

"So? That's a present?"

"It's paid up. I don't have to work nights any more. Not unless you want me to take another year so we can buy some more furniture."

And that was the end of it. Dennis was twelve. I was fourteen. We had a father again. Mom had Dad again. And we owned a house.

It had seemed like forever, but really it was only five years, it only took five years to pay off that loan, and it changed everything for us. That was the first time I ever really saw that you could do things, change things.

All this happened thirty-five years ago. We never talked much about it when it was finally over. Then last year, Dennis and I came together again in Jackson Heights to close up the house, after we buried Mom. Dad had died of a heart attack two years before, and then Mom got sick pretty soon afterwards, and we came together with our own wives and kids to bury her in the plot at St. John's.

The house was valued at just about fifteen times what my father had paid for it, a small fortune. It would mean all the difference for my children and their education, for my life, and surely for Dennis's, too. As we left the brick row house for the last time,

I looked back at it and said, "Boy, Dad really fixed things up for us."

"Dad? He would never have done a thing without Mom egging him on. We'd still be in that damn basement on Bliss Street."

For a moment, an old, bitter anger began to rise in me. I looked into my brother's dark, fine-featured face, coarsened some by the years, but still the same face I had bickered and laughed with through all the years we were kids. I was about to say something to him, something mean, but then I ran my hand through my thin red hair, thought the heck with it.

That's just my brother for you. We never could agree about anything.

(1996)

THE SINS OF GENERALS

I SLEPT POORLY last night and argued with my wife in the morning and was late for work today. Two tom cats were competing for a she under our bedroom window. I watched through the curtain. The she was hidden in the bushes, caterwauling, while the two toms stood silently facing each other down. The moon cast a silver sheen across them—the one a young trim tabby, the other a squat seasoned tiger with a gruff little stub of a tail. The contest was invisible and still—the force of the gaze, the posture, and of course the size. Suddenly it was over; the tabby rolled onto its back yowling submissively, exposing its belly and throat, whereupon the tiger backed a few steps away—showing, I thought, a certain tact and consideration with regard to the loser.

When I was a child I once came upon a cat eating a bird in our alley. The cat hunched at my approach and glared up at me, brown blood smeared across its maw, but seeing that I was just a child proceeded to eat, allowing me to observe, educating me perhaps. I was amazed. I tried to tell about it at dinner that night, but my mother smacked the back of my head and told me to be still. I recall we were having boiled chicken that night, my favorite.

This morning I went out on the lawn in my pajamas to get the newspaper, and when I returned my wife was glaring at me, her lips encircled in a white ring of tension. She said that I had just exhibited to the neighbors my complete and total lack of breeding. I told her that I had seen General Burgess on his lawn the week before wearing nothing but a bathrobe, exhibiting to the whole neighborhood the complete and total lack of hair on his thin yellow calves, but she said that General Burgess was a general and *ipso facto* well-bred, while I could not afford to risk a bad impression as I was nobody. I told her I thought this was middle-class bull crap, and she said, Yes, probably so, to a slum child, whereupon I reminded her that in fact she had been raised in working-class quarters whereas I had been brought up in a middle-class home. She laughed bitterly and noted that I had been raised in a middle-class family on the decline, while she had come up in a working-class family on the rise, and she did not intend to allow me to infect our children with the hypocritical pseudo-liberal attitudes of defeat.

At that point I might have mentioned how much worse it surely was for the children to have to witness this ugly scene, but I was disturbed to see their little faces looking bewilderedly back and forth at us, their eyes full of fear, and an argument has to stop somewhere, so I stopped. I always seem to be the one to stop when we argue. That is because she shouts and grimaces and has a technique whereby nothing I say seems to affect her in the least or even to register so that I generally give up for sheer hopelessness of ever achieving any kind of reasonable compromise. Perhaps this means that I have lost the fight. But if she thinks that this entails a meaningful victory of any sort for her, she is sadly mistaken, for it does not assist us in approaching the truth or wisdom, and there can be no such thing as a victory in love. Any triumph by one partner over the other of necessity entails a loss of equal magnitude for the pair, the objective of love being understanding, harmony, empathy, and mutuality. I feel that my wife's propensity to "triumph" in an argument is something she got from her father who is the same robust physical type as she and who, having had to fight his way out from a very poor background, uses sarcasm the way a wasp stings or a Finn pulls a blade—reason be damned, make the wrong move and you get it. I tried to tell her this once, but she immediately insisted that the real point at issue was that I was a weakling, trying to make a virtue of my weakness, as (she claims) had my father who (she claims) allowed my mother to walk all over him, a fact which (she claims) I have been unconsciously trying to avenge by treating her so badly and never allowing her her way without a fight, at which point I called her a dirty name, and she clawed at my eyes and I twisted her arm and smacked her in the face, knocking off her glasses. She stood there flexing her jaws, accusing me tremulously of having broken her eardrum, while I wandered into the next room and sat down on the carpet and wept into my fingers.

We have never been in harmony. I don't know why we married. If we were mere beasts we would part. But there are the children to think of. I was late leaving for work and while I ran alongside another commuter to catch my bus, an automobile swerved suddenly onto the sidewalk in front of us, and the driver leaned out to post a letter into a mailbox, blocking our way and causing us to miss the bus. My fellow pedestrian approached the car and, leaning down to the driver, pointed at the sidewalk and asked, "Know what this is?"

The driver, who had rolled up his window and had been about to drive off, rolled down the window again and held up his clenched fist. "Know what this is?" he asked.

The pedestrian extended the middle finger of one hand, jutting it vigorously upward. "Know what this is?"

The driver opened the car door and got out and smacked it shut, whereupon the pedestrian threw up both palms and took a couple of quick steps backwards. The driver glowered at him and made a sudden lunge which, although only an intimation of aggression, an incomplete movement, caused the pedestrian to cringe shamelessly. The driver lunged again, and the pedestrian cringed again. This was repeated several times—lunge, cringe; lunge, cringe—and appeared to be amusing the driver greatly. But then anger passed over him again. Things had now cooled down to the point where he couldn't really do anything to the pedestrian. He should have acted immediately if he had intended to, say, get him into a headlock or twist his arm behind his back or punch him in the eye, but he had quite naturally held back, having had no way of knowing how full of fear the pedestrian actually was when confronted with physical violence and how he could easily have punched him a few times without risking any retaliation. Now, realizing this, he seemed anxious to try to provoke an excuse to do something to the pedestrian, but the pedestrian was so totally cowed and submissive that the driver could not have legitimately done anything to him without having appeared to be a bully. He did push him a couple of times, rather hard, and cursed and spit on him, but the pedestrian simply cringed and accepted it passively. The scene was quite exciting to watch, but also rather ugly as I don't really approve of that sort of behavior, and I felt ashamed of enjoying it.

This made me even later for work, and I had to "hustle my tail" to the monthly senior staff meeting which is chaired by my boss, who is president of the socio-ethical humanistic foundation for which I work. My boss, the president, has a large body and a large face and a magnificent head of gray, white and black hair. He's not really the type to play big shot with the staff, even though he did once stab his finger deep into my tuna salad sandwich at lunch time, which I found rather childish and unfair because he did it as a joke so that I would have been a poor sport not to laugh along with all the others. Anyway, though, nothing significantly humiliating is entailed in any of this, which is all just something I do and has no real meaning, and after all I *am* a small person without powerful connections, so I consider myself lucky to be included as a member of the senior staff.

My chief competitor tried to take advantage of my lateness today by getting up alongside the boss at the head of the table and reaching out as if absently to remove a thread from the boss's lapel, but you could see that he knew what he was doing because when I showed up he leaned forward and jeered at me with all his teeth to try to scare me off from taking my rightful place to the left of the boss. I did hesitate for a second, but the boss invited me forward with a nod, and my competitor slunk away along the wall, grumbling and drawing back his lips.

I was inspired to ask if he were a student of Chinese literature. He sneered at the question, but his curiosity was piqued also, and he asked what I meant. I asked if he were familiar with the Chinese classic entitled, "The Brown Spot on the Wall" by Hoo Flung Poo, and every member of the Senior Staff, including the president, drew back their lips and showed all their teeth in laughter, slapping their foreheads and jiggling in their chairs, causing a very serious loss of face for my chief competitor.

On the way home from work, the evening was so lovely, so redolent of the spring times of my youth, and I felt so refreshed by my victory at work—even though I am not really that kind of person and was sorry that life has to be that way—that I couldn't resist stopping at a cafe on the square for a glass of beer. Spring. Ah spring! And memories. At one point three cows came sashaying past, their huge brown eyes so full of innocence, so soft and beguiling, their brown flanks glistening, their udders pink and full. I'll tell you: I've been married nine years; I need some strange stuff.

My wife and I have put an ad in the paper. Many couples are doing that now. We feel we have a right to do as we like. After all, whom does it hurt? The ad appeared today and just seeing it there filled our hearts with freshness and hope. All through dinner, we kept smiling privately at one another, and after the children were asleep we made love for the first time in nearly two years.

We had our first "applicant" tonight. We arranged on the telephone to meet him on the square. He was to sit in the café, wearing a red turtle neck shirt. My wife and I planned to stroll past in the crowd, arm in arm, and have a look at him, and she would flex her arm against mine once if she didn't want to go through with it, twice if she did. The man in the red turtle neck shirt was wearing blue plastic eyeglasses studded with rhinestones. He had a large stomach and a large nose. His cheeks and chin were red, his shoulders narrow, but his clothes had a certain flair, a certain fashionable drab—the cut of his slacks so perfectly unflattering, the colors so jarringly mismatched—which gave the impression of a man in the know. My wife squeezed my arm twice.

Back at our place we had coffee and talked about various meaningless things to try to get to know each other. Finally I asked him what he liked to do. He said, Lots of things. I said I meant what did he like to do, you know, sex-wise, and he suggested that he and I should wrestle, with the winner gaining the favors of the fair damsel. I was willing to go along with that if my wife were, and she said that yes she would be willing to give it a tryout in deference to our guest. He began to undress. I asked what he thought he was doing, and with a look of guilt and hunger in his eyes, he suggested that technically we ought to wrestle in the nude if we were going to play it by Hoyle. The fact that he tried to make himself appear so relaxed and casual about it when in fact he was clearly sick with nervousness about the mere suggestion turned my stomach. I told him that while I had nothing against homosexuals, if we had wanted a homosexual in our home we would have said so in the ad, and that he had better put his shoes back on now and blow, in the sense of *beat it.* Now. After he had gone, my wife told me that the thought of the two of us wrestling in the nude for her favors had aroused her powerfully, so we had a good night after all, just the two of us, without any need of help from that type of person.

General Burgess came over to speak to me today.

I was outside the house clipping the yew hedges, and he passed by on the other side of the street and waved to me. Highly honored, I waved back, raising the hedge clippers in a kind of Roman military salute, whereupon he stopped and squinted at me, then crossed the street to apologize for having waved. He said that he had thought that I was someone else, but now he could see I was shorter than the person he thought I was. I told him there was no need to apologize. On the contrary. I was honored. This seemed to please him and got him chatting about the weather. The day was quite hot and reminded him, he said, of one time back in the '40s in Nevada at a bomb test out on the desert. He and a lot of military officers from various lands had been invited to witness the detonation of a hydrogen bomb. They stood out on the desert at two in the morning and the temperature was almost down to freezing, but the second that mushroom showed, the temperature climbed right up to over a hundred. Terribly uncomfortable it was, all of them in their protective clothing and helmets and unable to strip down for fear of contamination. But at least the heat was dry. No humidity to speak of. The general said he can't stand the humidity. Bothers his sinuses.

This story seemed somewhat insane to me, but on the other hand I was proud that he told me about it and that he had instinctively trusted me enough to show his real feelings of indifference about it without feeling compelled to pretend to have humanistic misgivings about the Bomb lest I were in some way positioned to compromise him. I was anxious to go inside and tell my wife about this socially promising encounter, but he lingered for a bit, looking up at my house. He asked if I were aware of the fact that the senior Senator from Arizona had once been a houseguest there when it was owned by Mrs. Scott, the first wife of the former deputy ambassador in Dubai. Mrs. Scott apparently had been quite the hot little number in her time, and the Senior Senator had elected to be the one to debrief her on behalf of the relevant senatorial subcommittee upon her return from Dubai where everyone had been compelled to live a life of utter sanctity as representatives of the State Department and to avoid being lashed on the public square with a microphone before their mouths to broadcast their agony to the populace. I thanked him for this very interesting bit of information. I was quite thrilled. Even though I am a Democrat and a pacifist, I admit I was invigorated to stand there chatting with a two-star general about a famous hawk Republican Senator who had once been a guest in my house. Finally, the general squeezed my bicep in a manly way, both to measure my strength and to express affection. He said that I was a nice young man, and he liked nice young men. I told him I was forty-two, and he said that when you get to be his age practically everyone seemed young. I was quite flattered by his attentions. I hope that he is not a homosexual.

I've decided that if I'm going to be on chit-chat terms with generals and senators I had better catch up on my current events. From now on I plan to read one news magazine from cover to cover each week. I started tonight with *Time* and learned a great many things. I learned that the economy is still in bad shape, but that the President is trying to alleviate the tax burden on the people by cutting out social programs for the needy, who have been guilty of overusing them, and restricting them instead to those above a certain income level, who first of all are the ones financing these programs and second of all rarely apply for social assistance without good cause. These programs apparently siphon off a great deal of money from the productive members of society into the pockets of the non-productive ones, which damages individual initiatives. But under the new system, three times as many people could be helped for a third of the cost, and the tax surplus so produced could be partially siphoned off to other areas of pressing need such as defense. The main question here was whether the nation was willing to endure a long, interminable, dreary period of economic slackness or whether it would not rather get it over with fast with a brief, intense interim period of extreme hardship. I also learned that more young men are going into military service now because of the lack of job opportunities or social help and that, in fact, was a good sign for the economy because these young men would learn a productive trade such as how to run and repair a computer guidance system for an intercontinental ballistic missile.

My wife and I have felt no real change in our lives in spite of our brief sexual renaissance. We are still terribly irritable with one another. We argue over nearly everything. I went to a lawyer to talk the situation over, and he said that if we had reached the point where just to wake up in the morning and look at each other or to sit down at the same table or walk past one another in the hall were too painful to endure, perhaps I should contemplate divorce. I said that I guess things hadn't got that bad.

Then he began to tell me about some of the things his own wife had done to him. She had fed his canary to her cat and pretended not to know anything about it. She had filled his attaché case with five pounds of cocktail peanuts and two empty vodka bottles once when he was going for a very important hearing and when he opened his attaché case the nuts and bottles had come clattering out all over the courtroom. She would telephone him from time to time to explain to him how she was encouraging their son, who was in her custody, to become a homosexual as the only kind of men who had any real feelings were homosexuals. He became increasingly upset and excited as he told me these things. He began to weep. Then he got angry.

"So you think you have a bad marriage, do you?" he asked with bitter scorn. "Think you got problems? Poor you. Poor kid. You people make me sick, you know that? I could puke every time one of you comes in here so full of self-pity and disappointment. Sorry for yourself, hah? Hah! If I didn't need the money for my support payments I'd throw you right the hell out on your ass and just go take off for the woods and live on grubs and raisins and fishes. Why I'd rather live with horses than people like you!"

I left him determined not to allow that to happen to us. We would make a fresh start. I stopped off and bought a bottle of expensive Alsatian wine and some sliced smoked salmon and a loaf of sourdough bread, a piece of prime beef and a hunk of *gorgonzola* and a bottle of *chateauneuf du pape,* as well as a small bottle of armagnac and some vanilla ice cream, and went home and proposed that we give the kids some spaghetti and put them to bed and eat by ourselves later. My wife was thrilled. We prepared the meal together, cooperating and snuggling in the kitchen, oiling up with a good healthy vodka martini and nibbling high-quality peanuts. The meal itself was magnificent. The wine was superb, too. But unfortunately there was a little too much of it. We got drunk, and old irritations and testy topics began to crop up. She complained in a caustic, bitter way that I was smacking my lips when I ate and before I could catch hold of myself I had flung a spoonful of ice cream across the table at her, whereupon she splashed a glass of red wine in my face, and I came around the table and grabbed hold of her wrist, and she scratched my face. Then we started trading smacks and pinches, in an odd controlled tit-for-tat manner, managing to keep from unrestrained violence, but still the night was ruined. We were so bitter with one another that neither of us would deign to clear the table, and it was sad this morning to come down and see the dehydrated remains of that beautiful piece of beef on the cutting board and the melted dishes of ice cream and stubs of baguette and crumpled napkins on the dining table.

Sometimes I think the problem is that our lives have been too comfortable, that we have to learn the meaning of hardship again. Perhaps we're not fit for success. Perhaps the only way for us to hold together is to lower our sights to more reasonable goals and turn our energies back to the enjoyment of life within more reasonable terms.

I'm also worried about my wife. She has been very morose

lately. Even though I have a great deal of contempt and hatred for her, I care very deeply about her. She is worried that there will be a war. I suggested that she look on the bright side. A war now—which we would anyway be powerless to stop—would stimulate the economy in the long run, and our son would not have to fight as he is only six and then probably by the time of the next war he would be too old to serve. But she said that she was worried about a nuclear war so that everything would be ruined forever, our children would have no future, no civilization, nothing but slow death and disease or the prospect of torture as in certain South American countries, and there would be no more children after them, for the human race would end, and all would have been in vain.

I've never really thought of it as graphically as that, and I was both frightened by the vision and impressed by the clarity and force of her power to envisage and evoke it. I had forgotten that she had that power, which was one of the things that originally attracted me to her.

Sometimes I feel that we have departed from the things that we once held as valuable. When I was a student I was very interested in truth and justice and human dignity. I believed in the possibility of world peace, and in the perfectability of the law and in the possibility of enacting a truly just society. I feel depressed sometimes to realize how very seldom I think about any of those things any more. When I first stopped thinking about them, even consciously detaching myself from them, I thought it humorous in a way. I would make cynical statements to appear worldly in my own eyes: ethnic slurs or gleefully evil cracks concerning political expediency or the brutishness of human nature. I felt that I was zeroing in on reality, stripping myself of false niceties and the hypocritical mannerism of humanism. Now, however, I am beginning to wonder if I haven't just climbed down into a well of some sort. Or turned my garden into a jungle where no one can be trusted and where there is nothing but contempt for all the things I once believed of value.

On the other hand, sometimes I feel quite pleased with the progress we have made. After all, to be a member of the Senior Staff, to have sufficient money in the bank, to be living on chit-chat terms with a two-star general, and to own a house in which a renowned state senator was once a guest and which was owned by the first wife of the former deputy ambassador in Dubai are modest but real achievements. Perhaps these things would sound meaningless to anyone but myself, absurd even ("Senator Gridman slept here."), but I feel justly proud and pleased with them. These people are at least down-to-earth enough to come over and chat a bit, whereas I know a hell of a lot of self-professed so-called humanists who would think nothing of wiring you up to shoot a million volts through your genitals if they didn't have to do it themselves or see it or hear about it or know for sure that it was happening.

I no longer know what is important.

What are we anyway? Are we creatures whose lives have some meaning? Or are we just some kind of fluke whose existence is as devoid of significance as that of an ant or a fly or a monkey? And if so, does that give us existential choice? Really? Could a man have dignity under Amin's sledgehammers or Bocassa's moat?

What does it mean, existentially speaking, when you squab your thumb on a flea? Or, on the other hand, do fleas and ants and monkeys have just as much value as we do?

General Burgess dropped by tonight. He apologized for the intrusion. He seemed embarrassed. His fingers were trembling. He was wearing a red turtleneck shirt. My wife and I had been drinking coffee and watching television, so I invited him to join us. He seemed tense and strange, and I didn't know what to say to him, so the three of us just sat there in silence, looking at the TV screen. There was a nature film on about the Congo River. At one point they showed a boatful of baby monkeys clinging to one another. Their parents had been butchered for packaging as frozen dog food, but the babies would be sold as pets for the equivalent of about five dollars apiece.

Did you ever feel as though you would like to just go out and kill to avenge injustice? Not for the advancement of any kind of principle or for any kind of personal gain, but just because there are so many filthy unfeeling bastards in this world, parading around in the skin of human beings.

I once saw a film about a psychological investigation of the function of emotional bonding. A mother and a baby Gibbon were together in a cage, but with a glass partition erected between them, and they were weeping and reaching for one another and tearing the hair from their scalps and banging against the glass, while the researchers watched, silently recording the amount of time it would take before they stopped grieving and began to focus on their individual survival again. In another variation of the methodology, the floor of the cage was wired for electricity and each time the mother monkey would give milk to the baby a jolt of electricity would be shot through her, to see how long it would take for her desire for personal comfort to overcome her instinct to nourish her offspring.

I felt that I could gladly have extinguished the lives of those researchers. I could picture myself kicking in the door with a sub-machine gun in my arms and spraying them with lead so that the white walls and jackets were filthy red with blood and the air was filled with groans of agony from their objective mouths.

I began to think about the general, sitting there so tensely and quietly in his red shirt. I wondered about that shirt. I began to get a sinking feeling in my stomach that he thought I was some kind of a pimp flunky. Had he somehow found out about our liaison with the would-be nude wrestler and did he think that we were some kind of slut couple so hungry to climb that because he was a general and I was a nobody, he could just come in here in a red shirt expecting to help himself to whatever he desired? I admit that I was not unflattered to have a general sitting at my coffee table or even at the possibility that he coveted my wife, as this was some indication of the high standards of my own tastes, but on the other hand he appeared to be a sick, aggrieved, morose general. Why should we have to settle for a general who was less than healthy and whole? Are we so hard up? The Pentagon is full of generals.

Trying to keep my voice as neutral as possible, I asked him what the significance of the red turtleneck shirt was. He looked surprised that I should ask.

"Why these are our regimental colors,' he said. "This color was awarded us 200 years ago at the Battle of Dry Harbor. No other regiment is allowed to wear red dickeys or red backing on their brass." Then he fell back into his moody silence. I was somewhat relieved at this explanation, but on the other hand, I still couldn't fathom what he might want from us or what he was doing here.

I began to feel more and more agitated and bitter. *He* was wasting *my* time, violating my hospitality, sitting in the most comfortable chair in the room. I decided that if he got up and went to the toilet, I would claim that chair for myself and let him have the wicker armchair instead, which creaked when you moved to shift your position. My wife got up from her chair and walked out of the room, and the general's eyes followed her to the door. Then he turned to me and said, "Are you Catholic, young man?"

I said that I had been raised Catholic, and he nodded. "Then you're Catholic. And you should have been a priest. You're such a very nice young man, if you were a priest I would confess my sins to you."

Amazed, I stared at him. I hadn't known that generals committed sins. I hadn't even known that they *could* in a way. Somehow, it seemed, I don't know, outside their frame of reference. In a certain way I was touched to think of a general offending God and feeling remorse. I wondered what kind of sins a general would commit. Would they be run-of-the-mill type personal sins—violations of the commandments, failure to uphold the beatitudes—or would they be grandiose acts carried out on a great scale and with thundering pride like the sins of tragic Greek heroes?

He looked down at his great thumbs and jutted out the wet underside of his lower lip and said, "There are a number of things that I have done in my life of which I am not proud."

This moved me greatly, and although I had been curious to know what sort of sins he might have been guilty of, suddenly the opposite feeling took hold of me. I wished urgently to stop him from revealing his actions to me, to hold his secrets inviolate.

Before he could open his mouth to speak again, I told him that he shouldn't allow himself to feel so badly, that none of us is perfect, not one of us, for all have fallen short of the glory of God. I said, "Sin is behovely, general."

He looked hopefully at me. "Do you really think so?"

"I certainly do," I said, although I did not really know the origin or even the exact meaning of the statement. But the General had been so affected, that I repeated it, embellishing from some well of memory: "Yes, sin is behovely, but all shall be well. And all manner of thing shall be well. By the purification of the motive in the ground of our beseeching."

The general looked positively transported. His eyes were wide and his thin purple lips moved against one another in wonder, and he took hold of my hand in both of his and shook it warmly. "Thank you, son," he said. "Thank you and God bless you. And may God protect you and yours."

I think that my wife and I have found some sort of solution to our problem. Perhaps we were trying to do too much together, to be too much together, always following one another around, sitting at the same table, doing the same tasks together, watching television together, even *reading* together. Now we're trying to ignore one another more, not to tell each other everything that happens or everything we feel or think, trying to get out more on our own and do different things and establish a separate circle of friends. In any event we can't fight if we're not in the same room with each other. Last week at a party I was standing talking to a woman, while my wife was off somewhere else with someone else, and the woman suddenly reached out her hand to me and said, "Say hello." I took her hand and held it and she stared into my face for a very long moment, and it was not a sexual experience, but I felt as though something of her spirit, or her life, were entering my arm through her grip. The experience was an exhilarating one, and my first thought was to share it with my wife. But I didn't. I didn't. I kept it for myself. So I have a secret, a happy little secret, something all my own, which is lovely. But I also feel sad, defeated in a way. As long as we were fighting at least we were trying to reach one another. Now we seem to have given up. However now that the tension has broken between us, I feel hopeful that we might begin to be able to see one another as strangers again and have respect for each other and not hate each other anymore.

I was playing with my little girl out on the back terrace this evening. A warm red sunlight was suffusing the smoked glass wall which separates the house from the garden, and I was holding her on my lap and looking into her face, which was literally alight with joy, her eyes big and round, her mouth smiling toothlessly at me. A little girl of five months radiant with joy, laughing, chuckling, grinning, turning upon me the infinite depths of clear pure joy of her eyes. Where could such happiness originate from? How inexplicable that a creature could just appear out of nowhere being full of such joy, a creature who is totally dependent on others, the equivalent of a cripple, unable to walk, feed herself, dress herself, or even to speak or tell us what she wants or what's wrong. And yet as long as she is fed and dry and rested she is nearly always ready to light up with joy at the most trifling communication—a smile, the shake of a rattle, a tickle under her chin, whereas we adults who have our houses and cars and big salaries and fine clothes, color televisions, quadrophonic stereos, fat dinners, fine wines, vacation trips and pretty much more or less what we want, we are so full of bitterness and spite and misery. Why? Perhaps we have travelled too far from the source of existence. Perhaps an infant has just come from infinity and is still full of the glow of infinity's perfection. Perhaps we go back to that place when we die, all of us together again in perfect love and tolerance and harmony.

Perhaps there really is some meaning to it all. For when I look into the smiling face of that enraptured little girl, a wave of profound affection sweeps slowly across my heart, cleansing it, and for the time it takes to pass I have shared her joy and am renewed.

Perhaps what I told the general is true. Perhaps, despite it all, someday perhaps all manner of thing really will be well. Someday.

(1982)

HERE'S MY STORY
IT'S SAD BUT IT'S TRUE

THE BOX WAS quite nice. That's the first thing I noticed. That bothered me some. It looked expensive. I was already down five C's for the plane fare and pocket money, and a gaudy box seemed kind of silly, seeing as how they were only going to bury it. But that's my brother for you: why be reasonable when offered the alternative of ruining yourself?

He was already there, seated in a wooden armchair by the wall, gazing toward the box, talking to a woman in a blue veil, sitting beside him. She had nice legs in sheer blue stockings. I didn't recognize anyone else in the room except for my father, or what was left of him, lying in the box with a carnation in his lapel. The smell made me think of high school proms. I guess I can't really say I recognized my father either, although there was a definite resemblance in that skull of a face which I hadn't seen in nearly ten years. But of course it was his funeral, so it could only have been him.

I stepped up and clasped my hands in front of my fly. Propped up on the foot of the coffin were four photographs in chrome frames: a brown and white one of the old man in youth, smiling at the tiller of his boat; a studio portrait of my mother, wearing a hat that looked like a helmet liner, her full lips and long nose telling the story of her life; high school senior portraits of myself and of Al, both baby-faced with full-grown noses. The noses we got from my mother, who died when I was ten, thirty years before, in a car wreck with a man she had no business being in a car with. The man was still alive. On my twenty-fifth birthday, I looked him up with the intention of mashing his face in for him, but he got so scared when he opened the door and saw me there that I just laughed and told him what a sad bastard he was. I figured I had already won a moral victory, no sense taking a chance of blowing it in actual combat.

My father was twenty years older than my mother and out-lived her by thirty years. He never remarried, a fact which showed in his face, I thought, gazing down at him. There was a kind of egocentric innocence in that smooth, fleshless visage settled back on its satin cushion. It reminded me of all the lies he used to tell us. Every chance he got he used to go sailing off into the Long Island Sound to be alone with his illusions about humanity. He would never let us come because he said it was too dangerous to go sailing alone, and he didn't want to jeopardize our lives along with his own. He thought this noble, I'm sure. He loved martyrs, my father did: Dr. Tom Dooley, Senator McCarthy, John Henry, Big John. Jack Kennedy he excepted; Kennedy's death had been nothing but the wages of sin he said. Ditto Bobby, ditto King. But Hubert H. Humphrey's death he had followed with ecstasy, watching the ever-shrinking cadaverous frame, waving and smiling on the TV screen.

"Look at that man," he used to say, clenching his fist and jaws to indicate power. *"Guts."* That was the summation of a man's life in a word: *Guts.* Or, conversely: No *guts.*

Someone was breathing beside me. I glanced. Al touched my shoulder, firming his lips, nodding, face aimed at the dead old man.

"Guts," he said.

Asshole, I thought.

"Well, Jack," Al said. "How are you?"

"Can't complain."

He shrugged. "I could. But I won't."

"There's whiners and winners," I said. I had turned toward my brother and caught sight of the woman on the other side of the room with whom he had been speaking before.

"I lost a bundle on the campaign," Al said.

"Shame."

"The shame is all his," Al said. "I'm ashamed of him. I'll tell you, I flew that guy all over the country. From campaign to campaign. On the cuff. Owes me ten thousand. I need that money. Very badly. I remember when he used to laugh and say he'd make me chairman of the FAA. Sure. Couldn't make you chairman of the city pound now. I mean, you put your heart and your soul into something because it's your business and this is the man you believe in your heart should be president, and they turn around and do this to you. Dad was right about him after all. Said he had no heart."

"Sad."

"Did you vote for him?" Al asked.

I smiled. "Let me put it this way, Al: I couldn't bring myself to place my trust in a man who would place his body in a plane flown by you."

Al stared at me. "Are you being funny, Jack?"

"Hey, come on, can't you take a joke? You, yourself, said you were ashamed of the man."

"I earned that right."

I nodded, paused, asked, "Say, Al, who's the pretty woman there in the blue veil?"

Al glanced over his shoulder. I saw the tiny network of broken red capillaries along the side of his nose. "My secretary," he said. "We live together."

"Nice," I said.

"Nice is not the word. An angel, a saint is what she is. I could never pay back what she's given me."

I said, "If you want to keep a woman make her pay."

"How's that?"

The gaze was upon me again. Dangerous, but not yet lethal. "A woman will never leave as long as you owe her something. Old Japanese proverb."

Al continued to stare at me, blinked. "Do you think you're funny?"

I stand a head taller than Al and could always outwit him, although in a fight, if he got mad enough, even when he was ten and I was twelve, he could whip me. The trick always was to tease him to a lather and then apologize just before he tore loose. If you waited too long you could get hurt—as I could attest by a chipped upper incisor and two inch-long scars on my forehead.

"Aw, look, Al," I said, "You know I'm only teasing you. I love you. I never could resist teasing you a little."

A short, deep line of concentration creased his forehead. "You mean you tease me because you love me? Or you love me because you tease me?"

I grinned. "Allie, boy, I'm just envious. True love never came my way. How's Ginger?"

His gaze was steady, searching. "You don't know about Ginger?"

I allowed myself a dangerous luxury, the quick edge of a smile beneath the tip of my tongue. "Come to think of it, I did hear something about your separating, or something. Damn shame."

"Woman broke my heart, but I can't regret it. She made a man of me."

My eyes were flickering between Al's face and his secretary's which, if I wasn't mistaken, was staring from beneath the blue veil at me.

"Ginger fascinated me right from the start," he said.

"She was a fascinating woman."

"Not just how she was in bed, everything about her. She would hurt me and then laugh. My buddy, Walt—'member Walt? Walt Zipler?—he says, Al, the woman's a bitch; jettison her. I said, Walt, the woman is in pain. She's suffered. She's testing me to see am I the same bastard behind the face of every man she's ever known. I dedicated myself to that woman. I figured, make her feel loved, give her true love, and she'll bloom. I was devoted to her. Breakfast in bed. Shared the housework fifty-fifty, sixty-forty, seventy-thirty. I washed for her, cooked for her, bought her clothes, flew her to expensive resorts. I massaged her, told her she was beautiful, which in my opinion she was. I let her have affairs if she wanted. Took me fifteen years to find out Walt was right. Some people, you can't be nice to. She was a bitch and that's all there was to it. But at least I knew for sure. I mean, I wasn't just saying, 'Fuck her, the bitch.' I invested fifteen years in acquiring the right to say that."

"Well, more power to you, Al. I'm sure you did the right thing. Say, listen, I haven't eaten since this morning. Care to step out for a bite?"

"I'm not sure we should both go at the same time."

I shrugged. "I hate to eat alone. Well, how about your secretary? Maybe I could treat her to a sandwich?"

Al said, "You're wasting your time, Jack."

"Why? Doesn't she like sandwiches?"

"She's no tramp. You got the wrong idea. She and I are very good friends. But there's no cheap stuff to it. She's not that kind of woman. I've never laid a finger on her."

"I'm relieved to hear that, Al."

"Long as we understand one another."

"We do." I put my arm around Al's shoulder. "Isn't it something after all these years how nothing has changed? I mean five minutes together and it's like we've never been apart."

"On second thought," Al said, "I think I'll go with you."

"If you're sure."

"I'll ask Mr. Cooke to keep an eye on things."

"Good idea."

Al took us to a luncheonette out in Flushing, on the Sound. I didn't realize why until he motioned out toward the water, across the pier with its long rows of slanting, bobbing masts, and said, "Can't you just see Dad sailing off into the sunset?"

I said, "I can't even see the sunset."

The secretary giggled, one single note, like a wild hiccup, then put her sheer-gloved fingers over her mouth. Al stared at her, then at me. His eyes misted. I smacked his shoulder. "You were always a sentimental guy, Al. Always figured that was the secret of your success with women." This seemed to cheer him up. I didn't dare look at the secretary, though from the corner of my eye I saw her peeling up her veil and looking at me. Her name was Sharon and she had a strawberry mark on her cheek, which I knew was a good sign.

She said to me, "You have your brother's nose."

I said, "Wrong. I have my mother's nose. My brother has my nose, but he doesn't live up to it"

We ordered coffee and cheesecake, and while we waited for it to come, I watched Sharon leaf through the pages of the little jukebox extension at the edge of our table. It was full of golden oldies. I fished a couple of quarters out of my pocket and invited her to pick some tunes. I was fascinated by her sheer-gloved fingers as she punched the buttons for "Runaround Sue" by Dion and the Belmonts, "Tears on My Pillow" by Little Anthony and the Imperials, and "Sh-Boom!" by the Chord Cats.

"That's the original version, " I said. "You don't see that around much."

Our cheesecake and coffee came. I couldn't take my eyes off Sharon's fingers as she sliced into her cake. The gloves were like very fine blue nets with large blue clumps of material dotted here and there. My eyes kept moving from the fingers to the strawberry mark. She wore no make-up. Her lips were the color of pale berries. Her teeth were very good. She chewed cake, sipped coffee, wiped her mouth with a paper napkin. Her tongue was clean. I was hypnotized. I knew Al was watching me, but I was beyond caring.

"How's your wife?" he asked.

"Oh, didn't you hear?" I said. "She died."

"You're putting me on."

I stared coldly at him. "You think I'd joke about something like that?"

"Hey, Jack. You're telling me that Lucille is dead?"

"You heartless bastard," I said. "You want to make me repeat it?"

"Hey, Jack," he said, "No, honest, God, forgive me."

"So drop it, okay?"

"How'd she die?" Sharon asked.

"Car crash," I said.

Al said, "Oh, Christ." His mouth hung open.

I said, "Might've been a blessing in disguise. A few days later we got back the results of the smear. Routine screening, you know? Positive. She had 'C.' "

Sharon sliced a forkful of cake and turned it over as though she intended to plant something in it. Her fingers looked very kinky. I wondered if she were fond of perversion.

From the corner of my eye I could see Al staring at me, could see he thought I was lying.

Sharon raised her eyes from the cheesecake she was plowing. I winked. She bit the bottom of her grin.

I turned to Al to route him before he could get himself all worked up about whether or not I was lying. "What's Cooke going to sting you for the wake and all?"

"Five."

"Five? That's an outrage. I wouldn't pay it if I were you." Quickly, I added, "You have that kind of money to fork out? I'm impressed."

"We'll work it out," he said.

"Who's "we"? You got a mouse in your pocket?" Sharon's sheer fingers touched her lips.

Al half stood, holding onto the paper napkin he had opened on his lap. "Still the same prick as always, huh, Jack?"

I said, "Why the hell didn't you have him burned?"

He blinked. "You scumbag. You want to burn your own father?"

I said, "He'll burn anyway so what's the big deal?"

Al's open palm swung at me. I blocked it. He was on his feet, his hands gathering up my collars, lifting me from the seat of my chair. It felt kind of nice, his knuckles so firm against the under-side of my chin. I wondered if he would hit me. It was kind of ex-citing. I didn't resist. Some instinct told me that would be the most profitable course. He bounced me once so my glasses went askew.

"I could break your back," he said.

Sharon was on her feet. "Leave him alone!" she said. Al took his hands away at once. His face was all squished up as though he might cry. "Why?" he whimpered.

"Cause you're a big *bully!*" she said.

"*He's* bigger than me!"

I was tickled. I held my tongue, straightened my glasses. Then I said, "Why don't we all take it easy? This always happens when someone you love dies."

Al glared at me. "Did you love him?"

I said, "He was my father."

"Did you love him, yes or no?" Al shouted.

The man behind the counter was on his feet. The waitress looked over at us. The other customers looked steadfastly away. Sharon said, "Shhh..."

I stared into Al's eyes. "Figure you got the love market all sewed up for yourself, don't you Al? Figure you got a corner on it."

He pinched his eyes in thumb and forefinger. Tears welled up over his lower lids. He looked like a real jerk. "I'm sorry," he whispered. "I'm upset."

"Sure. Upset." I reached to my inside pocket as though to lift out a plane ticket. "I think I'll go right the hell back to L.A."

"No," Al said.

"No," Sharon said.

I sighed, glowered, took my hand from my pocket. "I'm not going back to that goddamned funeral home again tonight," I said. "I can't take it."

"Don't worry," Al said. "I'm sorry. It's okay. I'll take care of the whole thing for you."

Their apartment was surprisingly pleasant. The living room was all in white—carpet, sofa, easy chairs, white lacquered coffee and end tables. Al wanted Sharon to go with him back to Cooke's to help him close up the box and all, but Sharon didn't feel that I ought to be left alone. She whispered to him that she thought I was a lot more upset than I seemed.

"Well," Al said. "I won't be long."

As soon as he was gone, Sharon peeled up her veil again, which she had rolled down after we left the restaurant.

"How long have you been shacking up?" I asked.

"Since he left his wife," she said. "We're just very good friends. Is your wife really dead?"

"Not as far as I know."

She sniggered.

I said, "You have a beautiful mouth."

"That's a new one," she said.

"I mean it. I love your mouth. It's beautiful."

Her clitoris was also beautiful. It resembled an innocent young girl in a row boat wearing a Mexican hat. She kept her dark blue sheer stockings on and lay on the white carpet, and my tongue did a Mexican hat dance. What the hell, why not? We both liked it a lot, and we weren't hurting anybody by our behavior. I kept thinking of my father at the tiller of his boat on the Long Island Sound, wondering whether he ever got himself any strange stuff. Every time I tapped the Mexican hat with the tip of my tongue, it nodded affirmatively, and Sharon said, "Oh, you dirty bastard."

"That's right," I said and did it again. I was holding her wrists down as though she were my prisoner and had her thighs pinned beneath my shoulders. I had guessed that she would like it that way, and apparently I was right.

"Oh you dirty bastard," she said.

"You bet your sweet booty," I said. "Only way to handle a woman like yourself."

"Why?" she whimpered.

"Because," I said, "you have that desire. It's all over your face for anyone who can read it. You're an open book, kid."

"*Oh* you filth," she said.

It was lovely.

Then Al came back. I didn't even know he was there until my trousers smacked me in the back of the head. One pant leg plastered across my face, and he shouted, "Okay dirt: Out!"

"Take it on the arches," I muttered, extricating myself from the slacks and tipped the Mexican hat again.

"*Oh!*" she said.

"*Oh,* you filthy bastard," Al said.

The Mexican hat nodded agreement.

Over my shoulder, I said, "If you can't keep your woman happy someone else will."

Sharon's moans sounded like questions. I mounted her, and the moans turned affirmative. As I slid into her, I wondered if she were on the pill or what. I said, "I'm bareback. Can I come in you?"

"*Oh* you dirty fuck," she said. "Give it to me."

"You bet," I said.

I could sense Al standing behind me. "You two are totally shameless, aren't you?" he said.

Sharon's eyes were shut. I was staring at her strawberry mark as I rocked on her. Her fingers played in the short hair at the back of my skull. I felt really glad.

I heard Al sit down, heard the rattle of a bottleneck against the mouth of a glass, the sizzle of liquor pouring over ice. Al was talking to himself. "Sometimes I think the only pure love I've ever known was from a dog I had out in California years ago," he said. "It was a chow-chow. It bit me once, by accident, when we were playing in the dark. Just a nip. But it knew right away what it had done, and it started crying pitifully, running around in circles and crying. Christ, I loved that dog."

"I'm gonna come," I said.

"Not yet," Sharon said. "Not yet."

"Okay—I'll try…. "

"I'm the kind of guy who tries," Al said. "I don't believe in indifference. I'd rather get hurt than go free. And believe me, I've been hurt."

I said, "I can't wait any longer."

"Think about something else for a minute, *please.*"

I thought about my father at the tiller of his skiff sailing into the sunset on the Long Island Sound. I could see it now. I really could see it.

"I'm coming," Sharon whispered, "oh sweet Jesus mother of god I'm coming!"

Then she screamed out like a jungle parrot, and I could see my father smiling at the tiller, as his skiff slipped into the red sunset, and he waved, and I said, "Yeah! Yeah! Oh sweet motherfucking *yeah!*"

(1986)

THE AUTHOR OF THINGS

My name is Tom Dunne. I am an author. I am, in fact, the author of things. I am creating the world of this story into which you, hopefully, are being drawn.

But ordinarily this would be a lonely story. It would make you sad. Or at least it would make me sad. All my stories do. But this story is not going to make me sad. Because in this story I have decided I am going to meet a beautiful woman. I will create her just for myself, and she will be perfect, and we will not make each other sad. We will make each other happy.

She will be a redhead. A beautiful redhead, sleeping by a lake in late afternoon sunlight. There she is right now. Do you see her? She is lying in the grass on the bank of a lake—or perhaps a river. Yes, a river. The Seine. This story takes place in Paris. In the heat of August when most Parisians are away. The girl's brilliant red hair is fanned out in the deep-green grass. Her eyes are closed, and the hand of one arm, crooked at the elbow, rests languidly in her thick hair. The other hand hovers over her breast, holding a joint in her soft, ivory-white fingers. Yes. A beautiful redhead with beautiful pale red lips and skin the white of an ivory sculpture in the grass by the river, dreamy on pot. She could be the cover illustration for an anthology of British Romantic poetry. And she is mine. She is my creation.

I step closer to her and softly say, "Open your eyes. Tell me your name." I like to give my characters a little bit of free will—not much, just a little. It would be boring otherwise.

Her eyelids flutter open to reveal a surprise. I did not know what startlingly luminous pale blue eyes she would have. She stares at me, looking startled, as if surprised to find herself here, in this story.

"What is your name?" I ask again.

"I am Lorelei," she says. She has an accent I cannot quite place. Nordic perhaps. She looks at the reefer between her fingers as though uncertain what it is. Then she looks at me again with those luminous eyes.

"Who are you?" she asks.

"Dunne is the name. Tom Dunne. The author." I wonder if she will understand that when I say "the" author I mean the author of this story. As I try to decide what I wish to make happen next, there comes a splashing from the river, and another woman with red hair crawls up onto the grassy bank like a molting butterfly, water sliding from her close-cropped curly red locks, rolling down her shoulders and chest. She rises. She is wearing an aquamarine two-piece swim suit and her skin is tanned and alluring.

"Who are you?!" I ask, more an exclamation than a question. I didn't create her. What is she doing in my story? She may have come from my pen, but not from my imagination—in any event, she was not a conscious act of my imagination, and I wonder if my imagination has its own volition, if it hovers in shadowy corners into which I cannot see and subverts my purposes. I recall a debate between Forster and Nabokov in which someone asked Forster if his characters sometimes seemed to have a will of their own, and he answered that indeed they did, whereupon Nabokov said that he could well understand if the passengers mutinied on that dreary voyage to India but that *his* characters were galley slaves. Do my characters have free will? Do I?

The sun is in the western sky, sliding toward the horizon, and I notice suddenly how hot and muggy it has become. I did not ask this other redhead to rise from the water of the river. Nonetheless a quick glance at her and into her eyes—the same luminous blue!—assures me, as though it were the will of another, that I want her here.

"What is your name?" I ask.

"You can call me Bente, honey," she says in that same strange accent as Lorelei's. she looks me up and down and says, "And what should I call you other than honey, honey?"

Lorelei says, "He's Tom." She says it in a way that is almost a question—as though *I* were the intruder.

"Tom?" says Bente. "Well how are your caramels, honey?"

Lorelei claps her soft white hand over her lips and giggles.

"My caramels?" I ask, confused. Am I being goaded by my own creations. Made an object of ridicule.

Bente smiles owlishly. "Haven't you ever heard of Tom's caramels?"

"I'm Tom Dunne," I say and straighten my shoulders. "The author," I add with dignity.

"Author of the caramels," says Bente, and I feel the situation slipping from my grasp. In a bid for control, I ask, "Where are you girls from?" Yet feel that I should know the answer to that already. This is *my* story. And it is set in Paris, I remind myself. These girls, with their strange northern accent, could only be foreigners. Sweden, I think—perhaps I will make them be from Sweden. Like Anita Ekberg in Fellini's *Dolce Vita*, dancing in that Roman fountain, perhaps I will create a fountain for them to dance in!

"We're from Jutland," says Lorelei.

"In the land of Tom's Caramels," Bente adds, and they both giggle as though 'caramel' is a double entendre.

But not only do I fail to guess what it might mean, for a moment I can't even remember where Jutland is either. "Well you're in Paris now," I insist, still thinking with one part of my mind what kind of fountain I would like to create for them to dance in. They could dance in a fountain even if they're from Jutland.

"Well, honey, haven't you ever heard of a Jutlandish girl with a bone in her nose?"

"With a...? Say, are you getting risqué?" I demand. "This is not that kind of story. This is a romantic story." So the kitty is out of the bag. This is a story. That should put them in place. They are mere characters! I, *au contraire*, am the author.

"You *think* it's not that kind of story, honey. Once you let Jutlandish girls in the door, it could turn into any kind of story."

"You're kind of fresh," I say—but at the same time recognize that, despite myself, I am drawn to her

"You bet I'm fresh, honey!"

Lorelei at that moment slides the joint between her sweet, berry-red lips and takes a deep toke on it, as though suddenly discovering that after all she knows exactly what it is there for. She holds the smoke deep in her lungs, then coughs some of it out and begins to pass it to Bente, but draws back, saying, "Dry your fingers first, Bente." She says this in a familiar, even intimate manner as though they know each other already, even intimately.

Bente does as she is asked, then takes a perfunctory hit before passing it to me, but withholds it teasingly. "Don't Bogart that thang, honey!"

"He's Tom," Lorelei says again for some reason—as though imparting some other subliminal information, and as I take a hit they look knowingly at one another, then go into a dance routine, singing to the tune of "Juan Tanamera":

"Tom's caramel-els! Oh yes it's Tom's carmel-els! Tom's car- a-mel-els! Oh yes it's Tom's caramel-els!"

They kick their long shapely legs in unison, right leg left, left leg right, snapping their fingers and staring at me with their four luminous eyes.

Abruptly, then, they stop and Bente, with an amused smile, says, "You thought you could write yourself right into a big juicy ménage à trois, didn't you, honey?"

"No," I say. "No! That is not what I meant at all. I am not like that. I am not at all like that. I have respect for my characters. 'Almost astonishing respect and tenderness for his characters,' one of the reviewers said, in fact. And by the way, Bente: I didn't even write *you*!"

"Well, excuse me for breathing, honey!"

"Don't misunderstand," I say. "You're welcome in the story. I like you."

"But you're threatened, honey, is that it? Because you didn't know that we are authors as well. Anyone of us could be 'the' author."

"*What?!*" I demand. "What do you mean by that? *I* am the author!"

Bente looks into my eyes with a pity that is almost tender and, affecting a British accent, says, "Honey, *you* are the caretaker. You have *always* been the caretaker."

At that moment there is a splashing from the river and another woman emerges. She is shaved bald but has two lush clumps of copper red hair beneath her shapely arms. She is wearing a vest and jeans which are plastered wet to her, and she appears astonished to find herself in this company.

"Who the hell are you?" I demand, but Bente laughs. "Ha! That's the bitch you were so taken by at the Pathetic Bureau last winter. It was her debut reading. You couldn't stop thinking about her."

I gasp. "How did you know about her?!"

"Honey, I have *access*."

Lorelei and Bente begin to teach the bald girl their dance routine, and soon the three of them are kicking in unison and snapping their fingers, singing, "Tom's caramel-els!" to the tune of "Juan Tanamera" and staring at me with their six eyes—which are all equally luminously blue.

They are dancing toward me as I back away, gasping, "This is *not* the story I set out to write!"

"Oh, honey," says Bente with a mild smirk, rotating her fists beneath her elbows and shaking her breasts as she continues to dance, and the two others shake their breasts in synchrony—six breasts shaking in my face, but not in the way I would have written it.

"This *is* your story, honey—the story of your life, honey! You Dunne done it!"

"But this was meant to be a happy story!" I protest.

"Don't you think *we're* happy, honey? We're *very* happy. You just didn't realize that we are all authors, too. All of us. Maybe you created us that way. Or maybe *we* created *you*. To tease and torment. Or maybe to liberate."

"To liberate from what?" I ask, feeling a sense of creeping horror.

But Bente only smiles and, glancing knowingly at Lorelei and the bald woman with copper-red armpit hair, says, "Anyone's guess who 'the' author is here, isn't that right, honey?"

I back farther away as they continue to advance, kicking in unison, right leg left, left leg right, snapping the fingers of their six hands, rotating their six fists under their six elbows, their six blue eyes glowing at me, their six breasts quivering. With a glint in her luminous eye, Bente says, "It is a hungry dance we do on monsieur's sword," and seized by inexplicable terror—though I know it is unwise to do so—I turn my back and run.

Up the stone steps to the Pompidou Quai, across the Pont Louis Philippe and Pont St. Louis to the Ile de la Cité, through the shadow of Notre dame whose gargoyles are now all, unaccountably, stiff pricks—I hear Bente calling out behind me, "Are we keeping you up, honey?", followed by a cackling from many female throats. My leather heels sound against the cobblestones. I am panting. I feel a stitch in my side, and my face is slick with sweat in the muggy heat, my shirt plastered to my back and chest.

I cross to the left bank, not daring to look back for I can hear the tramp of their running feet close upon me, and there are certainly more than six tramping feet behind me now. I duck down Rue St. Julien and flatten myself in a narrow alley, and their pounding feet stampede past, and I was right, there are many more of them now, an army of redheaded women authors, taking over the left bank, taking over the story, taking over. What havoc are they seeking to wreak?

As the last of them trample past, I slip out of the alley and move with stealth in the shadows close to the wall, back toward the Seine. They are chanting. I can hear them in the distance:

"Dunne done it! Let's do Dunne! Dunne done it! Let's do Dunne!"

The city is bathed in shadow, the shadow of a de Chirico, of a Hopper black-and-white night shadow woodprint. I can see the redheaded women in the distance, running to and fro in the dark street, casting long frantic primitive shadows. Then the chant begins to move closer again.

"Dunne done it! Let's do Dunne!" A single voice—I think it is the bald woman—calls out, "Let's *undo* Dunne!" followed by a cacophony of cackles.

Panting, sweating, I slip into the next alley just in time to see two men emerging from the shadows. I gasp! It is Robert Coover. He staggers out, muttering, "Who fahrd that shot? Mart fahrd it!"

With him is Lance Olsen, red-bearded face smiling with

warm irony. "Hi, Tom," he says. "Burnt agin, hey?" Behind them comes William S. Burroughs, natty in a Burberry buckled around his narrow waist, saying with dry-throated sarcasm, "I never met a Dunne who was not bone dull." After him comes Nabokov, eyes brimming with disdain: "Cackling redheaded women taking liberties with the narrative! You, sir, are a poor author!"

As if inspired—perhaps by the unexpected appearance of this quartet of innovative writers, as this Redheaded Women's Liberation Army of Authors is moving closer with thundering footfalls, suddenly I understand *everything*—except who they are, and why they are after me, and what is going to happen. I stand sweating in the alley. It is August, and the heat is enough to drive a man mad.

And the story is not done yet.

(2010)

GETTING LUCKY

*...and to die is different from what anyone supposed,
and luckier.*

— Walt Whitman, "Song of Myself"

I. THE AWARD

LUCAS "LUCKY" BOHANNON lays the tux out on the ratty bed-
spread alongside his leopard-skin pillbox hat, black designer T-
shirt, and white suspenders. He wishes Lotte-Mia was with him—
he could tell her this hotel is the one where Joe Buck spent his
first nights in Manhattan in *Midnight Cowboy*. You have to be
quick to see it in the movie—it's only on screen for a second or
two—a long, vertical, neon sign hugging the side of the building:

H
O
T
E
L

C
A
R
T
E
R

Forty years later, some of the neon letters are burnt out, so tonight it says:

H
O
T

C
A
R

E

Back in the '60s, Bohannon remembers, you could get a decent hotel in New York for twenty a night. The Carter, then a couple of stars up from its current no-star status, could not have been more than fifteen bucks at most. Now with both his parents dead and his siblings scattered, the Carter is mostly where Bohannon stays when he comes back to New York. Even the Carter, at 99 a night plus tax, is a stretch, but it's midtown and isn't dirty, though he won't go so far as to describe it as clean. As much as he regrets that Lotte-Mia is not with him, he realizes she would not have been happy here—he would have had to spring for the Chelsea at two hundred or even the Algonquin at four-and-a-half Cs.

He knows the rooms in the Carter, always asks for 2324, on the next to top floor, from which, if he cranes his neck, he can glimpse the Hudson sliding past the Palisades. He fancies the beat -up furniture and neon letters shining across his sleeping face as stylishly *noir*. Especially now, he relishes the irony of it all with his glad rags at ready—tuxedo and leopard-skin hat—a 60th birthday gift from Lotte-Mia, the woman he adores, back in Copenhagen waiting for his call after the awards ceremony.

"It'll be like four in the morning Danish time," he protested.

"Wake me," she said.

He looked into her lovely aging baby blues. "Only if I win."

"Wake me whatever you do. I want you to wake me. *Wake*. Me."

She's convinced he'll win; he knows better. For Christ's sake, his essay was published in a literary magazine and, even after a quarter century of publication by small presses and university quarterlies, he is unknown to all but some of his fellow small-press writers and editors. And tonight he is up against writers from *the New Yorker, the Atlantic, Harper's, Elle...* Bohannan is the token small press person in the running, his essay is the American Society of Magazine Editors' nod to the quarterlies. For Christ's sake, he's up against a Stephen King essay about Harry Potter!

The ironies are multiple and piquant—too piquant for him to have resisted flying to the ceremony (at his own expense) from Copenhagen, his adopted home, back to New York, which he said goodbye to thirty years before, forsaking the bloody big-city literary arena to take his chances writing in isolation. He didn't want to have to mooch invitations to cocktail parties where he would have to suck up to people he felt ill at ease with for big-time writing assignments which paid well but deeply did not interest him. Didn't want to be a beggar at the banquet. He already had his moment of Satori by then: in Alphabet City in 1971; he was writing a story, another story that he knew would not be published, a story he had to care about with more or less every cell in his body even if he knew it would not be published, even if he knew it was yet another in a Beckettian row of fail-betters. He was in his East 3rd Street studio writing at his grandmother's beautiful, old, battered, mahogany dining table, and he looked up from his ecstatic absorption to gaze out the dusty window at the messy chain-linked back lots below and understood suddenly that what he was feeling right then was and had to be the most important part of it—the moment of creation. He no longer remembers what he was working on, but the process of creating it was engaging everything within him, and he understood then that was and is quintessential. Not money, publication, reputation, not even the possibility of getting laid by a lit-loving lass—but the process of creation. Climbing down into the darkness to bring up what he could discover and cast into language about his existence.

He was twenty-seven years old then. He had an agent and a grant for a novel-in-progress, part-time work writing an NGO newsletter. He had encouraging letters from editors, hyperbolic rejections, and had been trying to write for ten years with nothing published.

So quit! his girlfriend Claire told him. She was an artist. She had painted a picture entitled *Straining Man*—a picture that astonished him, the minimalist figure of a man straining all the muscles of his body as he grimaces challengingly upward. The figure was painted in thick rich pigments of oil, multi-colored lines delineating muscle and sinew, an abstract face, but

Bohannon had an immediate recognition that the figure represented human endeavor straining to overcome the opposing forces of circumstance. It was, in Bohannon's opinion, a very good picture. He would even call it a masterpiece. He loved her for painting it.

But as soon as the oils were dry, she threw a cloth over it and reorganized her midtown apartment, threw away all her oils and acrylics and brushes and rags, vacuumed and mopped and painted, bought an architect's desk on which she mounted a blue architect's lamp and started designing sofas. He asked why, when she had clearly just made an artistic breakthrough, she would go commercial, and she replied that those categories had no meaning, that Bohannon was trying to validate elitism, that all art was equal, that basically all art was either entertaining or pragmatic, and that this was what she wanted to do now.

What, sell out? Bohannon teased.

She was pale-haired and pale-eyed—her eyebrows and eyelashes pale, too—part of her beauty, but now her eyes flashed within their pale-haired frame, and she said, *If you got anything to sell, why not?* She peered into his eyes. *Got anything?*

He ducked his chin, but he was unrockable; he'd already had his Satori, and his choices were clear now, he knew what was important to him.

Claire, he thinks now. *Where is Claire?* Probably rich and highly respected among those who are satisfied with the aesthetics of a beautiful, entertaining, pragmatic sofa. *And, hey, who's putting it down?*

*   *   *

When he steps into the elevator car he is startled to see a young Latino fellow, shorter than himself, with a pencil-moustache and slicked-back hair, also wearing a tux and T-shirt, but his feet are shod in red basketball sneakers—a touch Bohannon wishes he'd thought of. Bohannon nods, and the fellow grins. "You the shit, mon," he says. "I dig you leopard hat!"

The early May evening is cool and dry, and Bohannon's black wing-tips walk him briskly up Eighth toward Columbus Circle. He feels self-conscious in the hat. Ever since '66 and Dylan put out *Blonde on Blonde*, he wanted a hat like this. Lotte-Mia knew that. She contacted the Royal Hat Maker in Copenhagen—and paid a small fortune to have one fashioned for his 60th birthday — from synthetic material, of course. You couldn't buy real leopard skin anymore.

My luck, he thinks, *someone'll splash me with red paint anyway*. Then he thinks, *Fug it —let 'em*. He'd welcome it. Add to the décor. He is willing to take whatever the evening might bring. He is sixty-four years old, one of six nominees for the so-called Pulitzer of magazine writing, a beefy little man with few illusions, trying to be stylish, and he considers himself lucky in a lot of important ways: Lucky to be alive (his essay is a humorous account of the pain and humiliation of a two-year cancer scare which he survived); lucky to have written and published as much as he has, even if it earns him little money or popular reputation; lucky to have a body of work which is, as far as he can tell, fairly well respected among his peers; lucky to have escaped twenty years of a loveless marriage (albeit at the cost of his one valuable asset, the house, which is now worth nearly a million bucks, owned solely by his ex); but most of all lucky to have a thirty-year -old son, about to earn his PhD in linguistics, with whom Bohannon has dinner two or three times a month and who, as far as Bohannon knows, enjoys his company as much as he enjoys the boy's (though he has not been answering his phone for a couple of weeks), and a woman whom he adores and who, as far as he knows, loves him right back, too, and with whom he still loves to make all manner of love.

So let them splash his synthetic leopardskin with red paint. Let a seagull drop a heavy green psittacotic bomb on it! Let Claire and all the others of his generation who dedicated themselves to earning big bucks live and be happy in their MacMansions while he and Lotte-Mia share a modest but sunny east-side, rent-controlled Copenhagen apartment, and let Stephen King of *Entertainment Weekly* or Walter Kirn of *the New Yorker* run off with the award tonight. Bohannon has the greatest prize of all—a fine son and a great woman who love him and no serious regret about the choices he has made in life. What more could he ask?

As he steps onto Columbus Circle, the ironies multiply in his consciousness. Forty years ago he worked in the building which used to be here—the Coliseum Office Building at Number 10. Now the whole block has been razed and in place of the Coliseum is an extension of Lincoln Center where in an hour or so, in the Frederick P. Rose Hall, the National Magazine Awards—the Ellies—will be handed out: fairly big potatoes for a small-potatoes, small-press expat writer, and he intends to enjoy every moment of it, right up to the instant that Stephen King or Walter

Kirn climbs onto the stage and accepts the Alexander Calder statuette.

By the elevator bank, Bohannon's editor, William Cross, waits with his wife, Mary, for his essayist. Cross is tall in his tuxedo, big forehead, smiling mildly. "Cool hat," he says to Bohannon.

"So stylish," Mary adds in a tone that clearly chides her husband in case he was being sarcastic.

Bohannon realizes this is more William's night than his own; this is a ceremony honoring the industry, magazine editors, magazines. It's the magazines that get the Calder sculptures. But Cross put his chips on Bohannon's essay, and an editor can't win in the essay category without a writer. Cross has been publishing Bohannon's work a couple of times a year for two decades. He was one of the first to believe in the value of Bohannon's writing. It occurs to Bohannon that Cross will be more disappointed than he himself will when King—or Kirn—takes the prize. The year of the K's, Bohannon thinks. No B. *That's me. A No-bee.*

Bohannon shakes William's big hand. Then, to keep his eyes from getting lost in her pretty face, he kisses Mary Cross lightly on the cheek.

"So what you think, Bohannon?" Cross asks quietly.

"I think you paid almost five hundred bucks for my ticket to the reception upstairs."

Cross blinks slowly. "Somethin' like that."

"So what about goin' up to the reception and havin' some expensive drinks?"

*   *   *

"Jesus," Bohannon says to Cross as they step off the elevator. The reception area is aswarm with penguin suits and their brightly feathered mates. Sweeping thirty-foot windows look out over Central Park South and West, and lights sparkle like jewels scattered amidst the dark green of the trees. Handsome, smiling young people in black livery, looking genuinely happy to do so, bear trays of canapés through the crowd—bits of goat cheese and beef on chips of toasted rye, small nuggets of *fois gras* with dots of truffle, shrimp big as crayfish tails, crayfish big as lobster.

Unlike Bohannon, Cross has not been away for thirty years; he knows people. He introduces Bohannon to a woman who smiles at his hat; then, when she hears his name, her brown eyes widen and light with a knowing look—though what her look knows he doesn't.

"Who was that?" Bohannon asks Cross.

"That was the Executive Director of this whole deal. That look she gave you was huge."

Bohannon knows that when Cross says huge, it means huge.

He introduces Bohannon to another man—tall, dark-haired—whose name slips past his ear.

"I hear your essay is very funny," the man says. "I look forward to reading it. Hope your health is okay."

"Who was that?" Bohannon asks.

"David Remnick,"

"*Who?*"

Cross smiles with amused compassion. "The editor of *the New Yorker*."

On a table near the bar stands a row of Ellie statuettes, a many-bladed sculpture designed by Alexander Calder, and Bohannon wants to heft one, but then his eye is drawn instead toward the glittering array of bottles behind the bar—he spots at least three kinds of vodka, two of them with black labels, one with blue.

As the immaculately white-coated barman pours copiously for him, Bohannon glances at the man alongside him and does a double-take. He hasn't been away so long that he would fail to recognize John Updike. An Uppy Sighting of the Third Kind. Even more astonishing is that Updike, who radiates star quality—his height, his mop of white hair, his Mongolian eyes and patrician nose, the aggressive brightness of his smile—turns to Bohannon and says, "Oh, you're that guy who moved to Denmark! Why in the world would you do that?"

Bohannon opens his mouth to let something out of the jumble of words clogging his brain and hears his own voice say, "I like it there. There's not so many people in jail. The last execution was 150 years ago. And when my neighbor gets sick and can't work I don't have to worry whether he has health coverage."

Updike's smile is insuperable—the smile of umitigated success perhaps. "I'm still somewhat amazed," he says. "But that's the beauty of the world. People move around in it." Updike takes his glass of white wine from the barman, looks once more at Bohannon, says, "Well. Good luck." And immediately is enveloped by a deep circle of admirers.

Bohannon feels as though he's sniffed a popper. *John Updike knows who I am!* Then—short-lived as a popper—his elation drops, and he moves away. He remembers a recent interview somewhere with Updike where the interviewer suggested that Updike's books would be read for hundreds of years because he had won two Pulitzers. Updike replied, "You know who also won two Pulitzers for fiction? Booth Tarkington. Ever read him?"

Actually Bohannon had read *Seventeen* by Tarkington, at his father's suggestion about fifty years ago, and remembers enjoying it, though he can't remember anything else about it now. He vaguely remembers it being something like a pre-neurotic *Catcher in the Rye*. Maybe in fifty or a hundred years Salinger will be a vague memory as well.

He doesn't want to meet any more famous people. Famous people make him nervous. He would feel better about it if Lotte-Mia was at his side. Why didn't he insist she come? He stands by the huge windows, looking out over Central Park in the light-speckled dark, sipping his tumbler of Gray Goose on the rocks, and his eyes are moist with memories of his personal history here. The years he worked in the now-vanished Coliseum Office Building, writing an NGO newsletter—the shop that used to be diagonally across the Circle where in 1974 for $150 he bought the dark suit he married his first wife in. Mistake. But then his son Robert would not exist. He thinks back on the years of night school at Fordham Lincoln Center just around the corner from where he stands now, sneaking a double Dewars at O'Neal's Baloon before his Victorian Poetry or Chaucer class. The pre-Giuliani years of being panhandled by the vagrants who clustered around the southwest entrance to the Park. Pale-eyelashed Claire Little, whose studio was just around the corner, on Eighth and 57th—he remembers necking with her in the kitchen there on Christmas Eve in 1970.

Now this: Bohannon wants to put it into perspective and keep it there. This is my fifteen minutes, he thinks, but he knows it's slightly more than that. He realizes that in some manner this affirms all his choices. He got his way. He left New York to do what he cared about without interference, and now they called him back to honor him (at his own fucking expense, he reminds himself—keep it in perspective), to rub tuxedo sleeves with the magazine magnificos of America. And it's happening on Columbus Circle around which so much of his life circulated back then. He leans in close to the window to see down to the center of the Circle, the statue of Christopher Columbus on his pedestal and thinks about how Columbus throughout Bohannon's boyhood had been huge—*In 1492, Columbus sailed the ocean blue…*—now tainted with post-colonial, revisionist correctness. Still, discovering America is bigger than winning two Pulitzers.

His gaze sweeps toward the large metal globe outside Trump International Hotel & Tower which, when he worked here decades ago, was the Gulf & Western Building, and he thinks about Donald Trump, the billionaire exhibitionist with his red comb-over (*and what am I but a small-potatoes aging exhibitionist?*), a man a couple of years younger than Bohannon, who owns a skyscraper that carries his name at Number 1 fucking Central Park West while Bohannon no longer even owns a house. He hears the sour note addling the melody of this evening. *There is no reason to be sour tonight,* he thinks. *In a couple of hours, I'll call Lotte-Mia and tell her I didn't win and then I'll join the post-ceremony party for as many Grey Gooses as I can guzzle, and life is good—or at least it is not so bad.*

Mary Cross, perhaps sensitive to his mood, comes over to stand beside him at the huge sweeping windows. Without a word she squeezes his hand, and for no good reason Bohannon almost loses it. He is *that* close to weeping and for no clear reason. He never cries. So why should he cry now?

Then William is there, smiling his mild smile that conceals all of what he is to all but those who know him. Bohannon fancies he knows him.

"So what you think, Bohannon? Feeling lucky?"

"That's my middle name."

"That's what I was thinkin'. Wanna go in and collect our prize?"

Mary is seated in the balcony, while Bohannon and Cross have numbered seats in the front rows, near the stage, but against the wall in about the fourth row. They have to climb over the thighs of several people to get to their places.

Bohannon tells Cross, "Figure this means we don't win—otherwise we'd be seated on the aisle."

"Hell, we can always scoot on out," Cross says. Bohannon is grateful for little things—like that he thought to visit the loo before going in to the theater because he sees from the program that the essay category is way toward the end.

"That's because it's an important category," says Cross. Then he looks into Bohannon's eyes. "When we get up there, on the stage, you don't have to say anything. I'll do the thank you's."

Bohannon snorts at Cross's stubborn belief that they have a chance, almost says, *In your dreams, Bill,* but he notices an alien emotion beginning to rise from his gut; each time a winner is announced and climbs the four steps to the stage to claim his or her Ellie and takes the mic to thank whoever he or she thanks, this alien emotion grows stronger. Feature Writing, Reporting, Profile Writing, Public Interest, Commentary, Reviews and Criticism, General Excellence...

The stage design is elegant. An enormous screen behind the presenter shows the logo of the magazine in question, a recorded woman's voice speaks professionally over the PA and the screen shows the words and names of the nominees, the winners...

As the essay category approaches, Bohannon's nostrils begin to widen with longing to savor that famous sweet smell of success, and he begins to suspect for the first time that if he does not win, he will be disappointed, perhaps seriously so. And then as they announce the essay category, he does not suspect that he might be seriously disappointed, he *knows* it. The transformation from content-to-be-a-finalist to lust-for-victory is instantaneous. Suddenly he wants it—*bad!*

Some guy is at the mic saying, "The essay has always been at the heart of the American magazine..."

"Who's he?" Bohannon whispers.

"Charlie Rose!" Cross whispers back. "You been away too long."

Cross's magazine logo is up on the screen and Bohannon's

words, while the recorded voice of the woman speaker, sounding at once professional and as though she's having the time of her life, is saying, "Wince-inducing, outrageously honest and wickedly funny, Lucas Lucky Bohannon's account of his cancer scare is essay writing at its most original..."

Then Charlie Rose says, "The winners are William Cross and Lucas Lucky Bohannon for..."

Cross yells in triumph, pumping his fist in the air, while Mary Cross screams from the balcony (a scream that will be reported next day in the *New York Observer*) and Bohannon whispers, "Holy shit."

Then they are on the stage in the spotlight and Charlie Rose is shoving the multi-bladed Ellie at Bohannon and saying, "Here— I'm going to give this to you!" while blitzes flash, and Bill Cross says his thanks.

As all 500 members of the audience bottleneck out of the theater toward the post-ceremony champagne, people nod, grin, say, "Congratulations!" and "Love your hat!" and "Is that a real leopard-skin pillbox hat?" Bohannon retreats to the men's room where the tuxedoed, cummerbunded guy at the next urinal smiles at him—something a man at a urinal is never supposed to do— and says, "Hey! Congratulations!"

As they move back toward the sweeping windows of the reception area, and a Wichita poet whose work Bohannon admires puts his grizzled beard in Bohannon's face and says, "If I was drunk I'd kiss you!" Bohannon laughs and hugs him, then thinks of Lotte-Mia. He fishes the tri-band out of his pocket, steps into a corner, and thumbs his contact key. It's quarter past ten in

New York, four-fifteen a.m. in Copenhagen. Her voice sounds more suspicious than sleepy.

"Did I wake you? I'm sorry. You said I should wake you."

"Congratulations," she says, but something sounds wrong.

"What? How'd you hear already?"

"I knew. I always knew, ever since you were nominated."

"You sound funny. Like you're crying."

"I am," she whispers.

In imitation of an infomercial salesman, Bohannon says, "Diced onions, mounds of them in seconds. The only tears you shed will be tears of joy." One of his bits.

"Thanks for calling," she says. "This will be expensive. And I can hear the party. All your groupies are waiting for you."

The connection breaks. He calls back, lets it ring six times, but there is no answer. On his way to the bar, he presses call and lets it ring until the answering service comes on. "I lost you," he says. "Let me try again." But it only rings next time, too, and he slips the phone back into his pocket. Before he gets to the vodka, he's had congratulations from half a dozen people and a half dozen more who admire his pillbox hat which makes him think of Lotte -Mia again with increasing urgency. He wants to tell her the hat was a hit, digs out the tri-band again, but thinks better of it, orders a double Gray Goose instead.

It occurs to Bohannon that he might never again be as happy as he is at this moment. *This is better than my first fucking Christmas!* he thinks. *If only Lotte-Mia was here.*

"*Tillykke, Hr.* Bohannon," someone behind him says in Danish. It's Valter Brandt, a journalist from *Politiken* who hangs out in Bohannon's serving house of choice in Copenhagen—Rosengaardens Bodega. They've been drunk together on more than one occasion, and Brandt has five-star reviewed two of Bohannon's books, but last time they got drunk together, Brandt said, "You realize this means I can't review you anymore? I know you too personally now."

"Do you cover these things?" Bohannon asks.

"Just happened to be in New York so they asked me to come over. Got in this afternoon. After a night at Rosengaardens. Lotte-Mia was there. Partying."

Bohannon just looks at him.

"How is she anyway?" Brandt asks.

Something in the tone of the question makes Bohannon look into the taller man's eyes. "What is it that you're not telling me?"

Valter looks sad which dissipates the little strain of jealousy that was insinuating itself in Bohannon's mood. Anyway, Valter is twenty years younger than Lotte-Mia. Valter's face looks like the face of divided loyalties. "She was a bit tipsy," he says. "She told me it was hard for her to see you having so much success."

"So much success? What success? One fucking award?"

Valter shrugs. "This is what she has told me."

II. Surprise!

On the flight home from Newark, Bohannon is pinned in by a window in economy, and the man in front of him—an enormous Mormon-looking guy in a black suit—immediately tilts his seat back all the way. Bohannon decides not to drink on the flight, so he doesn't have to climb over the other passengers to use the loo. After the meal, he pops a valium, nods off with his legs crammed up against the reclined seat and slowly his worry about Lotta-Mia seeps away into sleep.

At Kastrup, his one leg painfully stiff, he limps out to the moving sidewalk with his rolling carry-on, rests on the rail. He has no luggage to claim, nothing to declare, steps through the doors at Arrivals, halfway expecting Lotte-Mia and maybe his son Robert to be there waiting for him, but as he looks from face to face among the groups of people waving paper Danish flags and welcome home signs for other people, he sees no one he recognizes.

He limps over to the kiosk and buys a *Politiken* which he reads in the taxi home. There's a photo in the culture section of Bohannon in his pillbox holding the Ellie and a half page written by Valter Brandt—must have emailed it in—but Brandt's name only reminds him of what the man told him about Lotte-Mia. Bohannon looks out over the sparkling water of the sound, the steel blades of the windmills turning in the cool May sunlight, the patches of forsythia along Strandvej, bright yellow blooms already withering. Bohannon forgot to fill his eyes with them this year. The blooms only last a couple of weeks before they fade. How many springs remain for him to see these blooms in their full? he wonders. And he has missed his chance this year.

As he pays the taxi, Lotte-Mia comes out of their apartment building to the sidewalk to greet him. "Prepare yourself," she says.

"I know you don't like surprises but they insisted."

"I like surprises from you," he says.

She gives him a look. "Don't be so sure about that."

The apartment's 50-square-meter living room is crammed with people. The long dining table is lined with bottles of red and white wine, bottles of Tuborg, blue-and-white porcelain platters of *hors d'oeuvres*—she's made Danish meatballs and calf liver pâté and fresh baked rye bread!—red, yellow and amber tulips in vases, a forsythia branch, bouquets. *Politiken* is open and folded back to the article about his award, his photograph. There is another article in *Weekendavisen*. And there must be fifty people. Writer friends, publishing friends, his drinking companions, his psychologist friend Benjamin, his criminologist friend Dave, his doctor friend Jesper, a few reviewers, some of Lotte-Mia's friends and family.

If she were jealous, he thinks, *would she have gone to all this trouble? But she said "they" insisted. Who are "they"? And where the devil is Robert?*

Now he's doubly glad he didn't drink on the flight home. There is a gift table, too—books, bottles of malt whiskey, vintage wine, bouquets, cigars... His doctor friend Jesper, who is beholden to Bohannon because he once got him an autographed copy of a Tim O'Brien novel—Jesper loves war novels—an extremely tall dark-haired man who drinks even more than Bohannon—interrupts Bohannon before he starts making the rounds.

"What the devil's wrong with your leg?" Jesper asks.

"Was cramped in on the plane. Couldn't move around."

"That's not good," Jesper says. "Did you wear support hose?"

"Fuck no."

"You have to wear support hose and get up and walk around the plane every 20 minutes of the hour. Did you at least take an aspirin to thin your blood."

"No, but you'll be happy to know I refrained from drinking for once."

"That's not good either. Drinking thins out your blood. Keeps it from forming dangerous clots."

"Jesus, I love Danish doctors," Bohannon says and continues greeting his guests, shaking hands, hugging the women, a glass of red wine in his hand. In the kitchen, he finds Lotte-Mia pouring a glass from her own bottle of Merlot. She is looking out the mezzanine window into the courtyard. Bohannon clinks his glass against hers and asks, "Where the hell is Robert?"

She shrugs elaborately, and in the gesture, he can see that things are not right—not with her and not with Robert. "He said he *might* come. That he'd *try*." Her tone is a reprimand to him as well as to Robert, though what he is being reprimanded for he does not know.

He steps close to her, caresses her neck, peers into her eyes. "What's wrong, honey?"

"Is something wrong?" Her question is both a reprimand and an answer. *Figure it out for yourself.*

She steps away, and he is circulating again. A bookshop owner he's known for many years suggests he do a reading of the essay in his store. An old friend from Paris who edits an English-language magazine suggests he come down to read at Shakespeare

& Co., be interviewed for the magazine, give a talk at the American Library. His friend Dave who lectures in criminology at Copenhagen University invites him on a tour of Danish prisons to do an article series. From the corner of his eye, he watches Lotte-Mia. He can see that she's been drinking for a while. She's four years older than he but looks ten years younger, has just published her first book—her editor is there, too, and her publisher—and Bohannon helped her with it, helped her with the title, the structure, translated a chapter into English. It has sold out the first printing and gone into paperback. Why would she be jealous of him? She made more on that book than he ever made on any one of his.

He adores her. They've been together for fifteen years. For the first five years after his divorce they each had an apartment. He was wary of committing himself again, but in time, her gentleness, her passion, her loveliness, her devotion to him and to his writing won him over. She read everything he published; then she read everything he was working on and showed herself to have an excellent critical eye. Finally, it seemed inevitable that they should move in together and because her place was larger and cheaper—rent-controlled, five rooms, high ceilings—it was the obvious choice.

The centerpiece of the place is this huge living-dining room where now he is being celebrated, and as he chats with his guests, he marvels privately at how his investment of energy in his writing seems finally to be leading somewhere, albeit at an advanced age, but he worries about Lotte-Mia's undeniable distance. And his son's absence. He phones Robert but only gets the boy's answering service and leaves another message.

At one point, his psychologist friend, Benjamin, steps up to clink glasses and congratulate him. "If you need to talk," Benjamin says, "just give me a call."

Bohannon looks into the man's face. He is an Israeli, shorter than Bohannon, an aura of confidence in his posture, his eyes, a novelist himself who psychoanalyzes with literary metaphors.

"Why should I need to talk?" Bohannon asks him now.

Ben tilts his head, gazing downwards, which Bohannon recognizes as his prelude to an exegesis. "It is strange for a son not to attend such a party to celebrate his father. Maybe Robert is trying to step out of your shadow. You've done things a lot of people haven't."

"My son used to say he was proud of me. We were always so close…"

"Luke," Benjamin says. "You have this success now, and you should allow yourself to enjoy it. Have you ever heard of the German battlesip, The Bismarck? The Bismarck was designed to be nearly unsinkable by having each section of the ship water-tight from the others. So if a torpedo struck one section, the sea poured in there, but not into the whole ship. If you get hit, do not allow it to sink you—isolate the chamber."

By ten, only three guests remain—his Swedish friend Johan and two old colleagues from the NGO he used to work for—hovering around the gift table where there are several bottles of unopened single malt that Bohannon has no intention of cracking—he'll never get rid of them then. Bohannon steps into the kitchen to plan his retreat. Lotte-Mia is leaning against the new counter—Bohannon has just modernized the kitchen as a birthday gift for her—holding a full glass of red wine and looking at the novel he published three years before.

From behind, Bohannon rests his chin on her shoulder and whispers, "*Je t'adore.*"

She steps away. Her smile is crooked, her lipstick smudged. There is a lipstick smudge on the glass, too, as she lifts it from her mouth. "Wherever did you get the idea for this novel?" she asks.

"Wherever did you think of the woman who goes into the hospital to say goodbye to her ex-husband and he is dead and she thinks that if she kisses his lips he might awake."

"That's based partly on you," he says. "You know that. You gave me the story."

"I did?"

"You gave me permission to use it. You urged me to."

"Do you have that in writing?"

"You're kidding, right?"

Johan looks in the doorway, holding a bottle of Family Silver '71 wrapped in cellophane, tied with a red bow—a gift from the Danish magazine that wants to translate Bohannon's Ellie essay, and he says, "You, Bohannon? This is *good* malt whiskey!"

Lotte-Mia laughs—to his ear it seems a dark note—and looks at Bohannon with a smile that is not friendly. "The little man," she says, "with the big ass," and steps past Johan and is gone.

By the time he gets Johan and the others out the door, Lotte-Mia is already in bed, snoring lightly. Bohannon looks at her, his passion damped by the fumes of wine breathing out of her—something she complains about in him when he comes to bed with a snootful of vodka: *You smell like hospital spirit.*

Now he looks at her on the bed, the eiderdown bunched between her slender smooth bare blond legs, wondering what is going on behind her sleeping face. He has never felt there was something inside her that he couldn't reach, always believed she was on his side as he was on hers, that anything good that happened to him happened to her as well and vice versa. Yet suddenly she seems foreign to him, worse than a stranger, an enemy—the worst kind of enemy, one that you used to love.

Then he hears himself thinking these words and wonders at his thoughts. Why is he jumping to conclusions? He wants to dismiss it. Yet he recalls what she said to him in the kitchen earlier. *Do you have that in writing?* She encouraged him to write that novel, partially inspired by her divorce from the first husband, who was violent, and her estrangement from her sister. He was startled at the abruptness and finality of that estrangement, just a few years ago. They were entertaining the sister and her husband, and Lotte-Mia's arm was in a sling—she had fallen down the stairs and dislocated her shoulder.

"You *really* should not drink," the sister said.

Bohannon heard her say that just as he was on his way into the bathroom. By the time he got back they were all on their feet shouting. Lotte-Mia hasn't spoken to the sister since. That was about three years ago.

Bohannon steps out to the living room and begins gathering used glasses, dirty plates, crumpled napkins. A few of the tiny

Danish meatballs that Lotte-Mia made—for *him*, he reminds himself, for *his* celebration—remain on a blue-and-white Royal Copenhagen Porcelain platter. He pours a glass of Tuborg and pops one of the meatballs in his mouth—a mix of chopped pork and beef and halal lamb with chili, onions, various spices. He takes another, thinks of Lotte-Mia preparing these, the calf liver pâté, the loaves of dark rye bread she baked. His left eye is watering.

Soon he has eaten the rest of the meatballs, smears liver paste thickly on a slice of rye, forks on two chips of pickled beet, polishes it off in two bites. Both eyes are watering now, and he realizes that he is crying. He never cries. He must be drunk. He must be exhausted from the flight.

It's just past midnight. He tries Robert's number one more time, but there is no answer. Just as well. Why should the boy want to talk to a half-drunk father in the middle of the night. Anyway, he is not a boy—he's thirty. He's a man and free to do as he pleases. When Bohannon was thirty he said goodbye to his mother and brothers and left for Europe. A memory flashes of a late-night phone call from his mother a month before he left New York. "I couldn't sleep," she said. "I keep thinking what if you never come back?" Embarrassed, he mocked her affectionately, "Oh, come on, Mom, let's not be melodramatic. Of course, I'll be back to visit." Now, in the big living room among the leavings of the party, he remembers that his first visit back home wasn't for four years, though he did write, and he wonders now why he didn't try to comfort her on the phone that night. He tries to view his own son's avoidance of him in the light of that; sometimes young people don't always understand what they are doing to the people who love them.

Bohannon undresses, slides under the eiderdown against Lotte-Mia's back, wraps his arms around her, cupping her delicious breasts in his palms, touches his lips to the nape of her neck.

"*Je t'adore*," he whispers and listens to the indifferent oceanic whisper of her breathing.

III. G.O.O.D.B.Y.E.

Things change so fast sometimes. Look away for a second and people who once were bound by love are enemies forever.

When Bohannon opens his eyes, cracks of sunlight are seeping through the venetian blinds. He reaches for his watch on the night stand. 9:55. Lotte-Mia is not in bed. He stretches, wants her in his arms, in his face, closes his eyes again, remembers.

The living room is spotless, but Lotte-Mia is not there. Nor is she in the bathroom, her office, or the kitchen. In the kitchen there is a full pot of coffee in the electric brewer, bread and cheese, a jar of apricot marmalade (his favorite) on a plate alongside. And a sealed, peach-colored envelope with his name on it in Lotte-Mia's handwriting.

He weighs the envelope on his palm, can feel there are several pages in it. He dreads having to read this letter from Lotte-Mia. She has allowed him to read the letters she has sent to others— always solipsistic, written not to someone else but to herself: an aide-mémoire of self-justification, a catalogue of thinly-disguised discontents. (A question flashes through his mind—could that description as well be applied to his fiction?—*solipsistic, written not to someone else but to himself, an aide-memoire of self-justification, a catalogue of thinly disguised discontents.* Well, of course, he thinks, there's a little more to it than that: the exploration of the mystery of existence, the cohesion of art which justifies its song, the…Isn't there?)

Lotte-Mia has shown him such a letter every other year or so, and they are always verbose and tightly written, from gutter to gripper edge, top to bottom of the page, single-spaced. She has a lined sheet which she places under her letter paper to guide her handscript—a tighly-lined page. Over the years, she has written to her sister, to her oldest childhood friend, even to her priest, and the letter is always a goodbye. But she has never written such a letter to him before.

Whenever she showed him one of her letters—she copies them on the little photocopier in her office—it has already been sent. He suspects that the reason she does not show him the letters in advance of sending them is because she does not want to be talked out of sending them or talked into tempering them. So by the time he sees the letter it is always too late. No one is perfect, he always thought. This is her flaw. I can live with this because I love her. But she has never sent *him* such a letter before. He almost wants to tear the letter in half and half again, scatter the bits into the toilet and flush them away. But he knows she has a copy, so he fills a mug with coffee, sits in the sunlight at the little table by the kitchen window and tears open the flap of the envelope.

* * *

The remainder of their relationship consists of two letters. The first—this one—says, in a summary of four crimped, handwritten pages that she (1) calculated that he owed her seventy thousand dollars for the privilege of having lived in "her beautiful rent-controlled apartment" for ten years. He has been getting away with murder paying only half the official rent. He should have been paying rent to her which she has set conservatively at six thousand crowns a month which she would have been paid by renting the rooms they used as offices to a student or young professional as she had done sometimes in the past before he moved in. And (2) that she wanted him to put a bed in his office (which was larger than hers) and move out of "her bedroom" —just for a while, so they could both get their bearings and a little breathing room. "We can always come in to each other when we both want," she writes. "It could even be more exciting in a way."

Meanwhile, she was staying with "a friend" but he could leave his response in a sealed envelope with the owner of the convenience store on the corner. If he didn't agree with her two "points," she would give him a month —"standard notice"—to box up "his effects" and move.

She gives no other way to contact her —no name of the friend she is staying with. No phone number other than her cell, which he tries many times but she isn't answering or returning calls.

Is it a coincidence, he wonders, that the two people in the world that he loves most are not answering their phones when he calls? Or is he, unbeknownst to himself, truly some sort of miscreant who deserves to be treated this way? Who, unbeknownst to himself, treats them shabbily enough that they will no longer speak with him?

These are serious questions that he poses seriously to himself. But he is unable to make headway toward answers.

He starts to write a response to Lotte-Mia, but after three days and many crumpled up drafts, he realizes it is pointless. He cannot sum up his feelings in a letter to a woman who is clearly unbalanced. Maybe she was always unbalanced and somehow he blinded himself to that fact. Maybe he was living all these years with an illusion. Or maybe he is the one who is unbalanced. He closes his eyes and thinks of her beautiful face, her beautiful eyes, her beautiful body, her beautiful gentleness. He thinks of their friendship, the many trips they've taken—to the Ionian islands, to New York, Dublin, Edinburgh, Paris... She never traveled before... Then he thinks of the letters she wrote—to her sister, her old friend, the priest... To him.

On the fourth morning, he notices an envelope on the floor in the foyer. Then he remembers as he lay in bed last night, waiting for sleep, he heard an odd, brief, swishing noise. He tensed, listened, thinking it might be a mouse, but there was nothing more. Then sleep took him away, and he dreamed of a pig farm in a back barn of which old human beings were kept in a pit and fattened for slaughter. He wakes with a shudder and comes out to find the envelope and realizes that the sound he heard last night was this envelope being shoved under the door.

The sight of it evokes dread.

This one is in a plain white business-sized envelope with his name printed on the front. He turns it over to see if there is a return address and sees there is none, but that it is sealed with red wax. The sight of the wax seal makes him shudder. *This is fucking surreal. This is crazy shit.*

In the envelope is a single sheet, typewritten, with no salutation, no complimentary closing, no signature:

Get
Out
Old
Dude
Before
Your
Evicted!

The hair on his arms bristles. "Old dude" was an affectionate nickname she had for him. He sits by the kitchen window over his coffee, looking at the sheet of paper, reading down the words again and again with a dreadful fascination. Something about the grammatical error —"your" instead of "you're" —touches him. Makes him want to wrap his arms around her. To protect her. But how can he protect her from herself?

IV. Friends and Neighbors

He is thankful that they didn't marry. Since they aren't married, according to Danish law, he doesn't have to give her anything. He looks at a couple of apartments in his price range, realizes that Lotte-Mia asked for exactly half of what he sacked away over the years. He wonders how she knew, remembers that he gave her the password to his email, recalls a comment in her letter that he "even bragged to one of his friends about how cheap the rent on her place was, that she generously allowed him to live there by only paying half the rent—in all fairness," she added, "seventy percent of the rent because you took the big office"—but that all these years she waited in vain for him to volunteer more, etc etc etc.

He is incredulous at the revelations of her secret thoughts in her letter. How could he have so misjudged her inner feelings all these years? Yet he wonders how she knew what he had in savings, tries to remember in panic whether he ever gave her the password to his net bank. But he might have mentioned in a mail to someone or other how much he had. Maybe he even mentioned it to her. Why wouldn't he have done? Although it was stupid to have done so. She didn't have much—maybe she got jealous. But he wasn't stingy. He paid for their vacations, repairs, much of their food, whenever they went to a restaurant...

The apartments he looks at are depressing to say the least. Then he notices a two-room across the courtyard behind hers. It is small and doesn't get much sunlight, but large enough for him if he continues to live alone, and at his age and with his experience, he certainly doesn't plan on doing other than that. And this place is so close. He doesn't have the physical, emotional or spiritual surplus to move further away —here he could move by hand and foot.

The new apartment costs half his savings. The irony does not elude him as he orders the transfer from his net bank. He invests further in a bundle of thirty moving cartons which he assembles in the big living room of her apartment, and packs his clothes, his bedding, his manuscripts. He invites an antiquarian book seller to come by who purchases more than half his books for a few thousand. He takes the few pieces of furniture that he brought in with him, leaves her what he bought while they were together, but takes one of the plush red sofas and, of course, his art; he stacks it all in the center of their—*her*—beautiful living room.

He figures he can move in a single day if his son helps him, but his son is still not answering his phone or email or returning his calls. Bohannon walks across town to Robert's apartment, a sixth-floor west-side walk-up that Bohannon helped him buy and rings the street bell. He hears the intercom switch on and says, "Robert, it's Dad. I need to talk to you." There is no response. Bohannon waits a moment, rings again. Nothing.

At first, he's angry, almost leans on the bell, wants to press out a staccato message of his frustration, but he manages to restrain himself. Walking away along Istedgade, however, threading through the prostitutes and drug addicts, he begins to worry. This is not normal behavior. Back in Lotte-Mia's apartment, he sits on a footstool amongst the cluster of his worldly possessions and calls his ex.

"Oh, if it isn't you," she says. "Congratulations. Was it worth it?"

"What, you mean going to New York?"

"Never mind. What do you have on your heart?"

"Listen," he says, "have you heard from Robert? I'm getting worried. He doesn't answer his phone, doesn't return calls, doesn't answer emails, doesn't even answer his doorbell."

"The only thing I know," she says, "is that he said he needs a pause from family."

"A pause? But you're in touch with him, right?"

"You probably know more than I do. Sorry."

And that was it.

Whenever Bohannon gets to wondering whether he should have left after all or tried to tough it out, a moment of conversation with her generally reaffirms that he made the inevitable decision. Jab and dance away was her tactic, and her jab stung and sometimes injected poison where he was most susceptible to it. *Was it worth it?* Meaning what? That pursuing his writing had cost his marriage, estranged his son. What *bullshit!* But he couldn't shake the echo of her question. *Never mind.* She could always turn him around, make him doubt himself.

So, yeah, why did he marry her in the first place? Of course, if he hadn't, Robert would not exist —Robert who will not even talk to him. And why didn't it work out with Lotte-Mia? Why couldn't he ever make things work with a woman? Benjamin, his psychologist friend, told him, "We're not responsible for who we meet." *But are we? Did I make this happen somehow?* He thinks of some Greek poet. *If the soul is ever to know itself, it must look into the soul.* An impossibility, of course. He thinks of Sophocles: *Do not think that you are in command. And if you start to think it, remember how when you were in command you crafted your own destruction.*

Did I craft this destruction?

Next day is Friday. He rises at six, drinks his last cup of coffee in the sunlight by her kitchen window and begins to carry his possessions—everything he owns in the world—across the court-yard to his new apartment. Fortunately it is on the ground floor and Lotte-Mia's is only on the mezzanine.

But he is quickly stumped. Getting the sofa out, across, and in presents a logistical problem too great for his abilities. He knocks at the door of the superintendent, Knud, a 70-year-old man with dyed beige hair who can do practically anything. He single-handedly installed the new kitchen two years before. When Knud opens the door, he looks at Bohannon there, opens one side of his mouth while keeping the other shut and sucks air wetly into the opening, trilling the spit, and says, "Hannon, I hear you and the long-hair are splitting."

"Long-hair" is Knud's term for a woman, and "Hannon" is what he calls Bohannon.

With what he feels is appropriate solemnity, Bohannon says, "Unfortunately."

"Well ain't that a relief? Then you're free of all her screaming and all her red wine."

Bohannon doesn't know what Knud is talking about, but he needs his help, so he nods and says, "Yeah, whatever," then adds,"I've got a problem moving my sofa. Do you have time to give a hand?"

Knud grasps Bohannon's bicep and squeezes until it hurts. The man is no taller than Bohannon and probably weighs thirty pounds less, but he's strong as a gorilla. Bohannon manages not to squirm or yelp, and Knud says, "Are we friends and neighbors, or not?"

Knud not only moves the sofa—by unscrewing the feet and single-handedly lifting the front door of Bohannon's new apartment off its hinges, getting the sofa in and lifting the door back onto the hinges on the first try—but he moves the rest of the furniture as well. Then he looks at Bohannon with the same long slow evaluating look he gave to the sofa and the front door when he was determining how to manage getting the one through the other, and he says, "For the devil, you're limping, Hannon!"

"Think I pinched a nerve."

"Tell it to the priest," Knud says, "and you're breathing heavy, too!" He takes hold of Bohannon's hand as though he were a child and leads him into his new apartment, indicating the red easy chair that he has just moved for him. "Sit there and rest your nerve. Leave it to Knud." And Knud moves the remaining cartons by himself.

By late afternoon, the two men sit in the roughed out furniture arrangement in Bohannon's tiny living room, drinking Tuborg pop-tops straight from the can. The cartons are piled in the bedroom, and Bohannon's many paintings are leaned against the walls. Knud is not much of a conversationalist, and the expression on his face, when he isn't opening one side of his mouth to suck air wetly into it, reminds Bohannon of the blank, seeming look of utter stupidity as the man measured with his eye the sofa and the front door and silently calculated how to get the one through the other.

Bohannon fetches two more cans of Tuborg from the fridge and passes one to his benefactor. "Knud?" he says. "Before, when you were looking at the sofa and the door and trying to figure out

ɔblem of getting one through the other, were you, like,
g about the problem? Or were you just like *waiting* for the
answer to pop up into your mind? Like while you look at the
problem without thinking about it—somewhere inside, your
mind does all the calculations and gives you the answer?"

"That's it!" Knud yelps. "How in the devil did you know
that?"

"Cause that's exactly how I write. I just look around me and
wait for it to come to my pen. Thinking doesn't help the process.
In fact, thinking is a barrier sometimes."

Knud laughs, then opens one side of his mouth and wetly
sucks in air, looks at Bohannon with amazed delight. "That's just
it!" he says. "Leave the thinking to the long-hairs! That's what
they're good at!"

Bohannon opens another beer and remains sitting in his armchair. His phone rings—the opening riff of Coltrane's "A Love
Supreme"—and he digs it eagerly out of his pocket, thinking it
might be his son, or even Lotte-Mia, but it is the owner of a
bookstore where he gave a reading a couple of months ago, a man
named Carsten Kirk, a good-humored fellow who has always
seemed perpetually drunk to Bohannon. He once came into
Kirk's office in the rear basement of his bookstore and found Kirk
in his underpants literally chasing a young blond in a skimpy
summer dress around his desk. Instantly reframing at the sight of
Bohannon, Kirk said, "Oh —Liselotte was just giving me a haircut. Didn't want to get hair on my clothes. Drink?"

Now, on the phone, Kirk says,"I hear you're leaving

Lotte-Mia?"

Copenhagen is a small city; news spreads fast. "We're splitting," Bohannon says.

"You have to take care of her!"

"*She* asked *me* to leave!"

"She was probably drunk. You have to take care of her."

"How can I take care of her when she's kicking me out."

"She was probably drunk. Last time I saw her—at your reading!—she could hardly stand up."

Bohannon is confused. He didn't notice that she was particularly drunk at the reading. He himself could not have been particularly drunk or he would not have been able to read.

He continues to sit in his easy chair without turning on the light, looking around him at the many paintings leaned up against the walls of the little living room. He has collected them over the past couple of decades. Usually he buys a painting when it shouts out to him—if he has the money. It occurs to him now that he has never asked himself just *what* these paintings shouted out to him. He has several by Wiliam Skotte Olsen, the Danish colorist who died recently at an early age, brain-blown from drugs and booze, but undeniably in direct contact with images from the deep brain. Strange dream-like blurs of face, mostly with shoe-button eyes and minimalistically expressive mouths—grins, sneers, leers. The tiny paste eyes bore into him as well, and suddenly it is as though these Skotte Olsen faces are observing him in his new digs, boring into him. He wonders whether this feeling from a picture is of real value? True? Can you be sure art is of value? Well, look—just look at the value of Joyce, he thinks.

Portrait of the Artist freed him from the chains of nationalism, religion, and family; *Ulysses* freed him to finally look into his own mind without fear. What could have more value than that? he thinks. And that, he thinks, is why he writes, why he goes down into his mind, his consciousness, his unconscious to search for things he can bring back in language whether or fucking not he gets paid for it, whether or fucking not it makes him feel good. Whether or fucking not he has any control over his personal life… Then he thinks about the fact that Joyce's *Portrait* freed him of allegiance to family. But it didn't free him of allegiance to his son, only of allegiance to his parents.

As the evening darkens, it seeps through the window, blotting out the light and the Skotte Olsen eyes and mouths, the art fading away into the dark. Which makes him think of an ancient Mesopotamian animal—a big cat, a jaguar maybe—that he saw once in a museum, sculpted as a bas relief on a large medallion of stone. It was many thousands of years old, perhaps five millennia, and had all but disappeared, like the image on a coin handled by time. He felt he was looking at it for the final time before it disappeared, that it was almost gone, that after these thousands of years it was on the edge of obliteration, perhaps would even disappear completely before he himself did.

It is almost completely dark now in his tiny new living room. He thinks about that term, "living room." He thinks he should put on some music, but the TV and CD players are not connected yet, and he doesn't feel like rising or switching on the light or doing anything but sitting in the deepening dark, drinking beer from a can and thinking. Or letting his thoughts think him.

He thinks about the call from Kirk. Kettle calling the pot black. There's more to that knot than he'll ever unravel. He thinks about Lotte-Mia, thinks about how compatible they were sexually and personally, then wonders whether she had simply, quickly, sexually understood him, whether they really were in harmony or whether she just played along with her understanding of him and his desires. He wonders whether he will ever find another woman like her. But then he wonders what she was like really? Was her quick sexual understanding of him some kind of Scheherazade cunning? Maybe she had the instincts of a prostitute. And her sweetness, her kindness, was that all an act? Or had something gone wrong with her mind now?

He hears himself thinking that and wonders about himself thinking that. He thinks about the fact that Lotte-Mia's first husband, Henrik, the father of her son, had beaten her—punched and kicked her, pulled her hair out of her scalp, choked her until she almost died, and he thinks about how he hated the man and called him a coward whenever his name came up but Lotte-Mia always objected, saying that he was the father of her son and that Bohannon had no right to belittle him.

Then he thinks about the fact that he has no one's word for Henrik's having beaten her but her own. He wonders whether she was deceiving him about it, or deceiving herself. Then he wonders whether *he* is deceiving himself about *his* life, *his* actions, *all* of his past.

The thought terrifies him as he sits there in his easy chair, the disappeared Skotte Olsen faces boring into him from the darkness which has seeped into his new living room and taken over.

He goes to the fridge for another can of Tuborg. As he opens and shuts its door, the room is briefly illuminated with a flash of white light, then darkens again.

V. Getting Lucky

The tone of the cell phone on his night table wakes him—Coltrane's opening riff. He almost doesn't take it, can see by the light outside that it is very early, but then he thinks it might be Robert and lunges for it.

"Lucas? Samuel here."

His agent. Who has never sold anything for him. Not that he is a bad agent, but Bohannon is a small-press writer, what they call "a writer's writer," not commercially interesting. Whenever he writes a novel, he sends it to Samuel and when Samuel reaches thirty-five rejections, he returns it to Bohannon, who places it with a small publisher. Bohannon considers himself lucky that Samuel has not totally given up on him. At least he can say that he has an agent—which sounds more professional than not having an agent. He is currently at rejection twenty-something on the two companion novels he's been sending out for about six months.

"Did I get the time right?" Samuel asks. "It's morning in Copenhagen, right?"

"More or less." Bohannon looks at his watch: 5:00 a.m.

"It's eleven p.m. in New York. Are you sitting down?"

"Lying down, in fact."

"Good. Cause I just got an offer on the two novels. Hundred twenty-thousand."

"*Dollars*?!"

"That's right. And you can take that to the bank. And they want to reissue your last two novels also."

He waits until eleven to phone Robert, leaves an excited message, invites the boy out for the best lunch money can buy in Copenhagen, waits. By early afternoon there is still no return call.

It is Saturday, and the day is blessed by the sun, the sky a flawless blue. Bohannon sits at the Coal Square Bistro, at a table in the sun, orders a beer from the lovely Asian waitress, hears a woman's voice, a busker singing Joni Mitchell's "Big Yellow Taxi," and Bohannon thinks he might still be capable of love. When she comes around during her break with the hat, he drops in a handful of coins to make it jingle.

Bohannon signals the Asian waitress for another beer, and just as she places it on the table before him with one of her dazzling smiles, someone speaks his name. "Lucas?"

It is one of Lotte-Mia's friends, a woman named Marianne he has always liked. She is walking her bike past the café tables.

"Marianne," he says with feeling. "It is so good to see you."

"The same," she says.

"What the fuck happened? Why won't Lotte-Mia talk to me? Why is she so mad?"

"She's sad. She misses you."

"Well then why the devil did she kick me out?"

"There's more than one version to that story," she says, and he sees her face stiffen and her blue eyes cool. "Good seeing you," she says stiffly and rolls her bicycle further across the square as Bohannon tries to think what she meant, what Lotte-Mia might have said to her. *What the fuck is going on? Why won't someone tell me if I did something wrong? Admittedly, I can't be the totally innocent party here, but am I so bad that everyone I love has turned against me?*

This is madness.

He drains his pint and rises, crosses the square to Købmagergade, strolls on to Skindergade, where he sees a yellow Jag convertible parked outside the Café Theater there, top down, black leather interior, an EType V12. In the sunlight. This would cost pretty much his whole life's savings—at least before Samuel got him that fat advance. But he doesn't want to own it. He only wants to admire it, a work of art in the sunlight. He thinks about people whose main objective is to earn money, who buy houses, time-shares in Berlin or the south islands, summer houses, two cars, a yellow Jag sports convertible, thinks about the house that his ex got out of the divorce, worth nearly a million bucks now. He has no regrets. He thinks of his father, an insurance company executive who wrote poems at night and never got anywhere with them and drank in frustration and died before he was sixty. Thinks how the man had encouraged him to write, praised his early efforts, suggested books to read, given him books. Bohannon had to say goodbye to him in the ICU, his false teeth removed so he couldn't choke on them, a tangle of tubes in his arms and his face, his frantic eyes like an animal trapped in a cage, only fifty-eight years old.

Bohannon stands gazing upon the yellow Jag sports in the sunlight and looks at the cobblestones beneath it and thinks of Dan Turèll's poem about how the cobblestones contain all his life and all his dreams as all of everyone's life and dreams, and he doesn't regret anything really, but he wonders why his son won't answer the phone and why he cannot make a woman happy.

By dark he is in Pisseranden—The Pissing Edge—an old prostitute quarter that is now a cross between hip, yuppie, and bent, just around from the Town Hall Square. He wanders into Café Floss and is surprised to find it packed with people. Joni Mitchell's words are trilling through his brain—*don't know what you got till it's gone*. Apparently he is smiling because a young woman perched on a stool alongside of where he stands at the bar says, "Your smile does me good."

"Your saying that does me even better. What are you drinking?"

She's very young, possibly forty years younger than Bohannon, but they bridge the gap with conversation. She's drinking absinthe which the bartender pours for her through a sugar cube on a perforated spoon. The stool alongside her is vacated, and Bohannon hops onto it.

She studies his face. "How old *are* you?" she asks.

"Old as death," he says.

"What do you do?"

"Write."

"Anything I would have heard of?"

"Nah."

She takes a sip of her absinthe, looks into the glass, reflecting. "Let me ask you something," she says then. "And be honest, okay? Would you say that I'm beautiful?"

"Now let's see…" He examines her face with his gaze—her cheeks are round, her eyes strikingly green with dark speckles, her nose slightly broad, her chin slightly pointed, her eyes a bit close, her lips red as berries, skin light as milk. He leans backward to get a fuller view, sees freckles scattered across the skin of her chest, blesséd cleavage which he can see is enhanced by a bra under her V-necked shirt… *I see a valley where I could bury my weapon*, as the Celtic bard said and Bohannon refrains from repeating.

"So?" she says. "The verdict."

"Know what I think?" he says. "I think that *you* don't think you're beautiful. So if I tell you you're beautiful, you won't believe me. It will make you think less of me, make you think I'm a liar, trying to win you over with lies. But I'm an old dude, and you're not only beautiful, you're very young. Beauty is youth," he says, "Youth beauty. That is all ye know on earth and all ye need to know. And furthermore, furthermore, possibly there is some young man or men who don't appreciate your beauty and because they didn't appreciate you, you doubt your value. But you *are* beautiful."

This is some inspired bullshit, he thinks, hears that thought, feels shame, but then recognizes that she *is* beautiful and that he is a lucky old coot that she will even listen to his bullshit.

She parts her lips to respond, clearly at a loss for words, and at just that moment, a young mustached man in a faded Superman T-shirt pokes between them with his fat shaved head to ask the girl, "What are you doing talking to this old man? Is he your grandfather or something?"

Bohannon leans around to put his face in the young man's face. "Pardon me," he says quietly. "You are interrupting our conversation."

The young man ignores him. "So," he asks the girl, "you here alone?"

"*Hello*?" says Bohannon. "Would you please leave us in peace. We're having a conversation." He speaks quietly, but lifts his brow to emphasize his seriousness and stares into the young man's black eyes, wondering if he is going to have to eat a knuckle sandwich but has had enough beer not to worry a whole lot. He only hopes that he won't take a blow to his capped front teeth. Caps are so freaking expensive.

The young man glances at the girl again who says quietly, "Didn't you just hear what this gentleman said? So why are you still here?"

Bohannon is still staring at the boy with lifted brow, and the kid sputters his lips and smirks and slouches off, muttering.

The girl's eyes are sparkling at Bohannon's. "Know what?" she says. "That turned me on. You protected me. I don't ever recall a man protecting me before."

Her name is Beate, and Bohannon is amazed to find her sitting close in the back seat of a taxi headed for his dark and cluttered rooms, her hand on his thigh.

He apologizes for the mess, hooks up the CD player, puts on Counting Crows doing "Big Yellow Taxi," and he breaks out an ice bucket and bottle of black label Stoli and his two best crystal tumblers—his *only* crystal tumblers—while she rummages through his boxes of books.

"You translate Dan Turèll?" she asks.

"Guilty."

"And Henrik Nordbrandt?"

"Guilty again."

She looks at him with more admiration than he ever expected to be looked at ever again by a young woman. "You know there was a Turkish poet," he says. "Who said that translating another man's poem is like handling his woman. Without permission."

And to his amazement her green eyes with dark speckles are whispering unmistakable words: *Kiss my mouth.* Which of course he needs to have corroborated. "May I kiss you?" he asks.

She smiles, nodding, and he kisses her, and her tongue is fresh and sweet as strawberries despite the sour aftertaste of absinthe which has its own piquancy, and then she holds up her arms so he can lift off her pullover, and his ancient heart is racing so hard he fears it might explode, but of course, when they are naked and on the mattress, he can't get it up.

He excuses himself, fumbles into the cartons for where the medicine is, for the Viagra that he thinks might still be there, thanks god it is, sees the warning—*FOR ERECTIONS LASTING MORE THAN FOUR HOURS SEEK MEDICAL ATTENTION*—and he finds a vegetable knife to cut the pill in half with; the gleaming steel blade is sharp, and one half of the pill slides behind the stove, but the other he catches on the fly and swallows with vodka. Beate waits patiently, stretched out on the mattress, head propped in one hand, smiling, her plump 19th century beauty in the shadowy room something he never, ever expected to happen upon again. From the tiny basket on the bedside stand in which he keeps his French letters he lifts a phial of so-called "Quick Jaguar Room Incense," now illegal in Denmark but which used to be legal and which he has saved for a worthy occasion. He unscrews the cap and covers the bottle opening with his thumb, gives her a sniff, sees her eyes go fierce with pleasure, takes a hit himself, caps the bottle and with a grin on his face that he can feel is insanely idiotically ecstatic, he goes down.

Three hours later, she has come twice, he not at all, but his erection is still erected, and he's getting nervous, pictures himself in the emergency room, tries to calculate the logistics of it. He discusses it with her, tells her that in an hour his erection will become dangerous.

She chuckles. "It's been dangerous for some time now."

"Will you come to the emergency room with me if it's still hard in an hour?" he asks. He is afraid that if he shows up with a four-hour hard-on all alone everyone will think he took Viagra just to jack off.

She says, "I don't think that will be necessary." And she lowers her face to him as he lowers his eyelids and sees in the darkness behind them the face of Lotte-Mia, and she is doing what Beate is doing for him, and Lotte-Mia is smiling her succulent, teeth-glinting pleasured smile as he arches and sinks and lies back afterwards, saturated with that moment of beautiful weightless sadness as he wonders at a fleeting sense of having been unfaithful to them both, sinking down into the lovely nothingness.

His bedroom window faces east, and he wakes with sun on his face, alone on his mattress.

"Beate?" he says. Louder: "*Beate*?!"

Nothing. *Fuck.* He limps out to make coffee, sees a folded torn-out notebook page beside the machine: *Dear Dangerous Dick, thanks for a cozy night. Loving greetings, B.*

No phone number. No last name. No chance to cup her face in his palms and say, "Beate, let me make this perfectly clear: You are beautiful. A more beautiful woman I never hoped to meet in my life." But he is uncertain whether his thoughts are addressed to Beate or to Lotte-Mia.

The sun does not reach the breakfast niche in his new kitchen, but looking up the six-story walls of the courtyard, he can see a clear blue sky and sunlight at the top of one wall. He wishes Beate were here—he would have invited her out for a lunch complete with champagne—not champenoise, but champagne!—at Peder Oxe. And no expectations. Only to express his appreciation of her beauty, of her kindness, of her person. And he thinks of all the times that he and Lotte-Mia lunched on bubbly at Peder Oxe and wonders that that could be over.

He wants to get out of these dark rooms, so he shaves, showers, splashes his face and pits with Armani Gio, pulls on his best, most sparkling garments and plunges out into the sunlight. His Boss-jeaned legs, one of which is still dragging behind him, hobble him to the North Harbor city-train station, two stops from the Coal Square where perhaps that young blond woman busker is singing "Big Yellow Taxi" and the lovely Asian waitress will serve him a pint and a smile in the sunlight of a full-fledged spring morning.

He hobble-jogs up the steps to the elevated platform, as he usually does, defying the persistent pain in his leg, gets to the platform where he can see across the sparkling waters of North Harbor to the Swedish nuclear plants, as he always does standing on this platform, how preposterous it is of Sweden to put those nuclear reactors just *there*, so close to Copenhagen, but today something is different.

Today he leans back against a wall of posters, gazing out across the sparkling water of North Harbor and cannot get air down into his lungs. He cannot breathe. This is amazing and interesting and terrifying, standing in public and not being able to breathe, not even able to speak the word help. For one confused moment he looks right and left for Lotte-Mia who will surely be there to help him, but his back against the wall, he begins to slide downward, sinking, and thinks what he would like to write in his notebook: *Direct hit, Captain Benjamin! We're taking on water! Isolate the chamber!* But he is distracted by embarrassment, especially when he feels himself pissing in his pants.

He opens his mouth and his throat, but what comes out sounds more like gorilla language, the croaking of a frog, than words. A young couple standing not five feet from him look away, step away, and he understands that. Why should they get involved? He certainly wouldn't. Involvement leads to pain. Better to get out while the getting is good. *Get out old dude before your evicted.*

(2012)

Two: Unreal City

(1996)

THE GREAT MASTER

I DECIDED TO EAT everything in the house. It seemed a worthy project. To void the house of food. It would be a pure act in an impure world. Bottles, jars, biscuit tins would achieve an immaculate emptiness. The refrigerator would become pure in its frost, empty, sterile as the white tundra. My body would become a shelter, sculpture, art.

I worked at night while the others slept, teaching my body to expand. Red wine to thicken the gut. Milk, cold in the glass, to expand the belly capacity. I started by vacuuming off leftovers. Nothing was wasted. Salami heels. A bowl of congealing cold spaghetti. I sat at the kitchen table, work tools around me: a loaf of Wonder Bread, tomatoes, quarts of milk, olives, cloves of garlic, sliced cheese in plastic wrappings, oatmeal. Up on the pantry shelf a block of dark chocolate. Beneath the sink a can of brown beans in molasses, sardines, tuna chunks in oil.

Sitting alone, I chewed and swallowed, chewed and swallowed, belched and smiled and knew I had found my work. The happiness of my lips, of a full mouth, full throat, full belly which would continue to expand in capacity, continue to be full for as long as my work should continue, made me know I was chosen, blessed.

The world loved me then. Fat man. No, man of appetite.

Mensch. I drank till wine ran from the corners of my mouth, wiped it away with the back of my hand. Tore meat from the bone with my teeth, licked the glistening fat from my lips and fingers. I wolfed blue cheese on toasted buttered baguette, washed it down with bordeaux, gobbled raw onion on a cream-cheesed bagel, white bread buttered thick, packaged salami slices, a schooner of foaming draft.

There was no happiness like mine.

I worked hard, but all my best efforts seemed futile. Every time I eliminated a product from the house it reappeared the next night, or the next, or a week later. No sooner was a jar of grape jelly reduced to a sticky residue than a new jar appeared and those hours of labor, that sense of triumph and accomplishment as the blade clacked against the glass bottom gave way to futility, resignation. My body could never expand enough to contain this bottomless cornucopia. I would never empty this house of food, never.

How could I go on? I had to. I went on.

In the end they began to hide things so that my nightly labors became a search and destroy mission. The fruit cake in the washing machine, half gallon of red wine in the vacuum cleaner tank. Always beneath the rolls of wax paper in the utensil drawer, was a long flat pack of raisin cookies. Chewie ones. Powerful stuff, went straight to the colon, producing mighty farts, blasters in the kitchen, while the rest of the house slept. I smiled with crumbs on my lips, chewing on.

My son sometimes woke. "Ready on the right!" he would call down the stairway to me. "Ready on the left! Ready on the firing line! Fire one!" He salvaged the microphone from an old tape recorder in the basement and went around conducting make-believe interviews with me. "Please tell the studio audience how it feels to smell like a giant fart, sir."

In the eyes of friends and associates who at first had relished my behavior as a man of appetite, I began to see the subtle lights of revisionism. My wife was the first to reveal naked contempt. Her lips puckered, her eyes narrowed, her voice a whisper as she watched me climb out of the bathtub, water cascading from me as from a breaching whale. "Christ! You are disgusting!"

Many people did not see me at all, odd paradox in view of my bulk, and if I tried to call myself to their attention, they glanced at me briefly with incredulity, as if some stranger had mistaken them for an intimate, looked away, dismissed me with a totality that could only fascinate me. To be so utterly, unabashedly, unreservedly rejected—by a shopgirl, a colleague, a neighbor, people who knew me—is a special kind of distinction, acknowledgement that one has reached a purity beyond the perimeters of civility.

I knew then that what I was about had value.

Perhaps every greatness begins jovially and proceeds to labor, to transcendence of self, of gratification, of the need to be confirmed by affection. It begins with glamor, panache. In the beginning I was loved. A man who finds his work is an object of desire, a complete being amidst shadows. It is supposed the fat are loved, but not desired. That every party loves a jolly fatman, while no woman does. Not so. In all my years, I never was so desired as I was after cutting myself free of the mooring of restraint. Suddenly women were always near me, touching my belly as if it were a fetish.

At a barbecue, a block party, a PTA meeting, as I stood sipping punch and munching whatever had been provided, chatting amiably with my little girl's first-grade teacher, Mrs. Welch, suddenly her vivid blue eyes rippled with suggestion as her little half-grapefruit breasts touched my bicep, nipples hard as olives.

At a family baptism, my wife's grandmother sidled up to pat my corpulent butt with the palm of her scrawny hand and whisper, "I'll just bet you give 'em hell in the sack, buster!"

They were everywhere, and Yes! I said, Yes! I said yes to all of them, each and every one, but it was never enough: they would have me, have my dedication, my determination, my greatness. They would have my appetite! But I went on. No one could stop me, no desire could displace my mission. I kept on eating, drinking, growing, laughing.

But slowly, the gravity of my vocation began to dominate. The jovial boy who began to free the house of its ballast of edibles evolved into the serious-faced man hard-pressed to maintain dedication to his mission, the nightly tour of duty, the scouring away of all that could be eaten.

When I conquered the bathroom scale and then, after that, the medical scale, when my body weighed more than these machines were capable of registering, I realized something was happening. I was a freak, yes, but I was beautiful, too. I was beyond all the old measures and definitions.

I was post-modern.

There were times, of course, when I faltered, when the taste of food in my mouth was ash. But I did not give up. This was more important than me. I ate. Through the good and through the bad, I ate. I stuffed my mouth, chewed, swallowed, washed it down, filled my mouth again. I was loyal to this thing that had chosen me. I withstood all mockery, contempt, the staring eyes.

My wife's impatience festered. My children grew beyond their innocence to see me with the eyes of judgment. Their father was shameful, a beast. Finally, my wife requested that I see a doctor.

"For your head," she explained. "Clearly this is mental."

When I protested, they called a conference in the dining room and explained to me why it was necessary that I go away to a camp where small, slight beings of no consequence would program me to be like themselves. My son led the charge. He informed me, not without relish, that if I did not do these things they would leave me here alone in the house and would not return. I was given one hour to make a decision.

Two hours later, I sat in my two-man sofa in the living room and watched them carry their suitcases and hatboxes and garment bags and duffels out to a waiting taxi. From within my body I watched them. After they had gone, when the sound of the taxi turned the corner and was gone, when the street outside was silent, the house silent, I sat alone on my sofa and allowed the room to darken as the light of day slowly vanished. I missed my children, as they had been when they were innocents. I missed my boy's jovial mockery and the days before I grew so large when my wife still could gaze upon me without disgust. I sat there in the dark and thought back over my life, the things I had done and not done, the decisions fallen into, followed. They did not know, my loved ones, the nature of my quest, the necessity for utter dedication. They did not know. The remainder of my journey, I saw, would be alone.

When the house was completely dark, the rumbling mutterings of my stomach roused me from my stupor. There was still food in the house: lard and grains in the pantry, jars of condiments, preserves in the basement. When I consumed the last of that, my work would be done. I was afraid, but my fear was not unpleasant. It had the bracing edge of duty fulfilled.

On the fourth night, the electricity went out. Next morning, a FOR SALE sign was staked into the lawn. But no one came to see the house. Days passed, a week, two weeks, and no one came. The telephone was out. I ran out of flashlight batteries and searched the house for candle ends. I missed the air conditioner terribly in the summer heat, but took to living in the cool of the basement.

Sometimes at night I heard footsteps round the house, crunching in the pebbles of the drive or in the earth beneath the basement windows. Giggling sometimes. Teenagers daring one another. I blew out my candle and waited to see their eyes at my window, the glint of teeth. Sometimes I wearied of them and dispersed them with a bellow, listened to the rapid footfalls across the gravel as they ran for their lives, shrieking with laughter, exhilarated with terror. Children came during the afternoons and broke the windows with stones. I barricaded the door from the upstairs hallway. The only way in or out was through the hurricane doors to the side of the house front and I bolted them with a two-by-four.

One afternoon a man's face peered in one of the side basement windows and identified himself as a journalist. I did not answer. He cocked his head, listening, and I knew he knew I was there. With a stick he cleared the glass fragments from the frame and lowered himself in. I drew back behind the water tank and called out for him to stay where he was. A moment's silence ensued, filled with the breathing of two men in fear. He squinted through the dim dusty air at me. He wanted to interview me, to photograph me, to give me a voice for my cause.

"Go away," I said loudly. "I have no cause. I've eaten everything. This dwelling is pure of food. Let me be. I am who I am."

He called out questions to me, asked me about God, about spirits, about my purpose. He asked what I meant by 'pure of food' and whether I was fasting in an inner wilderness. He used his blitz to snap pictures of me cowering there and asked if I were a cult and if it were true what the local children said, that I slaughtered goats and drank their blood. He stalked me through the dim cellar, he would have me in his magazine, he would have me on film.

Finally he left. I did not know what was to happen now. What I told the journalist was true. The house was pure of food. Nothing remained but for my body to consume itself. I lay down on the old double mattress I'd dragged into the furnace room and contemplated this image of my being, like a snake swallowing itself. The final consumption to nothingness. The self consumes the self. This would be my end.

It began indeed as a consumption, pain in my gut, my belly, flanks, ribs. My head swam, my mouth was parched, my gums ached. My lips went dry and blistered. My dreams came as strangers at the windows. Once I saw a naked woman cross the basement floor, walking slowly in the shadows. Another time my father leaned into the doorway to encourage and advise me, and my son, innocent again, interviewed me with a banana I tried to catch between my teeth.

On the fourth or fifth morning, I woke to an aroma that caused the saliva to flow along the edges of my tongue. An aroma of fats sizzling over a fire. Groaning, sweating, I rose, followed my nose to the front window where I heard singing, some manner of mystical chant in the late summer morning. The grass of the lawn, ragged now, weed-infested, still glistened with dew. Kneeling over a fire was a black man wearing a white robe. A lamb leg roasted over the fire. The black man chanted a series of rising and falling syllables in a language I did not recognize. But the lamb I recognized. The juices dripping into the fire and exploding, the dark brown sheet of crisp skin, the brown-black fat, the graceful shank of bone and thick club of meats.

I took the stairway up into the garden, unbolting the storm doors, and stepped into the sunlight. The black man turned the lamb leg on its spit and continued chanting. On the other side of the street, a scatter of people murmured at my appearance on the lawn. Some had cameras. I heard the metal shiftings of time shutters, saw the flash of blitzes. I approached the black man who lifted the spit off its brace and held it forth at the end of his extended arms. His gold tooth shone in the daylight. One of his eyes was blind. I took the lamb leg and tore at it with my teeth, chewed happily as the fats and juices exploded against my tongue.

A young man stepped away from the crowd hesitantly, crossed the street toward me, knelt in the grass. His head was shaved to a beige stubble, and he wore a saffron robe and red running shoes. Others followed, sinking to their knees at the edge of the lawn. The sun was bright now, though still morning cool, the air redolent of cut grass and summer. The people kneeling before me began to hum in unison as I tore happily at the mutton, gnawed the meat down to white bone, tearing away every last scrap of crispy gristle and skin, poked my finger into the end joint for a clump of marrow I sucked into my mouth. Then I stood licking my teeth, belched into my fist and rose to my full height, fortified by the meat. The faces on the lawn turned up to me, and the boy in the saffron robe said, "O Great Master: Speak to us."

Noticing that he wore a bota looped over his shoulder, I said, "I thirst."

The boy held the bota out to me, and I took it, aimed the spout at my open lips and felt the delicious shock of well-tempered red wine mingling with the taste of lamb. When I handed back the empty wine bag, the boy said again, "Speak, Great Master."

My palm lifted, two fingers raised as I had seen on an icon once. I smiled, drunk on lamb and wine. All were silent, all faces turned up to me. I could have done with a spot of dessert, but could think of no dignified manner to request it. I opened my mouth, heard myself pronounce: "Waste!" And, "Want!" And then I was silent.

They watched me, eyes sharp with hunger for more, pleading for me to give them a god, but I could think of nothing else to say.

So I bowed my head once, and heard an OOO and an Ahhh rise from the crowd. Then I turned and squeezed back through the cellar passageway, and climbed slowly back down into the darkness. Someone behind me began to clap, and there was a ripple of applause as I withdrew.

The cellar was dim, dismal. All I could think about was dessert, how I yearned for a sweet, and knowing in that yearning and in my inability to voice it, the first flaw in my purpose, the first breach of my purity, the sour taste of defeat.

The greatness of my potential has eluded me. The certainty with which I began, with which my great body grew, has vanished from my spirit. I am no longer at ease in this basement. They come for me daily, the worshippers, fat most of them, corpulent arms laden with food, awaiting my blessing. I rise daily into the light to greet them, accept their offerings of food, but am no longer at ease, no longer engaged in the devouring of a world of insufficiencies, merely performing to fill a belly that will never fill, to still an ache that never will be stilled.

Sometimes many people come, sometimes few. When there are few, I worry, and when I worry, that worries me even more: that my appetite will abandon me, that I will begin to shrink, that I will lose my power to draw followers and offerings, that I will go hungry.

As gods we begin. And end in hunger.

(1987)

WHAT DOES GOD CARE ABOUT YOUR DIGNITY, VICTOR TRAVESTI?

"Happy is the man whom God correcteth; therefore
despise not thou the chastening of the Almighty."
Eliphaz: Job: 5:17

VICTOR TRAVESTI STOOD beneath the bus shelter, tall, hands easy in the slash pockets of his trenchcoat. The coat hung open on him, exhibiting the hand-stitched lapels of his silver suit. He watched for the bus, thinking ruefully of the copper Mercedes XL25 which Jewish people had sent an ape to take from him.

Seated on the bench at his back, two women in their late sixties chatted. Rain drizzled from the gray sky onto the pavement and slicked the road.

"It's sad for all the little boys who wanted to play ball today," one of the women said.

Let them drown, thought Victor Travesti, watching for his bus.

"And just think of all the families who planned to go on picnics," the other woman said.

"Such a shame."

Let them eat grief, thought Victor.

The broad glass face of the bus appeared at the corner. The

vehicle slid in alongside the curb, wheezed to a halt, clapped open its doors. Victor Travesti turned and with his arm swept a gallant, imaginary path toward the bus to usher the women ahead of him.

"Ladies," he said, and bowed to them.

"Such charms," said one. The other giggled, fluttered her eye-lashes, plumped up her thin, red-black hair. "Sidney Omar said my stars showed a tall dark handsome fella," she said.

"Your Stars Today," pronounced the first dreamily, with a smile of mystical ignorance.

Victor Travesti winked, poker-faced. Then his strong white teeth flashed as he guided the ladies up the steps of the bus, averting his eyes from the rolling masses of their flowered backsides.

"My mother always said to beware the Latin charm," the balding redheaded woman said, glancing sidewise and up into Victor's dark face, which replied with graceful forbearance.

Yes, he had charm. And scorn, too. He knew how much hand to give, and to whom, and how. For the upstart, for the Irish fornicator, two fingers, while the eyes look elsewhere. Full clasp for peers, for men of respect. He had all the tools of a good *paysan*. His people had been *Calabrese*. He thought it sad that a man of his dignity should have to ride the public bus with balding old ladies.

The reek of a rainy Saturday hung over the seats and passengers inside the bus—wet corduroy, yesterday's onions, breath. Victor Travesti sat by a window and watched the streets and neighborhoods of Queens roll past. Corona, Jackson Heights, Woodside, Sunnyside, the chintzy optimism of a people who would call their main road "Bliss Street." He watched the shops and houses and apartment buildings of people who were doing better than he, people whose dusty shoe shops and drycleaners hung on, decade after decade, despite the neglect and sloth of their owners, while to Victor, who rose early and worked hard and bore himself with the dignity of a *Calabrese*, fate had dealt failure as a crown upon his efforts.

Victor Travesti signalled his stop and rose, thinking of his wife and two boys and the Irishman who now lived with them, sleeping in bed with the woman who had pledged herself to Victor at the altar of God, sharing her marital bed in the same house where his children slept, eating food at the table with them. Victor's family. With whom a court had told Victor he had no right to be except twice a month at a time chosen by the wife who had violated her pledge. This they called justice. A woman spends afternoons in secret meetings, becomes drunken in public in company with a lecherous man in a business suit, and the court gives to her Victor Travesti's sons.

The judge had been a Jew. Silvermann. A tuft of dark hair jutted from each of Silvermann's nostrils and his eyeglasses had been dirty, speckled with dandruff and grease. When he informed the family of his decision concerning the fate of Victor Travesti's sons, Victor had clamped his jaws tight and risen. He had gazed upon the woman and her Irish lawyer in his shiny three-piece suit, forced them to observe the smouldering of his eyes, his dignity in the face of indignation. He raised his index finger to his eye and smartly drew down the underside of the eyelid: I see this outrage. I see your deceit. Victor Travesti sees.

Things had not gone well for Victor Travesti. Tribulation was upon him. His business had failed. He had had to go out begging to work for other men, companies. Victor Travesti had had to offer his skills and wisdom for money, payable by the hour, by the day, the week, to offer himself as a laborer in another man's vineyard, and even that was denied him. No one was left whom he even could beg. He had had to return to live again as a boy in the house of his mother. To see his sons, he had to ride in a public bus and wait with his hat in his hand in the foyer of the Irish fornicator who had cheated him of his family. A man named Sweeney with green creases between his teeth and the red veins of drunkenness across his nose.

The bus slowed. One of the old ladies, moving toward the rear doors, weaved off balance. Victor Travesti's hand leapt to her aid, steadied her by the elbow. She fluttered her eyelids at him. He nodded, dealt her a small, firm smile, held her elbow while she descended before him to the street.

The instant's delay which his courtesy produced decided the course of the brief remainder of Victor Travesti's life.

As he stepped off the bus, he heard a strange sound, very slight, yet somehow foreboding, a kind of hiss, a plop, and there was something familiar and strangely taunting in the sound. He heard the wings of a bird shiver overhead, the mocking scream of a gull, as he stood at the curb, hands in the slash pockets of his trenchcoat. Two men standing beside a carpet truck laughed raucously. Lettered on the side of the truck were the words Kipling Karpet Ko. The men were thick and red-faced. The one smoked a cigarette and smirked. The other wheezed with laughter. Pointing a thick hair-knuckled finger at Victor Travesti, he said, "I want to sing like the boidies do, tweet tweet tweet."

Victor Travesti clamped his jaws shut. The old woman he had helped off the bus was pushing a fistful of tissues at him.

"You poor dear," she said, "Don't you pay them no mind." She daubed at the lapel of his raincoat. Victor Travesti tipped his chin toward his throat and strained his eyes to see. Something green and white was sketched down its front. Victor grimaced, looked about him with chill fury. The red-faced man stood with his palms on his thighs and wheezed merriment.

Victor Travesti took the kleenex roughly from the woman's hand, wiped at his lapel. He pitched the crumpled, slimey paper into a refuse basket, shook his hands as though to shed water, fumbled into his pocket for his handkerchief.   The stuff was streaked on the lapel of his silver suit as well as on his Sardinian silk tie.

The old woman was shoving more kleenex at him.

"Please!" he snapped, palming her hand away from him.

"Well!" she said. "Some people."

The hand-stitched lapel of his silver suit was blemished with an ugly stain even after he had scrubbed it with his handkerchief, spit on it, scrubbed more. He could carry the raincoat over his arm, but the jacket and tie were just as bad, worse.

The carpetman watched with unconcealed pleasure. Victor Travesti looked at his freckled, pugged nose, his sandy-red, close-cropped hair. The man seemed to be laughing on behalf of all of Victor Travesti's enemies and tormentors: Judge Silvermann, the Irish fornicator, his adulterous wife, those who had taken over his business, those who had forced him to demean himself requesting permission to labor for their enterprises at a wage and then sent him away with no work. The blood raced to his face, his temples. A brilliant pain seared his skull.

Victor Travesti stood his full height and gazed with chill ferocity from the one carpetman to the other. The smirking one shrugged his shoulders and turned away, but the thick, red-faced man met Victor's gaze with a fury of his own. Victor found it necessary to avert his eyes, to turn away and walk from them.

A bitter taste rose to his mouth as he heard the man speak viciously to his back. "That's right, Salvatori, just keep walkin'. That's what ginzos are good at: walkin'."

"And fartin'," the other added.

"Yeah, that's right. And fartin'."

Victor's face burnt with shame. It was difficult for a man of culture and dignity to deal with rabble. Personally, he felt no shame over it, but he had begun to imagine how his sons might have felt had they witnessed the mockery of these orangutans. That they were strangers frightened him vaguely. That strangers should laugh in his face, select him as their target. Why? On what basis?

He remembered the woman at the bus stop with her smile of weird, dreamy ignorance: Your Stars Today. He kept walking, quickened his pace toward a sign in pale red neon script that said, Fortune Dry Cleaners—French Method. Inside, a tall Negro in a white short-sleeved shirt worked the presser, while a man in a lavender mohair sweater did paperwork at the counter.

Victor Travesti laid his coat and jacket on the counter, unknotted his tie and removed it carefully, trying to avoid touching the stain. The man in the mohair sweater took up each garment, examined the stains, laid them gingerly down again. He thrust out his underlip and shook his head. "I don't know about this," he said.

"I need it right away," Victor Travesti said.

The man laughed, tongued the fronts of his upper teeth. "You can have them next Monday."

"I need them now," Victor Travesti said. "As soon as possible."

The man looked at him with a smirk. "I could bulk them for you. You'd have them in a hour. But you'd need to pay a surcharge of twenty-five percent. Standard for a rush job. And no guarantes on that there Eyetalian necktie."

"Do you mean I have to pay a surcharge of twenty-five percent," Victor Travesti asked, "and still get no guarantee?"

The man shrugged. "Take em somewhere else."

"I need them now," Victor Travesti said.

The man said, "The labor's the same whether I succeed or not."

Victor Travesti emptied the pockets of his jacket and coat. He could not allow his wife or the Irish fornicator to see him like this. It would kill him.

"Come back in an hour," the man said and returned to his paperwork.

The Negro drew down the lid of the presser; steam hissed out around the edges.

Outside on the sidewalk, Victor Travesti lit a cigarette. The carpet men were feeding a long rolled-up carpet onto a pile of similarly rolled-up carpets in back of their van. Victor Travesti turned his back on them, walked past an Army & Navy Store, a cake shop, a glass doorway at the foot of a flight of stairs. Lettered across the glass was:

> *Madame Esth r*
> *Fo tun s*
> *While U Wait*
> *One $/One F ight Up*

Victor Travesti looked at his watch, flipped away his cigarette, opened the door. He didn't believe in such superstitious nonsense, although he had an aunt who could predict the weather by flinging drops of scalding olive oil across a scrap of red silk. He just wanted to get off the street, to sit, to have a woman hold his hand and purse her lips and touch his palm with the tips of her fingers and care for a moment or two about his fate. The religious medals around his neck, one of silver, one of gold, jingled lightly as he climbed the wooden staircase two steps at a time.

On the landing were three doors. The first two were locked. He turned the shaky knob of the third and entered a room which was empty but for a ladderback chair in which an old man in a flannel shirt and mustard colored necktie sat gazing out the window. His hair was white and trimmed close at the back and his body looked as though it might once have been powerful, barrel-chested, his hands thick and large, the skin now freckled and puckered with age. The room itself looked as though it were in a building that had been bombed. Plaster had fallen away from the walls in several places, showing the woodwork beneath. The floor was covered with dust and plaster flakes from the ceiling and rubbled with bits of wood and glass, broken bottles, a newspaper which looked as though it had been soaked in water and dried and yellowed in the sun.

"Pardon me," Victor Travesti said. "I was seeking Madame Esther."

The old man said, "I can't even bear to look at it anymore. It's no good. There's no pleasure left in it." He rubbed his eyes with the heels of his hands, then ran a palm over his entire face. "I could as well put it all to the torch." He sighed, clasped his hands across his stomach, closed his eyes. A tubular flesh-colored wart hung from one eyelid.

Victor Travesti waited for a moment to see if the old man would say anything further. He glanced around the room. Apart from the rubble, it was empty. No chair, no other furniture. Against one wall was a gutted yellow plastic radio with a crack in the casing.

As be began to turn away, the old man said, "Shut the door. There's a draft."

Victor Travesti hesitated. "I cannot stay," he said.

"Young men are impatient," the old man said. "It makes them uninterested and therefore uninteresting."

Victor shut the door, put his hands in his pockets, jingled his change, considering how he might amuse himself with this old man. He said, "Thank you for the compliment, sir. In fact, I'm hardly young."

The old man's eyes turned upon him in their pouched lids. "Ha!" he said. "You're all of what? Forty-two."

"Good guess."

The old man snorted, reflected, looked sad. He said, "I had such hopes for you."

Victor Travesti inclined his head in dignified query.

"You were so much greater than the monkeys," the old man said. He hawked gravel from his throat, spat it into a handkerchief which he returned to the pocket of his khaki trousers. "The monkeys were so stupid," he said. "All they ever did was fiddle with themselves and giggle and throw their crap at each other. Never much cared for the monkeys. What can you do with a great ape that does a cross-country hike just to find some bamboo to chew on? Stupid, vulgar creatures, really. But you," he said and smacked one palm with the back of the other hand. The report was startlingly loud. Victor Travesti flinched, wondered if the old man might get violent. Old as he was, he looked as though he still might have some power in his body, and Victor wasn't in the mood for a confrontation.

"You and all your kind," the old man said. "You had advantages. You had capacities never seen before."

He rose from his chair, crossed to the window, stared down over the elevated train tracks. Without looking from the window, he said, "What good does it do me? What can you do? You try your best, and it all goes bad. Then you start to question your own motives. Who or what was it for? It was sport, too. I was young. It seemed exciting. I liked them to be brave. I liked the men to be brave, and the women to be nubile. They were men, not rodents. I liked them to make spears and run after the tigers." The old man's deep blue eyes lit for a moment, staring into an invisible past which Victor Travesti could see only in the reflection of sudden vivacity on the man's face. "You should have seen them. Three men, naked in the woods, holding big javelins over their heads and chasing one of those great big tigers right through the trees. This was sport: See that big cat go down roaring and the three of them waving those bloody spears in the air, yelling out praises. Praise to the Lord! Hosannah on highest! That's how it was back then..." The old man paused and his eyes grew distant as his mood seemed to slide downward. His eyes were very blue beneath his white eyebrows, his eyesockets deep in sculpted pouches so that his gaze was like a pale blue shadow. The old man sat again, turned his chair toward Victor Travesti.

Victor Travesti's mind had begun to work hard as he listened to the old man's story. Slowly it had begun to occur to him that everything that had happened to him today, all his life, from the instant of his birth, every chance turning and decision, had been leading him to this moment.

When the old man had ceased to speak for some moments, Victor Travesti dug his handkerchief from his pocket, dusted a spot on the bare wood floor. Then he genuflected onto the hand-kerchief and bowed his head.

"My Lord and my God," Victor Travesti said with humble dignity.

The old man wet his thin purple lips with the tip of his tongue and watched this man on one knee before him.

"Dear Lord," Victor Travesti said. "I have a favor to beg of you. I have been to the courts and have had no satisfaction. My wife is an adulteress, and the man with whom she fornicates has been given to live with my children, my fine young boys, and I can receive no legal satisfaction. Now I am on my way to visit my children, and I cannot let them see me as I am. I must have some clothes. And if I could rent—or buy—a car, could show up in an expensive car, it would win their respect. It would refresh my dignity. But I have no money, dear Lord. Dear Lord, I need money. Very badly. I am really on my backside."

The old man gazed upon Victor Travesti and the light blue shadows of his eyes darkened.

"You. Ask. *Me*. For. *Money*," he said, his voice faint with incredulity. "You ask *me* for *money!*" As he repeated the question his face began to grow larger, his eyes flashed, and his hands swelled. The old man's face became the face of a radiant beast, huge and furious, blazing.

Victor felt his underpants get wet. He began to weep and dropped his other knee to the floor and clasped his hands together to beg for mercy, but the old man's rage continued to grow. The ceiling lifted above his head to accommodate it, and the walls bulged outward as the waves of fury radiated against them.

"YOU ASK ME FOR *MONEY*!?"

He was on his feet now, bellowing. Victor slipped onto all fours and crawled wildly toward the door, but the old man caught him by the seat of his pants and the scruff of his neck, lifting him with enormous hands, his voice now a wind tunnel of rage, the words no longer distinguishable. Victor was flung against the door, knocking it off its hinges. It toppled, smacked the floor with a hard flat report. Dust rose in small clouds around its edges.

Victor tried to scrabble to his feet, but the old man was on him again, picked him up by his shirt front like a suitcase and chucked him down the stairs. Victor Travesti tumbled, feeling the wooden edges of steps punching his kidney, his ribs, the bones of his cheek. He rolled to a stop against the entry door, which shattered, raining shards of lettered glass upon him. In terror, he looked up the staircase, but the old man did not pursue him. He only stood on the top landing, glaring with enormous eyes of fury down upon the heaped body of Victor Travesti.

Victor crawled out the door, took hold of a fire hydrant and hoisted himself to his feet. His one hand was pulsating. He cradled it in the palm of the other. The middle finger lay at a sharp angle from the middle joint and throbbed painfully. He tucked his shirt into his pants, buttoned the collar at his throat, tried to tuck down the torn flap that hung from his hip pocket.

Cradling his injured hand, he shuffled toward the bus stop, uncertain what to do. He would go home to his mother. She could call Dr. DiAngelo. Dr. DiAngelo would splint Victor's finger. He would drink an espresso and anisette and eat some stella dora bread. He would take a nap and when he woke again, his mother would have baked some zitti for him, and he would be calm.

The carpet men stood in his path.

Victor Travesti drew back, tried to circle around them, but they stepped to the side to block his way again. "Leave me alone," he whimpered. "I broke my finger."

"Oh," said the thick-bellied redheaded one to the quiet, smirking one. "He broke his finger."

"Yeah, gee, poor guinea broke his finger. He wants us to leave him alone."

"Have you no culture?" Victor Travesti inquired icily. "Are you *animali*?"

The redhead cupped a hair-knuckled paw behind his ear. "Come again, Salvatori? You said *what* to me?"

"That is not my name," said Victor Travesti. "Leave me alone. My finger!"

The carpet man reached for the lapels of Victor Travesti's shirt. "I'll leave you alone," he said. "Come 'ere, Salvatori."

Victor shrieked with indignation and fear as he was dragged down, kicked in the thigh, shoved and stuffed by the two men into a half rolled synthetic carpet. He flailed, was kicked hard in the buttock, the arm; he caught his injured finger, cried out with exquisite pain.

The thick man knelt with one knee on Victor's gut, pinning him, as the other, snuffling with laughter and excitement, began to roll the carpet. Victor kicked and twisted, and just before the carpet roll closed over his face, he saw, watching from the window above the street, the old man's blazing eyes.

Then the carpet was over his face, was lifted and tossed onto the stack of other carpets in the back of the van. Victor could not move. He felt another carpet tossed on top of his. The air was very close and tight. He could not fill his lungs. He realized—even as he heard the ignorant muffled laughter outside, as he heard the van's rear door smack shut, as he heard the ignition wheeze and catch, and his consciousness slowly began to dim from lack of oxygen—that he was going to die. He realized that he was going to die and that these two carpetmen, when they found his body, would be stricken with terror, would be baptized with a terrible guilt that might change the rest of their lives. All because of their stupidity in not realizing he would die if they did this to him.

It hardly seemed fair. Any of it. He had done nothing to deserve this. Nothing. Perhaps it was stupid of him to have asked for money, but he needed money. Very badly.

His eyelids lowered in the wooly airless darkness, and the tight gasping fury of his lungs stilled, and he knew that he was crossing the border to whatever awaited him—nothing or something, disintegration or the reflection of spirit for a time or forever—as the humming motor of the van faded off into a sleep which slowly ceased to dream him.

(1989)

Gasparini's Organ

1. The Birth of Gasparini

MY NAME IS Vincente Gasparini. I was born in sin, died in scorn. I gave to life my blood, my labor, my art. I do not rest.

My father was Arturo Gasparini, watchmaker, fitter of jewels, springs, minuscule gems and catches into intricate mechanisms to measure the rhythmic tick of that tedious gravity which melts the faces of beautiful women.

The day of my birth, I walked with *mon pére* upon the sidewalks of an unknown city—Vienna? Paris? Utrecht? Where? When? I do not know. I know only the warm, soft palm of my father, holding my own small hand as we stepped along the clangoring street. Fruit vendors screamed like fighters, fishwives in black skirts shouted, their red fingers fumbling amongst iced wares. Steel-rimmed wooden cartwheels rumbled over cobblestones. Scabrous cats slunk amongst sacks of grain to crack the necks of rodents. In taverns, alewives fed the furies of men who sought with spirit to escape their minds. Shouts, laughter, anger, mourning. Whores in brothels snored, happier in sleep than ever when awake, and amidst this clamor, a one-eyed man with pockmarked face stood holding a box in hands whose dirt had become the grain of their flesh, nails broken and grimed. His mouth smiled, his single eye saw beauties beyond that street—a pale eye it was, the color of boiled blue cotton, while the box in those hands gave forth the most delicate, exquisite melody my ears had ever sung. I was perhaps six. Or eight. I don't know. It hardly matters. I stopped. My father stopped. This ringing quiet melody overpowered all other sounds of that afternoon, all misery, all appetite, all, paused in the gentle, delicate shelter of that sound. I, Gasparini, was born.

2. Gasparini Learns His Skill

The box was at once so simple and so intricate. The hand of my father purchased it for me, reached into his leather purse and removed more tinkling coins than that one-eyed pock-marked face could master with a sneer. I, Gasparini, saw the light fade from the boiled cotton of that eye as he pocketed the silver and copper pieces, as my father fondly slung the singing box over his shoulder.

I, Gasparini, saw this one-eyed man vanish into the misery of that street, to the alehouse, the whore, to fill his belly, spill his seed, to buy a rope perhaps, to rent an attic with a stout beam.

I, Gasparini, had sinned the sin for which man is not responsible but for which he nonetheless must pay.

I, Gasparini, knew. Yet I did not know. I saw. But had first to experience before this vision, this knowledge became the reality to which man is sent. We all must see, must yearn, must labor. yearn, and die. Life is insufficient, yet in its very insufficiency, in the yearning for completeness, in the wound of that yearning, we live, and it must comfort us. It must produce the cosmic smile as fingernails rake pleasure from the itching flesh, as the box reels out music to fill the singing ears, as silver purchases the box that small boys take home and dismantle, seeking the secrets of its music.

It was of fine cherry wood, fitted together with pegs and the sheerest, finest glue, wood that shimmered at the touch of sound, that moved in the thrall of music. Wood. Wood transmits, but has no talents. It has features, but of itself is dense and still. The wood of the grand piano conveys the majesties of fingers to the ears that fill the concert hall, but fingers are fingers, keys keys, strings and hammers nothing but another insensate layer before dead wood conveys the art of these elements to the hungering ear. Yes. Within the cherry wood of that box which had stilled, for an instant, the misery of that city street, was a brass comb, a bronze cylinder fitted to a crank. Nothing more. Nothing.

When I saw these simplicities, the hairs at my neck stirred, my eyes opened. I sucked a draught of air into my nose. I understood at once that the tits on the cylinder were synchronized to the teeth on the comb, that the turning of the crank brought these two elements into contact, that the pluck of tit on tooth rang out a note, that the spinning of teeth and tits constituted time as it related not to the ticking of minutes but to the ringing of melodies.

Asthma struck me at that moment. I sucked in air. It wheezed in my throat, scarcely filled my lungs. My throat might have been the split reed of a woodwind. I recognized the appearance of misfortune. I recognized the first of my misfortunes. I realized that whatever price the universe exacted of my entree to these secrets would simply be paid. Choice? Yes, perhaps there was a choice of a sort. The sort of choice a lonely man might have gazing into the eyes of a smiling woman. And if the woman is a whore? Whores and whores. Prices and prices. Some fees are subtle. Some whores offer a love truer than the love of mother or wife. Some whores stand with God.

I, Gasparini, destroyed that box of music. I was nine. Or twelve. I don't know. I sat in my chamber. The four walls of the box laid apart in the red light of sunset through the window, a cylinder in one hand, an intricate comb in the other. I felt the mean evil of knowledge on my face as surely as if I had been gazing upon the nakedness of a woman—that was the way we used to gaze upon a woman's nakedness back then in those innocent years.

3. The Death of Gasparini's Father

My father on his death bed sent my mother to fetch me, Vincente, to say farewell. She came and departed as a whisper, the woman whose smiling eyes had lit my childhood, stooped now and silent as dust, her lovely face scored by time. My father, too, was old. He said to me, "You have learned my trade well, Vincente. Your fingers are clever, you know the way to correct the instrument which measures time so that it is devoid of all falseness, clear of the hungering ego which besmirches all human effort."

Did he truly say this? Did he truly take my twenty-year-old

hand in his old gray one? Did he smile upon his son? No. In truth, he spat bloody phlegm onto his bedclothes, clung to me as to life. His eyes rolled with fear. "Time," he gasped. "Time." And I helpless to comfort him. He said, croaked rather, "You... You ..."

And died.

You, what? A curse? A blessing? A request?

He was burned in a pine box. I watched his smoke rise from the high yellow brick chimney of the crematory on a bright winter day and wondered at my eagerness to get on with what I planned to do, had been waiting to do, aware without thought that only his death would free me to my task, unwilling to look into the heart of what his death had done to me, unwilling to feel the pain of losing the warmth his hand gave to mine, the gaze of his pale blue eye upon me, the approval of his nodding head as he saw my fingers clever at their interests in the mechanical objects of his factory, never guessing that his son was planning the usurpation of his entire industry.

I had inherited the business of Arturo Gasparini. Three shops and a showroom. Twelve employees. A stockroom of golden and silver models. Precious metals sculpted by skilled fingers, fitted with tiny gems of diamond and ruby.

I, Gasparini, cared for by my silent, dusty mother, sought out by the mothers of the city's maidens. I, Gasparini. Who among them could know that I had already long before bartered for my fate, given my future, exchanged it for the sound that rang from the friction of brass against bronze?

This was Gasparini's passion: Brass on bronze.

4. Gasparini Takes a Wife

There were years in which my vision fogged. I tired of the work room, the gearwheel, screwdriver, the watchmaker's pincers, the music box maker's pliers and saws and clippers and hammers and glue.

I constructed boxes for lonely gypsies who travelled with monkeys that tipped small hats for coins and flung their excrement at the children of their benefactors. I constructed boxes that sang of Jesus the Savior, that played minute masterworks, that tinkled great melodies on small teeth.

These wonders brought me a modicum of economic reward. I acquired a house on Staworski Boulevard, I acquired a second house on Staworski Boulevard. Yet somehow I knew that never would I have three such abodes. Two houses on Staworski Boulevard. This was the fate of Vincente Gasparini. Small music, small rewards.

And what of my passions? My dreams? I desired greatness. I desired immortality. I desired the power of music. I desired women. I had always desired women. My mind was filled with them, the music of them, the movement of a delicate hand, the bend of a knee, the pale nape of a neck, lips opening. My desires for women were such that they made me wonder. A woman's lips, what were they after all? A woman's thighs? A woman's fingers, feet, teeth, tongue... How could I be so powerless before them? Lovely creatures. God, I thought, could only be a woman, man an attendant angel. And how happy the universe if Woman were God. For then God created by desire, and we all were saved by the wishes of our flesh. No woman hated her child, not for long. Woman was earth and creator. And women did love, that was why they were slaves, that was why if God were woman we were fortunate, for then God was a slave of love. She may rage incontinently against us, but still would want us, for women and, thus, God, never ceased to desire.

These were the thoughts, the helpless bedeviled and beguiled thoughts of Gasparini as he tired of his cogwheels and cylinders and brass tits and little melodies vibrating through cherry wood. These, in any event, were his feelings at that time when the unfamiliar name of passion wove garments of flame which drove him from his work. Were those thoughts exaggerated? Did Gasparini deceive himself? Was he led by his own less than noble lance? What is true? From this side of the grave I ask myself what of this is true, and I do not know. I know only this: I burned. I wed.

Gasparini wed. Took a woman of black hair and plump thigh who admired his skills to bring forth music by raking a tortoiseshell comb across his thumbnail, striking wineglasses with spoons, whistling through the knuckles of his thumbs into the joined cup of his palms.

She had shining brown eyes and provocative lips, teeth that were strong and challenging and breasts that had never known humility. I, Gasparini, burned for her mysteries, for the secret music of her thighs, her breasts, her hips that were alien to shame, her lips and teeth which teased and tempted, glinted secret wishes, hidden fancies.

We wed, this woman and I, Vincente Gasparini, and both

were riven with disappointment. The season of our passion was comprehensive but short.

I constructed synchronized boxes which kept our love in symphonic structures, Wagnerian undress, Bachian ecstasy, Beethovian passion, Vivaldian joy and completions.

There was a time, a brief, fleeting time, that my lady's body was sufficient answer to all the insufficiencies of existence, her pink tongue between glinting teeth a succulent mystery more important than all the weight of cosmic ignorance, her shining eyes the master, the mistress of all weariness. The teeth of her smile shone and caused the blood to race toward the center of my body. She offered her knuckles for my lips and I knelt with joy, certain that I was chosen for a celestial visitation.

And Gasparini was visited. By new lives. Gregorius and Mathilda. Children of passion. I, Gasparini, could relate to you details of procreation which could form the basis of legend. I, Gasparini, maker of music boxes.

5. Gasparini's Children

These two little ones taught me love. To gaze into their small faces was to feel in one's own blood, in one's own eyes, in the movement and senses of one's own body the sacredness of life. If I shouted, and they trembled, I wept. If I smiled, and they smiled back, my heart lifted with joy.

On Sundays, we walked together in the city, one on either side of me, their small hands in mine, and I knew that if such love, such a sense of life's connection could exist amongst all men, amongst all creatures, life's beauty would be unbearable. Yet it was that beauty we sought, for life's lack of beauty was what led us to our deaths. I took them walking down the same streets through which my father had led me those many years before, my hand in his that afternoon on which the pockmarked face of the one-eyed man smiled, the life surrounding him transformed, my life transformed, with these small elegant notes and rhythms. And I said to my children every time we passed the spot at which I had inspired my father to aid me in committing my sin against that man, "In this place, many years ago, *my* father took me walking, and my fate was decided. You, my children, shall decide your own fates."

I laid a palm on either of their faces, their light shining eyes gazed up at me with such utter trust that cursed me for a fool. My eyes filled. I knelt in my morning suit on the muddy street and embraced them.

They fueled my work. Their smiles, the music of their laughter was lighter, more fluid than any musical instrument, certainly more so than any box. To see them in summer on the shore running naked on the beach, their small feet slapping the hard, wet sand as the breakers foamed round their ankles, as they ran, laughed, dove into the waves and came up again, in furious happiness with their bodies, filled me, somehow, with a pain of sadness I scarcely could bear.

I, Gasparini, maker of music boxes, realized that I had not fulfilled the contract drawn up for me that day so many years before when I caused the death of that one-eyed man.

The creation of life, procreation, is for us all. That which I yearned to create, which I had bartered my future for, was the completion of insufficiency, even if only an instant's completion, the production of a beauty strong enough to withstand the heart's sadness.

6. Gasparini Loses a Finger

Why? you may ask. What is this life, what asketh man to have? Now with his love, now in his cold grave? What requireth a man of his days? Wife, offspring, food, drink, shelter.

Yes. What? Nothing, other than to fulfill the destiny of his birth. That toward which he must labor in great agitation and hope and pain to find, if he is a good and just man, his undoing. Yes. I began again to seek the music I had heard on that city street that day years before, my small moist hand in the warm strong softness of my father's hand which, with silver and copper, had purchased the box whose illusions had so charmed me.

Yes, illusions. Illusions. There was no music in those boxes. There was only the friction of tit on comb. There was no human breath, no pluck of fingertips, no press of warm lips, no flick of intricately boned and blood-fed wrist. No. There was only brass on bronze. Mechanics. This could as well be the ticking of a clock as music.

I stopped building these boxes, stopped selling them, stopped producing the materials with which they were constructed, stopped oiling my tools, stopped.

I, Gasparini, stopped. I brooded.

We had a certain quantity of monies out amongst the lenders, a certain reputation, a certain respect.

But I drank geneva and beer and wine in public places, stood small and fat in the center of public squares and shouted insults at people I did not know, took upon myself to demonstrate against the bourgeoisie: I entered the shop of a cravat salesman. He approached me in his petit bourgeois finery, his son, apprenticed, at his heels, his posture equally bowed as his father's. Only my reputation kept me from being thrown out.

"Monsieur Cravat," I asked, "Can you be led by the nose?"

His shoulders lifted, his chin lifted, his nose lifted with it. He said, "By the nose? Not I, Sir."

Between the knuckles of my bent first and second fingers I entrapped that bulbous veined potato of a nose and proceeded to lead him round his shop from cravat rack to cravat rack. He cried out in pain. I was incensed. He whimpered. I laughed with fury. His nose began to run onto my knuckles. I whipped my hand away in disgust. Wiped it on my pants. Seized him by his own red cravat with its diamond stick pin. My aim was to lift him up, this little man, to lift him up to my own height until his face turned blue and he sputtered and gasped and begged for mercy, and when I did not give him mercy, until he seized it for himself, until he wreaked revenge upon me. But to my chagrin the cravat was not an ordinary one. It was a false cravat attached round his neck by a new substance called elastic. When I seized it and tried to lift him by it, only the cravat lifted. The elastic stretched. My frustration almost made me weep, but a sudden furious inspiration led me instead to drag the cravat down to his feet and let it go so that it leaped from my hand and smacked him on the chin. He staggered backwards, blushing. His eyes did not meet mine. He began to chuckle. A nervous, sick giggle. At that moment my eyes met the eyes of his son. The boy was perhaps twelve years old. His eyes were the color of pale amber, filmed over with salt and moisture. I saw at once what I had done. I raced from the shop. Paused in the doorway. Dug into my pocket and drew forth the bills that were wadded there after my visit to the wine room. I turned back to the cravat salesman, extending the crumple of bills toward him. It was more money than he would earn in a year. Two years. He gazed upon it, his eyes full of desire, lifted his face to mine.

I said. "I beg your forgiveness. I beg you."

He approached me, palm open.

In a voice slight as the sound of a tiny, unoiled hinge, his son opened his mouth and spoke a single word: "Father."

The cravat salesman drew back his hand, swung, smacked the bills from my grasp. I turned and fled. He followed me throwing the bills at me, crumpling them in his hands so that they bounced off me like small, weightless pellets. I ran back into the wine house. Dug into my pockets. but they were empty, found myself back on the street on my hands and knees gathering those small crumpled pellets of money. The cravat salesman watched me through the window of his shop, his eyes torn between dignity and regret.

Soon the name of Gasparini was without value, without interest other than to inspire laughter, or for those who sought the opium of their own superiority.

I, Gasparini, was a public fool. Even as I sought the music of the celestial spheres, even as I toyed with every manner of metal or wood for tunes that would thrill my god-abandoned heart, I continued to seek the bottom of my well, to insult my fellow creatures, to humiliate myself.

One night I drank so much that even the most jaded hangers-on turned from me. I was so drunk that I do not even know what I did or might have done, for the entire night was a blur, but I must have achieved the end I had sought for so long: my total, public humiliation. I woke next day in a pool of waters, alone, confused, in great physical and psychic pain, but clinging to an idea. The idea was of a system of belts and wheels which could create wind that might be driven by a funnel through a rubber gasket into the mouth of a French horn.

Where this inspiration had come from I could not know. It came to my besotted mind. It came of my degradation, of the abuse of my body and mind, came not as the reward of virtue, but as the reward of self-destruction. It came to me as light comes to a lit candle. The burning of its own essence. It came to me in terrible drunkenness, but stayed with me when I woke.

There followed years of trial and of error. I was determined that no matter what the world may experience, it must know the peace that I myself had known as a boy when I heard the music box in the hands of the one-eyed man, my own small hand warm and safe inside my beloved father's. I worked with tits and combs and bellows and belts, learned that punches in a sheet of paper greatly economized the amount of space required and thus potentialized a machine which could play an entire symphony. What I lacked were the sounds of violins, French horns, drums. Pianos we could duplicate to some extent. could even duplicate the exact performance of a particular player, though not his passion, and bells and such, we could manage, but real instruments we needed.

It was clear to me that this was the next thing I must do. I, Gasparini, must find a way in which the finest of all music could be played in the greatest of all detail so that music whose likes never have been heard before could resound amongst us all even when the violin, trumpet, or French horn were not present—or rather when no human talent was there to unlock their music.

I, Gasparini, built such a machine, and it cost me nothing less than everything. I labored all the hours of my days. Even as my wife lay dying, I labored, taking only a few moments to bid farewell to that poor disillusioned partner of my life with whom once, for a short time, I had shared passion. My children grew to be strangers. My beloved small children grew to be strange adults who did not know me. My fortune dwindled to nothing. My health failed. I lived on bread and broth boiled from bones salvaged out of trash barrels in the bloody yard behind the butcher shop. My brain, cleared finally of alcohol, labored in new fevers of exploration, vision, delusion.

At night as I slept at my workbench or huddled in a blanket on my pallet on the floor, a one-eyed face visited my dreams and in that eye all the resigned sadness of death and human misery shone, of the wrong death, for always, it informed me, one's death is the wrong one.

In fevered, sweating dreams, I was visited by the cravat salesman, the son of the cravat salesman. The son gazed upon me with burning eyes. "I have no father," he said. "You have taken my father," he said. "My father has died the wrong death." The boy and the one-eyed man together gazed upon me:

"Your death too, Vincente Gasparini," they said to me, "shall be the wrong one. That shall be the gift reserved for your age, to place the crown upon your lifetime's effort."

My wife, too, returned to me in sleep, reflections of her eyes on her death bed, her wrinkled lips puckering to breathe a single word: "Wrong." And, "You have taken my husband from me. You have sold my husband for fake music. Wrong. All wrong. I have died a wrong death."

The dreams were enemies, infiltrating my heart. They bore truths into the tender regions of my spirit. I woke in pain at night and stared at the dark ceiling with wide eyes and learned that pain has an upper edge, that it is not insuperable. I stared and let the pain enter me and denied it my will.

I labored through a cruel winter whose winds bit like tiny evil mouths at my flesh, whose icy waters soaked into my shoes, rotted my socks, my feet. I lost the tip of one finger to the frost. It aches. Still now, when all is taken from me, when I am nothing but the sighing of air in haunted evenings, still now that lost finger joint aches, aches like the loss of all the people that have been taken from me at my own bidding.

The machine upon which I labored was laughed at in the town. Gasparini's folly they called it, and laughed. Foolish men with puny dreams, insipid visions, laughed at me, Gasparini, who was driven by unknown furies to the accomplishment of this fate, this wrong death which the universe craved of me. This punishment which I had sought for myself finally by committing the worst sin of which I was capable.

I, Gasparini, labored to fulfill a destiny of greatness so that the gods could have their reason to strike me down.

I, Gasparini, rose to their sport with the shield of dignity; this, too, was snatched from me as one might snatch an object from an infant, as one might snatch the dignity of a father from his son, a music box from a beggar.

7. Gasparini's Organ

I built it on wheels so that it could be rolled into the street, harnessed to a horse, drawn into the center of the town, draped in sheets sewn together to conceal its mysteries until the moment of its presentation. Already burning in the furnace of its boiler were the last sticks of furniture in my workroom, the last hafts of my last tools.

They laughed at me on the main square as I fed these sticks into the mouth of the boiler. as the steam built to its moment of greatness. They laughed, the grubby merchants laughed. They said, "Ah! See! Gasperini pisses in his pants to get warm!"

I was calm. I unharnessed the horse and led her away, returned to shoo the arrogant children of arrogant fools who clustered with taunts round my Folly, lifting the skirts of its draping.

I, Gasparini, grasped the edges of the sheets and slowly drew them from the humps and contours of my machine.

A stillness began to settle on the crowd as the sheet dragged back, as the gleaming wood of a grand piano was revealed, a row of brass—trumpets, French horns—a cluster of violins in the corral of a circular bow, each neck grasped by ten delicate metal fingers, as a dozen sticks of varied weight hovered over snares and bass and kettle drums.

I, Gasparini, gazed slowly across the faces of the crowd, uncertain now of sornething they had so easily embraced, uncertain now whether Gasparini was indeed a fool. And their frightened eyes seemed to say, if Gasparini is not, after all, a fool, what then does that make us?

A single lever awaited my touch. The steam was released into the bellows, the conveyor belt moved into gear, the ten-yard long punch paper began to feed from its pile of rectangles into the brain of Gasparini's organ.

Gasket lips leaned forward to the brass mouth of a French horn and blew the opening notes of "Morning, Noon, and Night in Vienna." I knew my people. They needed not great music; they needed a music whose art entered them, not music which called forth their own art of human greatness.

The single brass voice was answered almost at once by the majestic synchronicity of the entire orchestra offering an introductory fanfare. The square was filled with the music of an entire orchestra, of a symphony.

Violins bowed forward in their harness to be sawed by the circular bow, plucked by metal fingers. Cellos roared quietly. Horns called out—trumpets, woodwinds, the French horns—it was these that gave the majesty. This was the greatest, the only moment of my life. I was filled with beneficence. For the first time in how many years I was able to admit to myself that I might have failed in my quest. Only now in success could I allow that doubt the air. I trembled at the risks I had taken, the prices paid all without guarantee. My entire life might have ended in my workroom with a failed instrument, my aged worthless body in the corner huddled under a moth-eaten blanket, frozen.

Tears filled my eyes as an elegant oboe line traced intentions into the air of the still square where the townspeople hung upon it, only to be dashed within the violent response of the entire orchestra in concert, building toward the conclusion, the last violent explosions of harmony stuttering to resolution behind a viola's wandering, an oboe's plaintive search for admission. lifting to a conclusion that revealed for me, finally, for but an instant, the secret ecstatic vibration which is the essence of all that is, before it all ended in a silent resonance of clash and harmony.

For a moment, silence. Then the square erupted in applause, cheers echoed upward amidst the encircling stone walls, palms beat themselves raw against one another. Coppers and silvers, too, were flung by the handfuls into the air to dance and jingle at my feet.

"Gasparini: Long life! Gasparini: Long life!" they shouted.

A stout man in a three-piece suit threaded through the crowd toward me. He smoked a cigar contemplatively, nodding many times before he spoke. "Gasparini," he said. "You are a great man."

I bowed in humble acknowledgement.

"But you are nowhere."

8. Gasparini's Greatness

This person with the thick lips and cigar also had eyes which could envision. He turned them upon my organ; his gaze was distant, focused not upon its gleaming surfaces, but on the magnificent horizons of its possibilities.

"Gasparini," he said. "My name is Rupert Pozzezioni. I, too, like yourself, have vision, but not your genius to transport those visions into this dimension of the senses." He slapped his chest with all his fingers, felt his face, his lips, his eyes, sucked on his cigar and inhaled the smoke, paused, raised one finger. "But," he said. "I have something you no longer have. A factory. My factory is flourishing. You traded your skills as a manufacturer for art. I do not have art. But I have the factory. Currently it manufactures steamship supplies. One entire department of that factory is at this very moment idle, awaiting a good idea." He touched his nose. "My vision, coupled with your genius, can make of you a man of international fame, of world-recognized greatness." He gestured with his palms to the heavens. "The Great Gasparini. London. Rome. Paris, Vienna, Moscow. Prague. Berlin. Utrecht. Philadelphia. The Great Gasparini. Gaparini's organ. They will flock to hear it and see it, to be transformed by it. They will marvel. Who, they will ask, is this genius who has made this thing. *Auteur! Auteur!* they will shout, and I shall say to them, He is called Vincente Gasparini, and they will shout and clap for you as they did today, this handful of insignificant bumpkins. They will shout *your* name, Gasparini. You: Gasparini."

Rupert Pozzezioni gazed into my eyes and nodded slowly. "Gasparini, I want you to hear me now. I want you to listen. I am a practical man. I will convey you to the greatness. And I do not and will not lie to you. You, Gasparini, your creation, Gasparini's creation will be known and hailed in each of these cities I have named for you. I say this to you."

Rupert Pozzezioni did not lie. Not very much at least.

The factory department was created, tooled, commissioned, calibrated. Pozzezioni himself did nothing. He walked about in a three-piece suit smoking his cigar, available for consultations and decisions. He had a team of engineers to prepare the conveyer belts and assembly line and mechanized operations necessary for mass production.

To me, he said, "Gasparini, I trust you. I am surely a fool, but I will take a chance to let the heart prove its love. I will not ask you to sign any papers. Think what you could do to me, Gasparini."

To his engineers, he said, "Improvise. Simplify. Use your fancies if you have them. Had Gasparini been bounded in his fancy by that which already exists, this great machine would not exist today. Now you men in building the machine that will duplicate this feat a hundred times, must look again beyond that which already is to discover the art of the possible. Cost-benefit. Think: cost-benefit. Eat: cost-benefit. Sleep: cost-benefit. The future of this very world, this expanding, hungering world depends on: cost-benefit. The most for the least to the most."

To me, he said. "Gasparini, the French horns have got to go."

"Never," I said. "Never. The French horns must stay. Without the French horns we lack noblesse!"

"Gasparini," he said. "The French horns are a twentieth part of the entire production and demand a tenth part of the economic outlay. Furthermore, Gasparini, the French horns cause an irregularity of contour which makes packaging for the hold of a modern steamship vastly more difficult and, Gasparini, that which is vastly more difficult is vastly more expensive."

"Without the French horns," I said. "My dream and vision is defiled."

"With the French horns," he said. "Your dream and your vision begin and end here, leaving you once again, old maestro: nowhere."

My lips trembled. I swallowed. I saw him see these signs. His voice lowered, became tender. "Gasparini." he said. "You are such a dreamer."

"And you, Sir," said I, "are such a shit!"

He shrugged. He smiled. He placed a fresh cigar between his fleshy red lips. He winked.

9. The Death of Gasparini

Still, I saw the day when my instrument in a rank of one hundred flanked the docks in huge wooden crates, hoisted into the holds of a dozen ships. It was an instrument which resembled mine, though it had only half the strings, half the brass, no tuba, no French horns, and only an upright piano. It was programmed to play a medley of Strauss waltzes and Sousa marches. Across the front plate of the piano, etched in porcelain the color of boiled blue cotton, were the words "The Pozzezioni-Gasparini Music Maker." The machine was activated by inserting a five mark coin into a brass slot.

On the dock, Rupert Pozzezioni, standing before the gangway of the flagship of the commercial fleet, removed his purse and scooped out a handful of coppers and silver pieces which he pressed into my palm.

"Gasparini," he said. "I want you to stay in your romantic workshop. Do not change a thing. When they learn of your greatness in the great cities of the world, when they come to bring you fame, I want them to see." He pulled down his lower eyelid with the tip of his finger. "I want them to see what it cost you. I want them to see that for the genius, for the true artist, cost is nothing, benefit all. I want them to see the great Gasparini in the truth of his greatness." Now he was mounting the gangplank. I watched him from the dock, holding my cardboard suitcase, mouth open, charmed, yet uncertain. He smiled, bit the end from his cigar, spit it into the sea, winked and ordered the withdrawal of the gangplank.

"Wait!" I shouted. the spell shattering like thin glass. "Thief! Liar! Take me with you!"

The ship's horn hooted. The ship slid forward in the waters. White smoke billowed from the stacks into the gray winter sky. Pozzezioni stood at the railing of the stern and called through a megaphone. "I never lied to you, Gasparini. All that I promised you has come to be. You are a nice man, Vincente. The world also needs your sort. Bye-bye!"

That night, seated on the concrete floor in a corner of my icy workroom, a tattered wool blanket around my shoulders, a bottle of plum brandy between my thighs. I drank myself dull, and froze to death. The process was gradual, death followed life as the nail follows the finger. The progression was logical: first the chill, then the stupor, then the letting go.

10. Gasparini's Afterlife

In the end, of course, all, all is vanity. All is gone. The merchant, Pozzezioni, dead now for many years, a great man in his own right, dead and forgotten, his riches squandered by his children and grandchildren, the fruits of his efforts, second-rate mass-produced music machines, forgotten. Three of the original hundred still survive in old cafés in unvisited sectors of fading capitals. All that was mine, too, is gone; my wife, never again met, not even in the afterlife. The same for my poor children, who nonetheless, I am pleased to say, found modest contentment; they lived simple lives as public clerks, shunned artistic inclinations, or had none. They even buried their neglectful father and once a year visited his grave, upon which they planted flowers and a stone with my name and dates and the words: "Inventor of the Gasparini Organ." Could I speak to them, I would say, "Make that 'creator,'" but a stone is a stone, better than no stone at all, and believe me, it was a comfort as I lay here in that cold, damp wooden box, to hear the gentle thump of their knees as they knelt on my grave, hands clasped before them, faces lowered, eyes shut, turning their thoughts to the earth where I lay rotting. Now, they too are gone, childless, and my family line has ceased. My grave is untended, my body long since turned to dust. Only I still pace the earth, unseen but breathing in the drift of air.

My organ, the original, sits as a curiosity in the National Museum in Utrecht, rarely played. though sometimes on special occasions, once a year or two, the curator, a black-haired big-nosed man named Dr. Dr. H. M. Blankenberg, of great charm and love of mechanical music makers, holds a special exhibition, and I always come to hear it play itself, and this is the reward of my infinity. This is the treasure that I laid up in heaven for myself. For every time I hear the organ play, I am again on that street with my small hand in the large, warm hand of my father, seeing the marvellous blue eye of that pock-faced man holding the music box which touched the vibration at the heart of the heart, which transcended all but love.

As long as the organ plays, that reality of love survives, and all of existence for those few moments transcends all threats to it. It is enough, I think, to run a world on.

(1987)

Murphy's Angel

Murphy walked slowly from the bus, smiling lazily into the calm evening sunlight. He yawned, shifted his briefcase to his left hand, fished a Pall Mall from his shirt pocket, lit it, filled his lungs. As he exhaled the smoke, he whispered an ejaculation: "Lamb of God who taketh away the sins of the world, hear my plea." Which he had learned as a child was good for a sixty-day indulgence from the sufferings of purgatory for yourself or the deceased of your choice.

On his street, a neighbor lady, middle-aged and blond in snug red shorts, stood watering her roses from a yellow plastic sprinkling pail. She smiled with her eyes at Murphy.

"Nice day," she said and bent to pluck a weed.

"You bet," said Murphy, his eye following the turn and pull of red terry cloth.

Lamb of God who taketh away the sins of the world, hear my plea. Another sixty days. If he kept it up, the accounts might soon balance out. There was an even shorter aspiration *(Lord have mercy on us!)* which could be ejaculated four or five times in the same breath space as the *Lamb of God* one and was said to be worth as many days off each time, but he thought it wiser to hold to the more demanding course. As a hedge against it all, he also prayed to the stars and burnt seasonal offerings of fruit and vegetables from his garden in honor of unknown forces of cosmos and chaos. His right hand never knew which god's back his left was scratching.

As he approached his own lawn, the shadow of a bird glided across the sunlit grass. He paused on the sidewalk and surveyed the house. *Who would know?* The house *looked* healthy. The eggcream beige stucco was freshly painted, the shingles free of gaps, rain gutter and window frames glistened with white acrylic. The pink flamingo lawn ornament lent an innocent, fairy tale air to the scene.

He sucked the last drag off the cigarette and flipped it into the gutter, strode past the side stoop to the basement window, squatted and lifted away the wooden skid which he had placed against it some weeks before. Peering in through the bars into the shadows of the vast dim cellar room, he could discern the water tank like some extraterrestrial insect on its four tall spindly legs, the powerful squat-bellied furnace, the clotheslines, his tool-bench. A discarded, hingeless, knobless door lay on its side, propped at a forty-five degree angle to the wall beside the sewer lid, bolted down since the rat infestation two summers before. There, seated on the floor between door and sewer, was the angel. Its wings had molted and lay forgotten beneath the clotheslines, golden black like desiccated banana peels. It was clutching the backs of its biceps, where the wings had hinged, fingering them as though they itched or ached, and its knees were drawn up to its breast.

Alerted perhaps by a shadow, its pale face turned toward the window and saw Murphy's face there, then ducked away, pressing to the wall, gaze locked toward the floor molding as it tried to squeeze in beneath the lean-to formed by the abandoned door.

Idly, Murphy tapped at the window glass. The angel slouched tighter to the wall. Murphy noticed that the poor thing had found his old Wellingtons and drawn them on over its swollen, chapped, bare feet. Other than the boots, it was naked, and very pale. In the beginning, when they were still on speaking terms, the angel had told how its feet had been ruined in the Russian campaign. *Never go into Russia,* it said. *It'll be the end of you. If the peasants don't kill you, the elements will.* The angel had never explained its role in the campaign or even which campaign it had been. Murphy had never asked. Only now, when it was too late, did the question even occur to him. It saddened him that he had not extended more interest to the poor creature.

He stared hard at the bent figure, hoping for movement, some sign of activity, intention, but the angel knotted tighter, drew closer in beneath the angle of the leaning door like a shy, diseased fish in a tank.

Murphy drew the skid back over the window. His knees popped as he rose, and the blood rushed to his brain, dizzying him for a moment. He blinked, shook his head as the world dissolved and reappeared before his eyes, then lifted his briefcase and mounted the stoop to his front door.

Inside, in the living room, his little girl was dancing a mambo in front of a sleek, black sound system. Trumpets blared "Cherry Pink," and the girl swayed there, running her fists beneath first the one, then the other elbow. She was quite good for a five-year-old.

His eldest boy sat sprawled across an easy chair, staring intently into a *Dungeons and Dragons* comic book; on the cover, a Dragonmaster in flowing cape manipulated a series of strange creatures like marionettes on strings of fire which extended from his fingertips. Murphy's eldest was an enormous boy of sixteen, six-five at last measure with fifteen-inch biceps. He wore an armless tanktop shirt and shorts which stopped midway down red-haired thighs thick as hamhocks. Murphy was always awed when he gazed upon the boy, that such a giant could evolve from his and his wife's loins.

"How'd the game go, son?"

The boy looked up and smiled with little white teeth. "We creamed them to bloody pulp."

"Great! You score?"

The boy's protruding brow clouded. "It's a team sport, Dad. That's what matters."

"You didn't score." Murphy wondered, looking into the boy's blazing eyes, whether he had ever killed anyone when he and his friends went out prowling on weekends seeking good-natured brawls like you see in the movies. But the boy had good manners. No one could deny that. It was a great comfort and consolation to Murphy whenever he observed the dignity with which his eldest son comported himself on social occasions.

"Want to watch the Movie of the Week on Channel 7 with me, son? Starts at eight."

The clouds passed from the boy's brow. His eyes grew placid once again. His little white teeth smiled. "Thanks, anyway, Pops, but I got practice." He stood and rolled his comic into a tube and stood beating out the mambo rhythms against his thigh with it.

"See you later, Daddy," he said and affectionately palmed Murphy's balding pate as though it were the curve of a B-ball. To his little sister, he bent and said, "Keep shaking that thing, Sis. Make you a fortune some day," and let himself out the front door.

Murphy shook his head with admiring hopelessness after the boy, placed his briefcase on the floor, took off his summer jacket and began to slip it onto a hanger. A figure, his younger son, darted in between his legs and grabbed the briefcase, backed out, and dodged down the hall again. Murphy heard the boy's door smack to, heard the click of a padlock mechanism meshing shut. He chuckled, then frowned: the boy had been so contrary and belligerent lately. Murphy had thought it a mere phase, but his wife was beginning to talk about a psychologist for the boy. Maybe she was right. After all, there was no stigma in it, not anymore: everyone was crazy now. But how could you be sure you didn't get a crazy psychologist? That was what stumped him. Only last week, he had read in the papers about a psychologist who had hypnotized his patients and performed pagan rituals on them.

He hung his jacket in the closet with the animal skins, and called out, "Hi honey! I'm home!"

From the sewing room, his wife's voice snapped, "Don't you start with me now."

Murphy's lips parted. "All I said was..." He felt a geyser of indignation boil up through his trunk. He pictured himself bounding in slow motion down the hall, shouldering in the sewing room door and grasping his wife's slender shoulders, shaking her until the expression on her trim, heart-shaped face rattled, watching her river-green eyes open wide with fear, dropping her roughly down into her chair again and leaping out like a TV narc to kick his younger son's door off its hinges, seize his briefcase from the fragile, agile, undersized little monkey. Saw himself call a conference of dependents: *All of you. Out here. On the double! Now behave! Do you understand me?!*

No! he could picture his wife shouting back. *I never have and I never will!*

Murphy stomped his heel on the parquet floor to vent frustration. In the basement, the angel groaned, shouted curses, wept.

"Shut up!" Murphy bellowed and clutched his head, thinking about how reasonably most of the people in his office behaved, how sweetly the neighbor woman had smiled and bent to pluck that weed so he could view the glory of her bottom. If only people would be more manipulative and false at home as well as out in the world.

His little girl mamboed over to him, smiling, running her fists under her elbows. Her lips were rouged, her cheeks and eyelids glitter-striped. She was wearing a tight Latin skirt with a split down its front, a strawberry-patterned bra that sat flat against her young ribcage, and a Chiquita Banana fruit bowl hat on her head. She danced on stacked, shocking-pink espadrilles, while Perry Como sang, "Papa Loves Mambo."

Murphy beamed down at her. "Say, those lessons are really beginning to pay off."

His wife stormed into the room and tore the phonograph arm across the record. The needle zipped crazily over the grooves, amplified through the sleek black speakers. His little girl stopped dancing and glared.

"Mother and Father need time to *talk* to each other!" Murphy's wife shouted.

"Oh, *boy,*" the child shouted back and stomped off down the hall.

Murphy's wife slumped into the easy chair. She pinched the bridge of her nose, a crumple of kleenex like a paper flower ready in the other hand to catch any tears that might fall.

He said, "All I said..."

"Sure," she said. "Alleluia. You're home. Roll out the red carpet. Strike up the band. Serve the martinis. Shake out the olives. The hungry hunter returns. And what about me? What about us? Have you considered how it is for me to watch my own son masturbating at the breakfast table right before my eyes?"

"Oh that. So that's what it is. Honey, it's natural. We have always encouraged the..."

"It is not natural for a thirteen-year-old boy to masturbate at the breakfast table. Masturbation is a private act."

"It's just a phase."

"Just a phase. That is you in a nutshell. *Just a phase. Give it time. Wait and see.*" She pinched up her mouth, mimicking with an unkindly nasal voice. "And *what,*" she demanded, "I ask you for at least the fiftieth time this month, do you propose to do about that angel in the basement?"

"I need more time to think about it."

"You have had *more* than enough time to think. Now it is time to act. I want that thing *out* of my house. *Out.*"

Murphy glowered at her to indicate that his patience was reaching its limits. "What do you want me to do? *Kill* the poor thing? Shall I *drown* it like a barncat? Set a trap?"

"What you do is your business. Just do it, so I can be free of its whimpering and groaning and foul language, and its *stink*. And the embarrassment of being the only house in the neighborhood that has an angel in the basement!"

"Yeah. Sure. That's what matters, right? The neighbors. The neighborhood. Fine. *Great! Typical you.*"

"Fine," she mimicked in the unkind nasal voice. "Great!"

The unkindness of her tone cut him, and he bled anger, fury. His passion crested. He opened his mouth to bellow, but saw reason: his rage would only fuel hers. There would be no end to it. The evening would follow as a stream of skirmishes, screaming, sarcasm. Nothing would be accomplished. They would all be miserable. He would miss the Movie of the Week, which was starting pretty soon. He closed his teeth.

"Honey," he said, "I'm sorry. You're right I'll talk to the boy."

"*Sure,*" she said. "*Sorry,*" quieting slightly, though not yet quite ready to lay down her arms.

He allowed a tiny flare of anger to burn off before he spoke again. "I'll talk to the boy now. And I'll get cracking on the angel after that."

"I'll believe *that* when I see it."

"You'll see it. Just watch. You'll see it."

She snorted, but said nothing more, and he knew he had won the peace. "I'll just change my clothes," he said.

She followed him into the bedroom. He pried off one shoe with the toe of the other and kicked them across the room, unstrapped his shockproof wristwatch and let it fall to the floor, broke open his necktie and dragged it off, flinging it toward the bed. His wife picked up after him, smirking.

"Men," she muttered. He unbuckled his trousers and let them pool at his feet, stepped out of them. She touched the small of her back as she bent to retrieve them. Her white denim bottom caught his eye. It looked good. He would never have known it was hers if he hadn't been aware for a fact that her head was on the other end of it. He laid his palm against the pleasing white contours, embraced her from behind as she stood, pressing against her, thinking, *Just think, this could be the bottom of a completely strange woman.*

"Your butt makes me feel so young," he whispered into the small of her neck. "It's worth more than the Pope's brain." He nibbled her ear. "More than existentialism itself. It precedes essence by a long shot." She nuzzled against his mouth, smiling, allowing him his fun while she went through his trousers. Her hand came out of one pocket with a thick crumple of bills.

"My God?" she said and stepped away from him. "What is *this?*" She sat on the edge of the bed, deftly smoothing and sorting the bills: tens, twenties, several fifties. "Where did you *get* all this money?"

He gazed curiously at her. "Why I stole it of course."

"You could get in trouble, honey," she said, stacking the edges of each little pile.

He turned up his palms, offering honesty in a bid for reason. "It's my job."

Cocking her head, she said, "All the same," busily arranging the bills again so the portraits of Hamilton, Jefferson, and Grant all faced in the same direction. Watching her fingers move, the obvious tactile pleasure in their long, slender ministrations to the bills, pleasingly unctuous from the caress of hundreds, thousands of strange fingers before hers, Murphy became excited. He grabbed the little pile of fifties and stuffed them down the neck of her blouse. She closed her eyes and smiled, letting him do it. Then he buried half a dozen twenties in a crumple down the front of his jockey shorts and smiled demurely at her. "Shall we go fishing?"

This was their signal.

She chuckled and waved him off mildly. "You promised me something. *Two* somethings. Or have you forgotten already?"

"Will you go fishing afterwards then?"

Her smile was teasing. "I don't have a rod," she said and pouted up her lips. Murphy had to breathe through his mouth. "You can use mine."

Her eyes twinkled at him until he began to move closer again; then she said, "My goodness, we haven't even had dinner yet."

"*After* dinner then," he said.

"And what about the Movie of the Week?"

Murphy hesitated, considered, panted: "Maybe between dinner and the film."

Abruptly, from the living room, Perry Como began to sing "Papa Loves Mambo." Murphy rotated his fists under his elbows, swaying before his wife. She watched him with a private smile for a moment. Then she stood up and said briskly, "You go get some clothes on and have that talk you promised to have with your son and with the angel while I put dinner on. *Then* let's see." She kissed him briefly and ducked under his arm. His palm closed over a breast of air. He squinted and gritted his teeth, punched himself a glancing blow in the chest.

Lamb of God who taketh away the sins of the world, hear my plea. Another sixty days respite from the furnace.

Murphy donned his velour smoking jacket and fez, stepped into his slippers and padded down the hall to knock on his son's door. He could hear rustling, breathing, a groan. "Go away," the boy muttered breathlessly, "you'll ruin my climax."

"Don't mess up my new *Penthouse*, son," Murphy called through the door. "I haven't even looked at the centerfold yet." He stepped away, but turned back to say, "Come on into my study when you're free. Like to have a word with you."

In his study, Murphy sat in his five-footed safety chair and lit a Pall Mall. The cigarette's extra length seemed to filter the smoke and make it mild as milk. The milk of death, he thought idly as he tore another match from the book and struck it, touched the flame to a pellet of incense in a shallow jade ashtray on his desktop. He drew smoke deep into his lungs, set down the cigarette on the edge of the desk, bowed his head, raised his palms, turned them to face one another, said, *"In hoc signo vinces per aspera ad astra."* Bowed, clasped his hands over his groin and said, *"Oremus,"* and, in alternating voices of celebrant and responder: "Nomini gomini. *Nomini gomini.* Nomini gomini. *Nomini gomini."*

From the basement, he could hear the angel caterwauling, smashing things. Then it fell silent and began to sing in a cracked distracted voice: *"Tantem ergo /* Makes your hair grow. . .

Murphy slid the concealed leaf out from the end of the desk; a laminated sheet of paper was taped to it. He read aloud from the sheet:

"O Nosey who comes forth from Hermopolis, I have not been covetous without cause.

"O His-Eyes-are-of-Flint who comes forth from the slime, I have not caused crookedness of any real importance.

"O Eater-of-Entrails, I have not practiced usury to a significant extent.

"O Wanderer who comes forth from Bubastis, I have not gossiped unduly.

"O Serpent who writhes forth from the place of judgment, I have not committed adultery beyond the privacy of my heart.

"O Hot-of-Leg who strides out of the twilight, I have not swallowed my heart except in deference to men who could bring me to disadvantage.

"O Dark One who comes forth from the black hole, I have not been abusive of those who did not request abuse by their low cunning or unpleasant manner.

"O Flowing One who streams forth from apertures, my voice has not been loud except to rise above noisy backgrounds."

From the basement, the sound of the angel's shriek raised the hair on back of Murphy's neck. He slumped shut the leaf, raised his face and recited loudly, from memory: "Evil will never happen to me in this land of the Two Justices because I know the names of these gods who are in it, and the sins which are repugnant to them."

He stood, genuflected, chanted:

"May the god who is not known be quieted towards me.

"May the goddess who is not known be quieted towards me.

"May the god whom I know or do not know be quieted towards me.

"O my god, my transgressions are many, great are my sins.

"O my goddess, my transgressions are many, great are my sins.

"O my god and O my goddess, my transgressions are null, I have not sinned more than the next man and in many cases perhaps less to the best of my knowledge.

"The prohibited place on which I have set foot indeed was unknown to me."

The angel was coughing loudly, causing the floorboards to shudder, as though its mouth were pressed up against the ceiling beneath Murphy's feet. Murphy raised his voice:

"How long O my goddess and O my god whom I know or do not know ere thy hostile, majestically vicious heart will be quieted toward me and turn instead upon others whom I do not like.

"Man is dumb. He knows nothing.

"Whether he has committed sin or done nothing, he does not even know.

"The sin which I have done I beg you turn into goodness.

"The transgression I have committed, I beg you let the wind carry away.

"My misdeed I beg you strip off me like a garment and let my nakedness be innocent as a babe's. The transgression I have committed, I beg you let the wind carry away."

Then he knelt and bowed his nose down to the dusty parquet floor, rose again, fighting a sneeze, and bringing his palms together and apart again, said:

"Free my house of this angel. Deliver this house from the angel. Invite this angel from my house into the place of the noseless one to leave us at peace with our humanity. We are but poor creatures, O majestic forces of the cosmos and the chaos! We have a hard time upon the earth. We are worms beneath the feet of giants. Spare us this troublesome presence. Let us be humans among humans, for no man is an island unto himself. We despise one another, but we cannot be alone. Therefore, deliver us of this foreign angel. Amen forever, sow without anus, goodbye."

He finished just in time to retrieve his cigarette from the edge of the desk before it scarred the wood. He puffed the last drag off the butt and stubbed it out in the ashtray beside the ashes of the incense. It squeaked against the polished surface of the jade, and the sound caused the hair on his arms to lift. The angel had fallen still. Murphy stared at his own face reflected in the black glass of the window above his desk: the eyes and nose and mouth were hollow in a pale, transparent oval. He blinked, snorted the thick sweet scent of the incense from his nostrils, wondered who he was, what he had done, why. He blinked again. A tear beaded on his eyelash.

Lamb of God who taketh away the sins of the world, hear my plea.

"Dad?"

Murphy turned to see his boy in the doorway.

"Dad, I'm sorry."

Murphy smiled. "What are you sorry for, son?"

"That Jesus had to die for my wickedness."

"Son, no one knows for sure why Jesus died. It is a matter of speculation."

"Dad?"

"Yes, son?"

"Is the Movie of the Week rated okay for kids this week?"

Murphy smiled, opened his arms, and the boy rushed into them. They embraced.

"Dad?" the boy whispered. "Am I a midget?"

"Why, no, son, you're just petite."

The boy was rubbing his palm with the fingers of his other hand. "Can that be caused by masturbation?"

"No way, buddy. Why just look at your brother. He jerks off like crazy and he's as big as a house. Course, he does it in private and keeps it secret."

After a silence, still looking into his palm, the boy asked, "Dad? How do you confess masturbating?"

"Masturbating is not a sin anymore, sonny."

"But when it *was* a sin."

"Well, I used to confess it as an act of impurity perpetrated upon myself by myself when in my own company."

"Do you still masturbate, Dad?"

"Practically speaking: never."

"Well, uh, do you and Mom, you know, get it on?"

"Yes, my boy, we do, as you put it, *get it on.*"

"Do you go down on her, too?"

"Let me put it this way, son: when you love a person very much, you wish to kiss them everywhere. 'Nuff said on that, I guess."

"Dad?"

"Yes, son?"

"What's on the Movie of the Week this week?"

"I don't know, son. But it's usually good. What do you say we two pals watch it together?"

"Yeah!" the boy said with an enthusiasm that warmed Murphy's heart.

"There's just a couple of things I've got to do first, son, so you run along now and I'll be with you in a snap. Why don't you set the table in front of the TV." He wasn't going to get any from his wife anyway. Maybe he'd get lucky later.

He watched the boy move off to the task and felt blessed, loved, graced by good fortune. Then he remembered the angel and felt cheap again, dirty, false. He doffed his fez and lay it on the desktop. Then he opened the center drawer, took out a tiny heart-shaped tin and pried off the lid, removed a key from inside it.

At the end of the long hallway, he ran the key into the lock of the basement door, twisted it, heard the bolt fall away. The staircase was dim. Peering down into the darkness, he experienced scraps of memory, a heap of broken moments from his childhood, stray fleet glimpses of remembrance swimming at him swift as fish up out of a black sea. He thought of his father, dead these half-score years; his mother dead but one; his brothers and sisters with whom he ate roasted turkey twice a year, grilled beef and boiled corn once a summer. He thought of Jesus who some believed had died for the sins of men and of how he had lost his love for the Lord when finally he had embraced the conditions required of him to engage in human love. He sighed. Climbed slowly down the stairway into the cellar.

The angel lay on its back beside the extraterrestrial insect of the water tank. The furnace growled as it burnt black gold within its powerful belly. The angel's breathing was unpleasant to listen to. *Die then. Die now and be done.* Murphy took out his handkerchief and blew his nose, honking like a duck into the cloth. He knelt beside the pale, fading creature. Its eyes rolled toward Murphy's face.

It said, "Death stands before me today as a man longs to see his house after he has spent many years in captivity. The light in the west is lovely, burning gently in that place beyond which the darkness has been smothered by the dark itself. The light is lovely. I shall sleep. You, old friend, shall continue a time in black darkness after I am gone."

Murphy asked, "Will it be tonight?"

The angel's only response was a hissing, labored breath.

Murphy heard the clock in the living room chime the quarter hour: almost time for the Movie of the Week. He asked, "Can I bring you something? Water? Food? Something to read?"

The angel inhaled sharply, jetted dead air from his nostrils. His skin glowed brighter for a moment, dimmed again. "I truly used to feel that you loved me, Murphy. At certain moments. When you smelt the rain, heard jazz, tasted gin. When you kissed your children or your wife, when you bathed your head in water. I truly believed that you loved me from the root of thy heart."

Murphy spoke softly. "I did that, angel."

"You do not love me now, Murphy, and I am sorry for you. I shall die, but you shall live without that love. With nothing but the other so-called love."

Murphy bowed his head. "You never wore the skin of a man, angel. You tried so hard to make us into radiant creatures. You—" Murphy stopped speaking and looked more closely into the angel's open, staring eyes, its slack mouth, its still, unlifting breast. The light of its body was dimming rapidly, fluttering up for a moment, dimming again, glowing like a phosphorescence shedding the last fuel of light absorbed over many years.

A sob croaked in Murphy's throat. He hiccupped. Shook his head and wiped the corner of his eye. He whispered, "Angel, what did you do in the Russian campaign? What did you learn there?"

There was no answer.

He crouched to lift the naked, cold body in his arms, but the first contact of dead flesh against his living fingers had him leap back in horror. The feel of lifeless flesh, he thought, is *dreadful*.

Up above his head, he heard the basement door open, and his younger son called down furiously, "Dad, the Movie of the Week is with Bing Crosby? I *hate* Bing Crosby, and I think it all *stinks*! I'm going to *bed!*" He punctuated the declaration by slamming the door so hard that flakes of plaster jumped from the basement wall. Murphy didn't much care for Bing Crosby either, though he would have gladly pretended to enjoy the film for the sake of his boy's company. Now he hardly knew what to do. His wife would be furious with the boy if he didn't join them at the table for dinner. And then she would be in no way inclined to play go-fishing with him afterwards. Not that he was much inclined just now either.

Murphy put his face into his hands. Upstairs he could hear Perry Como singing: "Papa loves mambo: Mambo, papa. Mama loves mambo: Mambo, mama."

He could hear the tiny feet of his daughter on her stacked espadrilles, dancing one-two, one-two-three. He pictured her sweet young face, thought, *The future, sweet child is yours: Please be happy.*

He crawled on his knees across the concrete, deckpainted floor to the wall, laid his back against it, drew his legs to his chest. He stared at the fading radiance of the angel's body. From upstairs, he smelled the roasted pleasures of supper, heard Perry Como's voice, his daughter's feet, saw her face, his wife's face, his youngest son's, his oldest's, the neighbor lady's snug red bottom, his wife's broad white one.

In a moment, he would climb back up the stairs and back into their lives. In a moment. For he needed them now, more than ever, needed to be close to them. But first he thought it only right and fit that he should witness this last fading of the angel's light.

Lamb of God who taketh away the sins of the world, hear my plea.

(1989)

THREE: DRIVE DIVE DANCE & FIGHT

(1997)

BONNER'S WOMEN

WHAT IT TAKES on such a day, to refresh a tired heart, is an Oak Bar martini in a cocktail glass—gin, rocks, dash of Noilly Pratt, three olives on a tiny wooden spear, and a little glass dish of quality peanuts. The uplift is instantaneous. Dry chill across the lips and straight to the brain.

Let this moment last forever, a magic circle within the best bar of the best hotel in the world, surrounded by the gathering darkness of unimpeachable December. Sleigh bells tinkle on the muzak and smarmy voices sing *Let it snow let it snow let it snow...*

Bonner agrees. Good blizzard do this city good. Whiten the desolate wind belching through the skyscraper canyons, make his kids happy. A woman at the next table, wearing a sprig of holly and two red plastic bells pinned to her blouse, has a crooked grin plastered across her mouth. Bonner glances away, sips his gin. He avoids handling the glass, not to melt the ice too quickly, helps himself to peanuts, feels good among all the well-dressed Christmas shoppers with their coats piled behind on their chairs, red-nosed, nests of colorful shopping bags around their feet, living Christmas trees sucking up sweet cocktails.

Yet no matter how he looks into his gin, straight down or from the side, held up to the light, he sees right through it to what he has promised Jenny he would do today after work. Still he lingers, studies the level of the drink, considers ordering another, sees Jenny's face in his mind's eye saying, *Another one, Fred?* thinks about Jenny, his son, his daughter, the promise to visit his mother, a promise which requires two martinis to fulfill.

Fred, we have been back from Ohio for nearly a year and you have seen her exactly twice.

I call her. Every other week. Almost always.

Either you go see her and invite her for Christmas dinner or I will!

The waiter moves within his field of vision; Bonner raises one finger and both eyebrows, points at his drink.

In a glass phone booth that looks one way into the bar, the other out to Central Park South in the dingy snowless afternoon, winter trees, stone wall, gray boulders, crosstown traffic, Bonner punches the number he knows as well as his own social security number.

As he listens to the ring, he watches a chestnut horse, nostrils spuming steam, step past in the road with a policeman on its back, thinks of his horse-crazy eleven-year-old Sandra, as his mother's voice, small, suspicious, noncommittal, New York-accented, speaks into his ear: "Hello?"

"Mom, it's Freddy."

"Freddy? Are you calling from China?"

"China! We were in Ohio! Mom, we've been back for a year. I spoke to you last month."

"From China?!"

"Mom. From Farmingville."

She chuckled. "I'm sorry for laughing, Freddy. Do you live on a farm now? Imagine that."

"It's the suburbs. I drove you out there last summer, don't you remember? We had a barbecue? Try to remember it, Mom."

"I have such a headache."

"Take an aspirin, Mom. Have you been to the doctor's?" As he speaks this sentence, he lifts his glass to his lips, and someone entering the bar catches his eye. A tall woman in an elegant linen suit the color of champagne, short hair framing her face in an array of delicate black curls. Bonner catches his breath, whispers, "Jesus, Mary, and Joseph," while his mother repeats Dr. Scrivane's detailed analysis of her headache.

"Isn't Scrivane getting kind of old, Mom?"

"Well he's younger than me, Freddy!"

The woman's gaze sweeps toward the phone booth, and Bonner feels his cheeks redden. He doubts she could have seen him, but she nods, once, curtly, and Bonner lowers his gaze, instantly regretting having done so. Beside her is a man he knows slightly, blue cashmere topcoat over a silver suit, a newly elevated vice president, a chunky dark man who looks something like a middle -aged Richard M. Nixon. Bonner notes the way the man squeezes her narrow waist as he guides her to a table. Bonner wishes he were home with his wife and children where he should have been. He glances once more at the woman. She looks older, but not much so. Her skin is still good. The curls on her brow. Eyes large and green. The way her face looks, smiling at her vice president there, envy turns inside him. *Catherine,* he thinks as he tells his mother he will be over shortly, places the phone back in its cradle, experiences a moment of extreme regret that he ever met her, that he had seen her again here, that he was forced to remember what knowing her made of him:

> *You should hear what they say*
> *About you: cheat cheat...*

A picture comes into his mind of his father kneeling to pray in the shadows beside his bed at night. He looks at the red stone in his St. John's College ring reflecting light through his gin on the shelf of the phone booth as he lifts the martini to his mouth and watches Catherine in her linen suit watch the vice president who is not her husband. How effortlessly she lied, simply did as she pleased and kept it to herself. Bonner asked her once if her husband knew. "Of course not," she said. "That would be cruel."

Her boldness seemed a new way of life to him. For a time. For the months he carried on with her. Then one evening, over drinks at the Bibliotheque, she told him something, and it occurred to him he had no way of knowing whether she were lying to him. It was an inconsequential matter, something about a cancelled appointment, a change of plans, but he looked into her face and asked, "Are you lying to me, Catherine?"

Her green eyes met his, startled. "Of course not," she said; and he realized he would never, ever know whether she were lying. About anything.

He hates the thought of the rest of his day, the visit to his mother, the Long Island Railroad home to Jenny with the memory of Catherine's face in the Oak Bar, green eyes looking up at the vice president as they once looked at him, the kind of look that could make you feel big for a while. He dreads that this thing is inside him, a smudge on his life. How he wishes he could tell

Jenny, be forgiven, be cleansed of it, tries to tell himself there is no such thing as cheating, you only live once, thing is not to cheat yourself of the few small pleasures available. But there is no pleasure outside his home anymore. And still there was that smudge.

The IRT Flushing Line screeches around the elevated track, curving up above Bridge Plaza. Face close to the glass of the door window, Bonner watches the Plaza turn past beneath him, sees the golden doors of the Bridge Plaza Savings & Loan Association behind which his father passed the bulk of his adult life, the Star Hotel, at the door of which a man and woman now stand in the eternal posture: negotiating. A perfect Hopper. The landscape of factories, neon Silvercup letters in the late afternoon dark in this place where as a child he rode his bike, roller-skated, fished for killies in the now-filled swamp, shoplifted at Sears & Roebuck's, adored his mother, loved his father, cherished his sister. A happy childhood. You had to learn discontent in life, as his brother James had, leaving them as he did, abandoning them to a life that was no longer ideal, a life he invalidated and then left them as a legacy.

His mother peers from behind a police chain as Bonner waits, sucking a mint, thinks about time, which seems suspended like Zeno's arrow, the little units of seconds it takes, half-life of seconds, for the chain to rattle out of its slot, the door to open, his mother's face to appear, body to enter his embrace, affording him time to recover from the shock.

So small and fragile against his palms, within his arms, she seems even smaller, her face older since last he saw her a few months before. His nails bite into his palm with remorse at his own negligence, having put this off. *I couldn't help it.* Her hair is totally white and wild. Bonner himself has just entered what he thinks of as late youth. At eighty, she is twice his age, a little old woman with a haunted look in her eye which used to twinkle.

The familiar smell of the apartment, neither sweet nor sour, a warm smell, close, closes around him as he shuts the door, watches his mother's fragile vein-corded hands carefully re-latch the chain. *You used to be so beautiful, Mom.*

"Would you like a Coke, Freddy?" she asks.

He looks at her, looks away, looks again, trying to reaccustom himself to his mother as an old woman. It occurs to him that he does not remember her this way when he is not with her. In his memory, she is still young, still looks a little like Donna Reid.

"You sit down, Mom. Let me make you some tea."

"I'd rather have a Dr. Brown's Cell-ray tonic."

Bonner in the kitchen pops open the refrigerator door, swears it is the same GE of his childhood, knows it couldn't be, rummages through the bottles and jars there, checks the date on a Hellman's mayonnaise, does a double take. Best if consumed three years ago.

As he prises ice cubes from a metal tray, his eye wanders over the array of plastic coasters, scraps of flowered paper, a flank of empty screw top jars, a lopsided, played-out stub of Brillo pad, which fills him with unaccountable sorrow. All at once he knows in his body that he cannot stay much longer.

He wanders the living room, a Bonner museum, museum of his childhood, ice cubes clinking in his glass of ginger ale, looking at bookcases, books, knickknacks. A white plaster Our Lady of the Television stands atop the old RCA console, a statuette Bonner won for collecting the most money in the class Might Box Drive of 1963.

Other mementoes are ranked behind the glass of his father's father's bookcases. One of them is filled exclusively with red books. "Who did this, Mom?"

"I'm not sure," she says and sips her Cell-ray tonic. "I think I did. Do you like it?"

"Nice." He opens a cabinet door and lifts out a little metal Roman chariot he assembled and painted thirty years before. He glances at his mother, a little old woman with wild white hair and terrified blue eyes.

"Mom, do you get some help here? Is anyone helping you?"

"Your Uncle Martin comes by frequently."

"What does he do for you?"

She stares at him for a moment. "I can't remember. Isn't that silly?"

The whip wielded by the charioteer is a length of string Bonner soaked in Lepage's glue thirty years ago so it would stand up, as if in the arc of a swing behind the Roman's back. And still it stands in arc. Testimonial for Lepage. Bonner holds it close to his face, studies the leather flaps of the charioteer's armor, the ornate handwork on the chariot itself, the wheel hubs. There are other figures Bonner painted, outfitted with armor he had made from bits of cardboard and tin, little cannons, tiny scenes of rebels defending a stone wall Bonner built of pebbles, glue, and grass clumps.

He remembers sitting in his room in the old corner house where they lived for his first nineteen years, remembers spreading newspaper across his desk, working with tiny bottles of paint and number-one brushes tweezed to a hair, copying coats of arms from a heraldry catalogue, remembers the smell of glue and paint and thinner, wonders what kind of a kid he was after all, what kind of kid would sit and squint over this junk.

"It's amazing you still save these things, Mom."

"What things?"

"These tin soldiers."

"James was so fond of them."

Bonner sips his ginger ale. "James?"

His mother's eyes lighten in the dust of her face. "Yes, he was so diligent. I'll never forget how he labored with the tiniest details, even their eyes! Why he even painted the eyes! The whites *and* the irises!"

Bonner sets his glass down on top of a bookcase, beside a jade Buddha, picks it up again and wipes away the water ring with his handkerchief, sets the glass down again. He touches the wall for balance as a single word, syllable, simmers in his consciousness: Me! I *made these!* He shuts his eyes tight, sees James in the chair in his apartment, smells him, sees the shattered forehead. No note, no reason, he never even said goodbye, the poor guy, poor Mom, think if Phillip ever, but he wouldn't, never.

Bonner picks up his ginger ale again, sips. "Jenny and the kids send their love, Mom."

He knows the smile she shows him, her polite smile, the smile she used to flash to hold off neighbors she was not in the mood to talk to. "When did you eat last, Mom?"

"Eat?" She is staring at her hand, a tiny fragile thing, turning it over in front of her eyes as if trying to figure out what it's for.

Bonner makes her a cream cheese and olive sandwich on whole wheat bread, puts the tea kettle on and sits staring at a picture of the *pieta* on the wall, while she eats the sandwich. In a cardboard frame on the sideboard is an oval portrait of his mother's sister, Constance. Bonner remembers her as a cynical woman whose favorite expression when called upon to care about something was, *What is that to me? Who is he to me? What are you to me?* Bonner looks at his mother intently munching her cream cheese sandwich, and a thought, a question enters his mind. *What are we to each other? What are any of us to one another? What is the meaning of our life together?* For an instant, the question seems an entry to the core of a great mystery; then it eludes him, the words go flat, he cannot retrieve the force of their first appearance. It occurs to him that love, emotion is not a thought but a feeling, and that too seems a brilliant observation for a moment until he recognizes how obvious it is, and it all slides through his fingers.

From the kitchen, the kettle shrieks. His mother sits at the table making sounds which Bonner slowly recognizes as a song. She sings, "Seventy-six trombones led the big parade!" She smiles at him. "James phoned me from China on my seventy-sixth birthday to sing that to me."

Bonner pours steaming water over a Lipton flowthrough. Should you humor them or not? "Actually it was *me*, Mom. I phoned. From Canton, *Ohio*. I was on a business trip and couldn't get home, so I phoned. James was already gone when you turned seventy-six, Mom."

"I wouldn't know about that," she says, warming her hands around the tea mug. Bonner has begun to notice how *very* quiet it is in the apartment, quiet and still, close. His breathing steepens. He watches his mother's blue hands lift the tea mug to her old woman's mouth.

"How about another sandwich, Mom?"

"Yes!" she says, her face alight. "I want one of those Greek ones!"

"Greek?"

"Yes! Where you take a piece of bread and some cheese and olives and *then:* another piece of bread."

"Is that Greek?" he asks, spreading cheese on whole wheat. She stares at him. "Well, why?"

Bonner just smiles. "It's okay, Mom," puts the sandwich in front of her, pours more tea.

"I'm so hungry," she says. "I haven't eaten all day." She reaches into her mouth, removes a piece of metal bridgework and puts it on the table, nudges it with her fingertip as though it might begin to crawl, mutters, "Damnation." Bonner watches her eat, watches her begin to collect crumbs from the plate on her fingertip.

"Mom, Jenny and the kids and I are looking forward to your coming for Christmas this year. I'll drive you out. Jenny ordered a great big bird."

She blushes. "Well, that's *awfully* sweet of you, Freddy, but I already promised James. I always have Christmas with James. He would be disappointed." She lowers her voice. "Otherwise he'd be all alone, you know."

Bonner smiles, thinking. "Well, James could come, too. It'd be great!"

She shakes her head slowly, skeptically. "I just don't know, Freddy. I'll have to discuss it with him before I say one way or the other."

Beneath the edge of the table, Bonner looks at his watch, says, "I'll have to be off now, Mom."

She pecks up a crumb and deposits it in her palm. "Be sure to give my love to James," she says, "and don't forget the Bufferin. I have *such* a headache!"

"Mom, I've got to go. Do you want me to call Uncle Martin?"

"He's such a prick," she mutters. "He said mean things to me and hit me, but my father gave him a good talking to."

"Uncle Martin loves you, Mom."

"Perhaps," she says. "Perhaps. With linen napkins on their laps. They loved me with a hundred hates, the dinner heaped upon their plates."

"It's fantastic how you can remember poems, Mom. Do you still hear from any of your old students, that girl, woman, what was her name, that always brought you flowers at Easter?" She does not answer, seems not to have heard. He is in the foyer, pulling on his topcoat as he asks this and hears her begin to sing again, low in her throat, a tuneless, gravelly murmur he finally recognizes as "The September Song."

"Dad used to love that," he says.

She stares at him. "He did? No, I don't think so. He liked

'Miss Fogarty's Christmas Cake' and that other one, that *terrible,* vulgar one about the goose."

Bonner chuckles, sings, "Don't give me no goose for Christmas, Grandma! Stop it! Cut it out! Now don't you dare…"

"*Stop* that!" she hisses at him, furious. Startled, he crouches by the armchair where she sits, puts his arms around her. "Hey, Mom, it's okay, don't worry, Mom." She sits stiffly in his embrace, like a child humoring an affectionate parent. It occurs to him that he cannot remember the last time she so much as mentioned his father. Her husband. He remembers the wake, the funeral, twenty years before. In the beginning, she used to talk about him: Your father this, your father that. He thinks back on their life, what he saw of it, tries to remember affectionate moments between them. He wonders if she still misses him, still feels love for him, would like to ask, but fears upsetting her, knows he cannot stay to try to calm her again if she gets upset.

He climbs slowly down the stairs and into the street, the papery feel of his mother's forehead on his lips, the lines of her poem ringing through his brain.

The light is gone. A few scattered flakes of snow float on the cold dark air above his bare head. He stops at the corner, knots his scarf around his throat, spots a flat empty wine bottle in the gutter. He stoops for it, studies the dirty, cold glass against his palm, the dirt-smeared Thunderbird label, pictures some bum, some lost abandoned man, huddled in a freezing doorway, sucking from this bottle. Abruptly, he smashes it against the dark brick wall beside the Chinese laundry, shielding his face from the spray of glass.

He ducks out onto the avenue, beneath the EI, grateful for the rumbling IRT that fills his brain, his body, plugs his ears from thought.

"Did you see your mother?" Jenny asks.

"Yes, sure."

"How is she?"

He shrugs, measuring gin, vermouth, spearing olives. "You want?" She nods. "Mom is not a young woman, Jen."

As the gin steams over the crackling ice, he recalls the face of Catherine gazing up at the vice president and feels dirt in his heart, and wishes to God he could tell her, beg forgiveness, but knows if she refused absolution he would hate her, and he knows he will not do it, thinks idly about all the big jets at JFK and how it would be to stick your head into one of the turbos as it revs up.

"Did you invite her for Christmas dinner?"

He nods. They are sitting in leather frame chairs by the front window. He sees lights in the windows of the other houses along the street, feels some comfort in the expanse of his lawn, thinks about how much it will cost to put her in a home, considers the alternative. Jenny might, but he can't, he can't have her live here, and the certainty of the knowledge makes him wonder who he is now, finally, at the age of forty. He wonders what it is about Jenny that she might do it, even for *his* mother, but he knows for sure he couldn't, wouldn't. What was the difference between them?

"Well?" Jenny asks.

Bonner raises his glass in salute. They sip. "She said she already promised James." Jenny stares at him. "She always has

Christmas with James, you see. But she'll talk to him and let us know."

"You have to explain to her, Freddy."

He nods, whispers, "I told her James could come, too," looks surreptitiously at her, sitting about five feet away from him in her chair, calculating what moves it would take for him to bridge that distance, thinking about the slight, feisty little girl she was twenty-two years ago when they met on the beach at Hampton Bays, and he sang to her so she smiled, *Jenny Jenny Jenny won't you come along with me…* He puts his drink down on the drum table, sits forward. Their eyes meet.

She reads his intention, says, "Help!" and dodges up from her chair into the kitchen, but he saw the light in her gray eye.

As they make love that night, Jim Morrison on the radio is singing *Hello. I love you, won't you tell me your name?* and he looks down into Jenny's gray eyes, whispers *Jenny Jenny Jenny.* Her mouth opens in a smile of pleasure, snow light on her teeth. He says, "I love you, Jenny."

Afterward she falls asleep against his chest. He switches off the radio, lies watching the dark ceiling, remembers Catherine's eyes in the Oak Bar, thinks of his mother, his father, wonders again if she still misses him sometimes, thinks tenderly of him. He wonders if she was ever glad to be free of him, and what that means, whether it matters. The gauze curtains float in a draft of chill night air. He tucks the covers up around Jenny's shoulder, studies her face, the wide pretty mouth, the almond, almost Asian shape of her Irish eyes. A novel question enters his thoughts: he wonders if she ever cheated on him, tries to remember times where there might have been opportunities, men with whom she might have wanted to. He knows he deserves no better, wonders if it matters. What might matter, he thinks, would be not the act so much as the lie, the secret life intruding between them. If she ever did. He read in an article the other day that women cheat as often as men but are better at compartmentalizing it. Still, he doubts it.

Downstairs, he makes the last drink of the night, trying to calculate which number it is as the gin fumes, cracks the cubes. He remembers something he read once, Kafka maybe—a book must be like an ice pick to chip away at the frozen sea within us. But he is using the drink to numb his mind. It is long enough since he was last drunk that he is not worried. He wanders barefoot through the dark house, not discontent. He has nothing to be discontent about really; only he wishes he could have just stayed a little longer with his mother, wishes he could somehow have done something for her. What good would it have done to stay another hour? He thinks with fear about if he would ever have to clean her if she soiled the bed, thinks about his Uncle Martin. He had always found Martin somewhat irritating, a fussy thick-lipped man who often nagged Bonner about his hair and his clothes and his studies those years after Bonner's father died and he was still in college. He tries now to compare himself to Martin, and it occurs to him he no longer knows quite who he is. Did I ever know? Do I have choices? Can I help being whoever the hell it is I am, the kid who painted toy soldiers, whose mother is so old now, whose kids are growing up, who cheated on his wife and has to carry that around?

At the wide front window he stares across the lawn, registers the fact that it is snowing. Big flakes fall steadily down the dark sky, and he smiles to think how the kids will cheer when they wake if it is still coming down. His son tonight made him laugh when Bonner told him, "Hey, sergeant, clean up that room, will you?" and Phillip said, "I'm no sergeant. I'm a major." Bonner said, "Yeah, a major disaster," and the boy shot back, "Well you're a general nuisance," as he dragged his butt off to clean up his room, but turned to smile at Bonner's laughter, pleased at the response to his wit.

They are growing away from him, both of them, especially his little girl, and he thinks of his mother in her apartment thinking of her dead son, Bonner's dead brother who shot himself in the head for reasons only he knew.

He wants to go up to speak to his little girl with whom he had been so close for so many years and who now mostly smirks at him as he had been warned would happen by more experienced fathers he knew, though he had doubted it, believed the love between him and *his* kids was stronger than nature.

He makes it to the top of the stairs, but stops outside her door, which is darker than he recalls it being.

Then he realizes it is wide open, the dark only the dark of the room. He sits on the floor with his cocktail and stares through the open black doorway to where his daughter sleeps in the dark, and tries to think about this person who rides on the backs of horses. He remembers how she told him about a game she plays with her favorite stallion, Phoenix, who she cares for lavishly with many small brushes, metal hoof cleaners, oils and apparati. The game is that she holds a carrot stub concealed in one hand and crosses her wrists in front of Phoenix's nose and says, "Which hand, Phoenix? Which hand do you want?" and Phoenix shoves at her hands with his snout until he finds the carrot.

Bonner sniggers at the thought of this little kid playing with such a huge animal like that. He leans back against the bannister behind him, cross-legged on the hall runner, smiling, thinking about it, picturing it.

He wakes suddenly there in the dim light of his home staring through a dark open doorway, frightened for an instant. Then he hoists his aging body up to his feet and shuffles down the hall to where Jenny Jenny Jenny sleeps, and the snow of a long overdue blizzard clicks against the panes. He can already hear the kids at the big front window, seeing the lawn white with virgin snow, cheering.

(1994)

KANSAS CITY

JOHNNY FRY STEPPED UP Columbus, sporting shades and suede, headed for City Lights. In from Copenhagen, high on jetlag and jumbojet booze, he had a plan, a mission. To buy a book of poems by Ferlinghetti. To meet Ferlinghetti. Ask him questions about all those years ago when Fry lived his life by the creed of poets. See if Ferlinghetti's thoughts of a gone time could help him understand what had happened to his own life.

In the store, he lined up at the register to give his money to a slender woman whose face, he could see, had rid itself of expression, a hardbody in baggie jeans and flannel shirt. To see her smile, he thought, would floor him, she was so cool. He wondered if she were gay. It occurred to him that, given the right moves and counter-moves, his entire life might deflect off this chance moment.

A young man behind the counter addressed the woman, calling her Velma. *Velma! Perfect!* She answered with no change of her expressionless expression, and Fry fell in love. Fry fell in love frequently and he was aware of this, a heart suspended in its own helplessness. Bimbo, he told himself. Middle-aged male bimbo.

Velma paid him no heed as she rang up the price of his purchases. As it should be, he thought, yearning for her. He removed his shades and asked, "Uhm, Velma? Is, uhm, Larry around?"

She assessed him with one eye, quickly registering, he could see, that he was nobody. She read the name on his credit card. "No, Johnny," she said. "I don't know where he is today."

"Think he'll be back? I'm only in town for the day."

"Couldn't really say," she said.

Fry shrugged. I'm nobody, who are you? He gazed over her shoulder at a tee shirt display behind her—black shirt with a silver logo he did not recognize, a straight-stemmed 'Y' containing a circle. It seemed important. If you don't ask, he thought, you'll never learn. "What does that stand for?"

The young man next to Velma smiled behind his tongue. "Martini glass," he said. Facetious.

But Fry saw something here. A message. He bought a shirt, stripped to the waist there at the counter, delighted to see Velma's gaze go to his chest for an instant. *She wants to see me naked!* He donned the black City Lights shirt, then his suede jacket, nodded once to Velma, thinking goodbye, you are not my new life, and stepped out to the street again.

He stood on the corner, glanced across at Tosca's one way, Vesuvio's the other, where he remembered years before sitting to watch the world walk by in its curious shoes. Yes, and he remembered, one particular afternoon, watching Gregory Corso at a table by the window, wearing an army field jacket, leafing through a book, a drink on the table before him catching the strange light of the afternoon. The scene was imprinted in him, Corso's wide flat nose, his toughie face, the book, the light, but only now did he recognize that drink. It had been a martini in a cocktail glass, colorless and luminescent.

Across Jack Kerouac Alley, he took a seat by Vesuvio's little front window, the very spot where Corso had been. The waitress, another hardbody heartbreaker, approached him with her face in neutral.

"Blue Cork gin martini, please. Shaken, straight up, with one olive." He figured she figured him for an asshole, but martinis were important, and she looked just as cute walking away as she did walking to him. You're a mess, he thought. Bimbo brain. No hope for an aging male.

From where he sat he could see both entrances to City Lights in case Ferlinghetti came or went. He took out his purchases—A Coney Island of the Mind and a City Lights postcard. Tacky, but what the hell? Like Jack Kerouac up on Mount Tamalpais with Gary Snyder, waving: Hi, Mom!

He planned to read the book, one eye on the street, one on poetry, and let his brain chill in gin for an hour or two. Maybe somewhere in there, he would write the postcard, too, to Vivi and Martin, his ex-wife and twenty-year-old boy. Take advantage of the fact that for eighty-two cents, you could send a message eight thousand miles, from San Francisco to Northern Jutland, to the house that used to be his home in a country where he lost his tongue for twenty years.

He met her here, in San Francisco, across this very street, in Specs, with her Danish accent and her Danish tits and was lost to her. Mystery of a mode of speech, shape of flesh, the sway of a hip, turn of a hand, a gaze, the light in the eye, and when she left, he crossed the country, crossed the sea after her, caught up with her on the tiny peninsula atop the peninsula of Jutland. She was charmed by his pursuit. He remembered her feeding him buttered radishes from a picnic basket in Skagen, beer and snaps on a blanket in the sand. Wild boar paté. Footy-flavored blue cheese on dark rye, there on the beach where the water of Skagerrak met the North Sea in a frothing seam.

What if I hadn't gone to Specs that day and what if she hadn't? What if I hadn't heard her accent, hadn't looked, charmed, hadn't spoken to her? Five minutes either way, two minutes, one, decides the whole fate of the bulk of your life. How? Why? Do things happen simply because they happen?

Across the street, several people entered City Lights, but none was Ferlinghetti. He'd heard Ferlinghetti read once, at the Jazz Cellar, twenty-five years before, had listened to him chanting "Junkman's Obbligato" and took it as existential prescription. Let's go, let's go, empty out our pockets and disappear into the soul still night of the flowery Bowerey. He remembered camping by the Big Sur River, reading it by flashlight, Let's cut out on the whole scene, cancel all our appointments and show up years later, old cigarette papers stuck to our pants, leaves in our hair, and his brain felt clear as the mountain river plashing past his sleeping bag. Clear as the hundred-proof Blue Cork gin delivered by the delicate hand of the waitress.

She put the drink before him and squeezed his shoulder, startling him with pleasure, to know he existed for her, whose face and body were so nice. "You really like City Lights I guess," she said.

"I've got to find Ferlinghetti," he said. "It's important. Goin' to Kansas City tomorrow."

"What's there?" she asked with a turn of her cute lip that answered her own question: Nothing.

"Twelfth Street & Vine," he said.

She watched him, not quite understanding but not quite put off. He didn't quite understand either. He only knew that Twelfth Street and Vine was another thing he'd never done, a place that had beckoned since he was thirteen when Wilbert Harrison sang to him about it. Who could say? The words had hit his mind like a window, a place where something waited for him maybe. Who could know what might be around this corner, that one, at some intersection you hear a song that says you've got to, all the difference made at every single turn of every single moment every single day every single face you gaze upon and turn from.

A tall thin man walked up Kerouac Alley, and Fry craned to see but was certain it wasn't Ferlinghetti. On the sidewalk a little boy, head round as a globe, bounced a spauldeen pink as Fry's childhood. He pitched the ball at a curbstone so it would snap back to him, but it hit a fault in the concrete, fluked, struck a lamp post. The boy lunged for it, missed, ran after it, bouncing crazily down the hill.

Fry sipped his gin and addressed the postcard, printed a heading of date and place and stared at the white message block. What? Greetings from Vesuvio's! Or Hi, small Fry's! Greetings from Yerba Buena. Maybe some poetry. High society is low society/the upper middle class ideal is for the birds/but the birds have no use for it/ having their own kind of pecking order/based upon bird song.

He sipped his gin, considered his jet-lagged brain. He must speak to Ferlinghetti soon. He had no way of knowing what the man might say to him. It was necessary to actually speak to him. It was not sufficient just to read his poems. This poet was very old and still alive. He had perspective. Fry had to hear the words of his very mouth. Tell me what you think, Mr. F. Is it still true?

A fact intimated itself; he had to pee. What if Ferlinghetti came while he was gone? He would have to take the chance. On the way to the gents, he passed two young women at a table, one of whom was saying to the other, "I got a revolver and he's got a semi-automatic. My attitude is, with a semi-automatic, is that sometimes they jam. A revolver never jams. It makes me feel safe."

At the next table, a woman holding a bottle of Moosehead was saying to a man, "That's nothing but attachment to the opinion of others about you, so fuck it."

He could still feel the touch of the waitress's hand on his shoulder, fueling his heart. It occurred to him that a touch was important, could be important, and wondered again why she touched him. Maybe she was just a touchy type. Or maybe she recognized his need, that he was fucked up and that a touch could help him. Maybe he should touch her? Or maybe he shouldn't. Maybe that would lead to unpleasantness, charges of sexual harassment. That is not it at all, that is not what I meant at all.

On his way into the gent's he came face to face with a guy on his way out. "I'll tell you what else is in Kansas City," the guy said. "I heard you said you were on your way. There's a picture, a painting. It's called *The Midwife*, painted by Francois Gautiere in 1776. It's at the Nelson Atkins Gallery. Check it out, man. It'll change you!"

The man's face was pale, his choppy hair tinted green. His breath smelled like a wound. Fry backed away, and the man's pink eyes glared into his as he slipped past. "Do it, man."

Fry was trembling as he stood at the urinal. Printed on the white tile wall at eye level was the message Second hand smoke made me do it. And, Women—just slap em around. And Vow. Vow? Vow.

On his way back to the table, worrying whether he might have missed the coming or going of Ferlinghetti while he was away, looking about nervously for the man with the wounded breath, the waitress touched him again, hand on his shoulder. He touched her elbow. She touched his wrist. "Julius," she said, "in the kitchen, says that Ferlinghetti is up on Mt. Tam today. Julius says he favors the Cataract Trail. Know where that is?"

Tears filled Fry's eyes at the sight of her, at the message that she cared to deliver to him, and he recognized that his interchange with this woman would go no further than this moment, even though he was certain he would remember her all the rest of his life and each of the three touches. He thought of the Housman poem of two persons' eyes meeting on a street in passing, then deflecting. Mystery of another road.

Fry steered his rented Mustang across the Golden Gate, March sunlight glinting on the green bay and remembered for some reason a day—when?—in a cab from Galway to Cong, asking the driver what water they were passing. "Ahhh... Now that would be sea water, y'know. Some people would call it a lake, but it is sea water for sure."

Vow, he thought. Vow what?

He rolled through a cleft in the green hills and turned north up past Sausalito, Mill Valley, onto the tortuous road up the mountain, twisting the wheel, leaning with the curves, past a sign that read Wind Gusts. A thick milky fog descended as he rose, and soon he could no longer see more than a foot or two beyond the nose of his car. He slowed to fifteen, ten, hunched over the wheel.

There was a breach in the fog to his left, and he looked down a sheer drop of some thousand feet into a marvelous valley. He felt his fear, recognized there was nothing to do but continue forward. He pictured himself missing a turn, slapped by a wind gust, careening over the edge. The fall, the pain, explosion, death by fire, trapped in a sculpture of twisted metal. How long would it take? How much would it hurt? Where would he go then? He thought with satisfaction of the fact that his insurance was in order. Vivi and Martin would suffer no want. But they would find secret things among his possessions that he had not yet got round to throwing out, things that revealed matters not meant to be known. Undignified. Private. Nothing to do about it. The truth at last. We all have our secrets.

The fog hung low and white over the Cataract parking area, but on the trail there was more visibility. He climbed briskly, urged on by hunger, the fear-sweat on his back cooling to be replaced by the healthy sweat of exertion. In the inner pockets of his suede coat he had a bottle of mountain red, a baguette, half a pound of Swiss cheese, a sweet Walla Walla onion, numerous small envelopes of French's mustard, and his Swiss army knife. At the top he would sit with his book and his food. Perhaps Ferlinghetti would find him there. Perhaps he would find Ferlinghetti first. Surely the coincidence of this meeting would overpower any resistance in the man.

The trail wound back and forth across a stream, mounted through the green, brown trees on a ridge slanting up from a rapids. He stepped over rocks and roots, jumped on his toes through a slog of mud, leaped from stone to stone across a washout where the stream had swamped the trail. On a tree stump he saw a banana snail. A bird articulated in the trees above his head, telling the woods he was there.

He came to an abandoned picnic area, considered sitting, but pushed on. He could hear his own breathing in his ears, felt an intense loneliness, a longing to see someone else, but recognized in these sensations a certain joy. The trail continued to rise, more steeply, and he breathed through his mouth. He passed a sign that warned of a sharp, slippery ascent, realized he was near the top.

The trail was very narrow now, corkscrewing around a grassy peak above the tree line. Here the fog was patched around him. From time to time he could see the expanse of valley and hill sweeping away down below, green of tree and white of fog blowing slowly across, glint of river in the crease. He paused to gaze down over it, turned and saw the peak just above.

He sat in the grass munching his food, sipping wine from the bottle, and watched the valley below him, the green of vegetation, the floating white smoke of mist. The food was excellent, the onion and cheese, mustard, the wine, and it was so still there, so empty and still and vast.

Spread between his legs was the paper bag, torn open to serve as a placemat. He set down his sandwich on it, dug a pad from his pocket and printed The Midwife. Francois Gautiere. 1776. Nelson Atkins Gallery. He stared at the words, bit off more sandwich, chewing thoughtfully, printed Vow.

The United Airlines Fokker Friendship taxied out onto the rainy Denver runway. He had seen one of the pilots—a woman, who had greeted the boarding passengers. She was cute, a trim petite blond with a nice smile, a pretty face. He had a daydream about her. Meet her in some bar in Kansas City, say, "Weren't you...? And, "Yeah," she says, "I noticed you, too..." And they're drinking martinis and Patsy Cline is singing on the jukebox. "Crazy..." Now she's locked in the cockpit. Did she have a wedding ring on? Vowed to be faithful to another.

Vow. A word. What did it mean? To vow with your fingers crossed? Only he forgot to cross them.

The little plane shivered in the rainy wind, waiting for take-off clearance. What is a vow? What is it for? Maybe it was a case of hanging your pictures where your nails were. I took vows in a church when I married Vivi. She took vows. We both broke them. But not without regret. Before we even realized what was happening, we were out of love and looking back wondering what it was we had and lost and never understood.

"I vow." A word. The word "dog" does not bite.

As the plane began to roll, pick up speed, lift, it occurred to him this was foolishness. The motor whined and wings wobbled, and Fry suddenly felt like an idiot, leaving San Francisco earlier than planned, changing his reservations to win a few hours—for what?— having to route through Denver. It was Ferlinghetti's fault. He had met the poet finally, a fluke, caught him floating like a ghost among his poetry stacks upstairs at City Lights, white-bearded, short-haired, with a green jewel studded in his one earlobe. He was arranging the shelves of his books, his own books. Fry cornered him and plied him with questions, while Ferlinghetti tried to get him to spring fifty bucks for his new Fantasy CD version of the old Jazz Cellar cuts.

"Fifty bucks to you is nothing when you consider how favorable the exchange rates are from kroner," the poet said. Velma looked on expressionlessly as Fry backed away: I am only temporarily a tie salesman.

Now, in the Fokker, he thought about the word vow, thought it really ought to be in a poem, wondering if he would write that poem, if he could. He plumbed his mind for an opening line, but his socks were askew and annoying him to distraction. On the horizon, the light sky ended in a ceiling of angry gray.

He took out the little notepad in his shirt pocket where he had copied down the details about the painting from the man with the wounded breath. Maybe it was a lie, fake. Why did I even listen in the first place? He tore the page out, balled it up and stuffed it into the armrest ashtray, looked up for the stewardess, to order a drink, but remembered there was no liquor on these little jobbies. A young man walked down the aisle toward the rear of the plane, headed for the loo, fair-haired like Martin, clear-eyed, moving past, away again. A pain of separation touched Fry's gut. He thought of Martin at three, running along the gravel driveway to greet him after work. Martin at twelve, chubby and serious with horn-rimmed glasses. Martin at sixteen, slim again, athletic, toughing it out. Martin at twenty, gone from him, an ocean away.

Behind him somewhere two children were arguing. "You big baby!" And "I'll 'pit on you if you call me baby. I'm gonna do it!"

Their parents were bickering as well. "Well why didn't you put your racket in the bag." "Don't worry, I'll carry it." "No I'll carry it."

"Well why don't we just start a fight in the middle of the airplane!" And "I saw that!" "But he kicked me in my shoe!" And "He kicked me in my shoe again!" And, "You're gonna get it, honey!"

Americans are so loud! he thought. Hollering into their mobile phones, into one another's faces, into strangers' ears. He opened his newspaper, read an article about Vincent "The Chin" Gigante, another about a boy who had won a science project with a visualization of surreal numbers, projections of infinitely large and infinitely small calculations, an article about the Tootsie Roll company which was celebrating its hundredth anniversary, describing the factory process, the never-ending sheets that look like brown vinyl turning into thick chocolate logs, becoming thin snakes dancing forward until they're dropped and wrapped at a speed far faster than the eye can see.

Fry was perspiring. In the row ahead of him two huge mormons sat shoulder to shoulder, blond giants in black suits, their beefy shoulders pressed together, their knees pressed against the seats in front of them. Fry felt for an instant as though he had always been here in this little plane, always would be, fate without end, headed perhaps through a machine that would press him into brown vinyl, dancing chocolate snakes at a speed faster than the eye can see.

At that moment, lightning struck the plane, bouncing off the wing. The plane dipped, dropped, bounced.

A woman behind him screamed, and Fry, sweating, heard himself say, "No need for alarm. Everything is all right. No need for alarm..."

For a fleeting moment, he glimpsed deep within his mind Vivi's face stripped of flesh. No lips. No fucking lips! Just teeth! Grinning hideously. "Everything is all right. No need for alarm!"

Across the aisle one row up, a dark-haired moustached man chewed gum vigorously, teeth showing as he opened his jaws wide and snapped them shut, eyes fixed hard on the seat back in front of him. Just over from Fry sat a man of sixty, slender in a double knit blazer, leafing calmly through a magazine.

The plane seemed to have stabilized, and then the woman pilot was speaking over the P.A. "You may have noticed we hit a little tur-bulence back there so I'm lighting the seatbelt sign. Please keep them buckled at all times while seated..." She had a nice voice. Imagine her singing. "Crazy..."

Fry had his shoes off, tugging to get his socks to sit right, won-dering what the fuck he was doing here in this stupid little airplane in a storm over the Rockies. For some reason he thought of Vivi grown old, thought how it would be if she died, the two of them apart after all those years they'd been together, having Martin, rais-ing him, splitting. Her mortality gripped him. Don't let me outlive her! Bending to tie his shoelaces he couldn't catch his breath, and he noted the fact that he needed a drink. Needed. First road sign on the way to twelve-step city.

He sat up, desperate for company. The man in the double-knit blazer, he noticed, was reading a magazine about fox hunting.

"Tally ho," said Fry.

The man eyed him. "Ware heel," he said.

"Pardon?"

"That's what you say if the couple—the hounds—get deflected from the scent of the fox and take off after a hare."

"Well ware heel, then," said Fry.

"You ride?""

"No."

"What do you do for danger?"

"Me? I fly. And I drink."

The nearest tavern was on Brushcreek, half a block from his hotel. From where he sat at the bar, he could see three things: (1) out the window, across Brushcreek, on a wide expanse of yellow grass, an enormous shuttlecock as if fallen to earth from The Badminton Game of the Gods; (2) at the end of the bar, a woman with short henna hair and a kind, vulnerable face, thin lips with lavender lipstick smudging the rim of her Manhattan glass; (3) mounted on the wall above her, a TV set showing CNN so Fry could watch her without seeming to.

Why must I constantly feed my eyes on women? The fuck is wrong with me?

On the screen above her head Bob Dole was saying, "You ask Bob Dole what he thinks the election is going to be about? Bob Dole thinks, going to be about bad news. Be about the future of this country, about foreign policy, about our defense policy. Be about youth, values, honesty, decency, self-reliance, jobs, family, leadership. Lot of issues left. I'm certain something will pop up in November so we'll be able to put it together. If that's what you want, I'll be another Ronald Reagan. One thing is pretty sure, though. I think it is pretty well ordained now that Bob Dole will be the nominee."

The woman down the bar signalled the bartender for another Manhattan.

"You got it, Nora," he said, and Fry took in her name, thinking it a few times like a smooth, pleasant object you might absently take up from a shelf or table top to soothe the fingers of your mind. He could speak to her. He could ask, Where did Nora go?

A Louisiana preacher was now on the screen saying, "We know Pat can not lose because God is looking for a man who will stand up against the Devil's man in the White House."

Above the cash register, a Schlitz clock shimmered with various neon liquid colors. It read half past three. Fry planned to book a ticket out early in the morning, but he didn't know where to go. He wanted to walk down the bar to Nora and look into her sad eyes, hold her hand, wanted to hold her naked body and hear Dylan sing, "Sad Eyed Lady of the Lowlands."

And he wanted desperately to do none of these things. He raised a finger to the bartender and let it dip toward his tiny empty martini glass. Three thirty-two on the Schlitz clock. The giant shuttlecock on the yellow field across Brushcreek, he knew, was a work of art by a Danish sculptor, Claes Oldenburg, and the building behind it was the Nelson Atkins Gallery where, according to the man with the breath wound, *The Midwife* by Francois Gautiere (1776) hung. The Gallery, he knew, because he had asked the cute black girl at the hotel desk, closed at four p.m., and the Schlitz clock informed him it was now three thirty-three.

Nora stirred her swizzle stick through the caramel-colored drink, and the bartender, who made Fry think of a tall gray alien, delivered another martini. The Schlitz clock said three-thirty four, and Fry thought again of the man with the wounded breath. *It will change you. Do it, man.*

Abruptly his heart lurched at the thought of leaving Kansas City without doing this thing, following the message carried on the wounded breath. Then he was on his feet, slapped a bill onto the bar, down past Nora, leaving that untapped potential fate behind as he ran for the corner to do what he could for another fate, crossed the boulevard, and sprinted across the yellow field to the Nelson Gallery.

*   *   *

There were four rooms of eighteenth and nineteenth century European works, but he could find nothing by Gautiere and nothing that depicted a midwife. His heels sounded along the marble corridor from room to room. There were portraits, family scenes, pastoral landscapes, but no Midwife. The rooms were vast and windowless, the light greenish-beige.

A black woman guard wearing an olive drab uniform watched him. "You look like you lookin' for something specific," she said.

He told her about the picture, the name of the painter, and she stood comfortingly close to him as he spoke, her side touching his arm, shaking her head slowly. "I been here fifteen year and never saw a picture like that you saying to me. You know I sometime might forget the name of a painter, but I never forget a picture, and I never saw that one here. Try Norm in the bookshop. He know a lot about what we got."

But Norm in the bookshop sent him to the information desk where a skeptical middle-aged woman with a tic that made her seem always about to sneeze confessed that the information desk files were not completely à-jour. Then Norm came out again with an out-of date exhibit catalogue. "If you find it here, it might be in storage."

A clock above the vaulted entry said three forty-seven and on page forty-eight of the catalogue he found a three-by-five black and white reproduction of Francois Gautiere's The Midwife.

By now, the black guard, Norm and the sneeze-tic information woman were all gathered around him. They clucked with pleasure at his find and sent him along the far corridor and down the back stairs to the office of a curatorial assistant named Nadine Flower.

"You're from *Denmark!*" Nadine said. The clock on the ledge behind where she sat read three fifty-six. "I've been doing some research on the Danish Golden Age painters which has led me to the Skagen group. Aren't they just marvellous?"

"They are," he said at three fifty-seven.

She rose, a file in her hands, led him along the hall as she spoke. "I hope to get there myself one day." She keyed in a code on a door, and he followed her through and down a series of blunt corridors. "I just adore the colors, the light."

"Oh yes," he said, remembering. "There is noting quite like the Danish light. I mean people speak of Mediterranean light, the light in Venice and so forth, but I've never seen anything like Danish light. You know Magritte's Empire of Light? That gives a clue to Danish light."

Her eyes followed him brightly as he spoke. "You must love Denmark very much."

"I don't love Denmark very much anymore," he said. "I mean I like it. I like Denmark. I love the Danish light. But..." He could not explain himself, could not bring himself to try to articulate what he felt about his adopted country, about himself, his life, about how he had savaged his own heritage by leaving his homeland, by living all these years in a foreign place that would never quite be his and that would never quite let him go.

They stopped outside a broad thick door with a single round porthole window in the center.

"It's like a woman," he said then, lunging at a thought that seemed to promise an explanation, and her bright, curious eyes watched him. "It's like you fall in love and then it ends but it never ends. You grow up in a place and then you go away and you come back and it's gone and you left something there that you'll never be able to retrieve now. Do you see?"

She nodded rapidly in a way that made him doubt she did, but he was thinking how good it might have been if when he was younger he'd been more stable and met a woman who was a museum curator with these bright light eyes. If he had married her mother this young woman could have been his daughter now. He wondered what her mother did for a living.

"It's like that," he said. "Everyone you love takes a part of you. Everywhere you ever lived has something that's yours. And what do you have? Memories. Longing. It's not all bad, don't misunderstand me, it's not. But nothing is ever the same as you thought. You read a poem and it goes into your heart and you live by it and thirty years later you don't know for sure what it meant, you see? Or whether you should have gone this way or that way, or, like, what does your mother do for a living?"

Her finger tips touched his arm. "Are you all right?" she asked softly. "Would you like a drink of water?" She pointed at a metal fountain on the wall. He bowed to it, pressed where it said Press and caught the cold arc of water on his tongue. It chilled his teeth and freshened his brain. Water, he thought, is everything.

Nadine keyed in yet another lock code, and the broad door with the little porthole swung open. Behind the door, a uniformed guard with a large pistol on his broad hip nodded, eyeing Fry. The room was huge, arrayed with aisles of raw wood shelving with rack after rack of paintings. Fry's heart lifted and dropped at the sight. All this art! Stored away. It occurred to him that these people did not own these pictures. No one owned anything. Everyone just bluffed their way to a piece of the action.

Gautiere was already out, set up on a raw wood stand for him to view. It was large, perhaps three by three feet, oil on canvas, and he caught his breath at the sight of it, simply because he had found it.

Nadine opened the file. "You've picked the best of Gautiere," she said, reading from a sheet in the folder. "This was painted in 1776. In a rustic interior are seen four figures outside a room, two couples, one aristocratic, the other obviously peasants, servants. In the room a woman is giving birth, assisted by a midwife. At left, behind the aristocratic couple, a woman who might be the mother of the woman giving birth stands gazing upon the scene with an expression at once benign and suffering. The midwife we see only in the shadows of the room, tending to the birth, but her profile is illuminated by candlelight. This was later engraved by Nicholas de Launay and enjoyed great popularity."

She turned a page. "It is interesting to note the moral Gautiere was teaching here, suggesting an understanding and friendship between the aristocracy and peasant classes several years before the catastrophic French Revolution. If this lesson had been heeded, the great upheaval of the Revolution might have been averted. Dismissing the subject matter, the painting itself gives every evidence of the ability of Gautiere which ranked him with any of the lesser painters of his period." She turned a page. "Would you like to hear the details of the frame maintenance done in 1983?"

Fry shook his head, studying the painting for some clue as to how it should change him, why he had been led to this moment. His brain teemed with wonder at the intermesh of a million details.

What led me here today to this moment? When I was thirteen, in 1957, wearing new black chino slacks I had bought especially for the event, for a day that seemed like the first day of my life, I went to the Brooklyn Paramount Theater to see Chuck Berry, Buddy Holly, Jerry Lee Lewis, Fats Domino, Little Richard, but the figure who caught me was Wilbert Harrison singing "Kansas City," up on the stage in a red suit with his glittering guitar, and at the first instant I heard the words Kansas City bark softly from his mouth, I knew one day I would go there, but how could I know the real objective at the end of the parade of tiny events and details leading me to the realization of that? What was the meaning of this painting? Why am I here? I haven't even seen Twelfth Street and Vine.

He figured that Nadine, watching him closely with her bright intelligent eyes, must think him mad. She could not know why he stood looking at this two-hundred-year-old mediocre yet skillful painting with water in his eyes, and he despaired of being able to explain it to her, how beautiful and pointless and lost it all was. He put his palms over his face, turned away, removed his hands and saw, on a large rough table before him, another painting on a frame.

"That's one of my Danish acquisitions," Nadine said. "Ancher's Meeting of the Waters."

To catch flight 911 out of Newark for Copenhagen that next day necessitated a hop from Kansas City to St. Louis at 6:05 a.m., which meant getting a taxi for the airport at 4:30 a.m. That taxi was driven by a woman of perhaps sixty-three, unremarkable in appearance, but talkative, and in the course of their conversation, her conversation rather, as the taxi rolled along the highway through the pure dawn darkness toward the airport, she said, "Well, I live in town now so I can't keep the kind of cats I'd like to anymore."

Still half asleep, Fry felt the phrase reach into some private areas of his mind, prodding gently at some lever. "What, uh, kind of cats did you mean?"

"Well at one time I had four mountain lion, a leopard, a cheetah and three bobcat. But all I'd have now would be mountain lion. Now your mountain lion is a sweet animal by nature, but she does smell, I'll tell you that, and you need room out in the country for her. My leopard was also a dear animal, but she took a liking to my little Bobby, and I tell you she'd go right after my knees, slash 'em, if I said a bad word to that boy. She followed him around wherever he went. She was a one-boy cat, she was. Bobcats are honeys, too, but they have a temper."

Fry peered out the side window of the taxi into the darkness rushing past, and the moment posed unanswerable questions. Did I seek Ferlinghetti to find the man with the wounded breath to search out Gautiere to be shown Ancher to send me back to Denmark so that I could be intercepted by this bizarre monologue at an ungodly hour in a dark vehicle in this city I heard sung about as a boy? Or is it all chance? Flash without meaning.

A mystery to ponder for the next many hours and thousands of miles of transport, over land and sea and land, plane to plane to train to sandworm, depositing him none the wiser in pre-Easter midafternoon out on the tip of Grennen, the branch of sand jutting out into the place at the tip of north Jutland where the waters met. He expected a revelation here, but nothing occurred to him. The sky, the horizon were gunmetal gray, the air a chill mist, and he felt the power of the water drawing him. In his mind he saw himself walking to it, felt the cold shock of it enveloping his feet, wrapping around his legs, his belly, chest, felt the power of the crossing tides tip and swirl him away.

No.

He turned away, half expecting to see Vivi standing there, Martin, a woman with a leopard, something, but no, there was nothing. Perhaps this little chain of events had reached its end. Yet the thought of Vivi led him back to his rented car and into the town, near empty at this time of year. He parked in the square and continued on foot, past the Ancher house, pausing for a moment to think of the Gallery in Kansas City, the woman Nadine with her Danish acquisitions. And stepping out of the little museum shop as he stood gazing at it was Vivi. Not so remarkable. She lived here.

They embraced—stiffly at first, then his arms tightened in around the warmth of her closeness, and they clung there on the breezy street beneath the yellow trees.

"One thing is clear," he said, "I'm sorry to say, I don't love you anymore."

"No," she said. "Me neither. I don't love you any more either."

His face found the warm crook of her neck, within her woolen collar. "I mean I like you," he said.

"I understand," she murmured. "I don't like you either. Your breath is unbearable by the way."

"Thank you. How is Martin?"

"He has had his eyebrows pierced and has joined a band of autonomes who de-stroyed a McDonald's in Copenhagen last week. He asked me to give you his love if I saw you. He did very well in his first year examins, and I said I thought you vould vant to give him something for that."

"Of course."

"You really should do something about that breath. I really can't bear it."

So when they parted again, it was with both relish and rue, waving once from opposite ends of the street before she turned the corner and was gone, the woman from Specs whose accent had so enchanted him, with whom he had joined to detour the bulk of his life, live here, create Martin, raise him. Perhaps Martin is who counts here.

Behind the wheel of his car, he keyed the ignition, pulled away from the curb, bouncing over the cobblestones of the town square, headed alongside the gray swelling coastal waters. He pulled in down a roadway of pounded sand and sat staring through the windshield out to the waters, the seam of their meeting. Two seas joining. A mystical thing. A place where matter was so clearly charged with the spirit of its existence. He thought of the airport, considering the things that had happened to him in the course of his years, the things that might lie before him in what remained of his life, wondering if perhaps his fate, everyone's fate wasn't in reality one, leading inexorably through time, through history, through all the days of all our lives to the same unknown conclusion that awaited us around one corner or yet another or somewhere in between.

(1996)

Drive Dive Dance & Fight

IT HAD BEEN RAINING for seventeen days when the lights went out.

Twomey fumbled into the cabinet over the sink for the flashlight and descended to his basement to have a look at the fuse box, discovering, as he stepped off the bottom step and water filled his slippers, that the basement was flooded. He cursed, wondered if it was dangerous to change a fuse standing in water, couldn't make up his mind. He climbed back up to the kitchen, socks and slippers squishing on the wooden steps, and sat at the formica kitchen table, thinking about who he might call.

He could pick a plumber, an electrician from the Yellow Pages, but they would be sure to scalp him. Maybe if he called Con Ed, they could tell him whether it was safe to change a fuse with your feet in water. It made him feel stupid and clumsy to have to ask that. His father had been a great handy man, except he was dead. His mother, too. The only family left was his brother who lived in Atlanta, a thousand miles away, tending the regional headquarters of a truck rental firm. Karen was gone, too. Even the cat had run off.

He thought of phoning Karen, actually went so far as to sit by the telephone with his hand on the receiver, on the verge of dialing the number he knew by heart now, Karen's sister's, where she was staying since she'd left. But then he saw again how futile it was, how ridiculous to keep after her. For whatever reasons, she did not love him. That would never change. The more he loved her, the more her lack of love seemed to grow, as though it were contemptuous of him to still care for her. Maybe she hated herself and could only have contempt for anyone who loved her. He considered that thought for a moment. How would it explain his own psychology? A guy stuck on a woman who didn't want him?

He went out into the living room of the little house and stood at the front window watching rain fall along the street. It was really coming down. Incredible how it could just continue like that. It was late September, already almost dark at six. Very dark actually. The trees were silhouettes, all the windows of the houses across the road dark. Then he noticed the street lights were out, too, and the traffic signals.

His chest lightened. He felt good again, connected to the world. We're all in the same boat here. No juice.

Across the way, a small boy stood on the front stoop. Twomey thought for a moment how it might have been to have children with Karen. The little boy turned around and went into his house. Twomey didn't know the boy's name. He didn't know the names of anyone on the street, only a few faces. He'd lived here for less than a year, in the house he inherited from an aunt he barely remembered. Perhaps Karen was attracted to the house, had only accepted his proposal because of it. The possibility roused pain and hatred in his heart.

The house next to the little boy's was a smaller house where a woman lived alone with many cats, a woman in her late thirties, maybe more, a little dumpy-looking, weary-eyed. She seemed lonely. He had tried talking to her a few times, and when she learned Karen had left, she gave him a kitten, a six-month-old tabby. Twomey brought it home, and it ran in under the sofa and wouldn't come out again. He got down on his knees and peered under. He could see it there, green eyes glowing, big with fear. One eye had a mote in it. Twomey tried to reach in with a shrimp to coax it out, but the cat spat and scratched his hand. It stayed there. Then, later, when he opened the door for the mailman, the cat darted out. It lingered around the house for days, but would not come in again. It sat up on the back fence watching the house, cried like a banshee at night. Then one day it was gone, and he decided maybe it wasn't such a hot idea to be friendly with the woman after all.

In the other houses were families, an older couple in their fifties with grown children, and further down a man a few years older than Twomey, thirty-five or so, who lived alone and had various girlfriends Twomey had seen coming and going. Twomey wondered how the guy did it.

At the corner, just visible if he bent and stared obliquely from the edge of the window, was a shop with a sign that said *Atlantic Plumbing Supplies.* The display window was empty, smudged with dust, *For Rent* soaped on the glass. Twomey experienced an unaccountable sadness. The word *Atlantic* made him think of the ocean, which he loved, and seemed to suggest an optimism crushed by a system as indifferent and unimpeachable as the weather.

He thought of the water at Atlantic Beach where some of his

old college buddies sometimes used to go scuba diving. He sat on the beach and watched them suit up in hot high summer or nippy early fall, watched them trudge out into the sea, slip under into another element. He compared those thoughts to the idea of the faceless person whose plumbing supply business had failed, and the comparison seemed filled with an almost overwhelming sadness.

A figure was coming along in the rain, the man with all the girlfriends. He wore a wide-brimmed hat and a blue trench coat, wet on the shoulders. Twomey watched him climb the brick stoop to his door. In the alley, shining with rain, was a bright red BMW. Twomey looked out at his own lawn, the single tree, a magnolia, bare now, like an empty candelabra, the spotty grass, the driveway where the old secondhand blue Vega he'd bought was parked, right where the Iranian cook he'd bought it from had delivered it, cultivating body rot along the edges of the quarter panels. Ought to put it away, he thought, out of the rain. But he didn't have his license yet and felt funny about driving, even just into the garage. He remembered Karen, early on, asking, "You don't drive! Why not?"

"I hate cars," he said. "Scourge of modern civilization." And remembered the old Ford skidding in the snow as he fought for the wheel, and it flipped, remembered hanging in the seat belt, listening to the drip of water from the radiator. "Amazing," the young emergency intern said. "Not a scratch on you. Can't see a thing."

"That's it for me with cars," Twomey said.

"Nonsense, you got to get right back on the horse."

"No."

He went out to the kitchen and sat by the back window. The rain stopped. A tall mass of dark clouds rose up against the sky, but at the top was a strip of blue and sunlight, bright red along the upper rim of the tall cloud bank. Fall sunset, the first in weeks. The hugeness of the sky made him feel small, agreeably so, a little creature in a great universe.

The kitchen light came on a yellow bulb in a glass shade that looked like a fancy clam shell stuck to the ceiling. He went out to the front door, crossed the street to the house where the guy with all the girlfriends lived and rang the bell.

The guy came to the door barefoot in a white open-collared shirt, combing his hair with a blue plastic comb. Twomey introduced himself. "I'm sorry to bother you, but my cellar is flooded and I wondered if you have some kind of pump or something I could borrow."

"Frank Getz," the man said and plucked some brown wispy hairs from his comb, dusted them off his fingers. "I guess I have a pump." He and Frank Getz stood behind his house drinking Jack Daniels on the rocks and watched the flexible pipe dribble water into the soggy earth of his back yard.

"Haven't seen your wife lately," Getz said, and Twomey thought, *That s how to do things, just ask.*

"She's not my wife actually," Twomey said. "Almost was. Got cold feet." He liked the sound of that. Her fault. No sweat. Win a few, lose a few. Plenty more fish and all that. He waited for questions, but none came. Then he realized it might have sounded as though he meant he got cold feet. "Well," Getz said. "With the best of them it's hard."

"You married?"

"Was. You know how it is. One's too much, two's not enough." He crouched by the window and peered through. There were still a few inches of water on the concrete floor. Twomey's scuba gear lay on the old wooden table beside the water tank. Getz tapped the window glass. "Dive?"

"Yeah. I mean, I will. Always wanted to. I bought this stuff to take lessons."

"Expensive investment if you decide you don't like it. "

"Oh, I'll like it."

Getz nodded, pursed his lips for the cold whiskey, but Twomey could see all he got was an ice cube in the tooth.

"Hey, here," he said. "Let me freshen that for you."

Getz shook his head. "Thanks. Got to be off." Twomey winked.

"Date?"

"Yeah, with my taxman."

Or would he like it? He sat at the front window again, into his second four fingers of bourbon, mindful he was drinking alone, listening to the chugachug sound of the pump draining his basement, found himself thinking about Karen again.

On a folded piece of yellow paper in his wallet, written carefully in black ink with a fine-nibbed fountain pen, were the words, *Drive, Dive, Dance, & Fight*. When he grew discouraged and depressed, as he was this evening, sitting by the front window with a drink, hoping he would not take another, he folded the paper out of his wallet and read the words there: a catalogue of things he always wanted to learn to do, but never had. The ink was slightly blurred from perspiration and the creases in the paper were fragile from handling, but that only increased its value for him. He had written the words down one evening about two months after Karen left him.

Over breakfast one morning, the day before his twenty-ninth birthday, she told him she was leaving, that it had nothing to do with him, it was *her* problem, had been a mistake, better end it quickly now before they were married and things were serious.

"I'm sorry, Daniel." She always called him Daniel, not Danny.

Twomey could not believe what he was hearing; yet he was not surprised, after all, that she was dropping him. He had always feared she would.

"Is it something I did?" he whispered.

She got up and went to the sink, her back to him, turned suddenly, crouched, bent forward at the waist, and rasped, *"Nothing!"*

Twomey flinched.

"You have done *nothing!* You *do* nothing. You *can* do nothing!" She turned back to the sink and he watched her shoulders slowly relax, and then she was herself again. Without facing him, she said very softly, "You seemed so *sweet.* I thought you were so *nice,* so unassuming and modest. But you're just...a wimp."

"What a thing to say to a person," he said, following her into the bedroom where she began to pack a large turquoise suitcase.

"I guess *you're* God's gift to the earth, then, huh?" She was fitting her shoes one at a time into clear plastic bags and lining them along the edge of the suitcase.

"Just like that, then, huh? So long, I don't love you, have a nice life."

She moved swiftly, folding blouses, T-shirts, jeans, her hands so deft, capable. He couldn't catch his breath.

Then she was at the door in her raincoat, the cute short beige one he urged her to buy because he loved to see her long legs beneath it. She placed her key on the formica tabletop with a click. He followed her to the door, watched her walk to the corner, turn down the avenue, the big turquoise suitcase bumping her leg beneath the short raincoat as he stood there thinking, *What should I do, what should I do, what in the name of Christ should I do?*

He slept in his clothes that night and didn't go to work the next day, celebrated his birthday fully dressed in bed holding a forgotten pair of her underpants beneath the sheet against his heart. He didn't go to work the day after that either. Several times a day he got out of bed to phone her sister Eleanor, who lived in Baltimore with a black high school teacher, to ask if Karen were there, but Eleanor said she hadn't heard from her at all. On the fifth or sixth day, Karen answered. "Stop phoning here. It is over, Daniel. Forever." He went back to bed and masturbated. Got up and washed his hands and went back to bed and masturbated again. Then he got up and washed his hands and phoned her again; this time Eleanor answered and repeated Karen's message, and he went back to bed and masturbated again, got up and washed his hands, went to the bathroom to see if he had any sleeping pills, and broke his toothbrush glass in the sink, drank half a bottle of prescription cough syrup, went back to bed, and slept until he woke in the dark.

He got up and sat at the kitchen table with a yellow pad to write her a letter, but only sat and stared at the paper, thinking about all the things he could not do, all the things missing from his life.

The basement was dry but for a few puddles here and there in the hollows of the concrete floor, and Twomey felt an enormous sense of satisfaction and accomplishment that he had managed that, at least. He unplugged and packed the pump motor into the cardboard carton Getz left behind, wound the flexible pipe around his shoulder and then, on impulse, grabbed a bottle of '85 Medoc from a case he and Karen had bought for the engagement party that never happened. He went across the street in the chill fresh evening.

It took Getz some time to answer the bell. Twomey was deciding whether to give it a third ring or go when the door rattled open and Getz stood there with a bemused smile on his face. He looked rumpled, though he'd put a tie on, red and black stripe, and Twomey could smell a ham cooking. He unloaded the pump carton and held the Medoc out by the neck.

"By way of thanks a million, neighbor."

Getz studied the label before taking the bottle, then lumped his lips. "Pricey," he said.

A woman appeared in the hall behind him. "Frankie," she said. "Don't you want your dinner?" Her face was in shadow, but Twomey could see its lean, angular highlights framed in an array of curls and the topography of her T-shirt. He fell silent. The woman pressed against Getz's back and traced his ear with a finger. Twomey was considering asking if she did taxes. Getz waved the woman off, literally, with his fingertips. "You've made your point," he said. And to Twomey, "Thanks for the wine." He passed it back over his shoulder to the woman. "Totally unnecessary. But appreciated."

Behind the wheel of Mr. Aziz's push-button Dodge Dart, idling at the curb, Twomey fiddled with the radio tuner and waited for Mr. Aziz to come through the glass door marked *Aziz Driving School.* He knew that behind the venetian blinds there, Mr. Aziz was downing a couple glasses of wine to steady his nerves because the student he had before Twomey, a South American woman psychiatrist from Elmhurst General Hospital, made him nervous. Twomey tried chatting with her once when they were waiting for Aziz. "That must really be interesting work," he said. "What are you, like, an actual psychoanalyst?" He was thinking maybe he could talk to her a little bit about things. "Did you ever have a patient that was, like, scared of driving?"

"Only me," she said and smiled. The skin beneath her eyes was smudgy and her teeth protruded slightly, and Twomey was trying to think of something else to say when Aziz showed up for his lesson. He got Twomey aside and said to him, "A man who must speak to a psychiatrist for help should have his head examined."

Now Twomey found an oldie on the radio, the Contours, and beat time on the steering wheel. "Do you *love* me? *Do* you love me? Now, that I, can, *dance!*"

He pictured himself with a license, wheels, flying along Sunrise Highway to the beach, scuba tanks in the back seat, some bimbo nibbling at his ear. That was his brother Mark's phrase, remembered from years before. Mark had had a ' 51 Ford convertible, beige, mint condition, which he totalled out on Cross Bay Boulevard. Cause of accident?

"Some blonde bimbo was nibbling at my ear. Distracting."

On the street, a tall slim woman in a plain pale green summer dress walked past. Twomey liked her face, her long body and graceful walk which made him think of Karen. His eyes followed her like a magnet. Actually, he thought, *I'm* the bimbo here, some kind of male bimbo. Fall for every woman I see.

The door of the shop front opened and Mr. Aziz appeared patting his lips with a folded handkerchief, short and potbellied in a white shirt with rolled-up sleeves, arms fanned out slightly from his sides. He beamed. "Ah! My prize student!" He slid into the seat beside Twomey and clicked off the radio, tapped his head. "No distractions. Concentrate." Then he patted Twomey's knee. "With you I can to relax. No problem. You can handle. *Big,*" he said forcefully and flexed his pale slender biceps. *"Strong!"* He fastened his seat belt. "Please to signal and proceed into traffic flow. At first corner, to make please a left turn. Left turn."

Twomey flipped on the directional, checked the sideview mirror, looked over his shoulder, steered out into the road. He could feel, as he did so, that he jerked the wheel a bit. "Sorry," he said quickly, to make it clear at least he *knew* what he had done.

"Dancing style," Mr. Aziz said, sashaying in his seat. "Easy easy, move and swing, easy easy, move and swing."

At the corner, as Twomey waited to make the turn, a black-haired woman in tight black pedal pushers crossed the street leading a Doberman on a leash. Twomey's eye followed her steps. "Beware of woman with large dog," Mr. Aziz said. "They do not want man. They prefer dog. But..." He lifted a forefinger. "If man does not take care of woman, she will find it another place. The man is at fault in such cases."

Twomey jerked the wheel into the turn. "Sorry!"

"Dancing style, easy, Mr. Twomey," Aziz said. "Move and swing, easy easy. You can handle. *Big! Strong!*"

Now he sat at the window sipping red wine and watching yellow leaves skitter along his street, his slip of yellow paper opened on his knee, trying to think of things he had managed to do. He'd managed *not* to lose his job. That was a plus—although the job itself was a minus. He was almost ready to take his driving test. He was considering dancing lessons. He was seriously considering diving lessons, even had an appointment. The health club had been a fiasco, though. He'd dropped that. Even now, he blushed to remember it. He made an appointment after work one day to go down and check out a ninety-nine dollar one-month introductory offer over in Rego Park and was met by a Vic Tanny type V-shaped guy in a black muscle shirt. The guy looked Twomey over, said, "We're gonna build that body up for you, Danny boy." He stared evenly into Twomey's eyes. "You like women?"

"Sure," Twomey blurted, annoyed with himself. *I'm* the customer here.

"You want women to want you?"

"Well, sure, of course."

"Good," the guy said. "Cause this is a strictly co-ed operation.

Come on meet the girls." Twomey allowed himself to be led down to the pool, a small square in a windowless room where three women wearing string bikinis sat in beach chairs, gabbing. When the guy appeared at the door with Twomey in tow, they leapt to their feet. One of them, a short busty blond, said, "Ooooo, let me see 'im!"

Twomey managed a grin as the girls circled him. "He's *cute!*"

It took him a week after signing a six-month contract to realize they were shills, and he felt so embarrassed at being duped that he never returned. He felt the heat in his cheeks and saw himself through Karen's eyes, fiddling with the wedding band he'd bought and never got to put on her finger and that he carried on a drain plug chain with his unused car keys. He saw Karen shake her head slowly, click her tongue the way she did when she was annoyed. He was on his way into the bedroom to masturbate when he noticed the little hand weights on the floor behind the armchair. Two-pounders. He took one in each fist and dropped into a crouch, started boxing, located his shadow on the yellow wall in the hallway and danced there, snapping off lefts, a right hook, trying to do it as his brother taught him years before. Snap the left out so it shoots back into position like a rubber band. Throw the right from the shoulder, grind the sole of your shoe into the floor and grunt as you hit, shoot air out your nose like a bull.

Hnh! Hnh! Hnh! He bobbed, stepped like a fencer, snapped lefts, combinations. Left-right, left-right, left-left-right, left-right-left. Who you punching, wimp? Huh? Who? *You*, you ugly fuck! *You!*

*   *   *

Twomey felt chilly and dumb standing at the edge of the pool with all his equipment. He had gas pains and didn't like the way the other people in the pool were looking at him, and he didn't at all care for the instructor, who talked like a pimp.

The instructor was thick and hairy with four tatoos on each arm, and a little devil on one calf. His name was Louis, and he told Twomey he could make a diver out of him in one day of in-dividual instruction—four hours if he learned fast, six if he did-n't—but on one condition: "Diving is not an individual sport. You do it with a buddy. You do not go in the sea alone, okay? You got me? The sea is not to be fooled with, my friend. You go into the sea alone and the sea may just decide she wants to keep you there, so do not fool with this, okay, my friend?"

Twomey learned all the theory fast. He had the safety-first principles down by heart and let Louis sell him a sturdy-looking steel knife with a black rubber handle and a calf sheath.

After three hours of theoretical instruction, he was too scared to show his fear when Louis ordered him to fall backward off the edge into the deep end of the pool. As he hit the water, he heard Louis call out, "'Member, nothing is done till the fat lady sings!"

Despite the fear, Twomey was thrilled: first moment in his life fully immersed in an alien element, breathing! The weight belt dragged him toward the floor of the pool, and he pinched his nose and cleared every three feet of the descent, landed, duck-walked along the shimmering bottom, sixteen feet of chlorinated water above his head, the slow eerie sound of his own breathing soughing in his ears through the Self-Contained Underwater

Breathing Apparatus strapped to his back.

Then Louis appeared before him, pale and hairy, swimming like a ghost, wearing nothing but a weight belt, no equipment. Twomey could see the greenish water rippling around the little red devil tatoo on his calf as he issued orders in sign language. Blade of one hand vertical at his sternum, blade of the other intersecting it like a cross, then sweeping up and down his body and away.

Twomey knew what he meant, but pretended he didn't to buy time. He was scared. *Wimp!* he thought. *Scared in a swimming pool.*

Louis did the sign language again, and Twomey, to his own chagrin, acknowledged he had received the message by nodding up and down like Stan Laurel. Now he would have to do it. Time for the SCUBA strip. He started with the knife, peeling the rubber sheath from his calf. Then the flippers, one at a time. The easy part. Now he had to doff the tank, the mask and, worst of all, the regulator and mouth piece. He did not wish to relinquish them.

Louis had to surface for air, and Twomey relished the interruption, watching the devil leg flash up past his face, but he was back in no time, his chest fat with air.

Twomey wanted to go home, but he saw his right hand go for the tear flap on the harness that held his tank to him. He yanked and it tore free and then he was hugging the yellow tank to keep it from rising, peeling the mask off his head. Louis jabbed in the direction of the regulator with a thick, commanding forefinger, and sheep that he was, Twomey took it out of his mouth. Unfortunately, he forgot to take a last deep breath first, and it was too late now. He wanted to claw for the surface but was too embarrassed to reveal his naked fear. He stayed put, watched Louis reach for the mouthpiece, press the button to clear it, blow through so bubbles fluttered up past his face. And then Louis was there, eyes smiling, sucking air through Twomey's regulator while Twomey stood barefoot on the slimy floor, weight belt dragging at the little lumps of fat at his sides, face fixed in a dissimulating smile, thinking, *Air! Give me my fucking air source back! I need air! Now!*

Louis yanked the regulator from his mouth and teased Twomey with it, keeping it back while he pointed out the features Twomey knew only too well, reminding him of what he had to do, keeping the precious glittering object from him.

Twomey felt the edge of anger, rage, rising up within the tight aching pouches of his lungs. He glanced up at the surface, the lights of the high ceiling shimmering above him. He was ready to split, sensed Louis's eyes on him, and knew what that gaze meant. It meant, *I see your fear, Twomey. Conquer it or you fail. You won't get the regulator. You'll have to run like a chicken, and you get no certificate from Louis Mallier, boy! Remember you paid in advance. And remember, nothing is done until the fat lady sings.*

Twomey put his hands at his sides, met Louis's gaze, decided to die there, to faint from lack of air and suck chlorinated water into his lungs and die, and it would all be over with forever then; he would finally learn whether there was a secret of life or not, whatever, anything, but he would not give this devil-legged comic -book Frog frogman the satisfaction of seeing his face decompose into terror.

Louis smiled, held out the regulator. Twomey reached slowly, suppressing his greed to be certain he was not being set up to be teased once again, felt the rubber and metal in his palm, pressed the discharge button, fitted the mouth piece between his teeth, mustered something in his lungs to blow with so the bubbles rose past his eyes. Now the proof: did he do it right? When he drew in air now, what would he get? Air or water?

His lungs made the decision to suck and were rewarded with a sweet thick flow of air from the big yellow bottle, and now already Louis was saying, *Gimme,* with his fingers. *Pass it back. I'm your diving buddy, my hose is cut, I need help.* Twomey remembered to fill his lungs first this time, passed the regulator, watched Louis clear it, fill his lungs, pass it back.

After the fifth or sixth pass, Louis grinned, gave underwater skin to Twomey, took skin back. *Give me five, jive! Take the change, strange! The fat lady has sung.* Louis said with his hands, *Suit up again, bud,* and Twomey restrapped the tank to his back, stepped into his fins, fitted the knife sheath to his calf, and followed Louis up through the water to the surface, watching the little pitchfork-holding devil tattoo on his calf wink and smile down at him: *Hell of a life, huh, pal?*

It was time to drive.

That which I have most feared is upon me, Twomey thought, hoping the line might give him consolation. It almost did, for an instant, but the pain in his stomach returned at once. *Fear and Trembling,* he thought. *A slight case of sickness unto death.* And, *Eat your grief, wimp.*

It all served to remind him once again how very low his fear threshold was. A moment of illumination. This is why I am a coward, he thought. This is why Karen left me and why she chose correctly in doing so. Why I am a zero. My accursed love of not having anything to fear. My unwillingness to expose myself to it. Recognizing this comforted him for a moment, seemed to indicate a path of self-awareness through the maze. But then he reminded himself what the source of this fear was: a lousy driving test!

On the pavement outside the testing area, Mr. Aziz stood with two women. Twomey recognized the one as the lady psychiatrist from Elmhurst General. She was short and plump, black-haired with dark smudges around her eyes. Twomey could smell wine on Aziz's breath as the man greeted him with warmth, embraced him, patted his back. "Ah! Mr. Twomey! You are all ready I can see!" The other woman was young, maybe twenty, with black polish on her fingernails and a pretty mouth. Twomey fell for her at once.

"Who must take this test first?" the psychiatrist enquired.

Aziz touched his side, as though the mere sound of her voice triggered organic pain. "This will be to decide by the Motor Vehicles Bureau persons, Doctor."

"Because I am very busy," she said. "As a doctor, I must return to my duties. And because I must take this test in other than my mother's tongue, I feel I should go first."

"I feel you should relax, Doctor!" Aziz said loudly and winced and touched his side again, just above the roll of fat on his flank. Twomey watched the woman, startled to realize that even though she was a psychiatrist, a *doctor,* she was just as scared as he was, *more* scared. He glanced at the girl with the black fingernails, but she was staring at the pavement, and all at once he could see she was nervous, too, he saw it in her posture, in the set of her face, the hunch of her shoulders.

"Nervous?" he asked with what he hoped was a warm and sympathetic tone.

She shrugged, chewed her lip.

A ruddy-faced man in a white shirt approached, carrying a clipboard. He greeted Aziz by his first name, "Hello there, Mustafah," looked at the clipboard. "Okay, we start with Miss Gomez."

"*Dr.* Gomez," she said. Aziz touched his side and glared at her. "I will to come in the back seat," he said.

Twomey reached out to the woman, touched her arm. "Hey, good luck, doctor," he said. She stared at him, her eyes blank, smudged, as though she had never seen him before.

He waited with the black-fingernailed girl and watched the Dodge jerk away from the curb out into traffic. Almost immediately it stopped abruptly, then took off quickly again, turned right at the corner with a shriek of rubber.

The light seemed dimmer now, chiller, and he felt a sadness as he regarded this girl who looked so young and was too frightened to so much as share a word with him. He stood there in his weathered suede jacket and wanted to say something that might make things easier for her, seeing her fear was harder than his own.

"Dig your nail polish," he said.

She rolled her eyes without looking at him. "Jam my head

maybe," she said. Her voice was clipped, her mouth hard. And he realized she in no way thought of him as a human being. It seemed a bad sign. Failure, he thought, turning away, closing his eyes to see a murky, gloomy blankness that was his future.

The Dodge returned from the opposite direction. The BMV man got out first. Aziz was behind the wheel now, Dr. Gomez in the back seat. The tester said coldly, "I'll be back in a few minutes, Aziz. Got to file a report."

Twomey noticed the right front fender of the Dodge was crumpled. Aziz got out and held the seat so the woman could follow.

"You have really done it this time, *Doctor!*" he said.

"I did not do that," she said.

Aziz's eyes burned at her. He touched his side. "This is the end, *Doctor!*"

"I did *not* do that," she repeated with conviction.

Oh, Christ, Twomey thought. It's all jinxed. There's no hope here. And occupied his mind composing an ad for the automotive section of the local newspaper: *Used Vega hatchback, blue, automatic....*

Three days passed before he received the results. He could remember nothing of the test. It was all a blur. He remembered making the first turn through an amber signal, trying to decide whether to brake, feeling his foot decide to go for the gas instead, making the turn, the rest a blur of following the tester's instructions to turn right, turn left, make a broken-U turn, parallel park.

Had there been a stop sign? Had he stopped? What about the traffic circle? Had he entered properly? Did he cross any solid lines?

The third day was a workday, and he wanted to stay home and wait for the mail, but didn't allow himself to. He went to the office and suffered, knew he had failed, and the knowledge made him hope perhaps he had not, and the hope made him certain he had.

At home, on the floor inside his door, was a small white envelope from the BMV. He poured three fingers of Jack Daniels over three cubes and sat by the window with the envelope on his knee. Across the street, Frank Getz trudged slowly up his walkway, a paisley scarf hanging open at the throat of his blue cashmere topcoat, a leather attaché case at his side. Looks tired, Twomey thought. He leaned out his front door and called out, "How you doing, Frank?"

Getz turned, lifted his eyebrows. Twomey held up the envelope. "Driver's test results," he said, immediately regretting having done so when he saw in the set of Getz's mouth that he neither understood nor cared to find out what he was talking about. Twomey watched his back disappear through his door, glanced at the shiny red BMW in the driveway, back at the envelope.

If I failed, I take it over again, right? he thought, doubting he could, and jabbed his finger into the glassine address window. Inside was his learner's permit on which had been stamped *Temporary Drivers License* along with a slip that informed him he would receive a computerized license form within three to four weeks which, on payment of a fee, could be redeemed for a permanent document, renewable in three years.

He looked into his whiskey, across the street at Getz's house, the red BMW in the drive. He checked his watch; there was still time to drive over to Mr. Aziz and say thanks, give him a bottle of Medoc, maybe get one final word of wisdom for the road.

The little Vega handled so easily after Aziz's big boat of a Dodge, Twomey felt smooth dancing the car through traffic along Northem Boulevard, down to Roosevelt. He pulled in along the curb outside the Aziz Driving School. The Dodge was not parked there. Inside, the dark-eyed secretary with big teeth who had always scheduled his lessons sat flipping through a magazine. Aziz's partner, a young heavy-set man wearing a banlon shirt and an athletic club jacket, sat in a swivel chair across the room.

"Hi," Twomey said. "Mr. Aziz around?"

The girl looked at him, said nothing. She had a beaklike mouth that made him think of an owl. The young man tipped his swivel chair forward. "He's, well, passed away," he said. "Day before yesterday morning. Heart."

Twomey looked into the young man's face, the girl's, saw nothing. "He was young," he said.

"Fifty-three, would have been, next week," the young man said. There was a silence. "Well you probably want another lesson. I'll be taking on Aziz's students."

"I just wanted to tell him I passed the test."

"Well you can't tell him now, buddy."

"I brought him a bottle of wine."

The young man chuckled. "That we can help you with."

Halfway back to Bayside, Twomey realized he knew nothing

about Aziz's life. Did he have a wife? Children? In his driveway, he turned off the ignition, switched off the lights and sat with his hands on the cool hard plastic of the wheel, staring through the windshield at the garage door, ancient wood planking, gray and weather-beaten, and it seemed he had never seen that door before, never looked at it, never.

So there was no mint '50 Ford, no bimbo nibbling at his ear, no blazing summer day—just an old rot-paneled hatchback Vega and Twomey in a lumber jacket behind the wheel, a brand new paper driver's license tucked into his shirt pocket, scuba gear in the trunk, on Saturday, 9 October, of his thirtieth year. I'm just a slow starter maybe, he thought. The day was cool and bright, and he speeded toward the past, determined to redo it, radio blaring a jazz station, Horace Silver pounding out "Safari." Destination, Rockaway. Broadway to Queens Boulevard to Woodhaven, past the long iron-fenced cemetery where a van sold hot dogs and balloons and teddy bears, past Justice Field where some kids in uniforms were playing football, Forest Park, beneath the gloomy Liberty Avenue El, through Ozone Park where Woodhaven changed to Cross Bay Boulevard.

Then he was at Howard Beach and saw the Bay up ahead, and his spirit soared. He rolled past Shell Bank Basin while Charlie Parker blew gentle wild variations on "Groovin' High," up over the free bridge and down onto the long straightaway that spanned the Jamaica Bay marshes and hassocks. Four, five miles without signals. He rolled down the window, turned up the radio, floored the gas. Salt air gushed across his face as he speeded through

Black Bank Marsh, Rulers Bar Hassock, Broad Creek Marsh— green and yellow sedge grass tipping in the breeze, the hushing water, yellow sun, the scream of gulls.

He eased down to sixty through Cross Bay, glancing from the wheel to take in the crumpled shimmering water, dotted with sand bars and tussocks of sedge: Black Wall Marsh, Winhole Marsh, Silver Hole Marsh, Yellow Bar Hassock, Ruffle Bar, Little Egg Marsh, Big Egg Marsh, Giant Bar Marsh. It was like a poet wrote the map; he loved that they all had names, some of them no bigger than a couple of backyards on end, nothing to stand on but sucking sand. He paid a dime toll and headed for Far Rockaway, through the poor streets, past a storefront church, a heavy black woman in yellow sweat pants walking with a little girl, an elderly white man on a rusted iron balcony.

At Beach 8, he parked at the edge of the sand and sat in the car for a moment. The sea was calm here, Atlantic Beach. The crumpled surface of the water glittered, silver, black, green, blue, combed here and there with gliding lines of froth.

He got his gear out of the trunk, carried it down to the sand and stood, by his calculation, exactly where he had *sat* all those years ago in college, watching the others do what he was doing now, suiting up. This is my life now. I'm the *man!* I'm the diver!

The buildings along the beach, large red brick structures, were abandoned now, looked bombed out. Long and squat, they sat with broken faces watching the surf slap at the hard yellow sand. Twomey's naked flesh crawled and puckered in the chill as he drew the harness buckle tight, pinched into his fins, and slap-walked to the water. It touched him like a shock, and he yelled out, the sound of his cry small and flat on the empty beach.

He spit in his mask and rinsed it, fitted the mouthpiece between his teeth, plodded out into the dark water, moving toward a broad shaft of sunlight that rippled chest deep on the water, as broad across as a garage door. He cleared his regulator, looked up at the sun, dove.

Now we are born, he thought, swimming down through the jade green water, listening to his breath, the water afloat with sediment, bubbles. It got colder as he descended. He pinched his nose through the mask, cleared, stroked down another yard, pinched, cleared. He counted how many times for a sense of depth—seven, eight times. Deeper than he had ever been. Now in the sea, descending.

He saw the gray-green floor of sand beneath him, pulled toward it, a climber climbing downward. A movement caught his eye, a flounder, belly down on the bottom. Make a nice filet. He reached back for his calf-knife, lunged, but the fish was too fast for him. Twomey doubled up and spun back. Ahead, the floor sloped downward into a hollow, much deeper than where he hovered now. He could not see bottom, and it was dark; only shards of light glittered there.

His fear, he knew, was reasonable. Yet the hollow beckoned, a place where only he would be. Who else had ever been there? I, Twomey, touch the floor of the sea. He cleared again, slipped over the edge, pulled downward. He followed the slope of the cliff into the hollow so the sand was under his chest at all times. This seemed a good idea until he realized it was causing him to lose his bearings. He no longer knew how far out he was, how far from shore. Then he noted he no longer felt cold. At first he thought that was because his movement was warming his body. Now he began to wonder if it meant he had gone numb.

Surface, Twomey.

He listened to the voice, considered. Then, *In a minute*, his mind whispered back, *a few minutes.* He only wanted to see the floor, to touch it once, to feel the floor of the bottom of the sea here, just once, this true first day of the rest of his life. A lobster scuttled past his nose. He grabbed for it, but it vanished in a cloud of muddy sand.

The cliff wall was levelling out. The bottom couldn't be far. He pressed the illumination button on his watch, realized he had forgotten to check the time when he went in. He thought he had been down for about twenty-five minutes, but was not certain. He had fifty minutes of air in the tank, but it wouldn't take so long to get up again. He would go straight up, then swim back to shore from where he surfaced. The empty tank would float him.

He could see something before him, the sand floor, and a dark mass humped up on it. A rock? No, he knew it was something else. Organic. Alive. The fear was strong now, a fear to respect, beyond mockery or self-pity. He pulled toward the black mass, but more slowly, watched it begin to take form. It was long and broad, and there was movement around it, small frantic movements.

The fear was alarming now, shouting for him to pull away, escape, but he stroked forward, down, straining to see through his mask. He tilted his head for another angle of vision and saw it then, a yard from his face, grinning with a white jaw and teeth, flesh half eaten from the bone, an eel supping on its glistening eyeball, crabs and small fishes digging at the torn flank: A horse. Grinning at him from the dark ocean floor, being devoured by a thousand tiny mouths.

Twomey shivered deep along his spine, felt his gorge rise, prayed to himself, *You must not, must not...* He swallowed, swallowed, saw himself strangling at sixty feet on his own puke, a fitting death for an idiot. His belly settled then, and he felt the cold again, opened his eyes on the far side of fear, where survival was a mere series of movements-upward.

But something caught his eye alongside the horse's grinning jaw, a tiny thing hovering elegantly in the stream, a seahorse, perfect sculpted head, graceful arch of spine, standing up in the water, no bigger than Twomey's thumb. He stroked toward it, reached slowly and caught it between thumb and finger, felt triumph course through his body as he turned from the carcass, the black feast, upward, rising slowly, clearing with his left hand, holding the little creature in front of his eyes, studying its placid gaze, its silent face.

Somewhere perhaps halfway up he became aware of himself hanging there in the water, no longer receiving the air his lungs pulled for at the mouthpiece. He could see the surface above him, but knew distances were deceiving in water. He had to hold what air he had, continue to keep down the speed of his ascent, continue to clear every three feet.

He spoke to himself as to a child now and realized that he was in the process of molting an old self, talking to a person he was about to leave behind, a child he had spent many years with, who understood wonderful things but had yet to grasp certain essentials about existence. We must always remember one another, Twomey thought, clearing once again, holding the child still so that he could not panic on the verge of suffocation and cause them both to be destroyed.

Look here, he said. *Look at the pretty seahorse. Isn't it wonderful?*

His head broke water. Then he was up on his back, on his side, mask off, regulator and mouthpiece dangling, breathing in the wonderful cold air, looking up at the blue fall sky over Rockaway, swimming on his back slowly toward shore.

What he wanted now were two things: hot coffee and a large brandy. He drove to 116th Street where the Irish bars clustered, hair still wet, skin raw beneath dry clothes, car heater on full. The seahorse stood in seawater inside a Hellman's Mayonnaise jar on the dashboard. He watched it sway as he steered the Vega in alongside the curb in front of MacNulty's at Beach 116.

The bar room was broad and dim. Three or four men sat scattered along the bar, hunched over drinks, while the BeeGees sang from the jukebox, "How Can You Mend a Broken Heart?" Behind the cash register was a faded yellow news clipping: *Men on Moon,* with a photo of Armstrong stepping from the ladder. A bright-faced woman looked up from the tap as Twomey sat and set his Hellman's jar on the bar top like a trophy. "Coffee and Courvoisier, please."

"Whatever have you there?" the barmaid asked. British. Syllables like a hard sweet. Blue-eyed with a bright mouth and shining face.

"Seahorse," he said.

"A seahorse!" She turned the jar before her eyes. The animal stood erect, unmoving, in the water. "It's not a well seahorse I would say," she said.

Twomey took the jar, peered in. "Now you mention it, it doesn't quite look itself, does it?"

The side of the bar led out onto the boardwalk. Twomey crossed to the beach, stood at the edge of the surf, unscrewed the top of the jar, and flung the seahorse back, water and all, into a breaker. The water rolled in over his shoes, and he leapt back, but not fast enough; his socks were soaked. From the boardwalk, behind him, he heard laughter, the barmaid. "You poor dear!" she called to him. "You'll catch your death. Come have your cuppa."

Twomey hung his socks on the water heater in the back room and sat barefoot at the bar, rolling brandy on his tongue while Eric Clapton sang "Let It Rain" from the jukebox, and he answered questions from smiling Viv about his exploits at sixty feet beneath the sea capturing seahorses.

"You're quite mad, aren't you?" she said, her eyes full of admiration.

"Dance?" he said.

"Really oughtn't, you know," she said, coming round the bar, and Twomey stepped back to welcome her, lifting his feet to the music, one foot, the other, one foot, the other. He felt like the man on the moon wearing lead boots to keep from flying away. He felt like a fool, but Viv didn't seem to mind. She smiled like a birthday cake as he watched her, watched the last light of the afternoon slant through the window, the colored lights of the jukebox, the dull gloss of the bar itself, a reflection of sun on the dusty mirror and backs of aging, balding heads scattered along the stools, his own naked red feet stepping in sawdust, and as Slowhand's guitar screamed, it occurred to him how beautiful matter is, he was drunk, how beautiful to see light, shadow, feel the dusty floor beneath your chilly wet feet, breath in your lungs.

(1995)

Landing Zone X-Ray

I picture the FBI that year on 83rd Street in Jackson Heights across from St. Joan of Arc's Church where, years before, I'd gone to dances, the spring I was fifteen, doing the lindy in a powder-blue suit with a plump, sweet-mouthed girl named Luanne.

But now it's another time; I am not a boy, but a young man, a senior in college with the Army behind me and political ideas that may have consequences. I picture two men in suits climbing out of an unmarked car, chunking the doors shut, entering the wide, dim lobby of my apartment house. I picture them crossing to the elevator; one gets in, the other ducks out back to cover the fire escape. I see him stand there against the wall, chewing gum with his lips closed, dawn light shadowing the acne scars in the pit of his cheek. I see the other man's thick finger stab the elevator button for five, hear the moment's silence before the machinery hums into movement and the car lifts up the shaft past floor after floor of sleeping families, the Cohens, Mendozas, Taylors, Rakovecs, O'Connors, Giannasios.

And I see those families in bed behind locked doors in their three and four room apartments, some with little kids asleep in cribs, some old, retired, some alone, divorced, never married. I can hear the newspapers thump on their door mats as a sleepy kid jogs from floor to floor, delivering the *Long Island Star Journal*. I see the FBI man in the dim light of the ascending elevator car.

I see him, but I cannot see what he is thinking. His face is impassive, his mind, his heart closed to my reach. He is, say, forty-five years old (my age now), has a family I can barely glimpse, a smudged vision in a dream: a woman in a bathrobe, a house somewhere, a suburb, kids, two boys. Does he cheat on her? Is he a bully, a tyrant at home? Did she give him a plate of eggs this morning before he left to do this? Does he think patriotic thoughts about what he is about to do? Is he reluctant, grim? Did he himself fight in WWII or Korea and feel cheated by our type? Is it a meanly agreeable task, cornering the enemy in their sleep?

Or just a job?

I see his face only fleetingly through the round window of the elevator door as the car lifts past, up toward where I see myself now, asleep in Apt. 5D on a box-spring mattress beneath the high ceiling, within the shadowy walls, pale bars of light falling through the slats of the venetian blinds across my sheet-draped body.

I open my eyes. Danny is no longer snoring on the sofa. He stands on bare feet on the dusty wood floor, buttoning his plaid shirt. I sit up on my elbows. He says, "Something wrong," cocks an ear, eye whites luminous in the shadowy light. A clock ticks on the window ledge: 5:00 a.m. The elevator grinds and echoes in the shaft. I watch Danny's sockless feet find tennis sneakers. Then he is through the kitchen door, mounting the window ledge, out onto the fire escape, looking down through the bars. "Damn!" he sobs.

I hear the elevator stop on my floor, hear the tiny creak of its door opening, hear a finger stab at my dead doorbell, then a fist slamming the door itself as Danny climbs up instead of down, and I see the fire escape trembling under his weight and the weight of someone coming up from beneath, hollering.

Sometimes on a winter afternoon I sit at my desk here by the window, miles, years away, and look out at the water and the sky, gray as lead and just as still, and everything seems to make sense. The sky seems to take me to it, take my heart, and my stomach moves like when you look off a high building, and you know in your body suddenly how small and fragile and frightened you really are.

All I want to do then is pack it in for the day, go down to the kitchen and have a cup of coffee with Stephanie or yell out to the kids, "Hey! Jack? Kathy? Emergency up here! Come on up and give the old man a hug!" And rejoice in the fact they will come running, they will still do that for me.

We get to thinking things are stationary sometimes, but of course they're not. Everything is changing constantly, from minute to minute. A week, a month is nothing. A year goes like a dream. I waited so long in my life before having kids and now, in five years already both of them will be teenagers, off on their own most the time, that great sense of closeness we've developed will turn to secrecy, aversion, impatience. They will begin to take their own positions on things, will take chances, risk themselves on actions whose meanings will later seem to change, open to question. This is what parents know.

It was the same for us with our own folks. It's all in the natural order of things. They'll be off learning for themselves, beyond my control, uninterested in my advice, and I'll sit up here at my desk, stare out at the sea and pray they come to no serious harm, knowing there is a real risk they will, and I'll have to face it on my own, whatever it is I see there which gives me this scary feeling of merging with forever. Stephanie and I will have to learn to live together with quiet again, see if we can face it together. "It's incredible how short a life really is," she said to me the other day, dazed by the sudden realization that it had been twenty-five years since her little brother was shot to death in the war. She said it in a way that went straight to my heart, made me feel the way I do when I sit here and look at the sea in the dead of winter.

When I was a kid, ten or fifteen, my father used to say, "That was, oh, twenty, twenty-five years ago," and I used to think how strange to be so old you can remember history.

Now I think of Danny that morning they got him and *that* was twenty-three years ago. I never saw him again. We exchanged a few letters, then I lost contact with him. I saw his mother once or twice on the street in Jackson Heights before I moved away. She was about fifty, I suppose, a tall, slim woman with short red hair and Danny's big broad nose. I don't think I ever saw her smile. She was divorced, and very strict with Danny, whose father lived in Florida. She stared at me on the street, watched me with her pale eyes. She despised what Danny had done, called him a coward and a traitor, praised his older brother in the Navy, told Danny he was just like his no good run-off father. And she never forgave me for hiding him, would not speak to me, only stared, with those hard, pale eyes. That was so many years ago. She might well be dead by now.

Danny got a dishonorable discharge and four years at Leavenworth, came out to do some small-time dealing, worked as a mule, lived in communes in California, disappeared in Mexico during the seventies. That was his story, history. I knew him since high school, a nice enough fellow to start with, a year younger than me, a tall big-nosed guy who seemed always uncertain of things, but good-humored. He was always nodding to some private music, rhythm and blues, or plucking an invisible electric bass and miming notes with his lips, singing blues lyrics, "You know I feel so bad! Like a ball game on a rainy day."

In 1968, after he finished advanced infantry training at Fort Dix, he drew orders for Vietnam. He was given a week's leave first, and he ran for it. He lived where he could for a couple of months, spent the last six months at my place until they came and took him away.

I learned later that it was his girlfriend turned him in, Kathy Giovanni, a small, slight, green-eyed girl with overlapping front teeth she used to hide with her tongue when she smiled. Why she did that to him I cannot imagine. She was always quiet with him. For a few years there, the two of them were always together. I don't ever remember hearing them speak, just standing together, or walking with their arms around each other, Danny tall beside her, going off by themselves, walking to Mass together on Sunday mornings, speaking quietly, intently.

Then he ran from his orders, and she turned him in. I try to picture her getting out the phone book, turning pages to *F, Federal, Federal Bureau of Investigation,* dialing, saying, "I want to report a military deserter." I picture her lips, overlapping teeth near the mouthpiece of the phone, and I try to look into her mind, her heart, but cannot understand why she would do that to him. Was she bitter that his becoming an outlaw also meant leaving her? Did she hope he would only serve a few months in jail and then come back to her? Did she have her own political convictions, that a boy should be willing to give his life for his country even in a war like Vietnam?

The one FBI man already had Danny in handcuffs up on the roof when I opened the door to see a broad-faced man in a suit flash a wallet with a piece of metal in it, say something, shove me into the room before him, looking around at the blankets on my sofa, my bed, the banged up furniture.

Then Danny was being stuffed back through the kitchen window from the fire escape, and the other Fed with the acne scars was there. Danny looked young and slight next to him in the kitchen, his pale hair and light skin, his features clear, still young, untouched. He was twenty-two years old. Legal age. Expected to fight for his country. Old enough to vote. But he looked like a boy there, standing beside that man.

"He don't know anything about it," Danny said to the cop, jerking his head at me. That was when I noticed his hands were cuffed behind his back and there was blood between his teeth and his mouth was swollen.

"Did I ask you something?" the broad-faced cop asked quietly, staring into Danny's face. Then his hand shot out, and he smacked him. Danny's head jerked to the side, and he looked at me, smirked. I was too scared to pull faces. I just stood there in my pajamas, shivering while the cop poked through my things.

I had a poster on the wall that was a close-up photograph of a derelict staggering down a city street over the caption, *We have all come from lovers.* The cop ran his hand in behind the poster, tearing one corner of it, feeling the wall. Then he looked at the picture, smirked. "Beautiful," he said. "Just beautiful." He opened my bureau drawers, jerked them all the way out so the contents spilled on the floor as he checked beneath them. He opened the freezer section of my refrigerator and ran the ice cube trays under the hot water tap, watching them carefully as the frost melted from them. He went into the bathroom and lifted the porcelain lid off the toilet tank and peered into it.

"Better watch out," Danny said. "Could be some dangerous shit in there."

I shook my head to silence him.

Then the cop came back inside and looked at Danny. "You *stupid* jerk," he said. "You're screwed. And for *what?*" He jabbed the tip of his finger against my chest and asked my name. I told him, Paul Casey, and he asked my draft status, what kind of discharge I had, where I'd served.

"Fort Ben Harrison," I said. "Adjutant General's Corps. Honorable discharge."

He snorted. "Chair-born cowboy. Private pencil."

The other cop put his face close to mine, so I could smell the coffee and cigarettes on his breath, and he said, "I want you to wait right here, Casey, 'cause I'm coming back for you with a warrant. Now don't you touch a thing here, I got it all memorized, and you touch a thing, I got you for tampering with evidence in addition to being an accomplice to a felony. You got that, Casey?"

They led Danny out, reading him his rights, and that was the last I ever saw of him, with his shirt hanging out and blood between his teeth, tennis sneakers with no socks, and his wrists cuffed at the small of his back.

As soon as they were gone, I flushed the two joints I had in my cigarette pack down the toilet. I watched my fingers tremble as I broke and emptied them into the water. Then I scrubbed the bowl with Ajax and washed my hands and sat down on my sofa and waited.

Five blocks away, my mother and father were just getting up out of bed in their shingle-and-stucco house on Hampton Street. My father, a squat, bull-faced man, would be standing at the bathroom sink shaving, while my mother put on coffee down in the kitchen. They never spoke about the war. If I brought it up they would only stare, or change the subject, look away. The only thing they ever said was, "Thank God you got out before it started for real." My mother said that. My father said nothing. He had never been a soldier himself, too young for the first war, too old for the next two. He was a kind, quiet man, who would never allow anyone to use the word *nigger* in his presence without calling them on it. For many years, I did the same.

They used to call me "Paul X" in the neighborhood, many of my old friends who inherited their parents' racism. I argued with them. If they said, "Nigger," I corrected them, "Negro." Then it became a joke, so that if I said, "Negro," *they* corrected *me*, "Nigger," and I had to give it up then because they turned it into a joke.

But for a while there, a short while in the sixties, it seemed as though many of them changed. In the end, none of them wanted to go to Vietnam, and those who did go—if they came back— returned opposed to it. Their general view of things seemed to soften. Racism went out of style. Everyone was suddenly more open to one another, or so it seemed, for a time.

I didn't know anyone who *wanted* to go. I knew one guy who said he was gay to get out of going and was haunted by that ever since, others who got doctors to testify to false disabilities, chronic skin diseases, back disorders. I knew two guys who moved to Canada before they were called, and several who were called and went against their will, a few of whom came back in bodybags or missing a leg or an arm or limping, or broken in other ways. One guy named Brian Macauley came back and never left his house, sat in the front window staring out at the street, and you could see tears spilling out of his eyes, although his face was perfectly still. My wife's brother got killed there, three years before they showed up and got Danny.

Danny is the only guy I knew who deserted. Aside from marching a couple of times, and signing petitions, things like that, sheltering Danny was the only active thing I ever did against the war. Nothing to speak of, really.

It is hard to fathom the mistakes a nation can make, mistakes that mean the death of thousands of men and women, blown-up, burned, maimed, shot. I sit in my living room or at the window of my study looking out over the sea, warm, comfortable, and try to imagine Danny, try to understand his life, or the life of my wife's brother, Jimmy, who got called in when he was nineteen and got shot in the stomach and the leg and the face. I see a rifle bullet enter his face alongside the nose, tear through his brain, open the back of his head, others burning into his stomach, shattering his thigh bone. I see Jimmy, with whom I used to play basketball in the P.S. 89 school yard, set shots, twenty-one, a black-haired kid with a quick grin who was called and went and got killed so fast no one even knew there was a war on yet. They didn't even have the notification teams organized yet. Stephanie's parents got a telegram delivered by a cab driver. I sit safe and warm in my home now, a quarter of a century later, and I still see Jimmy's grin, see him duck and feint and jump, drop the ball into the hoop. And I see him fall, know pain, horror, at nineteen, beyond anything I have ever known or am likely to experience in my life, hopefully beyond anything my own children will ever know.

I can't really picture it. I can *see* him hit, bleed, fall. I can force my mind to create an image of his face shattering around a rifle bullet, but I cannot really experience it in my imagination, no more than I can experience Danny's fate at Leavenworth. Was he raped, broken, *protected, educated?* He wrote me a few letters, but the information revealed nothing of what his real life there must have been like, and I didn't ask. When he got out, he headed straight for San Francisco, the Haight Ashbury, then full of criminals, as was the East Village in New York, and for that matter the whole so-called Peace and Love Movement.

Danny wrote a few more letters about *muling,* about trips into Mexico, about a score so good he bought a new Ford Fairlane, about a commune where he stayed out in the desert, in the mountains. And then there were no more letters and the ones I sent to his last address were returned *unknown at this address.* That was a good fifteen or eighteen years ago. I no longer know where his mother lives, or his older brother, and I have moved so many times that if Danny tried to get in touch with me it is unlikely he would succeed. Most likely he is dead. Or in prison in Mexico.

I sat for nearly three hours waiting for the FBI men to return to my apartment after they took Danny away. Finally I realized they were not coming back for me, that I was free, off the hook. Well, it actually took some time before I really felt free of them. In some respects I continued to wait, felt them watching me. Every tear at the corner of a piece of mail, every click on the telephone made me think of them, but they never came back, never made themselves known in any way. Maybe my name still sits in some file somewhere and would ring a bell if I ever applied for a security clearance, but at least I was never interrogated, never had to spend even a day in jail. My life was allowed to go on without any disruption. I did not have to enter a penitentiary, see the hard faces there, waiting for me, did not have to die.

I had gone into the army after six months of college, volunteered for the draft to get it out of the way, and was discharged in 1964, the year the Gulf of Tonkin Resolution was adopted and President Johnson started getting serious about Vietnam. So I was spared that. My first six months in college I was an ROTC student—that's how abruptly my life changed in the sixties; so if I had gone on to finish according to plan, I would have been graduated as a second lieutenant in 1967, would no doubt have gone right to combat in the Nam. I would have been forced to make a choice which might have drastically changed my whole life one way or the other, death or prison or exile. But I was spared that.

How arbitrary it all seems. Danny's life, mine. The fact that a nation, a president makes a bad choice, thousands of people die violent deaths. My life has been more or less normal. I married, have a house, children, a job. I live a quiet life. I wear my political convictions, such as they are, quietly. I am old enough now to glimpse that place up ahead where my days will end, a natural death probably, although who knows? Perhaps I will be killed by someone shaped into a murderer by poverty, misery, the chance turning of events. Or perhaps not. Perhaps I will die as quietly as fall becomes winter, a withering, fading.

Sometimes darkness, gloom, is a comfort. One chill dark day, early winter, you look at the frozen earth, and you know that some winter will be your last one, you will miss the next beat in the rhythm, we all will, and that is actually a comfort sometimes, in the way it is a comfort on a chill dark day to see a light in the window of a strange house, a yellow lampshade on a table behind gauze curtains. Mysteries.

Like the mystery of Danny's life. I try to picture what it was like for Danny in jail, but I don't really know. He didn't say much about it in his letters, not about the actual conditions, but it must have been a cruel experience. I ask myself why Danny did what he did, why I hid him. What was really in my heart, in Danny's? Why was he ruined by the war? Because he was altruistic? Naive? Did he simply decide he could not kill, could not bear to risk his own life for an historical mistake, and lost it anyway? Did he just use poor judgment? Try to save his skin in a foolhardy way? Or was he just unlucky? An historical casualty? We didn't really discuss it. We didn't talk much about the war. We watched it on TV most nights, of course, shook our heads, groaned, but we were not political, didn't discuss the whole situation. Danny just deserted and, when the time came, I let him stay with me.

What about the generals, the politicians, the people who marched, the people who stayed home, the people who supported the war, and the ones who were just indifferent to it all? I know what my father believed. He said it once finally to me, reluctantly. "We *need* an army, son. People can't just go and run off."

I smirked. "But do we *need* this war?"

I saw Danny's girlfriend, the one who turned him in, once more, many years later. It took me several moments to recognize her. She had gained a lot of weight, but slowly her face appeared from amidst the heavy jowls and sagging wattles. I could see her face, the crooked tooth, the pale green eyes. She was wearing a gray cloth coat, standing outside the projects in Jamaica, near where I teach, and she was shouting after a child of ten or so. I stared at her, recognized her finally, and she looked back at me, but her face showed nothing. It was an empty face, or seemed so, one without emotion, neither joy nor sorrow, but who can judge from a moment's glance?

Now, so many years later, I try to recall Danny's face. I can remember he joked a lot, that he loved rhythm and blues music, used to play an imaginary bass guitar and mime the notes with his mouth. I can remember him with his girlfriend, the two of them with their arms around one another off by themselves, talking quietly. But in truth that is all I can remember. I can hardly remember him at all, cannot call his face to mind in more than the vaguest details, cannot close my eyes and see it there. It is almost as though I never knew him, as though none of it ever happened, although of course it did.

He did run from the army, I did hide him, I did see two federal policemen lead him out of my apartment in handcuffs, shirt out, blood between his teeth, his young innocent mouth swollen.

Twenty-two years later, on an airplane flying to a conference in the Midwest, the stewardess offers me a magazine, and I select *US News & World Report,* in which I read a story about the 25th anniversary of a battle at Landing Zone X-Ray, judged to be the first real battle of Vietnam, on November 14, 1965. The story recounts in detail the five-day encounter which took the lives of 234 Americans and 2,000 Vietnamese. The article narrates the battle, discusses tactics and strategy, the use of helicopters, tells about many of the individual soldiers who fought, plots their movements on a map through each day of the encounter, describes their wounds, an eyewitness account of a lieutenant bleeding from the neck, another whose brains literally spill into his helmet, corpsmen squeezing bloodbags into the veins of men bleeding to death.

I know about this battle; it is here that Stephanie's little brother was killed. The article does not mention his name.

The story ends with a piece about a meeting between the two generals who ran the battle, the American Lt. General "Hal" Moore, the Vietnamese General, Vo Nguyen Giap. General Moore is now 65 years old, General Giap is 80, an aged smiling man. They meet and converse for ninety minutes under the observation of a reporter who had been present covering Landing Zone X-ray twenty-five years before. When the time comes for the two old generals to part, General Moore, a big redheaded man, graying, with an under-slung jaw, takes off his wristwatch and presents it to *Giap—A small gift from one old soldier to another.*

Giap cups the watch in both hands. Then he embraces his former enemy. The article leaves the two old generals in one another's arms.

I remember a friend of mine who told me one night when we were drinking a little bit about what it had been like over there. "Giap had us pinned down in foxholes for four solid days in the rain. Didn't dare stick your head out. You shit in your helmet and threw it out."

I stuff the magazine into the seat pouch in front of me, glance out the window at the landscape below which looks like quadrants of sheet metal riveted together. It occurs to me that, with a quiet impartiality, I am observing the history of my own years.

I feel no rancor. I have read the article with interest, with a certain enthusiasm even, curious to know the details of the men who fought that battle, to know what became of the survivors. I am sad for the dead, shaken by LBJ's mistake, America's mistake, baffled by the revisionism that would have us no longer feel shame about it all, baffled by my own quiet acceptance of it all. I feel no anger. Not toward Johnson or Nixon or the generals or those two FBI men who took Danny away, or the political mistakes that murdered my wife's brother.

This is my story, the story of my time. This is what was going on when I was young. I think of Danny, probably dead now, and maybe his last hours were terrible, his last years, or maybe he is still alive, huddled against an adobe wall in Mexico, broken, rotting in his own dirt, ill, soon dead. We all will be one day, and at the hour of our death, we will look back over our time and regret its passing and puzzle over it, and all of our friends and all of our enemies will be the people we shared our time with. All the dead men and all the women will turn their hollow gazes toward us then, and I do not think we will wish that we had done more or less or something else.

I think death, finally, will become the passage we choose. Resistance will dissolve, and the mystery of all the people we ever touched or who touched us will fold into our hearts at that final moment, like the embrace of an enemy, old now, and smiling.

(1992)

Four: Cast Upon the Day

(2007)

THE PLEASURE OF MAN
AND WOMAN
TOGETHER ON EARTH

SOMETIMES AFTER they make love, Donna weeps and smoulders.

Brighton holds her as her babies sleep in the next room, and she curses her life, the fate she has brought upon herself and her bastards, calls herself a welfare slut, blames her puttana mother, a topless dancer who killed herself driving drunk. Brighton shushes her, runs his palm down the silken skin of her back trying not to imagine her mother's body burning in the wreckage of her Impala convertible; he tells her she should be proud of her children, three healthy beautiful girls.

Sometimes he watches them for her so she can go to Mass. Only if she asks, though; he's no missionary. Often as not on Sundays she piles them into her beat-up Dodge and drives out to the Bay for a picnic. Sometimes he joins them. It's nice to see Donna in a swimsuit, to munch the veal parmesan sandwiches she makes, play with the little girls in the surf, sun on his back.

Other times he hears her shouting at them, slamming things. She slaps the oldest girl, Marta, he's heard it, and he doesn't know what to say.

Tonight, however, the kids are asleep and Donna is feisty as they lay above the damp sheets, soft music of a soul tape rolling through them—Al Green.

"Do you forgive her?" Donna asks, leaning up on her elbow to inspect her navel. "Your wife?"

"I guess," he says.

"Fool."

"It's better to forgive, let things go."

"For you. You're Irish. Italians never forgive. Remember that."

He wonders if he has failed to satisfy her. "Maybe it was my own fault," he says.

"Did you beat her? Did you cheat?"

"No." He watches the way her fingers stretch the brown skin of her belly, examining for flaws. "Not consciously," he adds.

She smirks. "If you abused her you would know. She probably beat you. She just ran out cause she was a discontented bitch. Probably ran off with another guy. And took your money. And your kid."

"That's enough," he says. He rolls out of bed and moves to the window, can see his house below in the moonlight, the bungalow that has been home to all his fifty-five years, first when he was a boy, then a husband, father, now a man alone.

Brighton sees Dusty Mike shuffle along the street toward the beach where he sleeps beneath the boardwalk in a cardboard box. He's lived here as long as Brighton, longer, used to be a construction-site watchman who went to work every night with a six-pack of half quarts. Brighton can hear the droning of his voice but cannot distinguish the words. He saw him earlier today on the way back from Mass, muttering his indefatigible, incomprehensible narrative. "He says to me you climb clay it's slow. Climb rock. Your foot bites, you move."

"The walls are thin," Brighton says softly, meaning the walls of a person's life, the walls that keep you from the street.

Donna lights a Viceroy and lays back with one hand behind her head as she French inhales. Now her appraising eye is on him. "You're getting a gut, Tomasito."

"Privilege of age," he says, although in fact he has been doing sit-ups on his dusty carpet each day since the two of them got together.

She blows a smoke ring, sculpting it elaborately with her full lips. "Actually, on you, it's cute. Sexy." Then, while he is pulling on his T-shirt, she asks, "You know that guy in the big house on the corner? William Swartwood? Where's he from, you know? Looks familiar."

"California I heard."

Swartwood recently bought the sprawling old colonial house, the second oldest building in the county, built in 1710. Brighton has heard Swartwood came here to retire, though he hardly looks old enough, late thirties maybe. IT bucks. He had the house restored beautifully, then erected a tall fence around the property with an automatic speaker telling whoever rang to go away.

"See his car?" Brighton asks, picturing the candy apple Mercedes convertible.

"What can I tell ya? Some guys got it. You won't get wheels like that at the A&P."

"Toyota's good for another fifty thousand easy," he says and looks at her from the corner of his eye, thinking at least I work, at least I earn my own, immediately ashamed of the thought. He goes to his shirt for a Pall Mall, lights it, says, "Pall Mall's extra length filters the smoke. And makes it mild," using the speech as an excuse to look at her brown naked body on the white sheet in the dim light of the little bedroom. His eye fills with the beauty of lines and curves of her, smooth tan skin sketched here and there with black downy hair that glitters in the light from the streetlamp. He wonders whether to go to her again. He wants to touch her. He remembers that lovely moment the first time they were together at a church dance and she stepped out of her heels, suddenly half a head shorter than him, smiling up with her dark eyes and lips glistening with invitation. It embarrasses him a little, how pleased he is to have a girlfriend twenty years younger than himself.

An Indian man up the street approached him one day and pronounced, "My friend: You understand, I trust, she is using you."

"We're friends," Brighton said, wondering that Sudeep, whom he scarcely knew, felt free to be so frank, to observe another man's life and pronounce on it, involve himself. It made him feel like an outsider, a marginal person in his own neighborhood where he had grown up. Then it had been Irish and German with a few Jews, Italians, Greeks, an occasional Frenchie like his mother. Now all the families and friends of his youth are gone; it's mostly Korean, Indian, Latino—he and Donna and Dusty Mike, a few others like old Jack Ward behind the bar of the Donegal, last Irish ginmill in the area, reminiscing about Rockaway duke-outs of bygone years, all that's left of the old days.

He wonders now as he watches her lying there, naked, musingly absorbed in the examination of her skin, whether she expects him to want to marry her. He wonders if he wants to. When he kisses her sometimes, when their naked bodies touch, a belief rushes through his blood that she is divine, like some ancient Mediterranean goddess. Her family was from Naples she told him once—Napolitan— and in the way she pronounced the word he pictured her on narrow streets at sunset by the hot sea.

Other times she seems to him a foolish woman with too many children and not enough discretion or self control, the daughter of a whore, alone on welfare with three kids, beset with prejudice she spouts like fiat. (Italians don't forgive. Remember that.)

He still muses over the mistake he made with his wife. Tired of being alone, he conjured an illusion in which her virtues grew huge, his doubts tiny. He still does not know whether the love of man for woman is an illusion that grows out of loneliness and desire or whether it truly exists. You know what you are? his wife once informed him with elaborate enunciation. A cold fish.

The only love he never doubted was the love he felt for his daughter, the little girl he hadn't wanted his wife to conceive or bear in the first place. The memory of that selfishness causes the back of his neck to flush; yet the moment he looked into his baby girl's eyes, his heart swelled with unexpected love. A gift. Or maybe just hormones.

If he marries Donna, he thinks now, he will have to marry the three children, too. He enjoys them, though he would probably spoil Therese, the little angel who always smiles at him with gleaming eyes, and might be unfair with the oldest child, Marta, whose manner and face he does not like. The one Donna hits.

"Maybe I'll go back over to myself," he tells her now.

"Yeah. Go."

"Want me to stay?"

"I don't care either way."

A nightcap on his porch, a cigarette, pungent smell of weed from his abandoned lawn, formal opening notes of Coltrane's *A Love Supreme* playing softly through the screen door behind him as he watches the gauze curtain suck in and out the open window of her second floor apartment across the road. He reads the notes on the CD case which say Coltrane composed this in gratitude to God for helping him kick both heroin and alcohol cold turkey. "We are all from one thing," it quotes Coltrane as saying. "The will of God. He will remake us as He always has and He always will. Blessed be His name." Brighton has never been able to listen all the way through to the last part of the symphony, the wild disturbing disintegration of the closing parts.

A black cat sidles along his low chain-link fence. He half rises from his chair to get a better look and the cat stops at the opening where a gate used to be, looks in, cries out to him. It is purely black which seems marvellous to him. That the cat stops and looks and addresses him seems marvellous, like something out of a forgotten dream. He hurries inside for a bowl, pours in skim milk, returns, moving gingerly toward the cat, making what he hopes are reassuring sibilant sounds with his lips. The cat watches alertly as he sets down the bowl, trots over, sniffs, begins to drink with small stabs of its pink tongue.

Brighton wants to stroke the sleek black flank, but the little girl with thick glasses from down the street comes by and stoops to fuss with the animal which rubs against her.

"Hi, Alma," he says.

"Hi Mr. Brighton," she sings out with that incredible sweetness of a ten-year-old girl.

"How's school?"

She flattens her lips in friendly reprimand. "It's summer vacation!"

He laughs as she walks off with the cat in her arms, disappointed she didn't stay longer, wondering how old she will have to be before she can have contact lenses, poor kid.

A Korean man walks swiftly down the street, and Brighton wonders idly where he is going, what he thinks about. How strange it seems to him that these people from a country at war with the United States a mere fifty years ago, in which his older brother lost his life, have now taken over the neighborhood he and his brother grew up in.

William Swartwood passes by, headed toward the Sound. The slow steady register of his heels on the pavement echo beneath Brighton's porch roof. Swartwood is tall and slender with elegantly trimmed tawny hair. He wears a silk tie and dark shirt and his pant cuffs drape perfectly on sleek black leather shoes that must have cost like two hundred dollars.

"Evening, Mr. Swartwood!" Brighton calls out and receives in return a cordial nod. The crying of a baby drifts across the dusky street, and Swartwood turns his face up toward Donna's window, as though he already knows who's who in the neighborhood. Brighton follows his gaze and sees Donna sitting by the window, infant at her breast. Swartwood pauses for a moment, watching. Even from his porch Brighton can see, in the light of the streetlamp, the dreamy expression on her face, and it seems one with the mild air on his bare arms and the green shadows of the trees and hedges.

The summer dusk thickens to night, and a yellow firefly winks beneath an elm tree. How they used to catch them in a jar and shake it to see them all illuminate.

Cruel, his mother said, though without much conviction. He

wonders about her reserve. Was she a cold fish? Was he? Already then, as a boy? And his father's skepticism when he knotted his lips beneath his red moustache, what was he thinking?

Those two people who were gods to the child so remote now in death, like strangers. Their pictures hang in the living room, black and white studio portraits with small smiles, photographic reflections of living eyes that see nothing now. With each year as the portraits fade, the faces seem more strange to him, distant. There is a graduation picture of his brother James, too, killed in Korea at the age of eighteen, which saved Brighton, as sole surviving son, from Vietnam where he no doubt would have died as well.

"Your brother was thirteen years older than you?" Donna said once. "You must've come out of a wine bottle, Tomasito."

They shipped James's body home in 1953 when Brighton was eight. Closed casket. You don't want to look, Mr. Foley at the funeral home advised, and when Brighton's father continued to insist, added in a hush, There is no face.

Brighton pictures meeting James again in eternity, if he could believe that, as Dante meets people when he travels into hell and purgatory and heaven, pictures meeting a figure with no face and turns swiftly from the image only to collide with the still unanswered question of why Mary Lynne left him, where his little girl Lorraine, now twenty-five, might be.

He has pictures of them in the hallway, together and alone and one of the three of them. Where did they go? Why did she never tell him? Because he was a cold fish? Because they had to live in his father's house? He only wishes he could know Lorraine was all right.

The Coltrane has reached a point where the music disintegrates into screeches, vibrations. He goes quickly inside and stops it. He washes the milk bowl he'd put out for the cat, crumbles in some left-over bacon and places it on the back step.

The wind ripples the waters of the Sound, dappling each little spire in early morning sunlight, red black yellow. Brighton strolls the boardwalk alongside William Swartwood, experiencing the pleasure of coming closer to another human being. A spontaneous occurrence: two men headed in the same direction join company. Just a day to skip Mass for a walk by the sea.

Dusty Mike climbs up from beneath the boardwalk and crosses their path. He wears baggy red swimtrunks and a grimey tweed jacket. "Was wondrous," he mutters. His eyes are unwashed, hands ashy as the gutter, bare legs ruddy. "Doorman touched my wrist just as I look up to the clock. Thing's froze, hands stopped at three."

"Poor guy," says Brighton when they are past him.

"Maybe he's happy."

Brighton shrugs. "Who knows?" Yet he cannot help wonder what right Swartwood has in his big house and expensive clothes to think a guy who has to sleep under the boardwalk could be happy?

"You seem meditative, Mr. Brighton," Swartwood says. "Are you an educated man?"

"Not really," says Brighton, embarrassed to be reminded he only did two years of college. "I read a little. Got some books."

"What do you read?"

"Different things. I have a book of art which I look in. And then the pictures have led me to other things."

Swartwood glances with his triangular face. He wants more and

Brighton warms to it. He tells how he saw photographs of sculptures by a French artist named Rodin. "My mother's book. She was French. Anyway, I thought they were corny. A man and woman kissing each other." He flourishes his hand in the air to indicate an overblown title. "The Kiss! Another of a guy sitting with his chin in his hand: The Thinker! You know the one, looks like a laxative ad? But then I read the explanations and found out these actually started as parts of a much bigger sculpture called The Gates of Hell. Two big wrought iron gates like, with a lot of smaller figures on them. The man and woman kissing represent Adam and Eve, but also the book says, the pleasure of man and woman together on earth."

Swartwood, who is setting the pace of their stroll, has picked up speed, and Brighton's breath quickens. He has never tried to express these things before and now, fumbling to put them into words feels like a test of whether his ideas and thoughts hold water. It is as though he is demonstrating how vacant and idle his life is, but he plunges on.

"And then The Thinker, it turns out he is the poet Dante Alighieri, you know, meditating the sins and trials of humankind. So I go to the library for some writings by Dante."

"The Divine Comedy. Greatest work of literature ever written. As I guessed, you are an educated man."

Even if he is being patronized Brighton doesn't mind. He remembers something else. "Rodin never finished that sculpture of The Gates of Hell and the people who paid him to make it asked him why. He said, 'And are cathedrals finished?'"

Swartwood chuckles deep in his throat, and Brigthton feels he is on a roll. "Yeah, then I also saw Rodin's sculpture of a French writer named Balzac. I saw a close-up of his face, and it was incredible to look at. This, this broad face, flat wide nose, thick lips like. Underneath there's a quote by Rodin that says, 'No one has ever before taken the thoughts from a man's mind and placed them on his face.'"

Swartwood slows, his back to the water as he peers into Brighton's eyes. "That is a fucking amazing quote," he says quietly. Brighton cannot see his face with the sun behind him, only the shape of it, a dark inverted triangle in a blur of white light.

"My mother had a book by Balzac, too, and I read this amazing story about a soldier who gets lost alone in the desert. He sleeps in a cave and during the night a panther crawls in and sleeps beside him. He's terrified. Has his hand on his sword but he's afraid even to move. In the morning the panther leaves, but comes back later with a deer it's killed. For him, the soldier, you know—how cats do? They become friends. He pets her. They play together. And she seems like beautiful as a woman to him. Then one day they're playing, and she puts her teeth around his ankle. She doesn't bite, but she could, and he buries his sword in her throat. As she dies, her eyes look at him and he can see a question in them: Why?"

"Fantastic," says Swartwood, as though he really means it, and he leads the way to a bench where they sit, facing the water. Brighton lights a cigarette.

"Those things'll kill you," Swartwood says, but Brighton goes on. "At the end of the story, after the guy has escaped and it's years later, someone asks him what it's like in the desert, and he answers, 'It is God without humanity.'"

A smile stretches Swartwood's lips, and he laughs that deep-throated chuckle again, a dark sound that makes Brighton think the man understands the meaning of the sentence which he himself has been unsuccessfully puzzling over for more than a year. He wants to ask what Swartwood thinks it means, but doesn't want to give himself away.

That sentence is a recurrent puzzle in his thoughts. in his consciousness, and he does not understand why this should be. The things he has read were all by coincidence—because his parents happened to have this book on Rodin which led him to Dante and Balzac, and what he read of them was just what he happened to put his hands on, and it filled up his mind and shaped his life in a sense, his way of thinking over the past few years. But there was no system in it. What if he read something else instead? Maybe he would have been another person altogether.

Brighton wishes he could discuss these things, but Swartwood rises. "Very enjoyable talking with you, Mr. Brighton," he says. "Let's do it again," and strides off.

There is still time for Mass before he goes to work. He climbs the steps of the shabby brick church, blesses himself at the holy water font, takes his place in the last pew. His thoughts drift in the muggy still air as the priest prays from the altar.

Perspiration trickles down his face, his wrists. He notices his shoes need polish, buffs the toes on the backs of his pant legs, remembers the elegant black leather shoes on William Swartwood's feet. It seems to Brighton there is some quality in the man wearing the shoes that makes them remarkable, and he recognizes envy in himself, recognizes the envy as vanity yet wonders whether he merely uses the thought of vanity to excuse his own lack of success. If I was rich would I care about anything? He pictures Swartwood tooling out of his driveway in the gleaming Mercedes, top down, breeze riffling his hundred dollar haircut.

He wipes his brow with the back of his wrist. Then the altar boys draw back the trays of vigil lights, and the few people scattered about the church line up to receive the consecrated host from the priest. With the unleavened bread on his tongue, Brighton returns to the pew, bows his face into his hands, smelling the damp meat of his palms and tries to think of eternity. He pictures it as the exhalation of air from a mouth that ceases to breathe, as a pillar of dissolving breath drifting from a throat toward the sky, as peace.

He believes that his soul then will become something else, freed of his ego, moving on to its mysterious destination. It has occurred to him some time before that the human ego is perishable. It makes him sad to think that that which he has known to be himself will not live on in eternity, will not enter another region where his father and mother and dead brother might be waiting for him, where his wife and daughter, when they die, might go, where he might be waiting to greet Donna and her children, Dusty Mike, little Alma, Swartwood even.

After he completes his report and turns over to the nightman at the A&P, Brighton picks out some milk and fruit for Donna, takes a newspaper from the magazine racks, pays at the register. She clearly is not in the mood for company so he drops off the groceries and reads his paper beneath the porchlight, munching a jelly doughnut he bought for himself from the German bakery on his way home.

In the last section is a retrospective article about the Korean War in which 37,000 Americans were killed. The article states that America entered the war with rash overconfidence and outdated ineffective weapons, convinced that their victory over Germany and Japan five years earlier made them invincible, that the bomb had made conventional warfare obsolete, that the North Koreans would flee at the mere sight of them.

It tells about a battle near a place called Kunu-ri where an American regiment, ordered to withdraw in subzero temperatures, was swarmed inching down a narrow icy mountain road by thousands of Chinese troops who clubbed and bayonetted them at such close quarters it was impossible even to fire their obsolete rifles. The Americans had to flee through a ten mile gauntlet of Chinese fire, abandoning the dead and wounded who were crying out for help.

Brighton tries to remember the name of the battle in which his brother James died, cannot, folds the paper shut and wipes his eyes, gazing absently at a front page color photograph of Tiger Woods wielding his golf putter triumphantly above his head.

Then he thinks of something, goes inside to check the book of Balzac stories, finds that he has misquoted the final line of that story. It does not say of the desert that it is "God without humanity," but "God without mankind." He carries the book across the street to Swartwood's house, stands at the fence thinking Swartwood might find this makes a difference. He rings the bell on the gate, and a recorded voice says, "We are occupied. If you have a message, please leave it in the mailbox beside the gate. Have a good day."

"I saw you go into church," Swartwood says to Brighton as they stroll past Immaculate Conception toward the boardwalk. They have begun to walk together in the morning. "And I got to thinking, about how you've read Dante. I was wondering whether you believe in that scheme of sins and virtues and punishments he sets up. Do you believe that eternal happiness is possible on the basis of obedience to the laws of the church? Or that those who disobey are damned to hell?"

"Hard to know," Brighton says. "I guess not."

"Well you know the Francesca canto for example? Remember that one? Do you believe that lovers like that would suffer eternal torment in hell?"

Brighton hesitates, feeling himself under attack and his brain offers little of defense. "Longing!" he blurts then. "I think it was the longing between them for something...eternal." He feels foolish, just manufacturing words to conceal the silence of his mind, but Swartwood nods encouragingly. "Two people who loved each other now together in death. Their love, in a sense, in the poem, triumphs over death, even if they are filled with the pain of longing for what is gone and beyond all recall."

"Yes! Yes," says Brighton, "Yes!" hardly able to believe his good fortune, as they climb the steps of the boardwalk. He feels he has stumbled into the company of a man who can put into words his own deepest thoughts, feels as though the broken words he blurted have been affirmed, enlarged, clarified. He feels a surge of gratitude for the man that is near love.

Swartwood gazes out to the stippled surface of the Sound and recites softly, "'And I believed myself transported to higher salvation with my lady. My desire and my will revolved like a wheel moved evenly by the love which moves the sun and other stars.'" His smiling face turns back toward Brighton. "You're right," he says. "It's hard to know. Dante never saw his Beatrice again in life. Anyway, good to know you're not a papist, I take it?" When Brighton merely gazes uncertainly, he adds, "You know, someone who follows the Pope."

"It's just my religion, I was raised in it."

"Do you know the first thing the current Pope did when he was elected? He called out for the need for a simpler way of life and on the same day had a swimming pool installed in his private quarters. He also had the bullet that was dug out of him when that Turk shot him, he had the bullet set into the crown of the statue of the Virgin Mary at Fatima. And then he had his minions spread the rumor that the assassination attempt against him had been predicted in a letter the Virgin was supposed to have have given the three little peasant girls she purportedly appeared to at Fatima. How about that?"

Brighton shrugs. He can think of nothing to say. "The Pope publicly forgave that guy who shot him."

"Right, he allowed him to be extradited back to Turkey where he was facing another murder trial. The Turks know how to handle prisoners."

Brighton cannot find a path of thought in his mind, realizes gloomily that he has not really applied his intellect to the things he has read, that he understands so little. He has gone too long without speaking. "What do you believe in?" he asks. "Do you believe in some religion?"

"I attended the same school and church as you. My father was an ecumenical minister at Immaculate Conception."

"I never saw you there."

"But I remember you. I was just a kid, and I got out fast."

Brighton can hardly believe it. "You remember me?"

"Sure. Your father was a security guard at Dutch County Savings & Loan. My father was a worthless drunk. He died when I was twelve and my mother took up with another character who decided I needed discipline. My mother stood there and watched when he beat crap out of me. Spiritual people, like Augustine, Per molestias eruditio. True education begins with physical abuse." He laughs bitterly.

"So you are from around here," Brighton says, eager to turn the conversation. "Donna, a woman I know, Donna Graziano, said she thought you looked familiar. You know the woman with the three kids who lives across from me?"

Swartwood stops walking. The breeze off the water is constant, a soft feathery current across their faces. "Does she remember me? What did she say?"

"Just like, we wondered, why you came back and all."

"When I was sixteen I ran off. To California. I was good with computers and I got lucky in Silicon Valley. Retired at twenty-five. I went back to school, studied what I wanted, where I wanted. Stanford, Harvard, the Sorbonne. I travelled. But I never forgot certain things here. That house for one thing. I remember it from when I was a kid in that pissy three-room apartment over on Northern with my mother and that bastard. I dreamed of owning that big old Colonial. Now I do." He lifts his chin and gazes down at Brighton.

"Well it never looked better," Brighton says, obeying an instinct he does not understand to reassure the man when, in fact, he resents his wealth, his bragging, his sudden arrogant manner. Still, he recognizes it must have been hard for him, with a stepfather like that.

Brighton's own parents never laid a finger on him. "Religion," he says carefully. "Mass and all, confession, was something I really found important when I was a kid. Before you were even born maybe. Then I turned from it, but I came back later. It's not something I think about so much, but that church, my family always prayed there, all my life. It means something to me."

"I don't doubt it," says Swartwood, and Brighton notices that the man's way of speaking sounds wealthy, too, can hear the vague echo of unspoken thoughts which belittle him.

"Well," he says, trying to keep his own voice neutral. "I have to get to work."

The new kid he hired doesn't show up, and Brighton fills in as a bottle boy for a few hours, then doubles on check out. By the end of the day his back aches from bending, sorting, lifting, leaning over the counter. He stops at a cafeteria for his dinner, glancing up from his meatloaf and mashed potatoes from time to time at the gobbling faces around him. So many people eating alone. Some of them he sees in church. A balding black-haired man. An elderly round-faced woman. They look at him, too, but their eyes dart away before their gazes meet.

Later, on his porch, he drinks a beer and nurtures the resentment Swartwood's manner and accent called forth that morning, nagging at him ever since. A wealthy man who no doubt pays no taxes. Brighton has worked all his life, even in high school, at the A&P, and now is assistant manager. That's not nothing, he thinks, but feels his life shabby and futile beside Swartwood's. Still, he works, pays his taxes. So he drives a twelve-year-old Toyota and will never have anything anywhere near the kind of money Swartwood can spend on houses, cars, studies, travel. He used to dream about travel, but can no longer remember why. He thinks about Europe, about how they came here and took the place from the Indians, which makes it possible for him to sit here right now. He thinks about Swartwood in his big Colonial, flying off on the Concord or something for a weekend in fucking Paris.

The telephone rings.

"What are you doing all alone out on your porch?" Donna asks. "Why don't you invite me down for a drink?"

"What about the kids?"

"Marta can watch them. I'll leave the window open so I can hear."

Something is wrong, but he doesn't know if it's him or her. She's edgy. Maybe he's edgy, too. It occurs to him they are making love in the bed that was his mother and father's, maybe the place where he was conceived. Donna is very passionate at first, nervously so it seems to him, which cools his own passion, and then they lay still on the sweated sheets, and the room closes in on him: The mahogony headboard, the chipped bureau, beige tobacco-stained walls.

"Let's go out and have a drink," he says and opens a bottle of red wine in the living room, puts on Coltrane.

"That sucks," she says and replaces it with Frank Sinatra singing about the summer wind. Now she can't sit still or keep her mouth shut. "I saw you with your newspaper the other day," she tells him, as she moves about the room. "I saw you eating your jelly doughnut out of the little white bag. So tidy. You looked so, what's the word? Tidy."

He wants her to go home. The way she carries her glass of red wine from the sideboard to the window makes him nervous. It occurs to him maybe they will stop seeing each other and he wonders if that is a good thing. Maybe she was drinking before she came over.

"You drunk?" he asks.

"What are you, a cop writin' a book?"

"You sit up there all alone and drink? That's not good."

"I think it's good," she says stepping quickly toward him and stumbles so her wine splatters across the beige carpet.

"Oh, Donna!" he snaps and hurries for a wet rag, kneels to scrub the spot, as she watches from the sofa, feet up, pours a fresh glass of wine. "You are such a practical little pig," she says. "That's what I like about you."

He wonders if she wants him to hit her, if that's what she feels she needs. There was a guy who lived with her before, the little baby's father he thought, and Brighton could hear bellowing and crashing around. Maybe she just gets crazy and feels she needs to be suppressed. He won't do it. He stands and faces her. "You're getting on my nerves. Go home."

"Now you're getting me wet again," she says and sticks her tongue between her teeth.

"Save it," he snaps, but laughs despite himself, feels his blood move. "You know the buttons to push, don't you?"

But she is already up and at the door, turns back. "Hey, would you watch my kids for me tomorrow night?"

"Where you going?"

"I gotta do somethin'. Will you watch them or not? If you don't want, I can get my aunt."

After a moment, he shrugs. "Okay," he says, although he mostly wants to tell her no.

The baby is already sleeping when he arrives. Stuck to the refrigerator door on a magnet that says If Mama Ain't Happy, Ain't Nobody Happy is a note how to prepare the baby's formula if she wakes.

"Don't you breastfeed her?"

"She's being weaned."

Donna let Brighton taste her milk once. He thought it was a wonderful thing, to be nourished by a woman's body. He wanted to try it again, but was too shy to ask. And he is too proud to ask again where she is going, all dolled up as she is in the foxy black summer dress she wore to the church dance where he met her.

"You have great legs," he says, and she hitches up the mini to show more, tongue between her teeth. His mouth goes dry, but then she is out the door and he is reading to the two older girls from a book of Mother Goose. They have their favorites he has to read— "Hot Cross Buns," "Doctor Gloster," "The Gypsy in the Wood." He reads the one about Anna Eliza who jumps with surprise from chair to pail to net to ball to ground and ends up forever spinning around.

Three-year old Therese giggles, her eyes alight, her laughter like music, while the older Marta just watches him. Then he goes into "Old MacDonald," the whole tedious litany of it. Therese sings along for several verses, but by the time he finally reaches the last oinking pig, she is asleep, open-mouthed, on a plaid blanket on the living room floor. Brighton carries her carefully into bed, and dark-haired Marta still sits staring at him when he returns.

"Beddie-bye time," he says, but she does not move, only stares with her dark eyes in her dark square face, her small hard mouth. It is a terrible thing, he thinks, to dislike someone because of their face, especially a seven-year-old child. "Want me to read one more?"

She doesn't answer, and he checks his rising annoyance, decides to let her sit there in the corner of the sofa as long as she wants, to ignore her. He helps himself to Donna's wine and stands at the window, smoking a Pall Mall. Across the road he sees the black cat sidling along his chain-link fence. That morning on his back step he found a rat's butt and tail. It makes him smile to remember.

"Want to see a cat?" he says over his shoulder to Marta. She doesn't answer. "Your mom sure looked beautiful tonight, didn't she?" he asks; then, when she still says nothing, "Don't you like me?"

"My mother promised me a Barbie," she says tonelessly.

"Wow, great!"

"But she forgot she promised and now she says she never did."

"Well that happens sometimes. When's your birthday? Maybe I'll give you a Barbie."

"I don't want that one, I wanted the one from my mother."

Brighton turns his back to the room, peers out to the street, trying to imagine himself into the child's mind, to find some idea that might relax her, or make him understand, but as he looks out he sees Swartwood's Mercedes glide past below. The top is down and there is a woman in the seat beside him, black-haired like Donna. He leans out, but cannot tell for certain as the car moves out of the light of the streetlamp. He puts his wine glass on the coffee table and hurries to the bedroom for a better view, but the car is already out of sight. When he returns, the glass is on its side, wine rolling across the formica table top.

"Shit!" He jumps to dam the flow at the edge with his handkerchief, mops it up, glares at the child. "That was not smart."

"You're not supposed to say shit," she says.

"When you're my age you can say what you damn please," he snaps. "Now get to bed!"

He sees she is near tears, but she obeys, and he sits on the edge of the sofa running his palm across his mouth, torn between anger and remorse, trying to rid his mind of the image of the child's face about to dissolve into tears. He feels foolish. He would rather be furious, but has difficulty supporting his anger. What right does he really have? She and Swartwood are the same age, and he is old. He remembers the Indian who told him Donna was using him and feels even more foolish. He thinks about all the groceries he brings her from the supermarket. Is it so obvious to everyone but me? And what right do I have? I use her, too. We just use each other. And the image of the little girl's face trembling on the edge of tears haunts him.

What do I want here? What am I after? Just to fuck her young body? To feed some false image of myself as young?

He rises, drifts around the room, picking up her pathetic knick-knacks, a clamshell ashtray, a five-and-dime porcelain panther with fake ruby eyes, a dusty little heart-shaped basket full of souvenir matchbooks, a plaster statute of the Virgin Mary, all white except for the lips which are painted red. The plaster feels unpleasant against his palm, and he puts it down, wanders into her bedroom.

On one knee, he rummages through her dresser drawers, wondering what he is looking for, appalled with himself, but he continues. He takes a pair of her underpants in his hands experiences grim

367

satisfaction to discover stains there.

"What are you doing? I'll tell!" Marta stands in the doorway in her faded Minnie Mouse pajamas.

"I was looking for matches," he says and slams the drawer.

"Liar!"

"Go back to bed! I was looking for matches!"

"Matches are in the basket on the shelf!"

"Go back to bed or..." He is moving toward her, worried that she stands her ground, uncertain what he will do if she does not run, but just before he reaches her she screams, "You hit me you hit me!" and bolts for her room, slamming the door, and the baby begins to cry, a nagging incessant sound.

As he stands in the center of the living room trying to decide what to do, he hears Donna's key in the door.

Her lipstick is smeared and she goes straight for Marta's room. "Is she being a brat again?"

"No, mommy, no, please..." There is a sharp crack and weeping and without knowing he will do so, Brighton heads straight out the still opened apartment door.

His phone is ringing as he lets himself in. He lets it ring until it stops. Then it rings again for a while, and stops. He peers through the venetian blinds of his front window. The light is still on in her living room. It goes out, and he can see blue cigarette smoke drift from her bedroom window into the light of the street lamp. He pictures her with smeared lipstick staining a wine glass, staining the filter of a Viceroy. He cannot understand that he would behave as he has, at his age, losing it like that.

He sits in the dark in his living room, drinking Jim Beam on the rocks and smoking. From where he sits he can see the portraits of his mother and father and James above the sofa and in the hall the pictures of Mary Lynne and Lorraine and himself—fading reflections of people who are gone, people he has not seen for decades.

The sound of a crashing garbage can outside draws him to the window: Loud voices, cursing, laughter, three teenage boys swaggering along the middle of the road. His heartbeat quickens as he watches. One is holding a can of some sort, places the spout into his mouth, takes it away and flicks on a cigarette lighter, spits out a mouthful of fluid which explodes into flame before his face. The others laugh and they move off toward the beach.

He can't stop thinking about little Marta, her mouth trembling, the ugly sound of Donna smacking her. He remembers once in his presence Donna whacked the back of her head, and he watched shock and hurt register on the child's face and said nothing. He pours another bourbon, puts on Coltrane's *A Love Supreme*, and sits there in the dark, listening to the formal, orderly opening progress to the chanting prayer-like male voices, drinking until his mind blurs into the disintegrating squawking of the sax as he nods off into sleep.

Dusty Mike lectures loudly from the boardwalk into the cool of the morning. "Idiots!" he yells. "With gasoline! Threaten a human being! For what reason?" he shouts. "Because he has no home? No child of a mother should face this! It could be you! You!"

Brighton steps hurriedly past him, thinking about the man's words, remembers those kids with the lighter fluid and wonders if there is something he could try to do. His head is soft from the night before, the whiskey, the memory of Marta's trembling mouth. He sits on a bench and lights a cigarette, considers selling his house, moving away, live on what he gets until it's gone, recognizing that his thoughts are out of control yet unable to calm himself. Just wait till tomorrow, he thinks. Tomorrow is another day, yet he still can see Marta's trembling lips, and he puts his face into his hands, feeling utterly useless.

"Morning, Mr. B!" Swartwood sits beside him on the bench. "No Mass today?"

"Not today." In fact, Brighton left home with the intention of going to Mass, but an ugly spray of grafitti on the church's wooden doors discouraged him. He kept walking to the beach.

"Well," Swartwood says. He inhales deeply through his mouth. "So much for that." Brighton says nothing, and Swartwood adds, "Want to buy a house?"

"You moving?"

"Make me an offer."

"I don't have that kind of money."

Swartwood chuckles, nods, says "And I believed myself transported to higher salvation with my lady." He looks into Brighton's face. "What a joke. What a fucking joke."

"I don't know what you mean."

"Well." He drapes his arms over the back of the bench. "When I was a kid, I had a dream. There was that house and there was also a woman. A girl. She didn't even know me, but I used to see her, and I said to myself, Someday. Someday I'll be someone, and she'll see me then. She was so damn pretty. I never forgot her. For years and years, I felt like Dante with Beatrice, you know? The problem is, when you fall in love from afar you never get a close-up. It never occurred to me that the Madonna might be like, you know: the house is lit up but nobody's home." He laughs that deep-throated sound. "Higher salvation, my butt."

"Yeah," says Brighton. "You deserve better." Then, for fear the irony might be lost, adds, "You and your fancy shoes."

Swartwood turns his face slowly. Brighton can see from the corner of his eye that he is being considered. He can hear the sound of his blood in his ears and does not know what he might do or say.

"Were you sweet on her? You know who I mean? I had no idea, but nothing happened if that's what you were thinking. We drove to the beach, we talked. The whole thing took no time at all. Twenty-two years I waited for that moment. What a joke."

Brighton doesn't dare to speak for he fears the tight ball of emotion lodged just beneath his voice, fears he will disgrace himself, lash out shamelessly.

After a moment, Swartwood lurches to his feet, says, "Hey, my friend. Respect to you. It's been a pleasure." He extends his hand. Brighton shakes it without rising, half looking his way, and listens to the sound of the man's expensive leather heels moving off across the boardwalk.

On the surface, little has changed. Swartwood drives off in his Mercedes one morning and Brighton never sees him again. He and Donna still meet, though less frequently, even though she clearly tries to win him back. Brighton would like to know exactly what happened between her and Swartwood, but he doesn't want to ask and she doesn't tell. He thinks, She would drop me in a minute for a younger man with money. Yet he can see, or thinks he can see in her gaze, regret after they make love—that she tried, that she used him that way. Maybe her feeling is deeper now. Or maybe it is all illusion.

One day Dusty Mike is found dead beneath the boardwalk, and Brighton has to phone in sick to the supermarket that day. He sits for a long time in his living room chair staring at a bottle of bourbon with all the various colored pills and tablets from his medicine cabinet emptied out on the table before him. Finally with the back of his hand, he sweeps them to the floor, puts on Coltrane, drinks until he passes out in the wilderness of sound and is back in work the next morning.

He goes to Mass every day now. He sits in the last pew wondering why he comes, what he hopes for. He does not listen to the priest or the litany, does not meditate the ceremony, the sacrifice of Christ. These things are without real meaning for him. He decides that his purpose there is to prepare himself for death. Too many things he has done in his life without preparation—school, work, marriage, fatherhood. He should have planned his life better, prepared. It never occurred to him to do so.

Perhaps if he sits here everyday and peers into the dark behind his eyelids he might glimpse something in time that will make it possible for him to accept his moment of extinction when it comes. Yet he recognizes that, accept it or not, the moment will come and pass, and on its other side he will have ceased to be, whether or not he prepares for it.

That afternoon at the A&P, he finds himself standing before a shelf of toys divided in two sections, one half for boys, one for girls. Blue and pink mostly. There are several Barbie dolls in pink cardboard boxes with cellophane faces. He picks up one that is a little larger and flashier than the others, called Safari Barbie. The doll is dressed in leopard skin shorts and halter, and beside her in the box is a panther cub on a leash.

At the cash register, he pays and asks the girl to wrap it for him, then buys a bag of jellybeans for Therese. As he walks home with the candy in his pocket, package under his arm, the crisp smell of early autumn reaches his nostrils with its agreeable, promising edge of death. A bumblebee plump as a baby's fist hovers in air, wandering among the wilting flowerbeds of a neighbor's lawn. Brighton wonders what the bee is doing, wonders idly what it's for. Then he thinks how it might be to have flowers in his own lawn again.

And he finds himself enjoying the sound of his heels on the pavement, the cool air on his face as he quietly hums the formal opening notes of Coltrane's *A Love Supreme*.

(2003)

Years in Kaldar

In the evening, after they coaxed the children to sleep with fairy tales and lullabies, small faces bathed in orange glow of nightlights, Jack and Evelyn Lynch sat in the living room in horseblanket armchairs on either side of the smoked-glass coffee table, facing the television screen.

Lynch took off his shoes and wiggled his toes, yawned, scratched, smiled, and turned his attention to the stack of papers on the glass tabletop. He worked there, glancing up from time to time at the TV, or to say a word to Evelyn, or reach for his drink. He read and took notes on a manuscript he was editing. Evelyn had her research cards piled unevenly on the table so she could work on the coding for her project, but mostly she only watched the television, sipped her coffee, smoked Newports, tapping her ash into the stained saucer beneath the cup. From time to time, she glanced at Lynch. He could feel the heat of her anger. She wanted a fight. He didn't know why exactly, perhaps just on the ground of general discontent, disconnection. She began to mutter, insult him, and once that started, he knew he could do nothing until she talked herself out and went to bed.

On the screen, Alan Ladd, wearing a flannel shirt, was saying to George Peppard, "I have seen you make grown men vomit with fear."

"Why do you stay here?" Evelyn asked. "Why do you stay with me?"

Lynch looked at her, then at the pencil which he jiggled between his fingers. "This is my home," he said, raising his palm.

"*Your* home. *You. Your. You.* You give us *nothing.*"

He closed his lips. Alan Ladd and George Peppard began to box.

"You know what you are?" she said. "Know what you are? *Paper.* A* bunch of goddamn worthless paper."

He nodded, smirked to himself, kept his mouth shut, aware from experience that she would run down in fifteen or twenty minutes if only he could keep from fueling her wrath. Actually, it was not bad spiritual exercise. And it was interesting to be privy to such negative observations about oneself. She criticized his appearance, his occupation, his family, his character, personality, and general behavior. He listened to the things she said, thought about them. The only danger was if he accidentally listened to her voice itself, instead of just the words; the sound of the voice, the loud, hard, constant substance, the grainy smoked-menthol texture of it could infiltrate his peace, rouse him into her game. Then he would be on his feet, shouting lies, distortions, vulgarities, or worse, concealed truths, things from which he had meant to protect her, things her mother had said behind her back, or veiled slights forwarded by the boss from his wife, or his own observations of how she had conducted herself at some party or function. When these rages took hold of him, he didn't know himself. He paced, grinned malevolently, struck for blood, pain. If she began to cry, he bore down harder. Sometimes he stood watching her, thinking that if she came close enough, he might do something, lash out with his knuckles, the back of his hand, lunge for her, could feel his eyes wide open, fascinated by his own meanness.

But essentially, this was her game. He let her play it alone, waited for her to run down and stomp off to bed. His own game was a quieter one, so quiet he couldn't even hear it himself, though he had listened, tried to, for he wanted to know himself, to be free of blindness.

At last, she rose, glaring, cocked her leg, kicked his shoes from beneath the edge of the coffee table. One skidded into the wall beneath the TV. The living room door whacked shut behind her. He flinched, startled by the sound, then knew he had peace until morning. He cherished these interludes of solitude. (Perhaps *that* was his game.)

First thing he did was switch off the TV (Alan Ladd's face, bleeding from the nose, vanished with a click), spread out his papers. He freshened his drink with a healthy splash of Glenfiddich, filled a dish with peanuts, sorted through his record albums: Morrison, Dylan, Parker, Getz, Vivaldi. He chose the Vivaldi, sat again and sipped his malt whiskey, nibbled Planters, wrote letters to friends, contemplated women he had known, meditated, thought about his father, prayed, tried to find a prayer to focus on a power he no longer believed capable of an awareness of men, until he could neither drink more nor stay awake longer. Then he made his bed on the sofa, slept in his underwear with his eyeglasses folded in his hand because he feared being alone in the dark and unable to see.

During the night, he woke to the sound of a slow rain striking the roof gutter, sizzling in the dead leaves across the lawn. Not because he missed her so much as in a lonely panic to deny that this had happened to them, that their life together had grown so strange, he got off the sofa and climbed the stairs to the bedroom, lay beside her in the dark, listening to the whisper of her breathing while he stared at the knotty pine ceiling and contemplated the burnt, strange landscape of their ten years together, the children they had made, the transformation of their feeling for each other from what they had once called love to a relationship stranger than any he had ever known or could have imagined—the intimate hostility of people too closely connected ever to be free of one another, whether or not they parted. No, not connected. Disconnected, like a limb torn loose of its socket, bone grating on bone. He could remember saying to her, "I love you." The words he had held back until he felt sure he meant them. And, "I *do* love you," the extra verb emphasizing the doubt it tried to annul. The word seemed so cheap, the mandatory lie of surrender. The sound of it was like a trap with all its springs of pledge and vow and unspecified future commitment. It seemed a word for people weak with loneliness, desperate to deny that they were sealed within their flesh, alone for all time; he wondered whether this was due to a deficiency in himself.

In the pale morning light, he opened his eyes, watched her lift the white sheet and rise from the bed, her face bruised with anger. The haloed silhouette of her naked body in the narrow parting of the curtains might have been a woodprint, Hopper, a bad mood in its best light. Lynch's eye traced the contour of her breast, perfect curve, bawdy tilt of stem. Admiration began and ended in the eye, went fallow in his brain.

He remembered when he had realized he wanted to marry her, a dozen years ago. He had been lying on her sofa, waiting to make love with her while she stood naked by the window of her apartment on 85th Street, rooftops and water tanks behind her. She had been taken from his arms by the telephone, which she stood chatting into while he lay there and admired her body. She stood with one foot on a chairseat, and she probed and caressed the skin of her leg as she talked, looking first at one side, then the other, evaluating. The long soft plane of flesh inside her thigh drew his blood toward his center, his center toward her. He had fancied that he knew the difference between love and lust. He did know the difference between wanting a woman you dislike and lying to get her and wanting a woman you like and not having to lie. But this was more, a more complete emotion than he had yet known for a woman, so lacking another word, he called it by that one, love, though still there was the doubt whether it was ever anything more than people just craving the touch of one another. Nevertheless, he had experienced his attraction as *love,* used the word, thought it, buried his mind in its flow and ebb of sound; as he watched her there at the window with the dark city behind her, melded with the sound of her voice speaking into the phone, the whole situation added to the cumulation of what he had already seen of her, which made him see she was the best woman he had ever known in his thirty years, the best woman, all told, likely ever to be available to him. And she was not pink and passive. She was a source of power, enlightenment. He had learned from her, grown stronger from her.

Then she was setting the telephone back into its cradle, crossing the room to him, the light behind her, her teeth in shadow, and he was telling himself to share what he felt with her, *tell her.* "I love you," he said. And to nullify any lingering doubt, again, louder: "God. I *do* love you."

She had taught him, opened him with the prying, agitating tool of her honesty. His friend, Jay, his best man, had advised him: "Listen, Jack. Two things. First, when she tells you you got lousy taste, all she really means is she don't like your tie. And second, with a woman like Evelyn, you might think what you got to do is take down your defenses. *Don't.* Strengthen 'em!"

Yet her truth, her honesty, was illusion, too, insecurity, youthful brashness, a flair for cruelty. Familiarity stripped it of power.

From the straightback chair, she took the kimono they had bought in the Ginza during more promising times, blue willow branches printed on white cotton, faded now with years of boiling. The print was not unlike what he could see through the parted drapes—white sky, scratchwork branches not yet curved and fattened with spring. He lay in bed and watched her tie the belt; her hands jerked the knot as though to snap a neck.

At breakfast, she looked at him across the raw wood table. "You have egg on your lips," she said, the blankness of her face eloquent with contempt.

Sure as a prophet, he knew this morning, its small range of possibilities, the threat of bitterness, the equanimity, transcendence they struggled to learn and teach each other. Sometimes, rarely, they *met* over breakfast or dinner, wryly affectionate, understanding, knowing how absurd they were, what fools they were, yet trapped in their absurdity, rare moments of closeness. *After all these years,* they thought, shaking their heads. He patted her shoulder, squeezed it; she touched his cheek. The children watched, open-mouthed: *what now?*

More often they fought. Quiet spite. Or hollered, snarled. Or, if the children were awake, they seethed, holding it in, taking succor from the anger which was the strongest passion left between them.

They could not part. He couldn't leave her. The children held them together. He could not upset their world, did not believe in divorce. They stayed together, ten years behind them, another ten or fifteen to go. No doubt they would part when the children were grown *(but how could they really? how could they?),* when *they* were, say, twenty-five, if he and Evelyn could last together that long— otherwise sooner *(but could they ever really?).* Lynch had lost his father at twenty-three, and it had been too soon. It afflicted him that he had never met the man as an adult. Therefore, he wanted to stay as long as possible, to preserve this world of family for his own two kids. Perhaps *this* was his game, his fiction, the void which was not void and held him from the chaos without. But who knew what their next decade would teach them about marriage? Perhaps a marriage had seasons, long periods of dormancy in which it gathered strength to assume another form. Something stronger than passion, strong as that feeling he had known as a boy, welling not from the blood or even the heart, from the soul perhaps. The love for father, mother, for his brother, Jeff. Gone now. Dead as strangers. A few flickers of memory, a few impregnations of his character. No, no, more than that, much more, but still so little compared to this pure feeling, this direct connection with the children, this love he shared with them which would not let him be numb or alien or immune to the world.

Lynch and his wife had not made love in more than a year. The last time had been after a year's abstinence, and had been nothing at all like love. What was it, he wondered, that drove them apart? Truth or illusion? Was it the cool truth in her gaze that turned him away? She was beautiful. Why didn't he want her? Or she him? Why was her body so cold in his sight?

He watched her stub out her cigarette, swallow the last of her coffee, rise, leave the table without a word or glance at him.

That evening, standing behind the ladder-back chair where his mistress sat watching the television, he laid his thumbs along the back of her shoulders and kneaded the muscle there. He relished the stiff, knotted tension, the resistance. Something good lay beneath it for him, like juice beneath a shell.

On the television screen in black and white sparked with blurs of green, Bela Lugosi was saying to Peter Lorre, his Hungarian lips supping on the words, "The soul is eaten. Fifteen years in Kaldar. Skinned alive. Day by day. Minute by minute..."

Lynch bent, placed his mouth against Cindy's ear. "Your body is the only truth," he whispered. It seemed as good a lie as any. He wanted it to be truth. He wanted to allow his passion for women, for a woman, to be the single, irrevocable, irreducible fact. His face turned to them as surely as plants grew toward light. His desire, his will for her was true, the lie irrelevant. He wanted to skin the tension from her. He wanted her will. When he broke the tension from her muscle, he knew the will beneath would flow into his palms. For a little while, he would own her, master her, the expression on her face, the light in her eyes would be things he created from her body. And then he would release her.

His thumbs worked at her shoulders, building slowly, carefully, in force, retreating instantly when resistance flared, the strength of his thumbs addressing the will that tensed the muscle, pressing harder, slowly, gradually taking control.

She moaned, exhaled, her shoulders lowered. He put his lips to her neck. Her head tipped back. Her shoulders moved into his palms.

Later, she lay on her hip beside him and picked gently at the cruciform of hair on his chest.

"Do you love me?" she asked.

"Yes."

"Why?"

"Because I don't love you."

She blinked, thought, smiled. "You're a fox," she said. He watched the teeth of her smile, the teeth and lips, white good teeth and full lips, a scrap of red meat lodged at the base of one canine.

"And you love me..."

"Yes, I do," she said.

"... for the same reason."

The lips went slack, closed, tightened. "Cynic."

He was stroking her calf, slim and muscular, downed with pale beige hair that kinked against his palm. She pinched his sideburn and tugged. Through her teeth, she said, "I want to hurt you."

"Why?"

"To make you jump. To drop your face."

"The face I have here is the bottom one," he said.

She looked into his eyes. Her blue-green gaze flecked with yellow and sienna, eyes soft and submissive with something falsely received, extracted. That was not the way he liked to own her. That was a way for her to own him. He did not want her to own him.

He said, "That was meant as hard truth, kiddo. *Hard* truth. *Hard. Truth.*" As he rolled over onto her and pinned her wrists above her head and watched her eyes change from openness to hurt to glitter.

On one knee before the television cabinet, he spooled the video tape back, triggered fast forward. He saw Lugosi's eyes in black and white with green sparks and let the film play, adjusting the volume down not to wake Evelyn or the kids. He sat in the horseblanket chair with his bourbon, Cindy's fragrance in his nose. The smell saddened him now, seemed to emphasize the ephemeral nature of everything, even that physical closeness. Here and gone. Flesh against your fingers, lips between your teeth, her will gathered in your palms. And gone. An hour, an evening, a few touches, a fragrance. *After coitus all animals are triste.* She liked his game, he thought. She didn't want to be allowed to love him. She liked it as it was. His control kept them intact, free to use one another, to enjoy one another, the illusion of not-void in void. His resistance gave life and direction to her yearning, his desire to possess gave the framework of strategy to them both.

The green sparks danced in Lugosi's mad black eyes. Lynch spoke the lines with him: "The soul is eaten. Fifteen years in Kaldar..." He and his brother Jeff had seen that film together thirty-five, maybe thirty-six years before, a Saturday matinee at the Newtown theater, up over the concrete bridge past the graveyard and the railroad tracks and the river. And those lines had been the mainstay of their repertoire for years. When they had nothing at all to say, they could always fill the silence with a black glare, a Hungarian Gothic accent: "The soul is eaten..." Hawk lips supping on the words. It had been a game—perhaps a game to prepare them for life.

Jeff was three years older than Lynch. Until Jeff was nine or so, he and Lynch had been devoted to one another. Their parents liked to tell a story of how they went out to the theater one night, leaving the kids to take care of one another. A thunderstorm broke out on their way home, and they got back to the house to find eight -year-old Jeff and five-year-old Jack huddled together under a blanket in the dark, arms around one another while the thunder cracked outside, telling each other, "We can't get hurt, so there's no reason to get scared, right?"

"Right. 'Cause thunder can't hurt you anyway, and anyway it can't see us under here, right?"

Lynch rattled the slushy ice in his glass, sipped the bourbon, and wondered how your love for a person could die, vanish. Maybe, he thought, you somehow just lose the capacity to keep it alive. People grew from one another and lost interest in understanding one another. He thought of Jeff's face, could call it to mind in detail, his turtle-like nose, thin lips, his smile, his cool, funny manner, how they once would have lain down their lives for one another, simply because a world without one of them in it was unbearable. And now, somehow, they couldn't bear five minutes alone together. *Why? Is it me?* He thought of Evelyn last night in terminal frustration: "You don't *know! You* don't *know* how you are!" Intriguing him. *Tell me how I am. Give me a hint.* But she could not explain further and, anyway, it wouldn't have helped. They were in disconnection. Nothing they said to or of one another at the moment was valid. They were not even capable of touching one another with their fingers or their gaze without their lips curling, nostrils cocking as though at a bad smell. Disconnection. He thought of the way his son sometimes touched him as they spoke together, unconsciously picking at the hair on his arm or stroking his shirt or tugging at his earlobe, running a finger across his lips. He thought of how his little girl's body clung to him when she was tired or frightened, the fragrance of sunshine in her auburn hair. He tried to remember how it had been to make love with Evelyn, closed his eyes, but smelt Cindy and saw her smiling mouth, lips, teeth, eyes so green, hovering over him in the dusky light, careening rhythmically, endlessly, shifting to the side, to the side, groaning inarticulate questions of pleasure.

On the screen, the shadow of Bela Lugosi flailed with a saber at the shadow of Peter Lorre tied to a rack, flaying the skin from his body. Vengeance for Kaldar. Screams. Mad eyes. Lynch tried to remember the gleeful horror the scene had given him and Jeff all those years before, but remembered instead the night that Jeff predicted their estrangement. Lynch was about seven, Jeff nine or ten. Jeff had been in school for two or three years and had begun to go places without Lynch, to see people Lynch didn't know, to play games Lynch was too small to join. This particular night was clear in Lynch's mind even after nearly four decades; he could remember it the way a person remembers being hit or jumped or thrown down by a car. He couldn't remember the pain, only hollow details, brilliant in memory.

Lynch had been lying in bed, the clean, cool sheets folded over the satin lip of a peach-colored woolen blanket pulled up to his chest. He could smell those clean sheets, feel the warmth from the yellow lamplight, smell the pages of the Superman comic he was reading. Jeff stood beside the bed, barefoot on the wood floor, buttoning his striped pajama top. He looked at his younger brother and said, "You know, Jack, someday, you'll have all your own friends who you'll always want to be with and play with. And me, I'll have all my own friends, too. But we'll still see each other at home."

"Sure, I know that," Lynch said and pulled the sheet up to his forehead so his brother wouldn't see the tears squeeze out of his eyes. But Jeff did see.

"Hey," he said. "Listen. I'm just talking. That'll never happen. That'll never happen to us."

They sat at the round glass coffee table, chatting, she leafing through a catalog, he halfheartedly trying to organize some footnotes. On the television screen, a swarthy man with a dark Vandyke beard was saying to John Forsythe, "I would smile at your agony."

Lynch sipped his coffee. He glanced at Evelyn, at the brochure in her hands. He could see women in spring coats on glossy paper, light glinting off them in white smears. She always dressed so well. Who *for?* he wondered. *Why?*

A tumbler of club soda stood on the table beside her. Lynch experienced *déjà vu,* recognized the source. When he was a boy, right up until he went into the Army, every night at nine, his mother went upstairs and brushed her teeth, then came back down with a tray of brushes and jars and tubes which she set on the table in the dining room, which was also the television room. Then, while she watched television, slowly, methodically, using all four fingers of each hand, she massaged her scalp for thirty minutes, moving the skin of the scalp against the skull bone, rubbing, stimulating the blood flow for thirty minutes—she timed it—exactly. When she had finished that, with the rubber tit on the handle of her   Pic-o-pay toothbrush, she would massage her gums, in between the bases of the teeth, front and side, top and bottom, vibrating her hand, moving on, vibrating, moving on, using a round chrome mirror on a wire stand to guide her work. Then she slipped the toothbrush back into its green plastic sleeve, clicked its cap on, and unscrewed the lid from a jar of Pond's hand cream, scooped up a blob of it on her fingertips and massaged it into her hands, wrists, forearms, elbows—another blob—neck, cheeks, the nub of her chin, her upper lip, forehead, down the top of her nose, her earlobes. Then, her face and arms glistening, she closed up all the jars and tubes and rearranged them on the tray and, when the next ad came on, climbed the stairs with the tray and returned it to her vanity table, after which she came back down again to fill a tumbler with water from the kitchen tap. She covered the mouth of the

glass with a pale green plastic coaster embossed with green floral de-
signs. She kept the glass of water beside her bed in case she woke,
thirsty, during the night. But first, she would sit at the dining table
and watch to the end of whatever was o n — *Perry Mason* or *Al-
fred Hitchcock* or *What's My Line?*—with the glass of water on
the table in front of her, her face glistening with a layer of Pond's.

Something about that glass of water had always been repugnant to Lynch. He used to sneak glances at it, watching the tiny,
lethargic bubbles which rose in it from time to time, sliding up
along the wall of the glass with its pink fleur-de-lis decal toward the
pale-green plastic-flowered ceiling of the coaster across the mouth.
She had always seemed to him perfectly oblivious of him or anything else throughout all these rituals, a person devoid of awareness, protected from it by insignificant purposeful motion. But
once, as he was gazing at the water tumbler and she was gazing at
the television, she said to him, without turning her eyes from the
screen, "You might not be so quick to sneer at it if you were dying
of thirst on the desert."

On Lynch's twenty-first birthday, his father and his brother,
Jeff, took him out drinking with them. Towards the end of the
night, Jeff went off with a waitress, and Lynch and his father sat at
the bar, while the bartender counted up the take. Lynch's father
was pretty drunk. He was staring glumly into his shot glass, eyes
fixed, brow wrinkled, the breath whistling in his nostrils. He said,
"You know your mother and I haven't had relations in twenty-two
years. *Twenty-two* years. They told her another baby'd kill her. And
that was the end of it."

It was not until next morning, as he lay in bed with a head

that felt like a kicked-in watermelon, that Lynch realized the significance of the statistic. Twenty-two years. *He* had been their last act together. Little Oedipus. Or, at any rate, when he came out, the door locked behind him. He wondered how any man would allow himself to put up with such a situation. But still he admired them all those years together, staying together. He couldn't imagine them apart. All those years of thirst, drinking tap water for the passion. And it had been important to him and to his brother, he knew that. The glue of their rituals, their self-control. He knew them. They were there. Always. You always got a fair deal from them, and you knew they would always be there for you. If you got hurt, they got upset. You lost, they cared. You won, they smiled. Always. A single, stable base from which to address the world. You knew the soundness of the wall behind your back. That one thing you did not have to doubt.

Palms cupped around the rock glass, he stared down into his drink, the remains of his drink, the deep whiskey he had poured over three steaming cold ice cubes which were now slush in a finger of pale amber. If he poured another, he knew he would also pour a third, and the third would cool the drowsiness from his brain, and he would put on the Doors or Charlie Parker and pour another and contemplate the fact that he was killing himself, but that that was fine because he was dying anyway, even as he sat there and puzzled over his life as it evaporated, as the once long night proved itself as ephemeral as all its predecessors, fading towards a dawn as fleet as all other hours, that emptied as quickly as a full bottle of whiskey.

He poured another, sat in his sturdy armchair, legs crossed, gazed through the parted curtains to the navy blue sky, the black scratch marks of late winter trees and branches imprinted against it, the unearthly high street lamps up above the sunken highway at the next corner, staining the darkness an unnatural pink.

He sipped his whiskey, considered himself, the increasing evidence of the mortality he only now had begun truly to understand awaited him. He was stout now, next year no doubt, or the year after, would be fat as his father in the last part of his life. He was not unlike his father actually. His eyes were bad, too, his teeth, his lower back. His excesses had left their mark after all. His joints sometimes ached. His toe (gout?). A grape cluster of varices swelled behind one knee. His internal organs—spleen, liver, gall bladder, intestines—complained from time to time, grumbled and muttered and bit. Their complaints were earnest, stern pains, needle sharp flashes, a shot of pain in the rectum which gave a hint of how death would humiliate, with pain in undignified places. Sensations too ephemeral to present to a doctor as symptoms, the opposite of a child's growing pains, perhaps—ending pains, advance signals of the last leg of the journey.

He studied the back of his hand: three pale liver spots, roughened, reddened skin, knotted veins, fattening at the blade. His father's hand, the way his father's hand had looked to Lynch when he was fifteen years old. Gone now: Father, mother, brother. Gone from him. Now there were the children, and Evelyn who had borne them. He remembered her swollen belly, the arc of her body in a sundress, remembered her on the table with her thighs spread, white belly humped up, while the midwife told her when to breathe, when not, when to push, when to wait. Lynch held her hand, rather made his own available to hers, felt useless.

The midwife, a dark-haired woman with a black mole on the edge of her upper lip, looked up from where she sat on a stool between Evelyn's legs. "Perhaps your husband will wet a cloth and lay it on your forehead," she said to Evelyn. He hurried to the sink, ran the tap over a cloth, wrung it out, patted the perspiration from Evelyn's face, touched the damp cloth to her dry, swollen lips. She smiled at him.

The midwife's voice, strained now, said, "Okay, now you push. Come on, do it now. *Push*. That's it. Good. Okay, now, again: *push.*"

Lynch looked from Evelyn to the midwife to the place between her bent, parted thighs. The midwife took up a shears. He heard the clip, the groan lost amidst other groans, and a slimy scalp appeared, swelling through a wall. Lynch was dizzy. Then the plastic gloved hands were drawing it forth, turning it, a face, glistening body red and purple and pink, a penis, pudgy thighs, knees, the body lifted free and laid on Evelyn's still swollen belly, the cord yet uncut. His hair was red, eyes open and blue, gazing, startled, embodied, while Evelyn's face, tipped forward, smiled at him, her palms at his frail purple arms, and Lynch stood apart, a pale attendant.

Cindy stood waiting for him at Rockefeller Center, looking down over the railing into the skating rink. She wore a tweed skirt and jacket, tailored, impeccable, skirt just above the knees, slender nylon-sheathed thighs, brown leather shoes with pocked toes, medium heels, pale brown hair clean and long and glistening in the evening light, as taped organ music piped out of the speakers.

Lynch held back, admiring her from the avenue: picture of a lady, hot as a cat. His happiness at the sight of her felt so pure. He wanted only to give and have pleasure of her. Only that.

* * *

Some moments lasted. He realized that now. Some moments lasted and were worth their price, were inevitable, cheated time. He sat in the horse-blanket chair, ears sweating in plastic earphones within which Stan Getz blew "Sophisticated Lady," and that moment of admiring her at the skating rink survived itself, reflected in his mind, and he saw himself cross the narrow arcade of elegant shops, past the long planters and water-spouting lips of stone fish, as he came up behind her, saw her jump, then smile, as he touched her shoulder. She turned, and he leaned to kiss her, his hand sliding up under her skirt, and she whispered, *"Jack!"* as his palm moved up against the inside of her nylon-skinned thigh to the warm center of everything. He could taste her lips, feel the smooth dead nylon against his palm, the rough tweed against the back of his hand with its three pale liver spots, as his palm took possession of her.

"Jack!" she whispered. "Everyone can *see!"*

"Let them eat their hearts out," he said around the spice of tobacco and gin on her young mouth.

Even now he could taste it, drunk, could taste and smell her, see the glow of her pale body on the white sheet in the dark room, the parted thighs, the smile, teeth, the reaching hands, open arms, even as the snores welled up the base of his nose, and his ears sweated against the now silent earphones, and his head nodded forward in sleep.

The smack of curtains opening in an angry burst and Evelyn's voice, muffled, woke him, caught him by surprise. He opened his eyes and heard her words, but could not understand them, saw the glare of her eyes looking down at him where he had slept in the horseblanket chair. He lifted off the earphones, felt cool air against his damp ears, tried to speak, but his voice was clogged with phlegm.

"Daddy! Daddy!" the kids shouted, racing in through the French doors, across the carpet towards him. His son stopped short, stared, open-lipped. "Why did you sleep out here?" he asked.

"Go and eat your cornflakes," Evelyn said.

"But why did Daddy sleep here?"

"Just *do* as I say."

"For fun," Lynch called after the boy. "Just for fun. So I wouldn't wrinkle my jacket."

"Are you prepared to talk sense?" Evelyn said.

"Course I am." He lurched forward in the chair, saw he still was wearing his jacket, his tie, his unlaced shoes. A half-full drink stood on the carpet beside his foot. The amp of the tape deck hummed, and sunlight slanted in across the windowsill through the parted curtains, as he coughed and dug into his trousers for his handkerchief.

"I'm taking the children to my parents for a few days," she said. "No scenes. I'll come back Monday and expect you to be gone. Are we agreed on that?"

"No, we are not."

"You've done it this time," she said and stared at him. "You've really done it." He felt the blood run into his cheeks, couldn't meet her eye. "Meaning what?"

His voice was thick; his tongue ran out to wet his lips.

She glared, her eyes bright with hot anger. "I will *not* be your fool!" she whispered. Then the coldness covered her again.

The breakfast table was set. "Daddy!" his son called out. "Sit next to me, okay?"

"We're going to gramma's," his daughter said. "Mommy said you were too busy to come."

He looked at them, at Evelyn, at the table, covered with food the way a family's table ought to be—sugar, butter, coffee, cream, toast, cornflakes, a pitcher of juice, napkins, plates, spoons, glasses, a waxed container of milk imprinted on the side with a child's crayon drawing of a cow. He sat down, meaning to explain, persuade, to speak and clarify everything, but as he tried to find the words, something rose up in him that seized control. He lifted his palm, swung, flat-handed, round-house. His hand smacked the milk carton. It flew across the table, sloshed a trail of milk down the wall, floorboards, struck the floor on its side, milk trickling from its spout. He rose, shouting, *"I do not want this ..."*

"Jack!" she whispered. "The children!"

He paused, felt the blood in his face, eyes bulging, saw their faces, their eyes watching him, suspended. He took a decision. They must see this. They must know. That it was not for lack of love or passion or fear of pain. He slammed the flat of his hand down onto the table. The cups jumped in their saucers, and he bellowed out: *"I do not want this to happen to us!"*

He was breathing hard, through his mouth, thinking, trying to think. No one spoke. Evelyn stared. The children moved behind her. The room was still. Lynch always remembered that. How very still they were, his wife, nonplussed, staring at him, his children gazing up in bewildered fear at their father, a man they did not know, as his own mind flashed with thoughts of his own father and mother, the stillness in which they had lived, the standoff they had survived, dead now, gone, all of them, as his lungs heaved for air and his heart banged against his chest.

(1984 - 1986)

A Cheerful Death

Jastovic has received a troubling letter from Internal Revenue. He knows somehow, or thinks he knows, that the phone he did not answer the evening before—and how did they have this number?—and the nasty buzz of the doorbell just now—and how did they have this address?—have some connection with the letter he has been ignoring for weeks, just as he ignored the three that preceded it.

He knows this is unwise, unpatriotic, illegal, practically sacriligious, but he has his reasons. And as surely as he knows the Revenue Man (or Woman) at the door will be indifferent to those reasons, he also knows that they are morally unimpeachable. The thing is if he opens the door now, he will cease to be happy. And it is his duty to be happy. It is his sacred responsibility to live and be happy because what he knows full well, and the Revenue Man (or Woman) only has a partial and unsatisfactory grasp of, is that while it is true Jastovic has cheated (yes, he must confess, cheated is the correct word) on his last three returns, it is also true that he had enjoyed rare and virtually irrefutable offshore business opportunities to do so, and equally true that he is fifty-eight years old and has already lived at least two thirds of his life and very likely a good deal more, and it would be an insufferable affront to the indefatigably friendly cells and fluids that have so kindly united and developed and propelled him through the years to force them into the unhealthy atmosphere of a prison cell for the relatively little time remaining them in the unity they have so kindly achieved in the form of the body that is him, Richard Jastovic—to his friends known as Jazz, to his CEO and Executive Board as Yestovic.

And to what avail should he go to prison? Would it improve the state of the nation? Would it make the world a better place? Is it even truly, in the true order of things, just? Legal perhaps yes, but just, truly just?

Jastovic has done his duty for many years. He has risen early and worked hard to fulfill the requirements of a position he never quite understood. He has paid very considerable sums in taxes and made it clear that he was in no way opposed to doing so: Taxes are an investment in the society which houses us. He was simply selective which dollars he paid on. He has also been faithful to his wife, right up to the point at which she decided, and perhaps not unfairly so, that they had reached the end of their time together, packed and run off with the shoe salesman who was so enamored of her feet. Truly! He wrote poems about them: Your foot, madame is divine/The subtle cleavage of your toes/In pale kid pumps my heart... Jastovic had been allowed to read one of these poems, and he had to admit that the happy flush of Lena's face as she watched him do so was impossible to deny or, for that matter, begrudge. Who could begrudge her the very apparent happiness this man had brought her, particularly since Jazz and Lena no longer did very well in the good old sack which had otherwise been a satisfactory playground for some decades, and the lives of their four children no longer required them to maintain their union: Eliphas, their oldest lad, now thirty-eight had made a fortune on the net; Winnie, sweet girl, now thirty-five, had parlayed a Penthouse centerfold into a small, but lucrative chain of motion centers; Ricardo, thirty-four, was a free-lance priest who specialized in corporate ethics workshops; and their baby, Feodora, with a Ph.D. in journalism from a prestigious non-accredited university, had already made her mark in a nationally distributed journal on alien abduction.

In truth, Jastovic is slightly envious of both the shoeman and Lena, that they have found new passion, but envy is beneath him. His life has been devoted to cheerfulness. It does no good to be sullen. And envy, well, of what use is envy?

Half Czech, half Celt, Jazz is devoted to the smile.

The naggy buzz of the doorbell persists, accompanied by a knocking. Jastovic has been cheerful all his life and wishes to continue to be so and will not be able to do that unless he breaks a few more rules even if he would not be supported in this by any public agencies or the officers representing them. It is hardly their fault. He can see their position, just as—he is convinced—most kind-hearted persons—and most people are kind-hearted—would see his.

So he opens the bedroom window, and with pleasingly bulging pockets and the agreeable heft of the manageably sized royal blue bag slung over his right shoulder, he climbs out onto the fire escape. Bidding silent adieu to the various objects, commodities, objets d'art and electronic devices peopling his little hideaway apartment, he quietly closes the window after him and proceeds swiftly to descend the four sets of rusty iron ladders through the bracing brisk autumn air to the yard.

*   *   *

It is a beautiful afternoon in the midst of perhaps the most beautiful of the fifty-eight autumns he has experienced upon this planet, and he is determined not to allow this current adversity to get him down.

As he hops off the bottom ladder and glances up, he sees a blond male head look out the window after him and hears a rich male baritone call out, "Mr. Jastovic? Is that you? Mr. Jastovic!"

But Jastovic is already jogging on his prized brown Bali wingtips through the foyer, noting that it is littered with red, brown and yellow leaves that have blown in through the lobby door. He salutes the decision of the superintendent—an excellent big-nosed fellow from Alabama named Clyde—to let them lay; they make for a lovely, poetical vision. He almost pauses to contemplate them, but thinks better of it and is out on the sidewalk, chuckling to think of himself in this filmically melodramatic situation as he quicksteps toward the avenue and climbs the staircase of the elevated train.

The best time to do something beautiful, he thinks, is when you are supposed to be doing something else. There is so much to be thankful for, so much to look forward to in the little time remaining us. Passion is important. He thinks of the shoeman—what was his name? Zilka, that was it! Walter Zilka! Himself a Czech, though of a later immigrant wave than Jastovic's own father, who left the old world in the thirties—perhaps a Jew, and that was fine, Jews were good. Zilka, Lena told him, had left Prague in sixty-six. Jazz thinks of Zilka on his haunches, fondling Lena's bare foot with its painted nails—good decision to use paint considering the greenish-yellow color that had begun to develop there—and almost unnaturally short toes. How happy they surely were, Zilka and Lena. He understood that they enjoyed dancing together, tangos and other ballroom varieties. It is good that people are able to find happiness. Why should Jastovic have presented obstacles to Lena's happiness? Just so that they could continue to engage in a life together which presented increasing obstacles to his naturally cheerful nature and to her, to his mind, somewhat unruly erotic desires?

No indeed. Let them live and be happy. Let Zilka press his thick red lips to the chubby instep of her no longer youthful foot, let him guide her through the melodramatic motions of the Tango à la Carte, and a blessing upon them to live and be happy.

The Flushing Line screeches in along the station and with a glance back at the stairway from the platform below, Jastovic boards. No blond-headed Revenue Man appears at the last moment to jam open the sliding doors, to squeeze in, to slap irons on Jastovic's admittedly slender wrists and tighten the iron bands to the point of discomfort or say unpleasant, vaguely sexual things like "Assume the position." Put your topcoat over your head as you are paraded past the gauntlet of crime papparazzi. And is that fair? Why should his name and face be smeared in the tabloids, even if he was technically guilty? Let us define your terms.

Should the success of his children be tainted by such untoward publicity concerning their papa?

Richard Ricardo Jastovic, this is your life. Or what's left of it.

Really it is not so complicated. A Trailways ticket from the Port Authority Terminal and you sit for a dozen hours in a window seat observing the lovely Jersey and Pennsylvania countryside roll past whilst two charming young African American women across the aisle engage in teasing, amusing repartée: "Yo fuck'n wit m'shit bitch!"

"Don yo be play'n wit me, ho, I toss you salat!"

Jastovic observes the color of the sky transform from gray-blue to an astonishing azure ceiling that hangs low over yellow gray fields and everywhere on the trees the leaves die with a splendor to make you wonder whether death is not the brilliant and desirable climax of existence.

He leans across and touches the nearest of the young women on the wrist. "Excuse me," he says. "See the moon?"

The girl gazes up from lowered brows at him, her face a magnificent shade of black, and says with elegant quiet, "That be the moon sho." Somewhere behind him a young stalwart's boom box issues a song about the wind and summer and the departure of a loved one and the heavens above and eternal love. Jastovic removes the pewter flask from his inner pocket and swallows warm vodka, not upset at the absence of ice for who could complain about the absence of shoes if he has feet? He sighs with pleasure at the marvellous world around him.

In Pittsburgh he bids adieu to the young African American women, extends thanks for the fine music to the young stalwart who looks incredulously at him and asks, "Hey you hah? You like educated all that shit, you hah? You ma man, hear?"

In the station, after surveying for blond-headed baritones, Jastovic purchases a Greyhound ticket for Toledo, rides the dog for several further hours and de-buses at Dayton where, after surveying the terminal, he hires a good old yellow cab for the airport and a nondescript flight with light snack and a diet tab to Las Vegas.

Really quite simple. This country so full of natural and man-made beauty clearly wishes to shelter him for the pursuit of happiness.

So it happens that Jastovic finds himself just before midnight on the second day of his new life dining on a three dollar and ninety-five cent prime rib in the Stardust lounge—and where else in the world could one dine so for such?!—drinking a large vodka on many slushy rocks and exchanging glances with a woman perhaps his own age with lips painted the color of the Queen of Midnight tulips which once grew on his front lawn in the now abandoned fifteen-room house in Bayside Hills. They have all gone away. The house is closed and still. There is nothing more to say.

Quite lovely, she asks him, "What is a Stoli?" having heard him order. She is smoking a small cigar from a charming little box and offers him one which he accepts with pleasure.

He blows a pleasingly slender stream of rich white smoke through pursed lips and tells her, "Stoli is, I guess you would say, a kind of yuppie abbreviation for Stolichnaya, which is the choice of many a vodka drinker. Russian distilled and I think probably one of the best I have ever tasted. When it comes to vod, these distinctions are pretty subtle since vodka has virtually no taste, they say, but that is why the little taste that is there is so important. A little bit like the colors of a landscape deep in winter—you have your grays, your whites, your blacks, your shades of gray smoke, white smoke, white and gray sky and suddenly you perceive a little splash of color—the blue coat and red breast of a woodpecker in a dark bare tree, say, and the senses go gaga. Anyway Moskovskaya is also good, also Russian, while Absolut—Swedish—I drink only if it is the only thing available. What right have the Swedes to think they can make vodka? Finlandia—Finnish, of course—is not bad at all and very modestly priced; I suppose after all their years of dancing with the Russkies they learned a thing or two, and the Estonian stuff is not only very cheap but perfectly drinkable. They take it like the Russians in big glasses, very cold without ice, and when they drink they say Tjervisex which sounds rather provocative, but simply means to your very good health. The Finns says kipis before they drink. The Irish make a vodka called Boru that I have never tasted, though I salute the name, which is for Brian Boru, the first king of a united Ireland—he drove the Vikings from the Emerald Isle in the eleventh century and was the father of the first Kennedy—which means ugly-headed by the way—but was my mother's maiden name, a lovely woman. There is also a Danish so-called vodka, Danza, but I have never been able to stop laughing long enough to order it. The American stuff is not bad by the way, filtered through mountains of charcoal, and they— Smirnoff that is—also make a black-label stuff that is distilled in Russia which can damn well compete with Stoli. One word of caution— do not partake of the Smirnoff blue label unless you are looking to get thoroughly bombed. Hundred-proof brain-cell burner. Stick with the red label if you must drink American or the black if you don't mind paying the tariff. By the way, though I have yet to taste it, there's an American-French co-production named Gray Goose that, I am told, is made by cognac distillers and I would imagine French cognac distillers know what they are doing, so watch this spot!" He draws smoke into his mouth, turns it on his tongue. "These little cigars are quite nice by the way."

The woman with the Queen of Midnight lips smiles with a pleasure that strikes him as definitely overclass. "You are quite the lexicon, aren't you?" she says in accents that make him think of Vassar, Smith, Princeton perhaps. He looks more closely at her, a handsome wench indeed. Well kept and more than worthy of pursuit. He cannot imagine her succumbing to sorrow and tells her so.

She smiles with self-possession. "After orgasm all creatures are sorrowful," she says. "Except for roosters and women."

How more perfectly could a new life begin than with an act of passion? Her gaze beneath him is challenging. Pleasure me her brown East-coast eyes demand, and their crispness lift him crisply to the challenge. In her Stardust suite they cry out in rapid succession, and the appropriately rumpled bed, white sheets glowing in the dim light, is all the home he needs for now. After a few timeless moments of post-orgasmic abandon, they proceed to the jacuzzi where they smoke small cigars and sip ersatz champagne from the minibar.

Her eyes, her freshly painted smile continue to watch him challengingly while soul music plays over an internal sound system. Jastovic is overcome with a sense of well being. "Oh to share this pleasure, this opulence with all the world!" he exclaims.

Her dark eyes slide sideways toward him. "Share?"

"Yes!" he says. "Share! Just think of that gorgeous meal we just enjoyed for a pittance. Just think that McDonald's should have such worldwide success with such an inferior offering when prime rib is available in that quantity for that price."

Her brown gaze is steady, cool. "And what?" she enquires, "is wrong with McDonald's?"

"Well it's pap really I suppose, isn't it?" he says, quickly amending, "Though some folk like it and I'm not putting it down."

"You bet your bony ass they like it," she says, the 'a' in 'ass' elegantly elevated. "McDonald's are de-licious. Are you some sort of traitor to the cause?"

"I beg your pardon?"

"Where is your money, then?" she asks. "In the fund to finance Clintonian obscenity? McDonald's makes a great country greater! Why it's all over the world, you sap! And that is sharing enough!" Abruptly she rises from the tub, water cascading from hips and thighs that already inspire the pain of regret. Who is he to mouth unrestrained socio-political-economic judgements anyway? Everyone has a right to a view.

She fixes him with her blazing eyes, pencilled brows arched. The curls on her love mount are a lovely shade of chestnut brown, a brilliant match to hair and brow. He lifts his glass and toasts. "It's a grand old flag," he says. "A high-flying flag."

"You bet your boney liberal butt it is, buster!"

You learn something every day thinks Jastovic, still wet, chilled after the warm frothing bath, drawing on his trousers. To the best of his knowledge he has never slept with a Republican before.

Still naked she watches him dress, head tipped back, chin raised, eyelids at half-mast.

Shirt unbuttoned, necktie untied around his collar, sock-footed, both wingtips in one hand, he says, "You are a lovely woman, I..." reaching to her, but she raises her palm.

"Read my bush!" she pronounces with severe Queen of Midnight lips. "No more sex!"

Jastovic's own room is down in the bungalow annex, equivalent to the poor streets, because he doesn't wish to call attention to himself, but how can he regret any of it? He hides his bundles of hundred dollar bills betweem the box spring and the mattress and dons the red swim trunks he has purchased from the casino shop, floats in the pool gazing up to the purple three a.m. Nevada sky.

I love therefore I am, he murmurs, but is uncertain who or what he loves, wishes he could be back in the thirteenth floor suite nuzzling the Republican lady. He can not help but admire her loyalty to the McDonald's stock she owns. After all, he reasons, if I owned McDonald's stock I might think the same. His comment was idle. Who is he to badmouth the majority of the world's burger of choice? Think of all the employment opportunities they provide.

In his bungalow again he towels himself with enjoyment, shaves with relish, applies with pleasure scented fluids to his entire body watching the television as he pulls on the fresh black socks he has purchased. No matter what channel, he finds what appear to be angry unhappy people—on Ricki Lake a man dressed as a not unattractive woman is angry that her boyfriend is angry at having learned he is a man; on Jerry Springer two very overweight thirteen year olds are cursing at their mother in a volley of bleeps; on David Letterman, David Letterman casts his pencil at the screen with a sneer; on Oprah Winfrey a very small wiry woman weeps while Oprah watches her with a gaze that says you deserve to weep.

"Is no one happy anymore?" Jastovic enquires aloud and goes to the casino to dance with a Lithuanian prostitute to a song about drying your eyes.

She whispers in his ear, "You want to come up with me?"

"Yes," he says, "but I already came up once today."

"With me you can always to come up once again," she says. "I haf my means."

"I would rather just hold you," he says.

"Hold where?"

"Just, you know, in my arms. But it would have to be free for me to truly enjoy it."

"This I can not to do," she says.

He tips her fifty dollars and goes to play the slots, first the quarters, then the dollars. He wins a few, loses a few, grows dizzy from the incessant jingling sound of them and sees out the windows on the other side of the huge room that the sun is up.

For about five minutes he wonders what is going to happen to him. Then he orders an enormous breakfast of sausage, bacon, mushrooms, fried tomatoes, homefries and eggless eggs which he wolfs down with two half liter glasses of salted tomato juice while on the sound system some women's voices sing that mama didn't lie.

Jastovic's own mama was a Kennedy. She was fond of Southern Comfort which she sipped while she ironed and often told him, "Ah, bullshit makes the world go round, sonny."

Refreshed he rents a peppy white sunbird and tools out into the desert, free as a sunbird himself, pockets full of hundred dollar bills, his shoulder bag tucked under the driver's seat where he can feel its reassuring bulk pressed up against his bony liberal butt. He wonders if he has done the right thing, cheating the government of their cut. Businessmen don't pay taxes, he once heard a very successful businessman say with great conviction, they create opportunities. After all, you have to draw the line somewhere. Do they really have the right to a bite of every single dollar? Dread descends upon him for a moment, so he turns on the radio, and voices come on singing about someone who gets knocked down but gets right up again which makes him feel better as he gazes out toward the shimmering purple horizon.

Towards sundown he sees an enormous grasshopper perched clean across the highway and decides perhaps he is pushing himself too hard. So he stops in the Whispering Winds Motel and collapses fully clothed on the bed with a bellyache, listening to the mournful sound of his own farts. During the night, someone rattles the door. "Go away please," he calls out. "I'm occupied." And whoever it is does just as he asks, confirming his faith in the goodness of the universe.

Next morning he has what he can only refer to as the shits. Hell, he thinks, shits happens. He crouches on the porcelain bowl thinking what a wonder modern plumbing is and hopes that the pain he feels does not not indicate blood, cancer or the like.

Somewhere between Vegas and Furnace Creek a phrase occurs to him: A cheerful death. He likes the sound of it, but takes a fork in the road that leads away from Death Valley toward Bullneck City on the Colorado River. The motel he checks into is right on the river and he asks the blond, pencil-moustached clerk if one can swim in the river.

The clerk glances up from his ledger and his moustache tips like Smilin' Jack's. "Sure," he says. "If you want to drown freezing."

That night he dines on prime rib and cola ad libitum, then carries a quadruple Stoli on shaved ice to the gaming tables and makes some room in his pockets. The croupier is a lovely woman, truly lovely. There is something about her smile that he wishes he could describe in words—a kind of shadow-edged smile, very very lovely. It makes him wish that he was younger. After losing nine hundred dollars to her, he asks, with a smile of his own, "Tell me, have you ever considered the advantages of an older lover?"

Her blue eyes sparkle. "And what might they be?"

"Patience. Consideration. A desire to please. Unconditional admiration. Fervor. Economic stablity."

For a moment she seems to waver. Then she says, "You old bull-shitter," and rakes in his chips.

He waits at the bar until she finishes her shift. As she passes she twinkles her fingers at him and he motions her over, but she smiles, shaking her head, as a tall narrow-hipped man wearing a string tie joins her, glaring across at Jastovic.

Slightly dizzy he empties all his pockets on the triple bed—four pants pockets, two inner breast pockets, two side pockets of his jacket and the money belt as well, then opens the zipper of his shoulder bag, removes the layer of ditties and dumps the bills from there as well. There are still plenty of hundreds left. He tries to count them, but falls asleep at five hundred thousand, or maybe four hundred thousand. He wakes with creases in his cheek from the crisp bills and stands at the window staring down to the chilly Colorado coursing along below his window. He remembers once—when?—that he and Lena had swum in the Colorado without drowning or freezing. In fact it had been lovely. Lots of other people were there too. A very hot day. He remembers an enormous black man in overalls who had walked into the river without undressing, plodded out again and appeared to be dry within a few minutes, so hot it was.

How lovely is the power of memory, he thinks, and remembers some book he read once about a man addicted to losing who gets lucky in Vegas, wins three quarters of a million dollars, goes up to his room and shoots himself. Now wasn't that a dumb story? he thinks. Why would anybody do that?

In the morning he tries to count his money again but there is just too much and the task is essentially boring, almost makes him lose respect for the lovely stuff. He estimates he has just over two million dollars. That ought to be good for something. He turns in the Sunbird and rents a larger model in a very pleasing shade of maroon, tires of that and switches to a Mitsubishi that handles like a dream.

Among the beautiful things about America are motels and ice machines, all the men and women who are today, and all the boys and girls who will become tomorrow. He salutes them as he tools along the desert road toward the Target Motel which is his objective of the day. He thinks of all the people in all the motels along the road, all their weary journeys, all their passionate explosions, the meeting of their eyes in wonder if for but a moment. It occurrs to him to buy himself a bottle of the best vodka—one of the rarest Russian or even better Polish brands, exquisitely spiced, if available— and entertain himself for a time in a motel room, possibly with a woman, even if he has to pay her to be there with him. After all, she is a person. They could talk regardless of their relationship or lack of one. He would not be cruel to her. He would be kind and enjoy being so, and what harm could that do?

In a little Arizona town called Bitter Springs, on the edge of the Painted Desert, he finds a liquor shop at a crossroads he has to ask directions to. It is a narrow deep place with one whole long wall of shelves of liquor bottles and coldboxes of beer and a picture of Clinton in a red-barred circle. There are more vodkas than he has ever heard of, rows upon gleaming rows of them, sheer happiness, bliss.

He buys a fifth of Boru in honor of his mother, then turning from the register sees that the entire other side of the establishment is a gun shop.

"You sell guns?" he asks the proprieter.

"Looks like," says the man, lean-faced, his protruding adam's apple bobbing.

Jastovic surveys the glass cases and wall shelving. There are pistols and revolvers, rifles, automatic weapons, shotguns, birdguns. There is a lovely little .22 and an elegant .38 and a dazzling nickle-plated .45 hardballer. "That one," he says.

"What you want it for?" the proprieter asks with his dusty gaze.

A cheerful death, Jazz thinks it not appropriate to say, so instead he says, "Going out into the desert to shoot snakes."

"Can't do that," the proprieter says. "Can't let you buy it for that."

"Well I was only joking," Jastovic says. "Why should I shoot a snake? Never did me any harm."

"Gun's no joking matter," the man says.

"You're right. No matter. Only wanted it on a whim."

"Didn't say you couldn't have it. Only said you can't go out and shoot snakes with it. Endanger specie. Go shoot Mr. Clinton instead why don't you. Ha. There's a undanger snake for you."

"Happiness," says Jastovic, "is but a breath away."

"How's that?" The man's mouth tilts unpleasantly, as though he might be considering annulling the transaction, but the lovely hard-baller is already in its box in a brown paper sack beneath Jastovic's arm, and possession, he has heard, is nine points of the law. "There's no point in being sullen," he says cheerfully. "And there is no shame in choosing happiness. Why squander precious time being gloomy?"

The man stares wordlessly at him with squirrel eyes, and Jastovic despairs of helping him to understand.

He guns the car through the night at astonishing speeds beneath the amazing sky blacker than a witch's lips and smeared with the silver Milky Way. A starburst shoots across the black expanse before his windshield, and he gasps, thinking how somebody or other who loves him might have loved to share this moment with him.

"See the moon?" he says aloud, watching the enormous pumpkin wafer of the autumn moon hang without a whimper above the road. "The sun suffers unendingly," he says aloud, "and owes us nothing."

It bothers him that the pistol is in a box so he pulls over to the shoulder of the road and lifts the brown paper bag from beneath the seat, pries the pistol out of its carton mounting and shoves a clip into its butt. It makes a lovely pleasing sound clicking home. He jerks back the cocking lever and hears a round kick into the chamber.

And he is lord of his universe. Now he can decide.

You have come a long way, Richard Ricardo Jastovic, he thinks as the dust settles along the long diversion he has made across the desert night, and he sits on the fender of his yellow Mitsubishi watching the headlights illuminate the magnificent desert floor before the nose of the car. From the radio a song called "Any Day Now" rolls across the vast dark night.

He hops down onto the sand, draws the hardballer from his belt and points it at the sky, goes, "Bang!" And "Bang bang!" Then he squeezes the trigger and the snout goes Boom! blazing in the dark, and he is on his butt on the sand, blinking. He stands up again, braces his wrist, aims at the moon and empties the weapon into the night. Take that and that and that, you uncheerful dark blue bastard!

The hot and redolent hardballer is stuck in his belt and he is smiling. A cheerful death is a cheerful possibility. He swigs from the fifth of Boru and thinks it an appropriate libation to salute this night with. "Sorry about that," he says to the black and silver sky. "I was only kidding. Like you're okay, I'm okay, right?"

On the other hand, all the money in his pockets could have been donated to a useful cause of his choosing, a kind of way of paying selective taxes. I pay but I choose who gets the benefit. Give it to some poor black kids or something. Visit some shanty clubs where unhappy lovers dance and palm them a fat wad of bills to start their love on.

Why not?

But this velvet milky smeared sky says now and the hard, cooled metaphor in his belt says you can do it, Jazz, you're the man, you decide.

He lays back on the warm hood of the Mitsubishi and now a sexy black voice is singing if you lose me you lose a good thing, just like that! And the Boru warm in his gullet, he watches the sparkling sky close above his eyes.

He dreams of sizzling wheels and whining howls, boots and clamor, and field upon field of waving misery, and wakes face down with a mouthful of sand, hands cuffed at the small of his back, flashing lights and crackling squad radios filling the air of the desert morning.

"Gol-lee," a pudding voice says, "Will you look at all those bills!"

The snout of his nickle-plated hardballer is pressed to his cheek.

"Who'd you kill with this thang, Mr. Jastovic, hhhmmm? Where you got all this damn money from?"

Jastovic's question is this: Did they, really and truly, have a right to take all his money like that? No. Surely not. Some of it was still his. But they just tickey tacked up the sum and it turned out he did not have dime one left. On the contrary. They figured that he owed them still, after all the arbitrary levying of fines and such. That's the thing. You cheat them, they cheat you double-triple back. No justice.

But no the real question at this moment, he would have to admit, is not that. What occupies him most at this moment, as he locksteps, clad in orange, with the orange-clad black man in front of him to whom he is bound at the ankle by a shackle, is the question of whether all the things you hear about what happens in prison are truly true.

How primitive and last century it all seems to be bound and shackled in this way. Why do they not realize the joy that is within our reach? In the truck that transported them to this facility, Jastovic, hoping to make a good start of things, offered his open palm for a shake, saying, "Richard Jastovic. New York." The black man smiled as though something were stuck in his nostril and murmured, "Fuck out mah face, cuntboy."

These words, spoken relatively mildly, nonetheless frightened Jastovic, though he did his best to exhibit a calm and friendly demeanor.

His question is this: Are there really people here who would want to perpetrate undignified acts upon his body? Surely they would respect his age, or at least be put off by it. Surely these stories are vastly exaggerated.

Whatever, it hardly seems necessary or appropriate that he should be shackled at the ankle in this way to this very alienated person in front of him.

The window in his cell is too high to look out of, but there is a window, which is after all something, and mopping out his cell that morning, he notes sunlight on the floor, a slanted shaft gayly adance with particles of dust, illuminating a patch of the concrete. Tomorrow, he thinks, I must look more carefully at that beam, study its movements, time it. This after all is something special, unexpected compensation.

Still it is extremely difficult to maintain his good spirits as he sits and waits to see whether the Latin fellow was serious who whispered to him in the showers with a goldtooth grin, "This night I fine you cuntboy por seguro."

Jastovic wanted to ask whether he really meant to say "fine" or had just mispronounced "find." He wondered about the idea of being fined, if that was really what he meant.

Jastovic thinks it was just a kind of power message and doesn't really believe it. But he does worry some as he waits. He knows one thing in this world, though. If you just keep doing your work, after a while people think you're good, and his own true profession has always been clear to him.

At just this moment he has no cigars, no vodka, no hundred dollar bills. Nothing but orange duds, nothing other than the determination to be cheerful and the power of his memory to illuminate this dark night trying to impose itself upon him. Nope, he thinks, and thinks of the sun through the window, and thinks, It's enough. Simple as that. It's enough even just to know it is there for a little while, that it will be there again. That, he knows, is what counts. Just keep at it and people will see and then, sooner or later, no matter what, they can try but they can't break the cheer of a cheerful man, and then it's like, for sure, you're home. No doubt. Home.

He hears a noise in the corridor outside his cell, listens, waits.

(1999)

Five: Last Night My Bed a Boat of Whiskey Going Down

(2010)

LAST NIGHT MY BED
A BOAT OF WHISKEY
GOING DOWN

THE WOMEN HERE are so damn beautiful you are in near constant danger of saying something likely to exact a snapped retort like *Old dudes should not hit on young chicks*, but it is a collision course, and at four p.m. you are already nipping down to the official conference bar. In truth you had already nipped over at lunchtime but that was for a purely reparatory beverage whose purpose was only to winch you back up to par after last night when your bed was a boat of whiskey going down, as Steve Davenport so aptly put it, and your bed no doubt will again be that tonight since you have undoubtedly just traversed the on-ramp to 12-Step City, but you have miles to go yet before Canada runs dry. Good evening, my name is none of your business, and I wish to remain as long as possible just where I am, in blithe denial.

So you had a single Stoli on the rocks, no fruit please, just to soothe your troubled mind and prepare for the series of meetings from two to four, and undeniably the meetings—also with beautiful women, each of whom has paid for thirty minutes of creative advice—went well, and this evening is the official conference banquet and dance but you are already now, after changing your shirt, slipping back under par so you steer back down to the official conference bar, this time for a *double* Stoli on rocks, no fruit please.

On the enormous flat-screen mounted above the shelves of colorful bottles like a celestial observation post a beautiful woman is embracing a man about your age and smiling into the camera as she says, "*He* uses Natural Male Enhancement," immediately followed by an authoritative male warning byte: "SEEK IMMEDIATE HELP FOR AN ERECTION LASTING MORE THAN FOUR HOURS!"

You catch the eye of the barmaid who reminds you of Gilgamesh's Divine Ale Wife, and you say, "Wouldn't happen here." She responds with a smile that is not quite sufficiently enigmatic so you decide to step out to the open-air tables in back for a cigarillo to recharge your respiratory apparatus. Beneath the sweltering August sky a wedding party is ranged around the tables, and as you look about for a place to sit, you spy yet another beautiful woman, a fortyish redhead who is attached to the conference's host university. She is sitting with another younger male colleague who was once your student, and they motion you to join them. They are perhaps twenty or more years your junior but seem sincerely to want you to sit with them so you do. You cannot take your eyes off the woman whose face is smiling and bright as a new minted St. Gaudens gold piece nor have you failed to notice her short trim tanned thighs beneath a short light summer skirt, but you make a point of looking from the one to the other as you speak with them, comparing life in the U.S. with life in Scandinavia where you have made your home for many years now. They tell you how puritanical America has become again as the three of you smoke and drink, and you speculate whether this delightful woman would ever consider the advantages of love with an older, shorter man who doesn't play tennis, but even well into the second round you manage to refrain from uttering that clownish question, fearing that anyway even if you did ask and even on the off-chance that she was interested you might wind up having to seek help for an erection that lasted more than four hours which no doubt is not all you might think it is cracked up to be.

These young colleagues insist on paying for both your doubles and you insist on paying for theirs or at least your own, and with her lovely fingers whose nails are the color of her hair, the gorgeous smiling redhead stuffs your double sawbuck back into your shirt pocket, causing an involuntary tumescing of your left nipple as she tells you that the young man has covered the bill and refused to take the money from her.

Then she asks you to save a dance for her after the conference banquet, but you really do not see yourself inflicting your creaky old dude moves on her so you refer her to another colleague who has agreed to be your surrogate dancer this evening because you are at best awkward, and she looks into your eyes with her beautiful green ones and says that in her experience it's the guys who say they can't dance who are the most fun to cut the rug with, and you do not tell her that she does not understand that you are not a normal human being.

You cannot stop thinking about her lovely green eyes as you hoof it up the hill, deep August sweat wilting your freshly-donned raw-silk shirt, to the main house where the official conference banquet will be held, and along the way you meet a colleague who is the wife of a jazz guitarist, and she asks if you would like to nip out after dinner and before the dancing to catch his last set in a local jazz club. You would like that very much although you also think of a blue-eyed Italian woman named Carlita who was once your student and whose Sicilian profile has always enchanted you and who has told you she would be at the dinner tonight and asked you to save her a seat. Her face resembles a shy Nefertiti, and you would so very much like to kiss and touch that fabulous face or at least to have a heartfelt conversation with it in which your eyes would be allowed to meet her enchantingly level gaze, and she would occasionally touch your hand and arm and shoulder and back as is her wont, but at the same time you advise yourself not to be an asshole because she is more than twenty-five years younger than you. You should stick to girls your own old-dude age or even just one half-a-dozen years younger like Kristina the gorgeous Norwegian even though she is a triathlon participant in far better shape than you so you would be subjected to painful embarrassment if things went so far you would have to expose your naked body which would certainly be a flabby mortification compared to her long lean tanned one.

Nothing is simple, you think, as old O. Jones used to say when he attempted to waltz on the slippery rocks, and as you sweat your way up the last of the hill, and step into the vestibule of the conference building, perspiration stinging your eyes, you blink and see Carlita with her so gentle mild smile. She pours a blue-eyed glance slowly down your face which makes you clutch your heart and think, Could it be *me*, Carlita? Could *I* be the one? And you hear yourself thinking those romance-comic-book thoughts and understand in a flash of illumination that you are a male bimbo too old to fulfill the part as you pretend not to feast upon the blue light of her gaze and tell her about the jazz club and ask if she would care to join you.

She thinks for a moment, and then she says, "I would love to. Thank you for asking me," and you wonder why she had to think for a moment but nonetheless are very glad even though you remind yourself to remember that you are an old dude and that old dudes should leave young women in peace. You once saw Carlita, as you spoke with her in a conference room, lift her blue Italian eyes to observe a tall slim black-haired square-jawed young man who stepped in and you could so clearly read on her countenance the intensity of her interest in his body, in his being, and realized you were out of this, realized how pathetic it was that that should be a surprise, cautioned yourself to be content that she was talking to you at all and touching your hand and arm and shoulder and back on occasion to emphasize a point and make the contact of your words more physical as Italians do so well. You love that touchie-feelie shit. So listen to some jazz with her and go to bed early before you get so blotto that you disgrace yourself by thinking that you can fire off your cornball lines to these gorgeous women, making them think of you as a horny old creep who does not merit the time of day rather than a nice clean old fatherly dude, but you remind yourself that no one can really know what you are thinking and that you can't go to jail for thinking it either, although very possibly all these women know very well what all old dudes are thinking as surely as they can read the map of Ireland on your nose.

Nothing is simple, you think, and sin is behovely but all manner of thing could be quite okay if you but keep your neck in your pants as the father of a girlfriend once said when you were in the basement with her decades ago, and the father called down the basement stairs, What are you two doing down there, and she stopped kissing you long enough to say, We're necking, Pop, and he said, Well tell him to put his neck back in his pants and escort you upstairs.

Before the dinner tonight there are drinks on the grassy vast terrace, and everyone is dressed so nicely, and have you lost all sense of proportion you wonder, turning a tiny circle to be dazzled by one high-heeled beauty after another, and you step over to the Stoli-less bar where you have to settle for a glass of red wine, employing your Dean Swift line when the Divine Ale Wife fills the glass halfway; you ask her, "Pray tell, Madame, what is the function of the remainder of that glass," and she, prepared, retorts, "It is for the bouquet to blossom in, Professor," and you, also prepared, tell her that since your sense of smell is in default she might as well fill it to the lip. She shoots you a skeptical look that quickly evolves into a friendly glance, and you compliment her pouring technique as her cute wrist turns to tip the bottle over your glass and complete the job, and you go off swilling wine and glad-handing the conference attendees, one of whom you spoke to the evening before in a rather blunt manner and therefore must take extra care to be certain she does not think you dislike her when it was only an excess of vodka that made you misgauge your repartee.

So you kiss her hand with an elaborate application of your lips, even though a gentleman never actually kisses a woman's hand but only holds it in his and kisses his own thumb, murmuring, "Enchanté, Madame," and she replies in classic New Yorkese, "You are so fulla shit but I have already forgiven you," and you happily smooch her hand again—a nice hand!—and say with real sincerity, "Your servant, Madame! Your liege!"

Then you are called in to the dining hall and the white-clothed tables and crested plates and cutlery and tented linen napkins, and there are speeches and more wine, and you step out back to smoke, and a lovely black woman you used to work with asks you for a cigarillo, and you say something or other that gets your face close to hers, and she lets you kiss her, but you note distantly now that you are experiencing a bit of tunnel vision and you realize that you are in danger of having one of these nights that occur perhaps twice a year where your short term memory will be seriously compromised, and you will wake next morning with only the patchiest recollection of how the evening ensued, how you got home or got to bed or how badly you slurred or staggered or even, as happens once every two years or so, whether you actually took a flop, and previously you would worry that you might have done terrible things during the blank patches of time where your memory was scratched out, but it seems you never did, or at least no one ever kicked in your door the next day to beat you up or lynch you or arrest you so you figure probably your ethics are deeply enough entrenched in your spinal column that you can continue to maintain the human potentialist mantra of I'm okay-You're okay though still you are unclear whether to-morrow you will have to apologize to the black woman for kissing her out back although she did seem to like it and did not resist at all, and it was really nice.

But then the dinner is over and you are in a car with Carlita and the jazz guitarist's wife, headed to the club, and you take the back seat, a perfect vantage point from which to study the elegant neck and profile of Carlita, and from somewhere inside the spar-kling ball of confusion that is your mind, the sparkles being brief points of profound lucidity, you sternly caution yourself to do all in your power not to make Carlita unhappy.

Then the three of you are entering the New Montmartre Jazz House and are seated around a table ten feet from the quintet who are doing a wonderfully wicked version of Miles's "Topaz," and you realize what a privilege it is to be here in this little club with such great musicians and two beautiful women and a double Stoli which could more accurately be called a quadruple and hear-ing those lovely sour trumpet notes and the cool cool cool fucking guitar, and you are hoping that Carlita enjoys the music, and then there is another quadruple Stoli in your glass, and the Chinese woman named Jin who owns the club comes over to the table to say hello and addresses you as "Dr." which in theory you are, hav-ing a Ph.D. on some marginal creative topic you used to know something about thirty years ago, but you feel so goddamned good there is no reason to elaborate, and you notice Carlita's gor-geous blue Sicilian eyes taking you in, and their expression is so warm that you decide that your next drink should be a glass of ice water to slow your progress toward oblivion but you forget and order a double quadruple Stoli because the guitar player is doing such a cool run on "Sienna" so you realize that you are not likely to avoid a vodka blitz in the not too distant future, and then the three of you are back in the car, returning to the dinner where people are dancing and congregated out on the grassy terrace where your good colleague Bob Giangrando with his warmly sardonic smile and cool understated voice says, "I have some shit you have *got* to sample," and then a very young very pretty very innocent-looking woman with black hair and blue eyes behind black-framed glasses hands you a very well packed bong, and you draw the hot smooth skunk into your throat, thinking "Holy fuckin' mackerel!" or maybe actually saying it , and at one and the same time it seems to you that all is lost and all is gained as your brain wraps around the cooling-down August heat on that grassy terrace, and a mosquito lands on the back of your hand and you bemusedly watch as it sips some of your blood and *why not, little lady, why not?* you think, as Bob Giangrando pats your back and smiles a smile you might think sinister except that you know it is a sweet smile and the very young very innocent-looking very pretty woman with black hair and blue eyes is packing another bong, but you suddenly realize that Carlita is nowhere in sight, and you are ready to propose marriage to her, and maybe you say that aloud because the very young very pretty very innocent-looking black-haired woman with heartbreaking blue jeans says, "I'll marry you. Why not? You could be my first husband." And she chuckles sweetly as you think, or maybe say, that is the kind of hyperbole that will help you make it through another winter of your discontent, and you wonder if you could get away with kissing her, but you have got to find Carlita so you venture in to the ballroom where everyone is dancing.

This is a very very dangerous place for you to be where someone might suggest cutting the rug with you, and if you say yes, and how can you not? you are in danger of taking a record-breakingly long Charlie Chaplin stagger halfway across the floor so you just stand at the door opening, and you see Carlita dancing in such a way that if you were the kind of a guy who *could* do so, *would* weep because she is doing some kind of a Middle-Eastern dance with her arms and hands extended and wrists turning, and your heart opens as you realize that you will never live long enough to see her grow old which means her beauty for you is immortal but also that she might well be around to see you turn into an ancient fossil, and you are stricken by the understanding that your life is over, that this Sicilian beauty has a whole life before her that does not include you, and with that understanding you take a step sidewise to right your faltering balance and fortunately there is a wall there that you stumble into rather than taking a header onto the floor, and as you hang against the door jamb, you realize that it is time for you to go home but that you will in no way be able to negotiate the steep hill down to the official conference hotel rooms, so you remain hanging there, hoping that your balance will suddenly, miraculously replenish itself and allow you the possibility of gathering what dignity you might have left to depart in a straight-enough line that no one will notice you or see you stagger disgracefully, and then for some obscure reason, you get the idea of mouthing a quote from "Under Milkwood," and you do that.

Pronouncing the words in the best stentorian splendor you can evoke, you proclaim, "Mr. Thomas: Is going to be sick!"

Apparently you say that loudly enough during a pause in the music that heads turn toward you, including Carlita's lovely Sicilian face, and then she is there in front of you peering with concern into what could only be the smudge of your puss.

"Are you all right?" she asks.

With some difficulty, you manage to say, "I think it is time for me to return to my room."

And that beautiful woman smiles at you the mildest of smiles and asks, "May I walk with you?" Even fogged as you are, you do not fail to recognize the elegant discretion of her wording. She might have said, "Would you like me to help you?" Or "Let me help you." Or even, "You can't make it alone." But no, she said, "May I walk with you?"

And you reply, "I should be very honored and pleased indeed if you would walk with me, Ms. Carlita."

The walk is not among the moments of greatest dignity of your life. You need to be held tightly under your arm, but Carlita does it with gentle firmness, her warm body snug against yours, and in no time you are down the hill, and you only drop your room key three times before you manage to open the door and concentrate on asking without a slur, "Would you like to come in for a nightcap?"

To which she replies, miraculously, "Yes." She lisps the word slightly. Not a full lisp. Not "Yeth," but more a slight shade of "Yesh."

And then in no time at all, the two of you are seated closely on your sofa, and you are thinking, Am I really going to get this lucky? Aloud you say: "Carlita: May I kiss you?"

"Yesh."

And you do that. Several times in succession. With great reverence and tenderness but increasing intensity. And you touch her lovely face with your fingertips which she actually allows you to do and to which she responds by closing her eyes and smiling with heartbreaking sweetness, moving her face in to catch your touches, and you know you don't deserve to be so happy, old profligate that you are, but you will take this good fortune and let it flood your aging pump, but then you say something you should not say.

You say, "How can you let an old guy like me kiss you?"

To which she replies the only sensible thing. "Why don't you shut up and just kiss me."

And you do that. You kiss her lips and her face and her eyes and her neck. You sigh with mighty pleasure and look and look into her baby blues and see beneath her gaze a certain sadness, sad but smiling and so very blue, and you whisper, "You are so beautiful," to which she replies, "Thank you," in such a sweet breathy whisper, and you say, "I have been crazy about you since the first moment I saw you."

She answers nothing, only looks into your eyes with her unblinking so-blue gaze, and in that moment you come to an understanding of passion's failure. There is no way that you would ever, even in your youth, be able to implement the fulfillment of your veneration of her beauty, your wish, your desire, your hunger to become part of her and for her to become part of you. The joining of bodies is only a symbol of what we so fervently wish we could, but never can. Even joined we look across a chasm at one another. And so you merely whisper, "Let's go to bed," and she whispers back, "Okay," and that whispered word on its way to reaching you has touched every part of her sweet mouth and moves toward your face, moist from her tongue, a gift wrapped in her sweet gin-scented breath.

There is no way, after all the vodka, that you dare ingest any Natural Male Enhancement so you need have no fear of an erection that lasts for more than four seconds even, but do your very best with the organs at your command to give her some pleasure at least and perhaps you do manage for you are rewarded with breathy sounds of joy and desperate sighs and you hope that she is truly pleased but what the hell, what can you do but your best, and you are just so bloody goddamn glad—so *glad!*—to be naked in bed with this lovely naked woman and that the lights are dim enough that she cannot scrutinize your aged flesh; even if nothing further ever comes of it, this is a moment in your life that time can never reclaim, and you are murmuring a hymn of admiration into the warm cherry-red cup of her ear as you reverently caress everything of her you can reach and tell her again you have been mad about her since the moment you first saw her, and perhaps you are gushing but there is a definite core of molten truth to your words, perhaps you could almost even call it love, but you manage to avoid that word with its four-lettered landscape of traps and springs, and though you wonder if she is skeptical because she says nothing, and you wonder if you understand the nature of your meeting, perhaps a woman of her age in this young century considers this a simple casual encounter, but you cannot consider this casual by any means, you are thrilled, you are wild about her and you see again that perhaps you are nothing but an elderly male bimbo or a self-deceived jerk, but what in the world matters at all beyond that this beautiful woman has allowed you to kiss her and she is here and naked and allowing you to touch and admire the beauty of her with all your senses and none of this would have happened if you had not gone through this day following each and every step that led you to this glorious series of moments, and in five-ten-twenty years at most, you will be in the house which none leave who have entered it, at the end of the road from which there is no way back, to the house wherein the dwellers are bereft of light, where dust is their drink and clay their meat, and they see no light, wrapped about as they are in darkness.

But not yet. Not yet. And you turn your eyes once more to the mild unblinking gaze of this lovely 21st century Italian Nefertiti, and what could you ever have said to this rare good moment of fortune but yes.

(2009)

I Am a Slave
to the Nudity of Women

"I do not know with what resolve
I could stand against it, a naked woman
Asking of me anything."
— Alberto Rios

He sits on his sofa, vodka close to hand, a book of poetry open on his lap, although he is not reading. He is ruminating, and he advises himself not to think about rising to step into his office to check the full-screen laptop opened on his desk to see if the email inbox is illuminated with the name of Lucia. Yet he does rise, the book closed around one finger, does step into his office and does look at the laptop screen and sees that there is no illuminated Lucia there and tells himself, Well *that* is no doubt *that*.

Did you think, he thinks, that the two of you were in love, could be in love? She is so much younger and lives so far away. And you who had always been suspicious of that word until Eileen made you see, or believe, it could be possible and then proceeded to withdraw from a love she had encouraged him to believe was lifelong? Still staring at the screen of the laptop, he thinks how all certainties he had once felt about the idea of love, both negative and positive, were now tipped over; the only certainty remaining concerns "chemistry." You know, he thinks, and have always known that "the chemistry" has to be right, and what *is* the chemistry. Lucia has the right chemistry, but what *is* that chemistry? Her gentle, kind smile. Her blue eyes, tender and sad and merry, yes. Her face, yes. Her body, its lines and curves and fullnesses and hollows. Her rump—how odd, he thinks, his heart captured by a rump. And the character in her chin—yet he has known people with receding chins who had character nonetheless—the features of a face deceive so why does a certain face make you see possibilities, feel that happiness is possible, trust. Yet there is no denying the chemistry of her face or her body. Or, for that matter, the chemistry of her intellect, the way she is able to see things, surprise him with a word of understanding, yes, so chemistry is more than the arrangement of features of a face and a body and a rump. Could he ever love a woman, at least initially, whose rump did not win him? And it is not even a specific kind or shape or size of rump but a rump that, well, makes him follow it. And what does that say about him as a human being? He finds it difficult to believe that he is standing there, disappointed, and thinking these things. Lucia is so different from Eileen yet he cannot deny that he "loved" Eileen and is on his way to "loving" Lucia (under Eileen's tutelage he had removed the quotation marks from the word "love"—now they are back in place for he realizes he does not know what "love" might be).

There is, of course, he thinks then, something more: The way she looks at him with admiration sparkling in her eyes; the admiring things she says. He realizes that he is a sucker for that.

This is ridiculous, he thinks.

He returns to the sofa and sips his vodka and looks at the book of poetry, a slender volume whose slenderness seems somehow to promise disproportionate depth and breadth. Still he does not read. He stares at the page and thinks.

He thinks maybe it was that Eileen, with her long chestnut hair and perfect lips and tenderness and appealing femininity (or was that an act?), kicked him out, surprising him when he still loved her by revealing that she no longer loved him, so that he still had his heart open, even though his pride or self-respect would never allow him to beg or even try to convince her of the genuineness of his love for her (he believed at that time, for a time, that he knew what genuine love was)—he thinks maybe it is for these reasons that he is ready, even eager, to love again or to keep loving for as long as he can, specifically to see if what he feels for Lucia and she for him might be love, because when he loves (regardless of what love may or may not be), he feels almost complete, so it is no good to be alone again as he was before he met Eileen, even though he was fairly content being alone for those few years, probably because, before that, for the last ten years of his marriage to Jessica, he did not love her at all, but only *tended* the relationship in a somewhat cynical manner, trying to avoid things that annoyed her, and there were so many things that annoyed her (to name but one, she would not go to the movies with him, an activity he had always enjoyed, because she so loathed the prospect of people munching candy in the dark), trying not to do things that would make her unhappy while simultaneously trying not to make himself unhappy.

Finally, of course, he failed at both things, made both of them unhappy, just as she had done (if she was to blame at all, though it takes two to tango and so forth) because, he suspected, of the basic lack of love in the relationship—(relationship, he thinks, what a clunky word! And of course, he thinks, what *is* love anyway, etc., although the love he felt for Eileen, in contrast to his feeling for Jessica, left him no doubt, though that lack of doubt reminded him of the necessity of maintaining a certain healthy skepticism about it all)—and therefore was not unhappy being alone, even though at times he was lonely, but there was the occasional woman (even if sex without love was ultimately unsatisfying, yet sex when it's bad is not so very bad, although it can be absolutely dismal to wake alongside another human being you do not love but whose body cavities, to put it hyperbolically crudely, you have merely made use of and so forth).

But then there was Eileen with her long auburn hair and delicate hands and beautiful mouth and feminine manner who told him he was the love of her life, winning him over by the force of her conviction that love clearly did exist, and she really did seem to love him to the extent that he actually began to understand that he did not love himself, but then in fact *began* to love himself, and then to love her, in the way a man can only love a woman when he genuinely has learned, preferably from her, to love himself (all these things, of course, being postulates built upon postulates when you have never in the first place answered the question of what, after all, *is* love, etc.) and there was the rub perhaps because just about when he began to love himself, and thus her, and began to think *she* was the love of *his* life, it seemed, she began to grow increasingly bored or annoyed with him (*Do you have to crunch your cornflakes like that?* kind of thing and so forth), ultimately showing him the door and giving him a verbal nudge toward it.

The mental image of him being nudged toward the door, though not precisely what happened, merely a manner of thinking, arrests him. He does not wish to think about these things, this recent history of his life. Living alone in his new apartment, small and lightless as it was in the depth of winter, as he negotiated the unexpected loss of Eileen, he began to be plagued by erotic fantasies of pain and humiliation that first repulsed, then baffled, then began to seem the inevitable next step for him to entertain and embrace. So he made a place for them in his psyche and allowed them to play out on the screen of his consciousness. Where, he wondered, were these scenes occurring? In what dimension did Eileen smile at him with such refined cruelty, laughing at his pain and him laughing along with her and taking pleasure from it all? Did he really entertain such thoughts? In what dimension did he welcome that cruelty? Perhaps he had thought (or convinced himself) that this entertainment would progress to some manner of release and perhaps it did on some level but on some other, perhaps more important level, he felt it involved an adulterating of what he had thought of as the closest he had come to a real experience of love, while at the same time realizing that this might all along have been the deeper point of all this, his imagined surrender to her imaginary cruelty, but no, no, no, you are confused, why would cruelty suddenly come into it when what had attracted them to one another was a mutual empathy and tenderness?

And he understands then that his intellect is limited such that he is capable of conjuring this cacophony of possibilities but not of organizing them in a comprehensible manner. Part of it has to do with the relationship of loss and lust but what is the nature of that relationship? The question makes his skull ache.

He looks at his drink and thinks, *Vodka: it keepeth the reason from stifling*, and sips, sips again, returns his attention to the open book in his lap where he reads, "I am a slave to the nudity of women…" The line takes his breath away, and he looks up from the page to contemplate those words. His eyes come to rest on a painting of an angel on the wall. The angel is slouched gloomily at a dining table before an empty plate and empty glass. Somehow the angel seems related to the line of poetry he has just read, which evokes the nudity of Lucia. He tells himself not to, but does lay the open book face down on the sofa cushion and does rise to go into the office to check the computer: No illuminated Lucia in the inbox. Of course. That *is* it. His vodka is empty so he throws two more cubes into the glass and pours in five fingers, returns to the sofa and picks up the book from the cushion, but a new thought strikes him:

That in the beginning, the very beginning, Eileen might have feared him and might have *wanted* to fear him and possibly confused fear with respect, confused that force she perceived in him, that she feared, with masculinity and possibly needed to have that illusion of him as forceful and masculine and fear-inspiring, which he never thought of himself as or even wanted to pretend to be, but perhaps was unconsciously inspired to do by a subliminal perception of and response to her fear, which caused an erotic reaction at that level, for he does recall how aroused he had been by her femininity, that she was small and slight and slender, that she seemed to enjoy cooking for him, even *serving* him, seemed to expect him to make demands of her, to seduce and undress her, to trap her wrists in his one hand as the other had its way with her body while her eyes met his in what appeared a kind of blissful surrender. Suddenly this appears to him as though illuminated along with the suspicion or perhaps understanding that it was the wearing away of her illusion that had led her to grow discontent with him and to the termination of their erotic life together.

Of course, he thinks, you have to realize that the fucking was important, and neither was the lack of fucking unimportant after she began to grow disenchanted with him. In the beginning, the fucking was the sine qua non and be-all-end-all, etc., a mix of instinct and consideration, of giving and holding back, of urgency tempered by reserve, spiced by the discovery and revelation of mutual secrets. But Eileen was also sometimes the aggressor in their erotic play, she was good at aggressing, was it a mistake for him not to have resisted, not to have kept her in that place where her illusion of him could thrive, but he didn't, he even discussed it (*How did you know I would like it if you did that?* and so forth), should have kept it pure of words, but he didn't, until there weren't many secrets left (there are always secrets, etc., no one can ever truly know another or even, perhaps especially, him- or herself, etc.) which led to a nakedness that went beyond the physical to the spiritual, the psychological, to what seemed to be a complete nakedness in their embrace but maybe just was based on that mutual feminine-masculine illusion so that they were building on an illusion, an unsound basis for love, which at first seemed akin to some kind of state of grace, to know and to be known (insofar as one can ever know or be known and so forth), to know another with reverence for the knowledge, to be known with tenderness for your vulnerabilities and so on and so forth.

Then came the moment when one or the other of them, both perhaps, used the knowledge without care, teasingly, took the gloves off. I-*know*-you kind of thing. I see right through you, and so forth, and Ha ha, you'd probably actually *like* that, *how pathetic* kind of thing. And then one or the other of them feels they're out on thin ice and in for a dunking from which he or she will emerge shivering and distraught. Or maybe the shadow part which was revealed is simply now illuminated, out in the light, and no longer has the force it had when it was locked away (you are, after all, what you are kind of thing), no longer interesting, or maybe just an illusion, self-knowledge being a series of lost self-deceptions and knowledge of the other being a series of disenchantments perhaps, the shadow of desire being dissipated in the light of awareness, and perhaps after that, perhaps when you get to that point, the beauty of real desire is possible, if by then you have any measure of desire left at all, but what it all led to finally was that he was no longer the love of her life, although she was still the love of his or seemed so (assuming that love is a real quantity or quality at all and not merely an illusion that each human being freely embraces because of his or her incompleteness.)

Or maybe, he thinks, it's just a matter of all passion eventually burning out regardless of what you do. Time limited. Or familiarity breeds contempt kind of thing. Desire an illusion as well as love, etc., on the other side of which is the cooling. But, he thinks, Eileen reached the cooling before he did. As far as he knows he might never have reached the cooling, although it is entirely possible that his love was perversely stoked to even greater life by her cooling, that his desire began to flourish more greatly in panic at the withdrawal of hers. Too late to know now, for now he is irrevocably separated from her and does not want to return, could not, even if she wanted him to, even if she implored him, that would only embarrass him on her behalf.

But his heart is still open to love ("love").

However, the chemistry has to be right. He can't just love any woman. The chemistry is right with Lucia, but is that a chemistry of passion which is also doomed to burn out? (And, again, of course, what is at the root of this *right chemistry* business is quite another question; it seems there are only questions upon questions and perhaps the only way out is to become a Buddhist and renounce all desire as illusion, but who in the world other than a damn Buddhist wants to live without desire, to ignore the jumping of your blood when it jumps; even if its jumping is only delusive, it does, in fact, jump, and that must be the bottom line: your blood jumps. *His* blood jumps, although perhaps one should seek a state of unjumping blood, the age of calm and wise blood, where a man and a woman live together beyond passion just as companions of different sexes without sex, How was your day kind of thing, And how was *yours,* etc., but would that really mean no more fucking at all forever; even if it is *but a tingling of the nerves* kind of thing, he does not wish to contemplate the entire rest of his life without it. And it is no mere tingling of the nerves, the dance to orgasm is surely sacred, or is that so much eyewash dispersed for profit by New Age and advertising mountebanks. We are in the dark, he thinks; *I* am in the dark. And there is another possible aspect to this chemistry business. What if the so-called "right chemistry" is in fact an unconscious formula devised by a variety of subliminal experiences and forces that has become his destiny merely because, say, his mother once looked at him in a certain way when his father had said or done something or other at a time when he was pre- or semi-lingual which then programmed his desire in a direction quite beyond his control or comprehension so that when the "right chemistry" presents itself, it merely turns him into a "fool for love" or as Milton put it, *Among them Hee a spirit of frenzy sent who hurt their minds/and sent them in a mad fury to hasten their destruction* or something like that, which could conceivably mean that when he longs to "love" a certain woman what he really longs for is to reinvent Eden and then the inevitable Fall from Grace, his own destruction or, to put it less melodramatically, his own nonproductive infatuation—a repetition of failure?)

Nonetheless, his heart was still open to love, it seems to him, after Eileen stopped loving him and he met Lucia and felt the first stirrings of love which led to the two of them putting their mouths together and intertwining their tongues and tasting one another's saliva which, though objectively might seem repellent, was subjectively quite stimulating—Wow indeed!—as was tasting and touching virtually all other parts of her body.

Actually, he knew Lucia already for the past couple of years, but never dreamed she was interested in him love-wise because she is so much younger than he, and anyway, when he met her he had just been taught by Eileen to love himself, and was not even thinking of Lucia in that way, being as he was so "fully in love" with Eileen, although apparently she, Lucia, was thinking of him in that way to his great surprise, and now he sees suddenly, as though scales have fallen from his eyes as it says in the Bible or somewhere, that he desires her also, in fact very much so. And what, he wonders, is the essence of his desire for Lucia? Surprise, perhaps? Surprise she would even for an instant desire him? There was so much against it. He is eighteen years older than she for one thing, lives two thousand miles away, and each of them has a life there, where he or she lives, from which they neither can nor wish to extricate themselves.

He thinks back over the girls and women he has been with over the six decades of his life—well, the five erotically active decades—and can only conclude that of the ten or twelve, he has only *approached* what he would think of as love (if he had a definition) with the two: Jessica, to whom, he was married for twenty years, and that love, if it had ever really been love ("love" which has still not been explicated) burned out in the first ten, even eight years; and Eileen, who taught him really to love, or so it seemed, and then, after fifteen years, rather abruptly gave him the boot, and now perhaps his passion for Lucia, too, was already at an end, or rather hers for him.

Now he is sixty-three (Liar! You're sixty-five!) (and Lucia— liar, again!—is more like twenty-six years younger than you) and hardly wiser about these things than he was at fourteen, albeit with a more complex confusion, and now is involved with Lucia who he feels he could love, maybe already does love—(if he is not merely setting traps of illusion for himself, falling for women with whom his relationship [relationship, what a word!] is by definition doomed and perishable [which is of course a real possibility—cf. Milton's *spirit of frenzy* etc.], although he cannot deny that he becomes extremely glad every time he sees or even imagines her face and her body and her kind and gentle manner as well as her wit and intelligence [blood jumping and so forth], and of course her rump, and who seems quite definitely to find something of value in him which tends to make him value himself—cf., Gene Kelly in some musical romantic comedy singing and dancing on roller skates: "Can it be, I like myself? She likes me, so I like myself...")—although he is by no means fit for roller skating any longer and in ten years will be seventy-five and she will only by then be forty-seven or so, so this prospect of love (perhaps extremely remote prospect of love is a more accurate term) seems doomed to fail (and there you have *that* again!), maybe has already failed, making him wonder if "love" is perhaps only a temporal thing (immortal love does seem a rather romance-comicbook romantic notion when it comes to the crunch of the cornflakes), and in truth what could she possibly see in him, he doesn't even like her to see his aging body naked although he does *extremely* enjoy seeing *her* in that state, trim and tanned and creamed and gleaming as her relatively young flesh is, *what an ass!* etc.

Is that what this is all about then, just lasciviousness? No, no, no, he has only seen her naked three times anyway (although his breath goes shallow remembering every detail of those three exhilarating experiences, nor does it have to do only with young flesh because Eileen was five years *older* than he and he was greatly enamored of her flesh even when it began to age and sag a bit, though he can't say how he might have felt if it had sagged a great deal more, but was spared that test by Eileen having ceased to love him when he still loved her), his primary pleasure has been taken far more from her (Lucia's) person, her manner, her words, than from her body (this went for both Eileen and for Lucia, although he cannot discount the piquancy of the fucking with Lucia—it was quite an experience for his sixty-five-year-old self to create the two-backed beast with Lucia's thirty-nine-year-old one—*wow, indeed,* to put it mildly!—although he remembers meeting a woman of thirty-nine once when he was thirty-four and the two of them kissing, perhaps the nicest kisses he has ever experienced, her lips and mouth so knowing and engaged that he still recalls the kisses nearly thirty years later, although he also remembers thinking, from the vantage point of his thirties, how much older she seemed than he, while now he is thinking that thirty-nine is quite young indeed. Everything, it seems, is relative or even worse. But wow! Could that woman articulate the art of kissing!

After his last physical meeting with Lucia, they sent lengthy emails to one another every day, filling the vast ether of their two-thousand-mile separation, sometimes twice a day, and every time he saw the name Lucia illuminated in his inbox, his heart leapt and his blood jumped, although he has to admit that then the emails began to come every other day, then twice a week, then once a week, and now he has not heard from her for fifteen days except for a couple of lines in which, however, she hastened to say she was *thinking* of him and which she signed "kisses"—though he is left in doubt as to whether she thought of those kisses in a literal sense or merely as a complimentary closing.

So, he thinks, what is he living off now? A word (kisses—an ambiguous word really) and the thought of his existing inside her pretty head (which might also be a hyperbole—what, after all, he thinks, does "*thinking* of you" really mean—thinking at the moment of writing those words or thinking more generally or even—do not rule this out—*wanting to tell him that she was thinking of him when in fact she was hardly thinking of him at all* or even thinking about how to extricate herself from this constant need to send him emails and from the prospect of having to be naked with him again?)

This is instructive, he thinks. This should be instructive. He thinks that he really should learn from this. What? he wonders. What should he learn? Perhaps, he thinks, this will finally teach him about the nature of love, the nature of loneliness, the nature of desire, the nature of life.

Don't be a fool, he thinks. Lucia is her own person and she owes him nothing at all and is free to decide against becoming involved with him and probably would be wise to do so because of the age difference and the geographical distance to name but two very salient matters.

Although he would prefer not to, he rises from the sofa, the slender book of poetry held open on his index finger, and pads across the carpet into his office to check his email. There is no illuminated *Lucia* in his in-box so his blood does not jump but sinks with resignation.

Don't be a fool, he thinks. Who could blame her? A young beautiful woman like that has no need of an old fool like me. This was merely a flirtation. A fluttering of the pulses. A pleasant interlude. A temporary jumping of the blood through the fiery hoops. So let it rest.

He clicks the "refresh" tab on his screen. Two new emails appear, but neither is from Lucia, and the absence of Lucia's illuminated name in his inbox makes him feel incomplete, but he thinks that probably everyone always feels incomplete anyway, it being a condition of being alive to feel incomplete and particularly a condition of a man of his age who should not expect to be completed by a relatively much younger and still beautiful woman. That *is* it, and he realizes that he is to be spared the mysteries and surprises and disappointments and vicissitudes of this "love affair."

He closes the book which he was still holding open on his index finger at the poem whose first line had so beguiled him and returns it to its alphabetical slot on his poetry shelf under Rios, Alberto. Then he goes in to his office to shut down the laptop, but does look once more to see if the name Lucia is illuminated in the inbox, which it is not, and he cannot help but wonder what he would do if the name should suddenly appear on the screen, and she professed profound love for him—would he be glad or frightened?—or, conversely, continued to offer ambiguous statements, complimentary closings of "kisses" and "thinking of you"—and either way, it seems to him now, is a kind of potential fall, a gateway to a kind of Fall from Grace where a kind of spirit of frenzy lays in wait for him.

He remembers then that in one of her emails Lucia said something about having been "naked in his bed," and he remembers the details of her naked body—particularly perhaps her rump, how odd, he thinks again, to surrender one's heart to a rump, though other parts as well—and of Eileen's naked body and her rump, which he also cherished (definitely part of the chemistry: *My soul then sold for but a rump?/By those hips parenthesized?*) And he remembers once then in Dublin at a conference when he was rather loudly entertaining a group of colleagues in his hotel room late one night and stepped out into the hall to get more ice from the machine and a naked woman was standing outside the open door across the way, a most appealingly naked woman, and she spoke in fury to him, shouting, "Ye can shut the fuck up, ye can, all of ye!" and his mouth dropped open at the paradox of her inviting nakedness and her furious anger, and he muttered simply, "Yes, I will, of course, forgive me," and she disappeared into her room with a flash of comely rump, and now he returns to his poetry shelf to find the book he has just put back into its alphabetical slot and thumbs it open to the page and the line, "I am a slave to the nudity of women," and it occurs to him that that perhaps is all he knows and all he needs to know. But *he does not know with what resolve he could stand against it, a naked woman, asking of him anything.*

(2009)

ABOUT THE AUTHOR

THOMAS E. KENNEDY'S many books include novels, story and essay collections, literary criticism, anthologies, and translation. Most recent volumes are the four novels of the *Copenhagen Quartet* from Bloomsbury Publishers in the U.S. and the U.K. (*In the Company of Angels*, 2010; *Falling Sideways*, 2011; *Kerrigan in Copenhagen, A Love Story*, 2013; and *Beneath the Neon Egg*, 2014) and two collections from New American Press, *Last Night My Bed a Boat of Whiskey Going Down* (2010) and *Riding the Dog: A Look Back at America* (2008). His stories, essays, travel pieces, interviews, poems, and translations appear regularly in American and European periodicals. His writing has won an O. Henry Award, a Pushcart Prize, a National Magazine Award, Charles Angoff Award and other prizes.

Kennedy holds a B.A. (*summa cum laude*) from Fordham University Lincoln Center, an M.F.A. from Vermont College and a Ph.D. from the University of Copenhagen and teaches in the Fairleigh Dickinson University low-residency M.F.A. program. He is an Advisory Editor of *The Literary Review*, of *Absinthe: New European Writing*, a Contributing Editor of *Serving House: A Journal of the Arts,* and Co-editor with Walter Cummins of Serving House Books and lives in Denmark where he is the father of a son, Daniel, and daughter, Isabel, and the mother-father of Leo Kennedy-Rye.

CPSIA information can be obtained at www.ICGtesting.com
Printed in the USA
LVOW06s0732200913

353169LV00003B/676/P

9 780984 943920